Vanessa

Vanessa

A NOVEL BY
Ann Pinchot

 ARBOR HOUSE New York

1ct

Library of Congress Catalogue Card Number: 76-39717

ISBN: 0-87795-157-8

Manufactured in the United States of America

For Julian Bach, with affection and esteem

Prologue:

THE PAST: THE BRASS-BED CASTING COUCH ON BROOKLYN HEIGHTS

THE NIGHT CLERK behind the desk was clearly bred to be a clerk. He had the deference of a born servant.

The night clerk, drab in a blue serge suit, celluloid collar and ready-made black bow tie, was a respectable man whom the manager trusted.

The hotel, too, was respectable, trusted by its permanent residents. Occupying a half block on Brooklyn Heights above the Esplanade, protected by space, sun and trees, it offered a home-like security to its guests. These substantial citizens divided their time between the hotel, the season in Saratoga, or Hot Springs or Arizona. In the spring they could be found in choice staterooms on the luxury liners bound for Europe. They were loyal, clannish

1

and demanding. They expected no scandal to disturb their womb-safe existence.

Scandal?

Oh, there's no chance of it, the clerk assured himself, ignoring the spasm of anxiety that clutched his stomach. The reputation of the hotel was as solid and upright as the Italian marble pillars supporting the frescoed ceiling of the lobby. Scandal might surface at Delmonico's, the Waldorf or even the Astor. But not here.

The gentleman was discreet.

And generous.

In no way could the clerk imagine him to be any threat to the hotel's impeccable reputation.

Still . . .

The clerk glanced at the elaborate gilt clock above the wall of mail slots. Eight-thirty. It wasn't likely that the gentleman in question (strange, wasn't it, how the clerk always thought of him as The Gentleman) would show tonight. He could be expected once or twice a week, and always before eight in the evening. Sometimes weeks went by and the clerk would wonder if he would appear again. But his room was paid for in cash on a monthly basis. The clerk suspected that the name on the register wasn't his real name.

From his station behind the ornate grille, the clerk surveyed the lobby, alert for strangers, but few appeared there. An unfamiliar face usually belonged to the guest of a permanent guest. Still the manager always cautioned the staff to be *aware*.

The last sweet notes of *Der Rosenkavalier* Waltzes faded in the Main Dining Room. Pages in scarlet jackets and blue trousers touched with gilt swung open the double doors as the *maitre d'*, stiff as a French civil servant, bowed to each departing guest. The diners, pleasantly stuffed on succulent beef and game, out-of-season vegetables and fruits, and the pastry chef's spun-sugar triumphs, moved at a leisurely pace to their favorite after-dinner seats. The lobby was rich with crimson draperies; the marble floor was covered with worn but valuable Orientals. There were delicate Louis 14th armchairs for the ladies who did not wish to discomfort their corseted bodies in the deep plump sofas. Members of the String Trio took their prescribed places behind the potted palms, making melodious background music for the ladies' chatter. The men soothed their digestions with fragrant Coronas and the financial news in *The Brooklyn Eagle*.

The clerk became suddenly alert. The main door of the lobby was opening. It was dark outside, and snowing, and a blast of cold air accompanied the entrance of two visitors.

A man and a young girl.

The man was probably in his mid-thirties, not handsome but distinguished. His body was a boxer's, but lean, an extrovert's manner at odds with his deep-set sad eyes. His gray wool suit and matching tweed overcoat were well tailored and conservative. Under his tan wide-brimmed hat, which he didn't remove, his skin had a healthy glow. The man had a presence, the clerk thought, watching his progress toward the desk. His appearance was faintly familiar. ("I've seen his picture somewhere," the clerk always thought, feeling troubled that he could not place him exactly in his memory.)

The man's companion was trying to match her steps to his stride, in order to keep abreast of him. The man didn't look at the young girl, as though this lack of recognition would divert the curiosity of the ladies in the lobby. The chill didn't seem to bother the man, but the young girl looked blue and pinched. She was of medium height, barely reaching his shoulder. A small flower-decked hat, inappropriate to the season, sat on her thick fair hair that fell in curls to her small sloping shoulders. In the tilt of her absurd hat there was a touch of the coquette, in contrast to her plain gray cloth coat, proper white wrist-length gloves and small Persian lamb muff.

The clerk recognized her, although she looked at him blankly without greeting. This was her second appearance at the hotel.

She was so serious, so delicate, so ethereal.

The other girl who sometimes accompanied him was like a sprite, full of laughter and mischief.

"Good evening, sir." The clerk was deferential but nervous.

The man nodded. "How're you this evening?"

"Very well, sir."

"And your family?"

"First rate, sir." He hoped the manager wouldn't make an appearance.

"And the boy?"

3

"Coming along well, sir."

"Glad to hear it." The resonant voice had a touch of authority. "My key, please."

"Yes, sir." The clerk was facing the mail slots, his anxiety less noticeable. The gentleman was unfailingly courteous and generous. Whose business was it if he brought a young girl to his room? Why shouldn't I close my eyes to it, the clerk thought. He isn't hurting anybody, and the young girls didn't look like the victims of white slavers. What business is it of mine if he ...

The clerk was respectable, tactful, a good husband and father at home. He wanted the best for his family. But they could afford meat only once a week, a small pork roast on Sunday. And at the Clinic the doctors said his boy needed more milk and liver.

He straightened his shoulders, wheeled around, held out the key. As it was transferred, the gentleman's handclasp left a neatly folded greenback in the clerk's moist palm.

"Thank you, sir."

The girl was watching solemnly, the eyes enormous in the small peaked face, the irises blue, the whites luminous. Her mouth was tiny, prim. She looked everywhere but at the clerk, who suspected she was trying to cover her fear with childish dignity.

"Come," the gentleman said. She followed him, docile, trying to keep up with his stride.

Chatter in the lobby fell to a lower decibel as the ladies watched the odd couple's progress to the elevator. The clerk felt sick. The girl was young enough to be the gentleman's daughter. Perhaps she was. *Of course she was!* Perhaps the gentleman was separated from her mother and was allowed to visit with her once or twice each week, never for the entire night. *Yes,* that made sense!

But if *this* was his daughter, who was the other—the small bouncy girl, all sandy hair and full of laughter and freckles, who looked like a tomboy?

You meet all kinds, the clerk reflected. He'd grown accustomed to oddities. Not in this hotel, but at earlier jobs, where he'd been obliged to cope with situations you wouldn't dare mention in this august establishment.

Earlier this evening, when the clerk checked in, the manager had summoned him to his office.

"Gus, if the man who rents 714 shows up tonight, let me know."

"Anything wrong, sir?"

"He's not desirable. From what the night maid told me, he's an unsavory character. Tell him we need his room, and no other is available. I don't want him on the premises."

"But he seems a gentleman, sir. He's caused no trouble."

"That because we weren't wise to him. I'm tempted to call the police. I must protect our reputation."

The elevator now swallowed the man and the girl. They reached the seventh floor before the clerk decided to take action. His puffy face took on a blend of anxiety and rectitude. He turned toward the manager's office, bracing himself for an unpleasant scene.

The room was empty. Not even a whiff of the manager's after-dinner cigar polluted the air. The clerk was spared briefly. Suppose he were to alert the gentleman; it would be helpful all around, save his reputation and the hotel's. Yet at the same time it would also deprive himself of a small but steady bit of extra income he sorely needed. Either way he'd lose out. Unless the gentleman showed his appreciation for the warning.

On his way to the elevators, the clerk was detained twice by garrulous elderly widows intent on making small talk. He finally broke away.

"Seven," he said to the elevator operator.

The corridor was soft underfoot with deep pile of crimson carpet. A white Hepplewhite sofa and a polished brass spittoon greeted the guest stepping out on Seven. The clerk waited for the elevator door to close and then he walked nervously down the hall, turning right to the wing facing the Bay.

He tapped lightly on the door.

Silence.

Perspiration dampened his forehead. He heard no sound inside. But the door was heavy, the building solidly constructed. He wavered, tempted to return to his post. He didn't want the maid to catch him when she came to turn down the beds. She was the manager's spy.

5

Another anxious rap, then the sound of the lock, and the door opening slightly.

"What'd you want?" The voice, usually so resonant and courteous, was harsh.

"Sir, I *must* speak with you."

"Well, what is it?"

There was a moment of tense silence as they stared at each other unblinkingly. Suddenly the clerk was certain he recognized the man, but still couldn't quite place him.

"Sir, I must urge you to leave. Immediately. Before the manager learns of your presence."

A pause, a weighing of facts and conditions, then the voice ordered curtly, "Don't bother me."

The clerk was in shock. Before the door closed, he saw something that added to his agitation. A ray of light shifting from the passage to the darkened room revealed a chair near the bed on which sat a pile of clothes. The clothes of a young girl, neatly folded. The absurd little flower hat was on top of the pile.

Trash was left in big cartons in the rear of the hotel. Before dawn, night creatures shuffling along the silent street, foraging in the trash, often unearthed treasures that could be exchanged for a few pennies at the junkman's. The old woman, bent with arthritis, wrapped like a mummy in her cap, scarf, sweaters, coat, lugging her worldly goods in two string bags, paused in the alley, searching by touch for anything left over by the scavengers who had preceded her. Her fingers crept like mice in the carton nearest to the street and she touched a fabric that felt good even to her numbed fingers. She scrabbled for it, yanking it from among the papers. Under the dim light, she held it up and peered at it. Fine linen. A sheet.

She dropped it hastily when she saw the blood stains. But her greed was strong, and gingerly she made a bundle of it and carried it off in the night.

It was eight in the morning when the night clerk snatched up his overcoat and hat and made for the employees' entrance. His relief was clouded by a sense of loss.

6

A valued elderly guest, a retired partner in a Wall Street brokerage house, had suffered a heart attack. Because of this crisis, involving the house doctor, the victim's personal doctor and the victim's hysterical wife, the manager had been too harassed to question him. While the clerk was genuinely concerned for the sick man, his mind was still grappling with the mystery of the gentleman and the young girl.

He plodded down the street, past the stores opening for business, past the nickelodeon where he sometimes spent a few coins to forget his problems.

The nickelodeon! He stopped short. *Of course!* The gentleman he'd suddenly recognized was the director, Joshua Fodor, who'd been written up in the papers. There was a picture of him and the young girl. She was the lovely little creature in *The Lost Daughter and the Gypsies*—Vanessa Oxford.

He shook his head sadly. Sometimes he wondered if his hotel clerk's facility for remembering names and faces was a gift—or a curse.

One:

THE PAST: VANESSA OXFORD
REMEMBERS: THE MAKING OF A LEGEND

"MAMA, TELL ME what to do. *Please*, Mama!"

"Vanessa, you must decide for yourself," Mama said.

I still have the image in my mind—an image more vivid than my dreams—of the girl I was, growing up in awkward stages, thrust into maturity I wasn't ready for, turning to Mama, always with the same plea, "What shall I do? Tell me what to do."

She invariably turned the problem back to me, and since then, I have often wondered if it was a deliberate effort to encourage my own decisions so I would develop self-reliance. Or whether being frightened and uneasy herself, she was at a loss to direct me. In her time, a beautiful young woman separated from her husband, with two children to support, wasn't likely to have wisdom. Poor Mama, so young, so frightened, and yet so brave!

Whenever she told me I must make my own decisions, I raged silently at her advice. I wonder if years later, when she'd look at me, so sad, so reproachful, so *reproving*, she ever blamed herself for not having given me direction, for having contributed to the tragedies in my life, however unwittingly. I never condemned her, I had too much love and respect for her. She was the center of my life from the days of my babyhood to the time I was a middle-aged woman, holding her hand, as she lay in an oxygen web, pleading silently with her, *"Mama, don't leave me."*

In our worlds, my sister Cassie's and mine, people still talk about our devotion to Mother. Well, no one deserved it more than she. Now, at last, I can understand her reluctance to influence my choices.

With marriage she had already taken on one child before Cassie and I were born—Father, who so needed direction but balked at the prospect. He was his own man. Looking at his photograph, my best friend, Rebecca, once commented, "Vanessa, he doesn't have a married look."

Because he didn't have a married look, I suppose I have become the kind of woman I am today. But perhaps I was destined for a life away from Muskenaw under any circumstances. I was such a serious earnest child, burdened with a sorrowful air. Rebecca often says that, like Kierkegaard, I was old in my mother's womb.

We were attractive children. Mama was delicate but her youth and good health were in her favor. Childbirth for her was uncomplicated. Both Cassie and I had well-shaped heads, unmarred by battering of prolonged labor. We were small-boned, with milky skin threaded with delicate blue veins.

Rebecca, who has always found our background fascinating, said our genetic strains—Mama's Scotch and German and Father's Irish and English—melded to produce the images that proved perfect for the great director Joshua Fodor's camera eye.

I love to listen to Rebecca, because even when we were girls, she had such intuitive knowledge. She is fascinated by chance. She's forever discussing it. Accident or fate, she asks, are they one and the same? Is our fate in our genes? In our choices, influenced by our genes?

If Mama's older sister, my Aunt Annie, hadn't come down with a quinsy sore throat one winter day and asked Mama to deliver a small item for her to *The Chronicle* about the Church Supper . . .

If Mama had refused, because it was bitterly cold . . .

But Mama lived with Annie and Annie's husband, Arthur. She wasn't likely to refuse her sister any favor, and this was such a small one. Annie was in charge of the affair and she wanted a good showing.

The Chronicle was edited, and printed once a week, in a long wooden structure (originally a log cabin) when Muskenaw, in the '80s and '90s, was the lumber queen of the West.

I often picture Mama, so slight, nearly albino fair, bundled in sweaters and weighted down by Annie's muskrat coat, losing her breath as the blasts of wind hurtled down from the Canadian wilds while she struggled along the snowdrifts on Occidental Avenue. Muskenaw was the second-coldest town in America, which may be the reason why I'm so well adjusted to frigid weather. But poor dear Mama suffered acutely in the cold, perhaps because of her lack of thyroid hormone. Mama, like many of her friends, had a thyroid insufficiency, the result of living on the lake shore where rains had drained minerals out of the soil.

She arrived at *The Chronicle* office, rosy and breathless. It wasn't old Mr. Hoogstraten behind the desk, but a young man with a green eyeshade over his dark eyes, celluloid cuffs over his shirt sleeves and a frayed cardigan sweater over his thin, bony shoulders.

Patric Oxford. More Irish than English.

Years later, when I played in *Mourning Becomes Electra,* the playwright, Eugene O'Neill, came to rehearsals every day. And whenever I saw him, so dark, intense, trembling; his brilliant, tortured eyes haunted in his gaunt face; his shy, unexpected smile, I thought of my father. Whenever I look at the picture of Mama and Father, taken the first year of their marriage, I think, *Papa, you needed someone to look after you. Papa, you needed me.*

The truth was he needed Mama. Rebecca has often comforted me with her insights. "Your mother looked like a bisque doll, Vanessa, but she had a reservoir of tender strength. Whenever there was a hurt creature around, a bird, a dog or a cat, it was always brought to her care."

Was Patric Oxford, barely twenty-one, a hurt creature, seeking instinctively the compassion of a gentle, forgiving mate? And then turning his back on her because he resented his need?

Rebecca and I have discussed this often, because sometimes I feel as though I'll never rest until I know the entire story. Mama never spoke of Father's background or his family, except to say, "Your Father could never live up to his dreams."

A church supper started their courtship. I wonder if Mama's response to Father was instant attraction or a need to escape from the monotony of her life. Aunt Annie was at peace with her destiny. Marriage and a family were quite sufficient for her. What young woman in the late 1890s, secluded in a small town cut off from the world, dared to hope for more? Mama, too, had been docile and passive—on the surface. I think she'd been afraid to examine her inner feelings.

But whenever Rebecca says of me, "Vanessa is the most reckless creature I've ever known, she has the courage of ten," she is also speaking of Mama. I suspect Mama longed to escape the straight-jacket of her future in Muskenaw, but saw no way to accomplish it until she met Father. "Your father was a cavalier," she once said to me, "so different from the boys I knew." Those stolid, dependable, dull Dutch boys.

Patric Oxford was mercurial, often exhilarated, sometimes moody. Mama credited these swift mood changes to his sensitive poetic nature. He was an itinerant printer, but she had belief in him, visions of his future as a publisher. In the spring he took her by trolley to the beach, where they sat on the dunes and watched the Milwaukee ferry boat on the horizon. He read Walt Whitman to her.

They were married in Aunt Annie's front parlor and moved to a light-housekeeping room on Terrace Street. Mama kept house and Father worked at the paper. There weren't many places a fellow could relax after hours, except Harry Goldberg's saloon on Western or the Red Light district on Clay Avenue. There was only so much time a man could read Walt Whitman.

Eventually Father got into an argument with Mr. Hoogstraten and was fired at a time when Mama was six months pregnant with me. When I was six weeks old, Mama left Muskenaw and joined Father in Detroit where he was working for a Polish-American newspaper. That he didn't know a word of Polish didn't seem to matter. From there, he moved on to a weekly newspaper, and my sister, Cassandra, was born in a light-housekeeping flat on Shiawasee Street in Lansing. Always the high hopes, the fresh beginning, then gradually the grumbling, the discontent. And always, just as he was about to be fired, Father would quit.

Mama followed him to a series of small dreary towns. Sometimes, after losing a job, he would launch out and when he sent money for our fare, Mama would follow him. Poor Mama, with two small girls, bundles, suitcases, loaded down and yet maintaining her calm manner. I remember some of the rooms Father brought us to. They were mostly dreary, with shabby furnishings and the smell of poverty. I remember, too, that Mama's first chore was always with a scrub brush, Fels Naptha soap and a powder for roaches and mice.

The last town was just below Buffalo, and afterwards she heard from Father in Toronto. He said he'd send for us when he could and why didn't she go back and stay with her sister Annie until his fortunes improved?

This was the end for Mama. Alone, with two children to care for—Cassie was four and I was five—she knew that from then on it was up to her to support us.

Whenever I reflect on that period in our lives I am truly in awe of Mama's courage. Rebecca says it was probably born out of desperation—that Mama had no one to turn to—but like a lioness she was obsessed with the protection of her young. Anyway, somehow she got to New York, found an apartment on the West Side near Hell's Kitchen and managed to buy some furniture on time. She took a job in a dry goods store and life became a daily exercise in making do, she existing in a persistent climate of anxiety that she tried to keep from Cassie and myself.

The fact that Mama finally found work in the theater was, frankly, less a testament to her talent than to her beauty and grace, and to her determination to take care of her children, *whatever* the cost.

"Chance," Rebecca says. "Chance, Vanessa!"

Whatever. Acting was not considered an attractive, respectable profession for a young woman at the turn of the century. There were, of course, the First Families of the Theatre. The Barrymores. The Drews. Otis Skinner and his wife, Maude Durbin. They were royalty, set apart from lesser members of the profession. Even the most proper hotels ("No Dogs, Peddlers or Actors Allowed") were hospitable to *them*.

But troupes of lesser reputation traveling through the country were subjected to humiliations and rejections. While they were performing, audiences gave them awed attention, these actors in their outlandish clothes, their painted faces, with their melodramatic voices. Their dramas reduced emotions to a simple common denominator. The audience identified with the characters' suffering and weeping, and rejoiced with them. Away from the footlights, however, these righteous citizens regarded the players with scorn and contempt.

Mama became a soubrette, a comic maid.

We became child actors.

Our theatrical careers, if you could dignify them by that name, came about by accident. Mama found a job with a company going on tour through the midwest. She took us with her, since there was no one to care for us. In the years of our growing up, Mama never left us once, except during the summer of my thirteenth year when she worked in a dry goods store in nearby Grand Rapids while Cassie and I spent the summer in Muskenaw. Usually when Mama toured with a company, some of their plays had roles for young children, and Cassie or I would fill the opening. Mama's salary was twenty dollars a week. The company paid for her transportation but not mine or Cassie's. Other companies often needed small children and Mama could've sent us off under the care of a woman in another troupe. But she never did. We were always together. That sense of togetherness was evident in our family photographs, starting from our childhood: Mama in the center, embraced by Cassie and myself. The Three Oxfords, we used to call ourselves.

All for one and one for all.

For survival.

Cold trains, icy theater dressing rooms, frigid boarding houses. Performances given in Odd Fellows Halls, opera houses, school auditoriums. The billboards, eight and twelve sheets daubed with garish scenes of the plays, and *East Lynne* was the favorite.

Every night after the performance we were on our way to the next town. I didn't mind train travel. The steady hum of the tracks, the shrill whistle of warning gave me a good feeling, as though the engineer was in control, like God. Sometimes, mornings, the train slowed down at village crossings and we'd peer at children bundled up and on their way to school. We waved to them, but usually they made awful faces at us and I wondered if it was out of envy. Whenever I am asked if I missed having roots, I answer, "Oh, I just *loved* our nomad life."

But so many times, just before I fell asleep stretched out on a red plush day coach seat, I'd look at Mama, sitting opposite me, and I would think, *Poor Mama. Some day you won't have to live like this . . . I promise. . . .*

It was an innocent age and we were among the most innocent. And most vulnerable. One evening, while we were having dinner in a small restaurant near the railroad station in a dreary little town, a child belonging to a family at the next table approached us, a tentative smile on her lips.

Her mother got up so quickly that she turned over her chair. She snatched her child away, as though we were devils.

"Don't go near those play actors!" she screamed at her child.

We were hurt. We were always hurt by the outsiders' behavior toward us. Even after we learned to accept it, the sting remained. The fact that we were regarded as freaks, no better than gypsies, became in time a kind of positive addiction.

"They may sneer at us," Mama once said, "they don't allow us into decent boarding houses or hotels, but don't forget, children, they pay their good money to come and see us act. We are the ones who bring romance into their drab lives."

I never forgot it. I often reminded Cassie of it years later whenever she balked at taking a role.

I was on the David Susskind television program recently with a psychologist who was discussing today's permissive parents and frustrated children.

"I've been self-supporting since I was five years old," I said. "There was never any time for me to get into mischief."

After I related some of our experiences on the road, the psychologist said, "It seems to me, Miss Oxford, that your life has been a continual adaptation to rejections, and that out of those experiences, your incredible strength was born."

THE PAST: VANESSA REMEMBERS:
A CHRISTMAS PAST

YES, THE PSYCHOLOGIST WAS RIGHT, I suppose. We suffered rejections everywhere, all the time. But it hurt the most at Christmas. . . .

Christmas was a family.

Vanessa remembered. In spite of the resolutions to block out pain, images bombarded the dark screen of her memory. Christmas in Muskenaw, when she and Cassie and Mama were beholden to Aunt Annie and Uncle Arthur. Christmases in so many alien places: boarding houses, shoddy small-town hotels, and, sometimes, when Mama was in desperate straits, back to Muskenaw again.

Aunt Annie's kitchen. Sanctity. Warm, with the black iron coal stove with nickel trim that Aunt Annie was always polishing; Mama's plaid shawl wrapped around you, while you sat in the rocker, holding Buster, the calico cat, and swinging gently, like a rowboat, rocking, rocking. And Mama and Aunt Annie, drinking coffee and talking in an undertone, while Vanessa, head against the rocker, knew without hearing that Father was the subject of their talk.

Christmas, over the years. One she remembered with a sharp, hurting vision. A Christmas party given somewhere on the road. Sleet, snow, ice overhead, ice underfoot, no performance of *East Lynne* on Christmas Eve. A party for the poor children of the town. The manager of the troupe heard about it. "Let the kids attend," he said, since the party was being held in the town hall, where the touring company performed. "They'll have a good time."

Vanessa and Cassie, aged six and five, dressed in holiday best, blue coats and full-length leggings and blue velvet hats, walking hand in hand up the steps to the town hall while Mama stayed in a downstairs office with the stage manager, "Uncle Harry," who traveled with them.

"I'm scared," Cassie said.

Cassie always said what Vanessa felt. Cassie was afraid unless Mama was there; and if Vanessa were afraid, she had truly forgotten about it. (Because whenever she now said, "I was never afraid," it was said with conviction.) She didn't dare show fear, not with Cassie looking to her for courage.

Behind the auditorium door, a band was playing. The sisters loved the old songs.

"It came upon a midnight clear ..."

She and Cassie stood at the door, Cassie nervous, her kewpie doll face pale, her eyes enormous, "I want to go to Mama ..."

"Look, they've got Santa!" Vanessa said, gripping her little sister's hand. "There're presents. Uncle Harry said so."

The splendor of the room dazzled them as the door opened and a heavy-set woman came out. Smiling, she allowed them to enter. Kerosene lamps overhead, candles on the stage, a long table spread with chickens, hams, turkey, cookies, candies; and a line of boys and girls waiting for Santa, who sat to one corner of the stage, ruddy and jovial in his costume, handing out little bags filled with whistles, candies, popcorn and real oranges. Vanessa ran her tongue over her lips. Once before, when Father was still with them, she'd tasted an orange.

The line of children, eyes focused on Santa, afraid the bags would run out before it was their turn. Children bundled up in sweaters, knickerbockers and boots, or wool dresses and sweaters and overshoes, sweating in the self-generated heat but refusing to budge. Santa, Santa, don't run dry! And the ladies, long skirts, full bosoms, pompadours, parading up and down the line, looking at the little scraps of paper the kids clutched in their hands.

A woman stopped before each child, asked something and the child extended the paper, which she collected. Oh, oh, Vanessa thought, sensing trouble. The line moved up and Vanessa figured they were saved. But the woman moved with it, and soon she was at their side. "Let me have your cards," she said.

Vanessa looked up at her, eyes soulful, a glint of tears in them, her small, perfect mouth turned down at the corners.

"I lost them," she whispered, so the woman had to bend down to catch the words. "I can't find them."

"Who gave them to you?"

Vanessa's eyes brimmed over.

"Who are you?" the woman asked. "What is your name?"

"Vanessa. My little sister is Cassie."

"Where do you live?"

Tears rolled down Vanessa's face.

The woman motioned to a man in a dark suit. "I don't think these two are entitled."

Cassie piped up, "We are with the *East Lynne* touring company. Last night we played here—*right on this stage!*"

"Heavens, they're *actors!*" The disapproval in the woman's voice made the sisters cringe. "You don't belong here. Get out, go on, *scat!*"

The other kids were watching. Vanessa held tight to Cassie's hand. With her head bowed, her small narrow shoulders stooped (a pose that was to become her trademark years later), she began to lead Cassie away toward the door.

"Hey, wait a minute!" The man put out his hand to stop them. "Wait a minute!" He walked down the length of the line, fished into a big carton, took out two large paper bags and came back to them. "Here, Merry Christmas," he said. The woman glared at him and began pushing Vanessa and Cassie toward the exit.

Vanessa held onto the bag with her left hand and Cassie with her right. But Cassie pulled away, picked up the bag and threw it at the woman, and the bright gifts scattered, and the beautiful orange rolled away, and the kids fell on it, fighting among themselves.

"I don't want your ol' presents!" Cassie screamed.

On the stairs, Vanessa said, "Don't tell Mama. Promise?"

Cassie nodded. They always spared Mama.

They went down to the office and Vanessa turned the knob. Mama and "Uncle" Harry were to one side, in the shadow, and

Mama got up quickly, but not before Vanessa saw that thing he had between his legs. It was thick and red and ugly, but she knew what it was like. Because once, riding on the train from one place to another, "Uncle" Harry had her on his lap and he was reading her a story, and she felt that red throbbing thing reaching out of him and onto her little bare bottom, only partially hidden by cambric panties.

A strange anger took hold of her. She thought it was against "Uncle" Harry. But forever after in her dreams, why was it Mama?

Despite her shock at seeing Mama with "Uncle" Harry, she was not too upset that day long ago to catalogue the presents in her paper sack. The whistle and Crackerjacks she gave to Cassie. The notebook and pencil she kept for herself. The handkerchief trimmed with lace she kept too. The long, ribbed black stockings she gave to Cassie.

"I hate 'em, I won't wear 'em," Cassie screamed as she tossed the ribbed black stockings at Vanessa. "I hate 'em. And I hate you."

I reflect often on Mama's lot in life. Young, attractive, with a winsome manner and enormous kindness, she must have had many admirers. Sometimes, when we stayed alone at night in our rooming house while she did an evening show, a man would escort her home. But she never lingered long; usually she came home directly from the theater.

Was her life a dramatic exercise? I suspect as much because I never saw her show an interest in any man. Except once, and I prefer to forget about it.

She was dedicated to bringing us up like ladies. Nothing pleased her more than to hear people comment, "The Oxford sisters are such little ladies." When we were traveling, she always counseled us, "Be quiet. Don't bother people."

I'm certain it must've been hard for her to spend so much time on the road without a home of her own, but Cassie said, "Nonsense," when I suggested it. "Mama was a gypsy at heart. She loved to travel. She adored new sights and new people. Of course, she detested the small towns and the bad food and the filthy rooming houses; and the way people treated us. But she loved it all anyway. If she were a man she'd have taken off for lands with exotic-sounding names—Canton and Cathay, Singapore and Kuala Lumpur ..." Cassie may have been right, but as usual she was, I suspect, mostly talking about herself.

Mama, you died too early. I don't have time enough to do for you what you deserved. Sometimes, I search for you in my dreams—not in the night terrors—but in my dreams, and my arms are full of gifts. But each door I come to remains shut.

I think I prefer the night terrors to those dreams, Mama. I cannot face them. I tried so hard to achieve success early, but the best came after you were gone. ...

At least if only you had enjoyed some happiness with Father the way other women did with *their* husbands. ...

THE PAST: VANESSA REMEMBERS: FATHER DESERTS US

WHICH BRINGS ME to Father.

His wanderlust was fueled by alcohol. Not a chronic drinker when he and Mama first married, he was becoming one fast. Why? Perhaps his dreams of accomplishment were not equaled by his talent. (I've seen it happen so often in my profession.) An itinerant printer, in conflict with his boss, he was an "almost" character. He *almost* achieved his dreams—but never quite. Inspired by his manic mind, his grandiose plans took shape, but whenever they were near completion something happened. His backer reneged, he lost an option, got into a terrible fight and wouldn't make friends with the money people who could help him. He failed at publishing a four-page weekly newspaper that was to be given free to readers and supported by advertisers. (He was ahead of his time.) Between these disappointments, he would go back to work for any paper or print shop that gave him a job.

After his disappearance in Toronto he drifted back in our lives once in a rare while, though how he kept in touch with Mama I don't know. Perhaps Aunt Annie was the go-between. She adored him. Father was no womanizer, but women were susceptible to the small boy in the gaunt, handsome young man. Why in the world the boy in a man appeals to women has always eluded me. Perhaps I lack a mothering heart.

Once when Mama was playing in Cincinnati, Father showed up at the stage door and asked for her. He wasn't allowed into the dressing room, which she shared with two other women and where we were playing with our paper dolls. He waited outside and I ran into the alley to look at him. I shall never forget his appearance. He wore a cape and a dark felt hat. Nobody we knew wore a cape. The men we knew wore heavy topcoats or plaid Mackinaws. We associated capes with villains in melodramas. I ran back into the dressing room and waited for Mama to bring us out to meet him.

Father didn't look like a villian. He looked inordinately handsome, his flat cheekbones flushed, his dark eyes glittering, his mustache neatly trimmed. Yet there was an unfinished look about him that I can still remember. He wasn't the father I remembered. He was a stranger.

Mother was cool to him when we came out of the stage door. They didn't seem to have much to say to each other. He kept watching Cassie, who was huddled against Mama's skirts, ignoring him—whether out of shyness or fear I'll never know. I thought he was foolish to pay so much attention to Cassie. I was a year older, nearly seven, and passionately devoted to my memory of him. I even thought how wonderful it would be if he took me away and we could live together, Father and I, and I could take care of him.

After a while, he gave up and said goodbye to Mama. Cassie wouldn't kiss him. When he turned to me, holding out his arms and saying, "Little Vanessa . . . ," I burst into tears and said, "Take me with you, please. *Please*, take me with you!"

Mama touched my arm, but I pulled away. I didn't dare face my feelings for Mama. I pressed my lips together and stopped crying and watched his figure disappear in the crowd.

Later we heard from Aunt Annie that Papa was in a hospital. She didn't explain what kind of hospital.

But somehow I knew.

Which is why I've always worried about Cassie and have tried so hard to look after her.

THE PAST: VANESSA REMEMBERS: THE LEGEND GROWS

THE YEAR WAS 1910. What was going on in America and Europe had little meaning to us. There were no means of communications except newspapers, which we seldom saw. In the New York papers Mama looked only at the want ads for work that would see us through the summer until companies left for fall tours.

When Mama got her first job in show business there were any number of touring companies, but this year the theater was in a slump. America was going wild for the nickelodeon.

Mama doggedly made the rounds. Finally she made contact with a new producer who was sending out a company of *The Branded Woman* in October. Fortunately the heroine had two children, so Cassie and I were chosen. If there were only one part I usually filled it because Cassie was too young. She was also high-strung and active. Today I suppose the doctors would diagnose her as hyperactive.

The Branded Woman company consisted of twenty-five people, including the leading lady and leading man, a soubrette and an ingenue. Mama, as usual, was the soubrette. The company carried not only luggage but scenery, and each member had his share of responsibility. I took mine very seriously. Today when I am in a film or on tour, the cast is usually shocked because I insist on carrying my own suitcase. I'm accustomed to it.

That tour was like the winter, long and hard. The company was stranded finally in Kansas, where the money ran out and the manager ran off to escape the awful responsibility of bringing his troupe back to New York.

The cast was in a terrible state. Everyone counted on each week's salary to keep going. No actor was able to salt away enough to see him through "at liberty" periods. The players met at the empty theater, trying to find ways to finance their return to New York. The manager had promised to send them money for their fares, but it would be a wait and they might not survive.

I don't know how the others managed, but Mama proved unbelievably resourceful. On Main Street, across from the post office, was a small dry goods store called The Emporium, which catered to the women in town and on outlying farms. She convinced the owner that she could help move merchandise by advising women on fabrics, helping them cut patterns, suggesting trimmings. Mama was wearing a dress of her own design, and her appearance and manner weren't at all what the owner, Mr. Muscowitz, expected of an actress.

Well, Mama worked in The Emporium for six months, earning enough to pay our room and board and adding every week a few dollars to the nest egg that would take us back to civilization. Cassie and I attended school, a one-room schoolhouse, and we even learned a little. Our classmates made fun of us but they were also drawn toward us; our acting experience fascinated them.

Mama finally was able to bring us back to New York in the spring, and we made theatrical rounds again of agents and producers, but for the first time in years there were no jobs. Mama, however, wasn't defeated. The six-month hiatus had given her the strength and assurance she needed. She knew she could support us. We would never again go hungry between jobs, because if we couldn't find acting jobs, she'd find another way to support us. Somehow. Some way.

THE PAST: VANESSA AND CASSIE: TWO
LITTLE GIRLS, TWO LITTLE TROUPERS

WE WERE a Sister Act.

You could see us doing a vaudeville turn on a Saturday matinee. Not in one of the major vaudeville houses, but in the second- and third-rate spots in Brooklyn and the Bronx, houses that put on several live acts between their showing of "flickers." We usually started the program and we were followed by a dance team and, finally, a comedian.

Picture the two of us, standing in the wings, waiting for the one-reeler to end. I was in a frilled, lace-trimmed pink dress, a fetching leghorn cartwheel hat on my curls. Cassandra was in a similar outfit. As the lady piano player swung into "Pony Boy," we pranced out on the stage, clinging to each other for support and courage.

We were pretty bad. The booker decided that a boy and girl act would have more appeal. So Cassie was ordered into a boy's sailor suit and a jaunty straw boater.

"I won't wear it!" Cassie threw a tantrum. "I'm a girl!"

As an addition to her misery, the booker suggested she appear in blackface.

In the end, Cassie accepted her outfit but hardly with grace. The odd thing was that she looked quite dashing as a boy. (Later, when she was a grown woman and long before pants suits were a part of every fashionable woman's wardrobe, Cassie bought her slacks and jackets in the boys' department at Brooks and had them fitted to her slim, flat-hipped figure. Recently she has switched to dresses. "The other side of my split is in ascendance," she announced.)

I remember that summer was an exercise in survival.

As I came into my teens, I was all bones and angles. Too old for child parts, too young for ingenues. But was obliged to earn my living. Mother, Cassie and I were staying in a small room in a boarding house on Broadway. I haunted agents' offices but with no luck. Then I happened to hear that Siegel Cooper, a department store, was looking for salesgirls. We had no working papers in those days, nothing like Social Security cards, so I tried to pass for eighteen. I put up my hair, borrowed a skirt of Mama's that I hiked up with a safety pin and went off, looking, I suspect, like a freak. The woman in Personnel must've been sorry for me, because she was kind and suggested my coming back just before the holidays when they'd put on more help. I walked out of her office, wondering where to turn, when I met another girl who was also looking for work. She was dark-haired, very pretty, and older than I was. Her name was Mercy Brown. She told me she'd heard about a studio that produced "flickers" for nickelodeons and suggested we try for work there.

So we walked down to East 14th Street to the Joshua Fodor Studio. Mr. Fodor was filming a mob scene that day and he needed extras. Mercy Brown and I were both hired.

We each got five dollars for the day's work.

It was a godsend.

And the beginning of everything.

THE PAST: VANESSA REMEMBERS: JOSHUA FODOR WAS LIKE A FATHER TO ME...

MAMA WAS CERTAINLY STARTLED when I arrived home that evening, after a long trolley ride from East 14th Street to our rooming house on the upper West Side (that's what Broadway and 48th Street was in 1913), and told her about my experiences at Mr. Fodor's movie studio.

She was even more startled when I handed her five dollars, my day's salary. I expected Mama and Sister to be shocked by my daring to work in "flickers," but five dollars was an impressive sum, more than I'd ever earned for a day's work. So I was divided between pride and a sense of having compromised myself.

The smell of lamb stew was delicious. Mama managed culinary miracles on the two-burner plate. But before we could enjoy the feast, Cassie sprang *her* surprise. *She* was going on tour for a month with the road company of a play by Anne Nichols. The role was for a young, pretty girl. And Cassie certainly filled the bill.

"If Mr. Fodor would give me permanent work, or even use me as an extra a few days a week," I said, "we'd be in clover."

Which is exactly how it turned out. Once Cassie was on the road, Mama found a job in a small family restaurant. She sat behind the cashbox, looking lovely, like the lady she was, and the proprietor of the restaurant treated her with courtesy and respect. The cook often sent home leftovers. So the summer that began so badly was coming along splendidly.

During the next weeks I showed up diligently at the Fodor Studio whether I'd been told to report or not, because sometimes, during the morning, there would be an unexpected call for extras. If you were there, you got to work. The rest of the time I sat in

26

the lobby with some of the extras, mostly older women and a few men, who talked about their past glories.

"They're nothing but a bunch of has-beens," Mercy Brown said, sitting nearby on the steps of the grand staircase, "who've never made it in the legitimate theater."

"Well, it must be awful to be *old* like that," I said. "And nobody wants you . . ."

Mercy Brown was also reporting as an extra nearly every day, but she had been used more often than I. We became friends and we shared thoughts about the studio and staff. Since I had met with no success at all in my efforts to find another job, I decided to work my way into the Fodor company. Mother never let me be aware of my looks, but others said I was pretty. The young girls in the company seemed no more attractive than I. They were experienced because they had been around longer, I told myself, and so it was important I learn to be like them, to accommodate myself to what was acceptable to Mr. Fodor.

But movie making for the nickelodeons was a bewilderment. So utterly unlike the theater, even the second-rate road companies that we'd known. Nothing the actors and the director were doing made any sense to me. In the theater the director rehearsed us until we were letter-perfect; then we were on our own for the rest of the play. But there, Mr. Fodor rehearsed his players endlessly and then directed them with the camera grinding, a scene at a time. Scenes didn't follow each other. There was no sequence. No wonder they were called "flickers" and "galloping tintypes."

Still, in the midst of all this confusion Mr. Fodor seemed to know what he was doing. He was an imposing man, nearly as old as Father, but where Father was dark and moody, Mr. Fodor was light, his blond hair straight, center-parted, and always neatly combed, not a hair out of place. His eyes were deep-set, his nose flat, his chin square. He was immaculate: his shirt starched, his suits pressed, his shoes shined. Mama would approve of him; she loved people who took meticulous care of themselves. She said you could always tell what a person thought of himself by the way he dressed. She taught us from childhood always to be scrubbed and neat.

I suppose you could describe Mr. Fodor as being a Personage. His staff felt his influence and responded to it. He was everywhere in the studio with that quick nervous stride of his, as though he needed seven-league boots to cover all his territory. Between rehearsals he would confer with Hans, the cameraman, and the electrician ("Let's try something different, Fred. I'm relying on you to get the effect"). Often he went out with his staff for dinner; other times he stayed in and worked through the night, editing the day's rushes, or preparing for a new film, or conferring with the Bogan Brothers, his backers, in the front office.

Before he started a film, he would often give the cast a little preparatory talk. "What we are doing here today will be seen all over the world. In time, people of all nations will find your faces as familiar to them as those of their own families. What our stories will tell them will influence their lives, for good or evil. We have in our hands the most powerful medium the world will ever see . . ."

I listened and found myself tremendously excited. I still remember the goosebumps on my skin and thinking that he must know what he is saying. And if it's true, why, this place can be the most important one in the whole world!

It was fascinating to watch him direct his company. His hands were expressive and mobile; he used them like an actor, slicing the air for emphasis with his upturned palms or punching the air like a prize fighter. In spite of his inspiring talks, none of us had any idea then that with his dreams and his little company of actors he would leave a permanent mark on our lives and the entire motion picture industry. As I grew to know Mr. Fodor I realized that he made us all see larger visions, and those of us who listened to him with all our senses were soon stretching our capabilities to the farthest reaches, toward him . . . His daring, imagination and courage that he incorporated into those early films were the genesis of the film industry. The ones who came after Joshua Fodor, men like Cecil B. de Mille, King Vidor, Josef von Stern-berg, Erich von Stroheim, all agreed that he'd gone a giant step forward, even beyond D. W. Griffith, to create the basic technique of motion pictures.

Today, everything in film making is compartmentalized. Everyone has his job. Well, in those days Mr. Fodor did everything himself. When I first came to work for him, he was already unique. Audiences preferred Joshua Fodor Productions, films that had a story with a beginning, a middle and an ending. Using the lens the way writers use the pen, he rose above the limitations of techniques and created a kind of compassionate humanity that's missing in many of the newcomers in the field. He often even wrote the subtitles to his films.

I heard some of the older actors talking about him more than once.... He came from Austria, a country where freedom of expression was a dangerous exercise. They said that his father had been a patriot who worked for the overthrow of the Emperor, and that Mr. Fodor had inherited the family hatred of injustice and feeling for the underdog.

All you had to do was keep your ears open at rehearsal and you could learn from him. Society, he said, made us feel guilty if we dared to be different. We were taught that conformity means acceptance. A wayward step and we lost forever society's love and approval and were banished to the darkness of loneliness and rejection.

"He sounds more like a preacher than a director," Mercy Brown grumbled during one rehearsal while he was explaining the reason why the actors were to behave in a particular way.

I made no answer because my mind was attuned to Mr. Fodor's remarks. Even if I didn't understand some of his language, I got the gist of what he wanted from his actors. I could visualize myself as one of the leads, taking direction from him.

Looking back now, I realize that he had the ability to make us see ourselves as simple human beings, well-meaning if perhaps misdirected, full of doubt and guilt but having the courage to overcome and survive. His film characters often seemed to cry out for maturity—"Let us grow up before our weaknesses destroy us."

Only a man who had suffered deeply himself could bring up these dark feelings at a time when self-knowledge was virtually unknown.

No one, of course, knew about the dark secrets that tormented him.

I did. Eventually. And the knowledge changed my life forever.

As I said, when it came to his work he was a one-man production unit. He read, he wrote; he designed costumes and sets; he produced and directed. To work sixteen hours a day was not unusual for him, and the company was inspired to share his intensity and dedication. In no time I understood that nothing mattered but the film in the making. If you got tired, you ignored your fatigue; if you were sick, you never mentioned it, and as long as you could walk, you were there.

Naturally I didn't understand him in the beginning, but from the first I honestly think I sensed that he was a great man. I dedicated myself to him. I based my hope of arousing his interest on the fact that I was new and he was always seeking new faces. I hoped to accumulate a knowledge of how he made his films, so he could talk to me, when the time came, as he couldn't talk to the other girls. I realized that the company, both staff and performers, were his family, and that those who turned to him for advice, those who listened, those who obeyed him unquestioningly, were his favorites.

Not many of the young actresses were fired by ambition the way I was. Perhaps they couldn't grasp the magical future he spoke about. They weren't girls with great expectations ... films were rent money, food on the table, clothes for younger brothers and sisters and a widowed or abandoned mother. Films were fun, but only a way station until Mr. Right came along.

Often, when the players were rehearsing, I'd station myself near the set, observing the way Mr. Fodor explained the characters and how he expected the cast to interpret them. He had unbelievable patience and he expected no less from them. He rehearsed until they were exhausted before he decided to begin filming. But the strange thing was that he seemed to know when they got their second wind, when their defenses were worn away and their inner powers emerged and they were at the peak for the performance.

My dear friend Rebecca once did a critique of his early work for *Theatre News*: "*Joshua Fodor combined drama, sometimes cheap melodrama, with social criticism. As a result, his audiences were startled by his insight into their own sufferings, their plight as a result of cruelty and injustice.... Fodor's films were never disguised to give untroubled pleasures.*

"*His greatest handicap was emotional, a tendency always to overload the scales against evil.*

"He was blatantly melodramatic. The cause may have been his youthful exposure to the Yiddish drama on Second Avenue, where plays pandered to the most elemental emotions of their audiences.

"Although he was Austrian, he never learned the subtlety of Austria's dramatists and writers."

Perhaps not. But he had humor, although it was mostly put on display for the benefit of his cast when he was having problems with a film—a simple, boyish humor that transformed him from the great director to just another member of the company.

It was easy to understand why they all loved him. There was a warm sense of unity among members of his company. They were mostly young. To them, going on location was exciting; location trips took on the casual charm of a picnic or an excursion. If a film did well, there were bonuses for everybody, and sometimes when Mr. Fodor was in high spirits he took the entire company over to Lüchow's for dinner. He loved the oompah band and the romantic waltzes of the orchestra. During the day, in the studio, as he moved from the carpenter to the set painter to the photographer, he'd be humming in his off-key voice.

Sometimes I overheard the men at the poker table talking about him. With the greatest respect, although there was something more...a pause if Peg Dalton happened to be in the studio. Or Jenny Mayran.

Years later, when I met his secretary Thelma again, that devoted woman said, "He was the kindest man I ever knew, but sometimes he'd do something mean, like he was teasing. Then if you cried, he'd get all upset and make it up to you. He was always friendly with the staff, he played ball with the men or took the girls out for dinner and dancing, but there was something about him...you just couldn't get close to him. I always thought he was rather sad, and lonely."

Historians of the Silents certainly agree he was the right man for his time. He was there when the raw material for films was begging for a creator. He absorbed, he exploited, he used courage and talent in a burst of brilliant, compulsive creativeness.

In eight years he turned out three hundred and fifty films, mostly one- and two-reelers, but toward the end there were also the long masterpieces by which his reputation has endured. He didn't quite equal his mentor D. W. Griffith. But he was close enough....

It wasn't too long before the important members of the Fodor company became individuals to me.

Richie Doyle. I counted on him even though he was the office boy. He was about sixteen, tall for his age, thin with the kind of poetic face that Gregory Peck made famous many years later. You felt the romantic streak in him, the dreamer under the practical boy who did his many jobs so well. He was the first in the studio to show me real kindness. The wardrobe lady said he'd started as a choirboy but because he was so good-looking she suspected that in time Mr. Fodor would cast him in a film. Meanwhile, he made himself useful, sweeping floors, showing the extras where to dress, running errands, fetching lunch boxes for everybody. Even carrying the camera for Hans Rolfsma.

"That camera looks awful heavy," I said to him one morning as he was lugging it into the studio.

"Weighs eighty pounds," he said when he caught his breath.

"And you carry it all by yourself!"

My admiration seemed to please him. "I do a lot of heavy work around here. Mr. Fodor kinda depends on me."

I discovered that he wasn't exaggerating. Mr. Fodor did seem very fond of him, and Richie worshipped Mr. Fodor. Mercy Brown heard from one of the extra ladies that Mr. Fodor had paid the medical bills when Richie's mother was in the hospital and had arranged for the care of Richie's eight brothers and sisters, hiring one of the middle-aged "extra" women to serve as housekeeper until Mrs. Doyle returned to her family. Richie's father had died of cirrhosis of the liver, so Richie was now head of the family. I don't know whether it was his gratitude to Mr. Fodor or whether he was an eager beaver, but he opened the studio and seldom left at night before Mr. Fodor, and Mr. Fodor kept an eye on him, gave him books to read and had the office manager help him with mathematics.

Richie Doyle was a good friend to have.

Hans Rolfsma. The cameraman was first after Richie to check in mornings. He collected equipment, the tripod and the movie camera (which was the Edison camera and gave him a lot of trouble), and he grumbled. He also gathered the plates for the still camera that would be used for still photography. He marked off the outline of the set so the actors would move within its boundaries. He was a tall, angular man, with a mass of coarse white hair that stood up around his face, which was all cheekbones, forehead and Prince Albert beard.

One morning, when I was there early, I just happened to bump into him. "Oh, excuse me," I said.

"That's all right, little girl."

"Mr. . . . Hans . . ."

"Yes?"

Now he was looking at me; now he *really* saw me.

"I am from the theater, but I'm just an extra here. I'd like to do my best, just in case I get a chance to act. Could you tell me . . . I mean, about my face and my hair . . . ?"

"Didn't Richie tell you what makeup to use?"

"Yes, sir, he did. But I am so fair-complexioned and my hair is so light, I thought that maybe there was something I could do . . . I mean, to look better for your camera."

He laughed. He had a big mouth of teeth, nicotined from cigarettes. "You're ambitious, aren't you?"

"I have to be, Mr. Rolfsma. I am the sole support of my mother and sister."

"Are you now! Well, I'll tell you. Sometimes when I'm not busy, I'll let you sit for the camera and we'll have the electrician try out different kinds of lights."

I took his hand and kissed it. "Oh, thank you, sir."

"If you've got that much ambition," he said, "you deserve a chance."

Lorraine North. She was beautiful. She looked as though she'd never suffered all the growing pains most girls are subject to. Her hair was thick and chestnut, coming down to a widow's peak on her forehead and framing an oval face of classic beauty with well-defined brows, enormous expressive dark eyes and a mouth that was full and bee-stung, in contrast to the small mouths of the other girls. She carried herself with a certain elegance, even when wearing the awful skirts and shirtwaists from the wardrobe trunks.

The wardrobe lady said Mr. Fodor bought her evening gowns from Madame Regina, a designer who dressed many of the Broadway stars.

During a filming I would stand back in the shadows and watch Lorraine North. It seemed to me she was more professional than the other girls, more confident of what was expected of her. I wondered if Mr. Fodor coached her privately. She put on airs, acting superior to the other girls, and one day when she was snippy the wardrobe lady said, "She won't last much longer. Mr. Fodor likes young girls."

"I suppose it's because any girl over fifteen photographs like an old hag," one of the women extras suggested. "I'm told it's those Cooper-Hewitt lights."

"Is Mr. Fodor married?" I asked. Nobody ever spoke of a wife and he seemed to work all hours, which meant he couldn't have much of a home life. The wardrobe lady said he was married but no one had ever seen his wife.

Jenny Mayran. She was younger than Lorraine, maybe a year or two older than I, and the most beautiful girl I'd ever seen. Everything about her was exquisite: her pale, straight, golden hair; her deep-blue-violet eyes; her porcelain skin and perfect teeth. Her hands were like sculpture. Mr. Fodor used them often—just her hands in a closeup to portray a feeling or prayer or fear. I think Jenny's hands gave him the idea of using fragments to express emotion, an innovation the reviewers later singled out for praise. (In film classes today they always mention Fodor's skill in using a fragment of the body, even once a daring suggestion of a bare breast.)

Peg Dalton. Richie told me about Peg. She was the newest girl in the company. She was small, like a sprite, with short blonde hair (the only girl in the company with short hair, cut like a boy's), and a freckled face with features that the camera loved. The first time I saw Peg on film and compared her to the girl on the set, I couldn't believe they were the same. Richie said she first showed up on the lot about six months before to visit a cousin of hers who helped Mr. Fodor's secretary with office work. She was usually dressed in a serge dress with a sailor collar, and Richie said she always bubbled with high spirits.

Mr. Fodor was always on the lookout for fresh talent; sometimes he stopped people on the street and asked them if they'd like to be in the movies and gave them his card. He put Peg on the payroll right away and she was his choice for a role in his next film, a role that was supposed to be Lorraine's. But he thought Lorraine was getting too uppity so he gave the part to Peg.

The wardrobe lady said Lorraine's nose was out of joint, and there were loud words in Mr. Fodor's office after the day's filming was over. The wardrobe lady said she overheard Lorraine say that Pegs didn't look like a girl at all, with her short hair. And Mr. Fodor said she'd had typhoid and they'd cropped her hair, which was falling out, and she needed a job. It was almost like he was apologizing to Lorraine, and afterward he took her out to dinner at Lüchow's.

(I thought how lucky these girls were, going out to dinner at Lüchow's, with the music and delicious food and deferential waiters. I didn't dare hope theirs would be my good fortune one day.)

When I first came on as an extra, Peg was in favor more than Lorraine or Jenny. Sometimes, Monday morning when she arrived at the studio, she let the staff know that Mr. Fodor had spent Sunday at her family's home, having dinner with them. I guess Mrs. Dalton couldn't believe her good luck, I mean about Peg being an actress with Mr. Fodor and he taking such an interest in her. When Peg wanted to go out with one of the neighborhood boys to a party or to the beach, Mrs. Dalton wouldn't allow her to make a date until she was sure Mr. Fodor wouldn't be calling on her. The Dalton brothers and sisters couldn't believe Peg's fortune either. She was supposed to be the homeliest girl in the family.

From the talk at lunchtime or in the dressing room, I learned that although Peg was plain-looking compared to such great beauties as Lorraine and Jenny, Mr. Fodor considered her very sensitive. He said she could weep through her smile and smile through her tears.

I found myself thinking a good deal about Peg, because she seemed to be the greatest competition I'd have if I were to make a place for myself in the studio. Then one afternoon, when I was walking toward the dressing room, I heard Peg talking to her kid sister, who'd spent the day watching her perform. I heard this childish voice, piping up, "I know something you think I don't know."

"Oh, stop your foolishness."

"I know what happens when he takes you for a walk in the woods. I know what you do. *I saw you!*"

And Peg's voice, not like her own: "If you ever tell, I'll kill you. I'll kill you with my bare hands."

She sounded as though she meant it.

That set me to wondering. When the company went on location and there was a break in the filming, Mr. Fodor would take the hand of one of the girls—not Lorraine, but Jenny or Peg— and say, "Let's take a walk," and off they'd go, Mr. Fodor whistling a Strauss waltz; his favorites being, I learned later, "Tales from the Vienna Woods" and *Der Rosenkavalier.* The men and women in the company, gathering up the paper from sandwiches and pie, would look at each other. There was a curious quality about their looks that made me feel they had communicated something they understood and I didn't.

When I made an attempt to talk about it, even the wardrobe lady clammed up. The staff loved Mr. Fodor, who was so good to them, and there was never talk about him either on or off the lot.

He was kind even to the extras. Many days he put in a call for them but never used them, and they got lunch and a day's pay, which most of them desperately needed.

They said, however, he had a streak of temper. Once when a carpenter's helper who was hired for the day got fresh with Jenny Mayran, Mr. Fodor beat the living daylights out of him and threw him off the set.

After that, he got bodyguards for the girls in the company. When they worked on a city street there was a danger of street fights with bullies, who thought it was smart to put down the performers. He saw to it that there were strong men to protect the girls, the older women, the expensive Edison camera. Richie usually roped off a part of a sidewalk or street for the filming, but the filming invariably attracted spectators.

Peg was present for all rehearsals and she was getting many choice parts the others girls felt were rightfully theirs through seniority. The wardrobe lady said Mr. Fodor worshipped youth, which was why he surrounded himself with the girls who clowned around, and this was the reason Peg Dalton was the current favorite. She seemed brimming with life. She giggled when she was happy and blushed when she was teased. Whenever Mr. Fodor saw her, a smile eased the tense lines in his face.

None of the girls could compare to Lorraine in poise and elegance, and I admired her and watched her, trying to learn what gave her such style; but it was Peg I was wildly jealous of. Unlike Peg, I was by temperament sober, serious, lacking in humor and social grace. I was usually ill at ease unless I was working.

In the studio, though, I came alive. Even if I were not Mr. Fodor's final choice for a part in the current film, I felt a sense of belonging. I was somebody. Others were watching me, perhaps even admiring me.

My education was so haphazard that words often confused and baffled me. I wasn't very articulate so it was simpler to remain silent (a trait that later gave the impression of mystery). But when I acted I could express all sorts of emotions I couldn't put into words, and in the process I somehow could feel bigger then myself.

It was a feeling I'd never been able to demonstrate during my early childhood, but in the secret places of my heart I think I always had a sense of self-prophecy. During our summer in Muskenaw, when I was all gawky arms and legs, I still convinced myself that all things were possible. And this absurd faith gave me the courage to refuse Eric's attentions, which that summer could have been my salvation: I loved him and he loved me. He was the doctor's only son. They had a house on Muskenaw Avenue near the library, and a standing in the community several levels above my Aunt Annie's.

"I must not turn my back on my dreams," I once actually said to him when he was annoyed with me. "I am an actress ..."

Poor misguided Eric. I never believed he would take my promise so seriously. For me it was just a lovely summer's idyll. For him ... but I cannot talk about that terrible day even now. ...

I was right in returning to New York; it led me to the Fodor Studio, and within three months from my first day as an extra I was to become a part of his company. I saw Mr. Fodor every day. Soon he would become truly aware of me. His prophetic words about the future of films gave me the courage to hope.

That an abundance of pretty young girls were frantically in search of a film future didn't divert me.

After all, I already was more successful than the eager girls waiting in the front hall for the call for extras.

I was Vanessa Oxford and a member of the Joshua Fodor Company. The fledgling movie industry paid great respect to Mr. Fodor. Every struggling company imitated him, which was perhaps the reason he was so secretive about his new projects. Any player who'd worked with Mr. Fodor was assured of a job with another film company if he wanted it. To take part in a Fodor film meant recognition, respect, prestige.

My first assault on the studio staff was to make them aware of my good manners and breeding. As I've said, whenever we traveled on the road Mama had always cautioned me, "Don't be a bother to anyone dear. Just be good."

Being good meant locking up your real feelings.

Being good meant being polite to your elders, being considerate and helpful. ("Such a lovely little girl ... Mrs. Oxford has certainly brought them up to be ladies.")

So I kept bad thoughts and bad needs down inside of me and denied them. Except, as clever Rebecca said later, when they came out in nightmares.

Whenever I got depressed, afraid that Mr. Fodor would never become aware of my existence and that I was doomed to remain an extra, I reminded myself sharply that I had more experience than the other girls. I thought of the tours Mama, Cassie and I had made, crisscrossing the east and midwest. People flocked to see us. They drove in from the hinterlands and they forgot about crop failures and family problems. Because what we brought them was delightful escape, the magic of an evening that left them feeling happy.

Mama taught us to be pleasant, never to gossip or speak unkindly of anyone. I obeyed, hoping that if I didn't gossip about others, they in turn would never slander me.

My skills were few, but the talent for innocent seduction was high among them. Hans and Richie both liked me and they were close to Mr. Fodor. My strategy might depend on their good will, yet it was important for me to keep my distance. Often when I was sitting at home in the Morris chair after supper, with my eyes closed as though I were sleeping, I would be formulating plans. I devoted myself to survival at any and all costs for our little family.

Cassie, all impulse and spontaneity, never planned ahead. Not then, nor in later years when she was an internationally known and loved film comedienne.

But I was all careful planning.

My goal was clear.

Mr. Fodor was obsessed with the making of films. He created his own atmosphere, but there was a pervasive friendly feeling in the studio. The young actresses amused him. But for how long? Not one of them showed an interest in anything but her roles. Not a single solitary one cared how the cameraman worked, or the electrician, or how film was developed and cut and spliced. Once the day's rehearsals or shooting were completed, they dashed out, as though school was dismissed. Except for Lorraine. And sometimes Peg.

The camera loved me, it was verified by the stills Hans Rolfsma did of me. "You photograph like a beauty," he said. "Now, you hang around, watch Mr. Fodor rehearse. You'll learn plenty."

I obeyed him.

Abel Levy and Jay Ritori, who developed film and worked nights with Mr. Fodor cutting and splicing film, were pleasant middle-aged men. They were surprised and pleased by my interest in their work. They explained their techniques and they didn't mind my hanging around, watching, listening, sometimes asking questions. Once in a while Mr. Fodor stumbled over me in the dark cutting room, but when he was absorbed in his thoughts he had a way of looking through you, as though you didn't exist.

He *had* to see me! To become aware of me. To remember me.

That curious girl Vanessa? You mean she's interested in the behind-the-screen technique? Remarkable. Which one is she? The bony little blonde?

It would be more fun for him to discuss films with an attractive, seductive young girl than the middle-aged men, wouldn't it?

But how was I going to make him aware of me?

This is how it happened.

THE PAST: VANESSA CREATES
A BLUEPRINT FOR SURVIVAL

THE MORNING was wickedly hot. The humidity was so heavy that our underclothes that Mama had washed in the communal bathroom wouldn't dry. Mama made breakfast, but I couldn't swallow a mouthful of cereal. The heat bothered me. I felt weak and inert. But we were schooled to keep our schedules, regardless of how we felt. Hans Rolfsma had been so kind, seeing that I was now always included in the extras. I couldn't stay away; Mama was counting on my having a minimum of four days' work each week.

The film Mr. Fodor had been rehearsing was about a society girl who makes an appearance at a settlement house to award a prize to a young immigrant, and falls in love with him. Her family disinherits her, naturally, but his family takes her to its collective bosom and celebrates a real ethnic wedding ceremony. I was among the players who were the groom's sisters. (That was Hans Rolfsma's doing, although I heard Mr. Fodor object, saying that a blonde was out of place in the beautiful dark Italian grouping. Hans said, "Haven't you heard of red-haired Italians? This girl is a strawberry blonde.")

Even the breeze on the open trolley car wasn't cooling; it simply stirred up the heat and dust. I was wearing a wide-brimmed leghorn hat, a white shirtwaist and a long skirt to make me look older, although we were no longer afraid of the Gerry Society that swooped down to arrest child actors. I walked crosstown, and the smells of heat, manure and dirt made me even more squeamish. The cobblestones bit into my thin soles; but it seemed faintly cooler as I entered the studio.

Richie greeted me like an old friend ... there was something so sweet about him. "You look kind of pale," he said. "You all right?"

"It's the heat," I told him.

We rehearsed all morning the various moments of the wedding ceremony and the joyous festivities that followed. Then Hans and Richie, who was acting as his assistant, worked from the rolling platform where the camera rested. This platform was approximately six feet square and between rehearsals or takes the cast used it as a place to rest. Although I was sensitive to the smell of sawdust and paint, I always found a place at the platform. But it was scalding under the Cooper-Hewitts that day. I felt as though I were in a roasting oven. The morning seemed interminable, but I clenched my hands and held on, smiling for the post-wedding party, dancing with another young girl, pretending to be frightened and scurrying away when a young man asked me to dance.

"When do we break for lunch today?" I asked a girl.

"Whenever Mr. Fodor decides. They said he's going to film the rest after lunch."

My body was drenched with rivulets of perspiration. My eyes were burning. But I kept up the animation. Finally, Mr. Fodor said, "Lunch, children."

We all trooped down to the basement, some of the girls flopping on the floor, others draping themselves on the wardrobe baskets. We were all breathing heavily, panting like exhausted puppies. Then Richie came in carrying a basket with the box lunches—ham sandwiches (the bread thick, the filling skimpy), an apple and milk. But we had appetites; even I, in spite of my morning squeamishness. However, after a couple of mouthfuls, I put the sandwich down. "Aren't you hungry?" Richie asked. I said I'd love some extra milk if it was available, and he brought me a glass. I didn't know until later that it was his own. When I walked out of the room and climbed the stairs, holding onto the balustrade, he followed me. He asked me how I liked working for Mr. Fodor and I said I didn't know yet, I felt as though I were wasting my time, and I told him about my stage experience.

"You better stick to the movies. Mr. Fodor says they're the coming thing. And the girls, Peg and Jenny and Lorraine, they make good money."

"I expect to be returning to the theater in the fall," I said, looking haughty, so he wouldn't guess that the theater had no place for me.

"Gee, I'll miss you," he said. "But you think about it. I did tell Mr. Fodor about you the other day, but you know, it's kind of funny. Sometimes he's listening to you and while you're talking he walks away. Hans says he don't mean nothing by it. It's just that his mind is filled with so many things."

In the afternoon there was more of the celebration to be filmed. Because there was dancing, Mr. Fodor had an accordion player on the set. Usually there was no music, in spite of what you may have read in film history books. But a squat, dark-haired young fellow was coaxing lively music out of his accordion, squeezing it shut, then pulling it out like an elastic band. Opera arias interspersed with popular songs. We danced and whirled and laughed in this sequence and the lights burned into our bodies, sending down the perspiration, and the next thing I knew, somebody was shouting, "Give her air, give her air . . ." and Mr. Fodor was saying, "Hans, keep the camera rolling." Then he added, "Richie, you help the groom pick her up, both of you. And you there, what's your name?"

"Vanessa." Richie answered for me because I was too faint to answer.

"Miss Vanessa, open your eyes and look at the groom. Let's see pain and reproach; he two-timed you, he deserted you and you kept it all to yourself until now, in a weak moment, your face tells them all the tragic truth."

As usual, he accepted the moment, improved it, and used it to give a film a fresh dramatic turn.

Meanwhile Richie helped me into Mr. Fodor's office, where Thelma, his secretary, a tall angular woman with a long horsy face, fussed over me, putting a cold compress on my forehead as I lay on the tufted black leather couch. The heat didn't let up; the afternoon sun poured a fierce blast over the city and into the room. I lay exhausted, flat on my back, but after a while I felt better, not sleepy, but remote, almost in a spell. I was thinking of Mr. Fodor, letting my imagination roam, as it did sometimes at night when I made up my own film in my mind. I saw myself in Lorraine's place, the focus of admiration from the company, the object of jealousy from the other girls. Lorraine was southern and she had a you-all kind of accent, and at times when I saw her talking to Mr. Fodor and they thought they weren't being watched, she seemed clinging and boneless. She looked at him worshipfully, her gaze fixed on him, her hands up, the wrists nearly touching, the fingers curved out like petals of an unfolding rose. If only I could learn grace from her, the exquisite use of her hands. I walked like a peasant, there was no use denying it. Cassie, though, had a graceful walk; she bounced with vitality and high spirits. I moved like a clod.

Lorraine's image kept nagging at me. To be like her, so feminine that men were drawn by a magnet more powerful than good sense! She was more of a siren than Theda Bara, to my way of thinking. I studied her whenever she was around. She was unfailingly sweet to everyone, men and girls. The wardrobe lady once said, "The southern girls are different from the girls up north. They're so soft and helpless. Lorraine makes each man feel like a cavalier."

Watch her, Vanessa, watch the way she uses her eyes, her face down, her eyes upraised, full of laughter without a sound coming from her lips. Sometimes her head was raised, her eyes lowered, her lips parted.

The leather couch was hot and sticky; I turned on my back and raised my skirt, hoping a draft of cool air would find my thighs. I raised my legs, setting my feet flat on the leather so my skirt made a kind of tent for the breeze.

"Feeling better, young miss?"

I was startled. Mr. Fodor was in the room standing beside me. I flattened my legs and sat up quickly, blushing deeply.

"Yes, sir. Much better."

"Take the rest of the day off. The cashier will pay you in full."

"Thank you, Mr. Fodor."

"Take care of yourself."

"Yes, sir."

He walked out and I was alone in his office. Then I realized something awful. I hadn't worn panties this morning, my everyday ones hadn't dried. Had Mr. Fodor seen my nakedness, as he walked in? I went to the door and looked as it must have looked to him. Yes, I had been in the direct line of his vision.

43

I was terribly upset. Mama had taught us to be proper young ladies. What would Mr. Fodor think of me? Back on the couch, I kept my cheek against the tufted leather, my eyes closed, trying to make my mind blank to shut out the embarrassment. And then something drifted into my head, a fragment of talk I'd overheard between Hans and the actor Allan Southgate.

Mr. Southgate had said, "Sometimes Mr. Fodor thinks like the Little Emperor." He went on to explain how Napoleon tried to divert the people of Paris after the losses of men and equipment in the disastrous Russian campaign. He sent an order to the dancers of the Opera demanding that they eliminate their undergarments.

"Can you imagine bare asses under those little tutus," Hans had said after he'd recovered from his outburst of laughter.

"Mr. Fodor's been doing research on Napoleon and he thinks it's a great idea. He's given an order for his little actresses to strip themselves of underpants and corset covers."

"What makes him think the censor will let him get away with it?" Hans had asked.

"I doubt he gave it a thought. He said it would give the girls a naughty air—they'd be aware of their sex and it would show up on the screen."

"Jesus Christ!"

"Don't take His name in vain," Mr. Southgate had answered. "I understand he's toying with the idea of doing the definitive life of Christ. He's actually serious about it."

"I don't believe it," Hans said. "Even Griffith wouldn't tackle Christ."

"But Fodor would—and will. After all, he's on his own now. Griffith can't tell him what to do any more. No one can. No one ever will."

THE PAST: JOSHUA FODOR
AS THE WORLD KNEW HIM

JOSHUA FODOR DIDN'T GO out on his own, he was pushed. Griffith fired him. It was as simple as that. Of course, Griffith made it sound as though he were doing Joshua a favor.

It was a psychological trick Joshua would remember. And eventually incorporate into his own style.

Meanwhile, he was dismayed. He wasn't a kid, he was pushing thirty and his prospects were grim. There was no future for him in the written word: he had failed as a journalist and as an aspiring novelist.

Where could he turn? Back to the Help Wanted columns of *The World?*

To plunge into gloom was dangerous, what with his introspective nature. It wasn't that he was so keen on the "flickers," but it was the only thing he'd done reasonably well at. It was also a new field where there were few experts. There had to be nickelodeon operators who would want him, particularly if he mentioned his previous association with D. W. Griffith. Everyone had a tremendous respect for Griffith. If you'd worked with him, your chances of finding a job were greatly improved.

Joshua was looking for a job.

Lambros and Delos Bogan were looking for a producer-director.

The Bogan brothers owned a string of nickelodeons that chewed up film faster than the Exchange could supply it. They decided that the dearth of available films made production the logical next step in their expansion. They would have not only enough films for their own nickelodeons, but films to lease to other operators.

45

"Money we have got, plenty!" It was a boastful but honest statement from the handsome young Greeks who only five years earlier had served as countermen in a greasy spoon.

The brothers urged him to start immediate film production. They had faith in him. Directors were still scarce. Everyone was learning by doing. The Gold Rush was in celluloid.

Joshua began his search for suitable quarters at Fifth Avenue and East 23rd Street, and checked the next blocks going south without success. Finally, on East 14th Street he found a townhouse that met his requirements. He knew the reason for his choice. At number 11 East 14th Street D. W. Griffith had achieved success. Joshua felt it would be a lucky street for him, too.

Once he staked out his own quarters, Joshua walked past the old Griffith Studio with great calm. Griffith had already deserted Manhattan for the climate and topography of California, where it was rumored he was involved in an epic film about the Civil War. Joshua had no such grandiose ambitions. Not yet. His lack of success as a writer had deflated his ego. Yet his nature and education had prepared him for future triumphs if only he could discover the right medium. He was familiar with the Metropolitan Museum, where he had studied the great paintings. Rembrandt's contrasts of light and shadow fascinated him. He came by his knowledge of music through his Austrian immigrant parents, who considered music as essential as bread in their lives. He observed people as an artist, seeing them as subjects for visual analysis. He often followed pedestrians on the street, watching, listening, creating characterizations from their dress, their walks, their mannerisms. He was a shameless voyeur.

At this early stage one- and two-reelers still satisfied him. Working with Griffith had allowed him to experiment with fiction, and he'd even sold the director several story ideas, though what he saw in his mind somehow always came out on paper as routine. Still he kept on trying and whenever he needed a little extra money he'd sell the story line of one of his unsold epics to Griffith for fifteen dollars, which was the going rate. He was drifting when D.W. let him go.

His reaction was that of an angry son to a cruel father: "By God, I'll beat him at his own game!"

Alan Southgate, the handsome young Southerner who was Griffith's favorite in spite of his weakness for spirits, first comforted Joshua and later joined his company.

"It's not that the old man is so great," Allan said, "but that the other directors are such clods."

Before he left Biograph Joshua discovered several other truths about film production: The difference between the stage and films was the art of compression. In a stage play the director had to get an actor on stage to speak his piece and then get him off. Film directors were slavishly following stage technique. The camera remained stationary. This entrance-exit procedure exasperated Joshua; it was such a time waster, it slowed up action. In the films he directed for Griffith, he developed a kind of shorthand that kept his story line sharp, his scenes generating excitement and mystery. He recognized the importance of suspense. It gave the film pace. He came to believe the film was superior to the theater because of its ability to use space and time as the theater never could.

Of all the young Griffith assistants, Joshua made the greatest progress in the technique of storytelling, developing on film the equivalent of the "page turner" in novels, a sense of "what happens next?" that made viewers sit at the edge of their seats.

Films also, he realized, required a new technique in acting. The physical movements of stage actors looked exaggerated on the screen. The only emotion they aroused in audiences was laughter. "I'm trying to develop realism in pictures by teaching the value of deliberation and repose," Mr. Griffith had told his assistants, Fodor among them.

Even Griffith was still learning. He'd refined the closeup, where actors' faces filled the screen, so the audience could share in their emotions. The closeup had been used originally in Edwin Porter's *The Great Train Robbery*. In 1905 Porter used parallel stories in *The Kleptomaniac* to dramatize his effects. He gave films their basic tools—suspense, terror. He was the original master of the rescue, which both Griffith and Fodor borrowed and improved upon.

Until that time most directors allowed the camera to take in every person who happened to be in the scene. As a result any actor who wanted to steal the audience's attention could do so easily. He could play for laughs during a scene meant to arouse pity, thereby confusing the audience and ruining the film.

Joshua decided to concentrate on the actor whose behavior was at the moment important to the story line. It heightened the drama of his films.

He had worked with Billy Bitzer, the cameraman who suffered Griffith's impossible demands. "It can't be done!" Billy Bitzer would cry out in frustration, "it can't be done!"

"Do it, Bill," Griffith would say.

Experiments in lighting. Camera tricks. The camera's iris focusing on the principal figure or the action, leaving out the others, and then returning to the full scene. Black gauze on the camera lens, the center a hole burnt out by a cigarette. The idea was to break away from the sharp-cornered pictures, to achieve a blending that was, according to Bitzer, like a wash drawing.

No question, Joshua had acquired from his apprenticeship at Biograph a headful of practical knowledge. He had already come a long way from his meager beginnings. . . .

The physical distance between the dark tenement on Fourth Street and the elegant Georgian townhouse on East 14th wasn't all that far. But Fourth Street was a dead end.

And 14th Street was the beginning of a new life.

The dank, depressing ghetto was, hopefully for Josh and his parents, a way station. The Vienna his parents had fled differed from the *shtetls* of the Eastern Jews. But their migrations had much in common. A flight from oppression into freedom.

The elder Fodor, a violinist, found a place for himself in the Jewish theater on Second Avenue. But the family never again attained the comfort and grace of their life in Vienna before their political views had made them fugitives. The tenement was a far cry from the light and space of Vienna. Maurice, Joshua's father, who scorned a society that was divided into ninety percent poverty and ten percent affluence, managed nevertheless to adjust to the new world. In the Second Avenue cafes, among the coffee-house intellectuals, he found a haven for his political convictions.

The new world was less satisfying for Joshua. The rude, noisy environment crushed his spontaneity. An only child, he clung to the security of his mother's love. He never became a member of the gangs, either the Irish or the Jewish, because he was neither. He was already a loner.

The two years he spent at City College, with its exacting academic standards, were enough. He dropped out. City College prepared its lean, hungry, ambitious students for medicine, law or teaching. None of these appealed to him. When he finally hit on reporting as a profession, his parents were pleased. They had respect for the written word.

He was an attractive young man, lean because of a siege of tuberculosis, the scourge of the tenements, that was undiscovered until years later when the lesion was already healed. He was a great walker. He was indifferent to food and his tolerance for drink was low. There was a haunted expression in his deep-set blue eyes that suggested inner demons. The sophistication of Viennese writers offended him. His sense of morality, so stern and unyielding in a young man, accepted the Victorian standards. His jobs on *The World* and *The Sun* didn't last. He was a maverick. Everything in his character that prevented him finding permanent work in a solid company shaped him into the ideal candidate for the new medium—the "flickers."

He first encountered D. W. Griffith in a small coffee shop on Park Row that he frequented after losing his job on *The World*. He was drinking coffee, smoking a cigarette and wondering where in the city there was a place for a young man with literary pretensions, when a tall, well-dressed stranger asked if he might share the table. The man had a long, strong face, deep-set hypnotic eyes with heavy lids, and a Semitic nose. The man introduced himself as a director of "flickers." He was on the prowl for new faces. He offered Joshua a job. Acting and helping on the set.

Joshua accepted. He didn't care what kind of work it was, short of larceny. His father had developed rheumatism in his left shoulder and could no longer play his violin. Maurice needed Joshua's support.

Joshua soon gave up the idea of trying to make a living as a writer. He was familiar with a wide range of writers, from Horatio Alger to Shakespeare, and he could offer Griffith outlines of their works. He knew music, which meant he could arrange for suitable melodies to parallel the action of the film, while showing, instead of depending on the good will of some mediocre pianist who sat in the pit of the nickelodeon and pounded out inappropriate tunes.

He enjoyed his work at Biograph, but over the next two years he was aware of a troublesome trait in Griffith. Not only did D.W. pit one actor against another, fostering rivalry that peaked to jealousy, but he seemed to lose interest in any member of his company who received any special recognition.

Griffith would let go anyone who fancied himself a "star." The director demanded your best, he expected you to succeed, to justify his reputation. But acclaim was soon followed by his rejection. He was delicate about it, being a courteous man, but fear of competition for the limelight impelled him to unload potentially great talents, among them a girl named Mary Pickford.

Working with Griffith, occasionally as an actor but more often as an assistant director, Joshua came to appreciate more and more the marvelous freedom of the new film form. You could experiment, try out ideas. Instead of writing with a pen, you wrote with the camera eye.

After the trauma of Griffith's rejection eased, Joshua was elated. The Bogan money gave him the opportunity to put his vision to work. He'd build up a staff and an acting company. The girls he would choose would be young and fair.

Very young. He would have to be discreet—and careful.

East 14th Street promised to rival the glamour of the boulevards of Vienna for Joshua Fodor.

THE STREET AS IT WAS:

THE GILDED AGE had bypassed 14th Street, but the thoroughfare still retained a certain distinction. The street was originally a farm owned by Peter Stuyvesant. In 1912 the Academy of Music seemed more like a music salon in an aristocrat's mansion than a showcase for international talent and the cultural center for the old Knickerbocker families.

Joshua found the street a colorful bazaar, shops spilling over with fine dry goods, satins from France, brocades from China, laces from Belgium. Decorators were calling for a layered look and mansions were stuffed with fine furniture and fabrics.

After the Bogans gave him the money to go into business, Joshua strode down the street each night, his head alive with plans. At Steinway Hall, a block away from the Academy, an actor was offering a series of readings of Charles Dickens. Joshua attended several sessions, eager to hear the works of the great writer he admired and longed to emulate. He was particularly impressed by Mr. Dickens' sense of humanity, his talent for making the reader care for the plight of his characters.

Griffith had cribbed from him.

Joshua resolved to do no less. But do it better. Old wine in new bottles.

THIS IS THE HOUSE THAT JOSHUA BUILT:

JOSHUA'S CHOICE for a studio was a graceful Georgian edifice situated on 14th Street not far from the Academy of Music. An influential Knickerbocker family with five marriageable daughters had abandoned it for a French château just below 34th Street, the new fashionable section of the city. The family solicitor consented to lease it in order to preserve it from vandals and decay.

Joshua was elated with his good fortune, except that in certain moments of introspection he feared it wouldn't last.

In converting the space into a studio, he preserved the wood paneling, the parquetry floors, the fireplaces framed with rare brown-and-white Dutch tiles, the intricate cornices, the painted ceilings spilling over with cupids, plump maidens and satyrs, creating an atmosphere to inspire his rich, some might say lewd, imagination.

Unlike brownstones, where the main door opened at the top of a flight of stairs, leaving the ground floor to the kitchen, scullery and servants' quarters, the entrance of Joshua's new house was directly off the street. The heavy door opened into a spacious hall with an imposing circular staircase leading to the upper floors.

The dining room, to the left, was converted into the business office. The sitting room opposite became the smaller studio, while the drawing room on the second floor, which had served also as a ballroom, was converted into the big studio. Most furnishings were sold before he took occupancy, leaving only a few tables and chairs and a rolltop desk he claimed for himself. Here he would work on future ideas and make out vouchers that the actors would present to the business manager for their day's pay. The needs for sets were few, depending on the interiors, usually a table and a few chairs were sufficient. Gradually Joshua found basic furnishings to serve a multiple of settings. He accumulated a supply of costumes, although dress suits were rented.

He built up his company from the young people who found no place in the theater and who turned to the "flickers" out of hunger and a need for identity. He was searching for a girl to become the symbol of Joshua Fodor Films, just as Florence Lawrence was the Biograph Girl.

The fact that experienced stage actors came to the "flickers" only when they were out of work didn't bother him. The film backers had great respect for stage actors. Joshua too was intrigued by the theater. He admired Stella Mayhew and Al Jolson at the Winter Garden and David Warfield in *The Music Master*, the Drews and the Barrymores, and Maude Adams in *Peter Pan* (something about her, the combination of delicacy and a certain boyishness stirred in him dormant, carefully controlled fantasies.)

If he couldn't attract names, he would create his own stock company of young, malleable actors. Meanwhile his studio welcomed any good actor out of work. Competition was keen but he wasn't depressed. He had something more going for him.

His father was a Socialist. His mother admired Emma Goldman and served as a midwife for many tenement pregnancies. It was inevitable that Joshua should become aware of social wrongs and that his anger against injustice should be dramatized in his films.

He dared from the beginning to disturb the status quo. Hunger, deprivation, loneliness, injustice—these were themes his audiences identified with, and which he fought against.

Critics later suggested that it was this social rebellion, combined with his inventive talents, that brought him recognition in the pre-World War I years. The truth was that he understood his audience. They reacted best to melodramas filled with raw emotions and with a kind of black-and-white delineation of character. They wanted laughter and tears, pure heroines and dastardly villains. He called on an ancient wisdom in his genes, and his knowledge of the Second Avenue Yiddish theater, and gave them what they wanted.

"Fodor never wanted to make films that could be enjoyed on a mindless level," Vanessa once replied to an interviewer's question. "There is an implied moral lesson in all his work.

"His finest pictures were based on realism as *he* saw it. Even when he used a tawdry melodrama for the story line, his compassion gave the film truth and conviction."

She sighed deeply.

As much as he loved music, Joshua seldom allowed music on the set. It was a distraction, he said. He wanted his actors to concentrate and he had no faith in their attention span. Especially his little girl actresses, who were lovely to photograph but sometimes gave him the impression that God had forgotten to give them brains.

His first "flickers" were one-reelers, but with a style uniquely his own. In each there was a tag line, a surprise ending that had been carefully planted early in the action, a visual O'Henry touch.

The unexpected was also part of his style in dealing with his acting company. During the endless rehearsals he would choose any man or girl who happened to be on the set to rehearse the roles. He often alternated the players so everyone in the company had the opportunity to rehearse. Sometimes the very young girls like Peg Dalton and Vanessa Oxford went through the roles of outraged wives or middle-aged mothers. He had a near-hypnotic intensity that often stirred greater depths in his players than they believed themselves capable of expressing. His imagination was completely visual, which of course was perfect for the medium.

He seldom made his final choice of the cast until just before he started filming and, was a result, his players all qualified for the roles in case they were chosen. They were keyed up until he decided who was best for each part. He was convinced each one would do his best to prove himself. It worked for Griffith. He also believed that each film had an inner life of its own. In spite of endless rehearsals he managed to strike a spark of spontaneity during the filming that was enhanced by his own excitement. Film, he discovered, by its intimacy could arouse a sexual tension in an audience that wasn't possible on the stage.

During rehearsals Joshua dressed in a dark business suit, a shirt, stiff collar and tie, and high-laced boots. His head was bare, his eyes shaded by a celluloid visor. Walking back and forth, his gestures often synchronized with those of the cast. He shouted, cajoled, pantomimed, exaggerated, then suddenly turned gentle, coaxing as one would with children. He reminded them between scenes that the eye of the camera was sharp and cruel and stripped away all pretenses. And whenever an actor exceeded himself, Joshua would give him a bear hug, saying, "Now that's how it should be done! Take a lesson, children!"

Rehearsals exhausted the company. Often it was two o'clock before Joshua remembered about lunch and called for a break. He, Dudley Norton, Hans Rolfsma, and "Uncle" Owen would walk west on 14th Street to Lüchow's for sauerbraten and beer, or German pancakes. Meanwhile Richie Doyle would check with the cast for their orders and fetch roast beef sandwiches, coffee, tea and milk and often cake or apple pie. The men usually sat together and the young actresses gathered around the two older women who played mother or auntie roles. It was all very companionable, except that the younger girls, like Vanessa, were wary of the presence of Peg Dalton and Lorraine North, who were Mr. Fodor's favorites. Vanessa not only learned the whereabouts of the girls on the set but she grasped quickly his manner of playing one girl against another, arousing jealousy that he used to heighten the intensity of his film.

She also learned early to use it to her advantage. She was there whenever he was looking for a girl to rehearse a role. Indeed, she was always where his glance could rest on her.

Lunch over, the carpenter and his assistant set up the background, marking off the stage so the actors and camera would stay within the lines. Now, at last, Joshua Fodor chose the actors for their roles and put them through one brief final rehearsal before the camera started filming.

His direction was quiet and well thought out, yet in spite of the long rehearsals he managed to bring to his films a sense of improvisation that gave them reality. He'd mix high drama and low comedy in a single film, often using Peg Dalton in comic roles with a touch of poignancy and Lorraine North for melodrama.

The curse of poverty, one of his most successful themes, reflected, he felt, his audience's struggle for existence. How to get money, by honest or dishonest means, was the core of their fantasies. Dramas in which the young heroine was frail, perhaps crippled, and always suffering, her honor sullied by villains, were always popular. And after she had suffered sufficiently, a fine upright young man would make an honest woman of her.

Joshua's convictions set the tone for his films. He dramatized the young gangs of the ghetto and the more vicious gangsters. The rich in his films were always pictured as greedy, corrupt, heartless, exploiting the poor. Money lenders were often leading characters, and they usually ended up with punishment for their cruelty and avarice.

But he avoided the violent prejudices common in other films—Irish, Negroes, Jews were treated fairly.

After Thomas H. Ince's *Typhoon*, in 1914, successfully created a natural catastrophe, Joshua tried to outdo him. Helped by Hans Rolfsma's photographic genius, the next series of Fodor films featured fires, collapsed buildings, and floods.

He was the first to use symbolism—the roar of the sea, waves bursting on rocks—as a fadeout for a love scene, and his films used animals—birds in flight, dogs frolicking, cats slinking—to make a dramatic point.

Hans Rolfsma always kept a pad beside him to record the scenes that were shot, the time of day, a description of the set (interior or out-of-door), and a list of actors used for the day's shooting. (No description of what they wore. Each actor was supposed to remember his costume and be consistent in dress during filming.)

Joshua and Hans worked as a team. Joshua was always demanding the impossible. Hans always fought him and came through with what Fodor wanted. As a result, a Fodor film was always visually exciting, filled with scenes the audience would remember for a long while.

When Vanessa first came on the set, Joshua was using the 14th Street house for all interiors. Location shots were scheduled for Fort Lee, New Jersey, or occasionally Greenwich, Connecticut. If the call was for location each member of the company was notified the day before. They usually traveled in small groups and, after a ride on the subway to the 125th Street station, they would rush over to the ferry building and catch the 8:45 A.M. ferry across the Hudson River to Fort Lee. Once on the Jersey side, Richie Doyle led them to a small restaurant nearby for breakfast. Rooms over the restaurant were rented and here they made up, got into costumes (which a horse-drawn wagon had brought from the studio) and prepared to drive out on location.

Joshua had an uncanny feeling for locations. He loved the lush, beautiful Greenwich countryside. After a while he eliminated New Jersey and concentrated on Connecticut. When they were photographing outdoors on a cold day, they often had to warm the camera by placing it near a bonfire.

From the beginning, in order to satisfy the demand, Joshua turned out three and four films a week, at first one-reelers, although he graduated very quickly to two-reelers.

The Fodor company could count on no social life. Meals were communal. There was no outside world. When you worked for Joshua Fodor, *he* was your world.

He never lost patience. If tension built up during a long rehearsal, he would call for a rest. Sometimes he would break into song, a melody from *Madame Butterfly*, or even "Wait 'Til the Sun Shines, Nellie" or "In the Good Old Summer Time," songs the young actresses preferred to opera. Or he'd reach out for one of the girls and dance a few steps with her. And then when everyone was relaxed he'd call out, "Back to work, children."

His capacity for work was phenomenal. Hans often said, "There goes the boss to the darkroom. Mark my words, he'll die working." Often he stayed up half the night working on plots for future films.

Abel Levy, his cutter, spliced the film negative and put it together in a coherent and effective sequence. From the notes Joshua and Hans Rolfsma took during the final rehearsal Abel would know how to unite the negatives. The first cut was rough; the final cut polished. For the finished cutting, Abel used a little machine he turned by hand. The cutting became so fine that he and Fodor would cut two frames and run them for effect. Because the film and lights were so primitive, Hans had a tendency to wash the actors with too much light. This was fine for the young girls, it gave them an ethereal air; but it made the men look effeminate. Gradually, though, Joshua, with Hans' help, became a master at lighting, just as he was at editing. He experimented with montage, perfected the rhythm of cross-cutting and emphasized symbolism and contrasts. It all came from some mix of wisdom and intuition deep inside him, but the memory, the drive of something else, primitive and brutish, seemed to crush his pride of achievement and kept him tossing, angry and frustrated, with suppressed violence in the dark of the night.

Once Joshua made a film built around a traveling circus with a brutish strong man and an innocent frightened waif. The little circus was a gallery of freaks. While he was filming it, the company was startled by his fascination for the strange freakish creatures that were hired for the film. The company wondered what he saw in them. He was such a proper, respectable man.

But Vanessa guessed, or sensed, why. So did some of the other little actresses Mr. Fodor was so partial to in his films.

THE PAST: CASSIE'S FIRST ENCOUNTER WITH THE MASTER—WHAT EVEN THE HOLLYWOOD UNDERGROUND HAS NEVER UNCOVERED

CASSIE CAME HOME two weeks later than expected. The tour was a success. In the six weeks she was away from us, she was transformed. Mama said Cassie was developing into young womanhood and Mama was buying more of those monthly pads in the dime store. What the new rush of hormones did for Cassie was remarkable. The sun had brought an apricot glow to her skin, her mouth was fuller than I remembered, her pudgy little waistline had thinned and her hips rounded. It was such an extraordinary change in such a short time.

Cassie went to sleep right after supper, although our room was unbearably hot. The front window was open to the humid, stale night air. We heard people on the front stoop, on the fire escapes, strolling in the street at all hours because the outside was preferable to the hot rooms. Mama poured some cold milk and we sat near the window sipping it. Poor Mama was exhausted. She was under a strain because business at the restaurant was off on account of the weather, the owner was talking of letting some of the help go, and Mama was afraid he'd put his wife behind the cashier's booth.

We spoke quietly, so as not to disturb Cassie, about what we should do. It was the beginning of the nightly conferences Mama and I were to have, to decide on the best step to preserve ourselves from possible disaster.

It was Mama's suggestion that I take Cassie to the studio.

"If she could get several days' work each week, we could manage," Mama said.

Frankly, I wasn't too eager but I agreed.

The next morning, Cassie and I caught the trolley to the studio. I warned her how to behave; to stay close to me in the hall until I could find out if there'd be work for her.

Mr. Fodor was shooting a film that required a group of girls who were supposed to be students in a private school. Cassie would be in the group. I showed Cassie around the studio with a familiarity that duly impressed her. Wearing a jumper and a shirtwaist and her hair in curls, she looked as though she really attended an expensive school. I saw Richie watching her, and I thought, these two will like each other. Funny, I had an instinct about it from the beginning.

After he distributed the lunch boxes, Richie came over and sat with us. All the leading players were in the studio or wandering around. The crew were playing poker in a corner, and Mr. Fodor stopped to watch their game. Then Mr. Fodor strolled by and paused as he recognized me.

"Feeling better today?" he asked.

"Much better, thank you." I could scarcely talk, being so excited, knowing the others were staring at us, as they always stared at anyone Mr. Fodor singled out. "Mr. Fodor, this is my sister, Cassie."

Mr. Fodor looked at her with that serious, intent look, his eyes half-closed as though he was peering through the camera lens. Cassie was obviously excited, her cheeks flushed, her eyes sparkling.

"Well, little miss, how would you like to be in flickers?"

Cassie glared at him. She said with enormous dignity, "I am a legitimate actress, sir."

Even the poker table grew quiet. And Lorraine, drinking coffee near the camera platform, turned around and glared at Cassie. Mama's old precept of keeping ourselves quiet and unobtrusive sent a warning signal and I wondered how I could spirit Cassie out of this unexpected limelight.

"Little miss, would you condescend to play in flickers for the sum . . ." he paused, ". . . of fifty dollars a week?"

Cassie didn't reply. I was stunned. Was he actually offering my younger sister that huge amount or was he merely making fun of her? No, that couldn't be. He had a reputation for being kind. I had never seen him show anger or disfavor toward anyone.

"You have to ask my mother," Cassie said primly.

"Well, little miss, you go home and bring your mama and if she says you can be an actress for me, we'll talk."

Then he turned away and clapped his hands and said, "Let's get on with it."

After the day's shooting we went downstairs to change back into our clothes. Cassie was scarcely in control. She was radiant. I thought it wise to quiet her down but couldn't decide how to do it. Then, through the open vent in the ceiling, we heard Mr. Fodor's and Lorraine's voices. We couldn't make out all the words, but enough came through so that we knew it was a real explosion. She screamed something about his not loving her, about him robbing the cradle, and then there was a silence. I said, "Let's go upstairs, Cassie." And as we scurried up, Lorraine came running downstairs, and we collided.

I don't know how it happened. I think she was furious at Cassie, who'd caught Mr. Fodor's attention. I held out my arm to protect Cassie, who was teetering on the stairs, and somehow Lorraine tilted. She was wearing high heels and was wobbly as she caught at the bannister. She lost her hold and tumbled. Before we could help, she fell the full length of the staircase. It was a terrible sound. We were screaming and so were the others on the set and in the hall. Several men lifted Lorraine and carried her into Mr. Fodor's office and laid her on the black leather couch. The screaming didn't subside. But none of the shrieks came from Lorraine. She was silent, deathly silent.

Cassie and I waited in the front hall, where Richie found us and went to get our pay.

"They've called a doctor," he said soberly.

I suggested to Cassie that we leave, otherwise Mama might be worried, but she wanted to hear about Lorraine's condition. Finally I persuaded her and as we turned toward the door, the wardrobe mistress joined us.

"Vanessa," she said in an undertone, "let me give you some

advice. *Take your little sister home and never let her come here again.*"

After she'd left, Cassie asked, "What did she mean?"

"Nothing. She just thought you where kind of young to be in Mr. Fodor's company."

But she wasn't. She was just the right age to be in Mr. Fodor's company.

Two:

THE PAST: VANESSA REMEMBERS: WHAT YOU WOULD NEVER READ IN *PHOTOPLAY*

To FACE THE UNKNOWN makes us feel helpless.

At least this is what Rebecca maintains, and she has within her the unconscious wisdom of her people, the Jews, who have faced the unknown and endured and survived for two thousand years.

"Turning points in your life mean that one way of living is over," she reminded me whenever I met with disappointment. "And your emotions will shape your future."

"I can survive every indignity but gossip," I said. "This I cannot take, for Mama and Cassie's sake."

Whenever she doesn't approve of my decisions, Rebecca will remind me tartly that during my peak years with Joshua Fodor my behavior sometimes shocked my mother and sister. But I always reassured them. "Don't worry. It will be all right."

And it always was.

Cassie often complained I had blinders that kept my eyes on my goal, allowing nothing to divert me. Well, what's wrong with that? Isn't a clear vision of the future you want a gift from God? I was well aware of the danger of scandal touching me. Mr. Fodor had warned all of us that our reputations must remain unsullied. The studio was barred to outsiders. The young actresses were chaperoned by the older ones and we were discouraged from attending parties except those that Mr. Fodor gave for us. There was no after-hours mingling between his actresses and his growing number of assistants. Many young players on other lots in those early days met with shame, humiliation, even tragedy. No touch of scandal ever degraded the Fodor company.

The world regarded us as pure, undefiled, spiritual.

It was a cruel age for young women who defied propriety. And for those who abetted them. Mr. Fodor was very aware of that.

Mama went to see Mr. Fodor about Cassie and, sure enough, he repeated his offer. He was willing to put Cassie on the payroll for fifty dollars a week because he had a hunch about her ability.

"You cannot create talent," he told Mama. "You can only hope the actress will listen to you, create an image of the character she is playing and react to situations as that character should react."

Mama was impressed by his presentation and by his courtesy. "He's the most charming man I've ever met," she said later. When she mentioned my future, he said he would put me on the payroll for thirty-five dollars a week.

My little sister would be earning more than I, who had been working with him for three months! It was humiliating. I complained about it to the wardrobe lady. She advised me to keep quiet. She said Mr. Fodor expected his people to be loyal to the company and to him and never expect to be singled out for special treatment.

He wanted us all to be good children, compliant to all his wishes. If a player did unusually well in a role and, as a result, got inflated ideas about his value, Mr. Fodor would scout around until he found another actor as a replacement. Naturally the company became jealous of any newcomer, and arrogance became humility, sometimes real, sometimes feigned. I know I got the part of Dollie because Jenny Mayran began to put on airs after she scored as the fifteen-year-old child wife of Edgar Allan Poe in Mr. Fodor's film about the tragic writer.

With eighty-five dollars a week in salary for the two of us, we were able to move out of the wretched rooming house to better quarters on the East Side in the Madison Avenue section. Our new apartment, while small, was more attractive with its Murphy bed and a tiny kitchen. Mama scrubbed the place until it was clean, and although the woodwork was dark, the linoleum worn, and the furniture sagging, we felt it was a step up. We didn't know how long Mr. Fodor would keep us, so Mama banked a third of our salaries, saving toward the time we might be at leisure again.

I wouldn't allow myself to admit any discouragement or anxiety.

Our future was with Mr. Fodor.

It was up to me to prove it to him.

Putting myself on a new routine, I got up earlier than Mama and Cassie and took a hot bath, even in the August dog days. I scrubbed my body and then blotted off the almond oil from my skin (an extravagance, but there's nothing like almond oil to keep your skin supple, especially if it's thin like mine).

Then I let down the rag ribbons that kept my hair in curls overnight. My hair style was copied from Mary Pickford and Lillian Gish, who had such rich, abundant curls. My forehead was a problem; it was high and bulging, unformed like a child's. I usually covered it with tendrils of hair, but after Hans took a number of stills, experimenting with lights, he said I should always keep my forehead bare, that it reminded him of the Renaissance ladies. I was puzzled until he showed me pictures of Italian noblewomen. This taught me that obstacles could be transformed into advantages. It was a lesson I would never forget.

Cassie hated breakfast and always fussed if Mama urged her to eat. But I swallowed what was good for me and would give me energy. I was already aware of the importance of good nutrition. Years later when I explained my regime of self-nutrition and exercise to Harold Kellog, who was the first great nutritionist to stress the value of less meat, more vegetables, salads and fruits for his patients, he said, "Vanessa, your instincts were absolutely superb. You ate what was right for you."

I ate a lot of oatmeal, which Mama cooked overnight on a low flame with milk and honey, and black bread, which Mama bought in the Jewish section of town. If the morning was still cool, I walked down Fifth Avenue to Fourteenth Street and turned toward the East River, where yachts of the rich were anchored. In my imagination, I saw myself a guest on a richly appointed boat, with the owner in a jaunty yachting cap, double-breasted jacket with gilt buttons, and cream colored pants, deferring to my every wish. I suppose my dreams were no more far-fetched than those of any young creature whose dreams were nourished on the Hearst newspapers. The girls in the company were always talking about the poor but beautiful girls who made it. Rich young men might be destined to marry within their own class, but they liked to sow their oats with the pretty chorus girls, artists' models and young actresses who blossomed in Manhattan. And sometimes, making dreams come true for many a poor girl, the affairs ended in marriage in a fine church.

My body, though, didn't suggest those delicious curves and the creamy flesh that attracted Stage Door Johnnies. My appeal had to be more dignified and therefore carry an even greater market value. And since Mr. Fodor had such faith in the future of films, I decided I must dedicate my life to him.

You understand that I did not think in the manner of the ordinary poor girl. Most youngsters, when they are humiliated or punished, think, *You'll be sorry! When I'm dead, you'll be sorry!*

I never pictured my death and/or the sorrow of adults.

I pictured my success and the *envy* of adults.

I saw myself as a young Joan of Arc, commanding them. They would listen to me, respect me, obey me, because their lives depended on my tolerance and forgiveness.

As I paused before the townhouse studio I saw myself as Mr. Fodor's favorite actress, his adored princess, his confidante, his advisor. My heart and mind were rich with the promises of what I could offer a great man. One day, sometime in the future, I saw him kissing me chastely on the forehead, admitting, in a voice rich with feeling, "I cannot express what you have contributed to my career and my life."

66

I believed it would happen because I believed I could *make* it happen.

His car was already parked at the curb. A black Packard touring car. That meant we'd probably go on location to Greenwich. Now that I was part of the company, he sometimes included me in the group that traveled in his car. (Mr. Fodor was not given to personal extravagances. Except for his automobile.)

Mr. Fodor had a Negro driver and, whenever the weather was fair, the top of the roadster was taken down and he sat beside the chauffeur. He loved being in the sun. Even in New York he acquired a summer tan that made the cartilage in his flat boxer's nose less noticeable. His prominent white teeth sometimes suggested a faintly wolfish expression and his jaw was rather long in contrast to the blunt nose. He had what interviewers called a "Hapsburg look," although there was nothing royal in his genes. So far as I know.

I checked in at the studio before Cassie. Sometimes I felt guilty about leaving earlier in the morning, but she already had a tendency to dawdle that drove me crazy. After all, she was earning more than I and there was no reason for my babying *her*....

The studio was the source of my enchantment. My reality was in the studio, not in our apartment. I felt alive here, the person I longed to be and saw in my imagination. The rejection of casting directors at the theaters was forgotten. I had a future here, alongside The Master.

He had savored Peg's high spirits, Lorraine's dark, mysterious allure, Jenny's pure Nordic beauty. Now he would have me. The girl who was "different."

Somewhere I'd read in a guidance book, "If you can see it, you can do it."

I saw what I had to do and I was determined to do it: be Mr. Fodor's greatest star and the one indispensable girl in his life.

Mr. Fodor cautioned his girls, "Always be nice to the people who work with you."

Most young actresses paid little attention to the rest of the staff except for Richie and a few of the male actors. I made it a point to be friendly with everyone, from the set carpenter to the wardrobe lady. I spent time with Hans Rolfsma, who couldn't have been nicer. I was patient when he experimented with lights, sitting for hours while he tried out his ideas, making a gilded halo of my hair or washing my face with a flat light so that the shadows under my eyes would blend with the bones.

"You are one of the lucky girls." Hans withdrew his head from the dark cloth shading the ground glass. "The camera finds you perfect from every angle."

I realized he was saying that I was genuinely photogenic. He added that there was a touch of the waif in my face, as though I were lost in a dream. He taught me to look up, so the half moons in my eyes would show. "The camera transforms you, Vanessa," he said. "It brings out an elusive quality. Make use of it. Men love what eludes them."

I listened avidly.

"Fodor is David," he said with a faint smile, "but he's also Goliath. Remember that, Vanessa."

Did he suspect that I might ignite a spark of interest in Mr. Fodor? Was he investing time in a future friend at court?

It was an exhilarating thought. When I become an important star, I reflected, Hans will be my personal cameraman.

He said something else I've never forgotten. This happened later when Mr. Fodor turned his casting plan topsy-turvy and chose me for Mary, Mother of God, and also for Mary Magdalene.

"Success comes when you're ready for it, Vanessa. Good luck. Make the most of your big chance."

I already had. But of course Hans was in the dark about it. Mr. Fodor had taught me to be circumspect and discreet.

At that time, if you had asked me, "What do you want in a man?" I couldn't have answered the question simply.

Somebody to look up to? Intelligent? Romantic? Kind? Protective? Yes, those qualities were important, certainly.

Someone who would believe in my talents? Who would help me to achieve my goals? Definitely very important qualities in any man I would be interested in.

Who would love Mama and Cassie and never be jealous of my devotion to them? Absolutely. My mother and sister would always be the most important people in my life, no matter how much pain they caused me.

Mama always stressed good manners. Professional actors, I had found, were self-centered to the point of rudeness unless you were rich or influential or could be of benefit to them. Perhaps I overstressed the amenities, but I responded to courtesy and thoughtfulness: the helping hand with the coat, the opening of a door so you could pass through.

And Mr. Fodor was courtesy itself.

He had the manners of a Viennese gentleman, Mama said approvingly.

Even when I wasn't on call, I made myself useful in the studio. The darkroom staff, Abel Levy and Jay Ritori, became my friends. I often brought my box lunch up to the darkroom and ate with them.

I had asked Richie to keep Cassie from getting lonesome and he took me literally. He was Cassie's self-appointed guide and I must say she was delighted. They became friends easily. From the beginning, their interest in each other was an accomplished fact. Cassie, fourteen, Richie, a couple of years older, were "the kids." Everyone was indulgent with them. They would wander off into a corner talking or just sit together quietly lost in each other's company. Cassie had a distant, almost shy, look those days; she was less active and more quiet, sweeter.

I hoped she wouldn't waste herself on Richie but I kept silent, except to apprise Mama of their close friendship. Mama seldom came to the studio, although Mr. Fodor obviously approved of her and would have welcomed her on the set.

With Mama away from the studio, and Cassie absorbed in Richie, I had less worry about my family and more time to think of our collective future.

Abel Levy wasn't aware of how much information he fed into my hungry mind. I learned how a film was developed and how it was spliced into a suspenseful, completed film. The endless patience needed filled me with awe. This is where the movie was really created. The pieces the cutter put together with the director could make a film a failure or a success.

Just before World War I, other studios were expanding their staffs, supplementing them with writers and scenic designers. But Mr. Fodor wouldn't allow a single facet of production out of his grasp. He wrote many of the scripts, he gave his ideas to the set builders, he chose costumes. While he was filming one picture, he was rehearsing another and planning a third. And still his energy and temper held steady, except when schedules fell behind and the carpenters made excuses or the actresses didn't show up on time.

Cassie was sometimes the victim of his irritability. She was irresponsible and often wandered off the set. He'd sound off and Cassie used to scurry behind the scenery so his eye wouldn't light on her. But after he told us off, all was forgiven and that evening he'd take us to dinner.

In the many pictures I was to make for Mr. Fodor, my role was invariably that of a gentle, passive creature subjected to cruelty at the hands of the villain. He loved the theme of betrayal and seduction of the innocent.

On location we were obliged to do our own stunts—the stunt man was still in the future. I felt it necessary to learn to use my body well: to ride a horse, to dive from a high board, to drive a car, to dance. A circus acrobat taught me to fall right, cuddling my face in my arms, rolling up into a fetal position. I even fell off a horse, which turned out to be a painful exercise with scraped skin and bruised knees.

"Don't ever try that again," Mr. Fodor warned me as the wardrobe lady was patching me up. (After that, he had men dress in women's garments for our dangerous stunts.)

I was hurt but not scared. As a matter of fact, the challenge of a stunt appealed to me. Dear Rebecca disapproved, though. She sensed a need in me that I really didn't understand, a force stronger than myself that nagged and urged and drove me often to excess and danger.

Mr. Fodor became aware of it early in our relationship.

"Miss Vanessa, you mustn't be so ... so ... wild. It is unbecoming." He sounded as though I'd betrayed his image of the ideal girl.

THE PAST: VANESSA REFLECTS
ON THE SEXUAL POWER OF WOMEN

TODAY'S YOUNG WOMAN is different from Cassie and me.

Her ideas on sex and seduction are different. She has the kind of courage and independence my generation lacked.

But then our times and circumstances were different. We didn't dare relate to men as equals. We didn't dare show honest feelings. Sweet smiles, flattery, helplessness were our weapons and, for us, they worked.

I learned early in life what men expected from their women. Mama thought she was protecting me from the grosser aspects of sex, but as a child trouper I saw a good deal. The adults were indiscreet when they thought I wasn't watching. Or perhaps they didn't care. Some probably enjoyed knowing they were being observed.

It was enough to turn some young girls against sex. Some.

Seduction had a market value. And I had an instinctive knowledge of its worth—that a girl had more latent power than people would have you believe. My feeling was fortified the day Mr. Fodor took me, along with his other young actresses, to see the new D. W. Griffith film, *Judith of Bethulia*.

I'd overheard Mr. Fodor discussing the film with Hans Rolfsma. He said Mr. Griffith had made it two years ago but it was only now being released and talk in the trade was complimentary.

That day there was enough Indian summer left to warm the November air. The studio was unseasonably hot, and we suffered under the cruel Cooper-Hewitt lights. Fortunately, I wasn't perspiring, but Peg was dripping under her makeup and Mr. Fodor was offended by it. He was very fastidious. At lunch, I'd taken the precaution to eat lightly: only the roast beef in my sandwich, none of the pie and just a sip of milk. Then I found a dark corner of the studio, closed my eyes and visualized myself in the film going into production.

My part was small. Peg's was more important. As usual, she played so well that the staff watched her, fascinated, and Mr. Fodor forgot his irritation. Afterwards, he touched her on the shoulder, a signal for her to accompany him to dinner. The thought of the hours they'd spend together at Lüchow's or the Astor depressed me. She could be most effective and influential when she was alone with him. Lorraine North was no longer with the company. The wardrobe lady told me in confidence Lorraine was having trouble with her broken hip and that Mr. Fodor was paying all her expenses and sending her a weekly check. I felt terrible, but in a way it had been her fault, quarreling with Mr. Fodor and then charging down the stairs.

When the day's filming was over, I saw Mr. Fodor nod to Jenny Mayran and Mercy Brown. Was he including them? Would he hint during dinner about his plans for a new film? I felt terribly left out. I thought I'd better go home and sit with Cassie, who was in bed with the grippe.

Before leaving, I stopped in the darkroom where Jay was checking strips of developed film. I was watching over his shoulder when the door opened on Mr. Fodor.

"I hope you don't mind, Mr. Fodor," Jay said, "but this little girl is the only one who shows interest in film *after* a scene is shot." Dear good Jay, he was fast becoming a friend to me, like Hans and Richie.

"I know what important work is done here," I said solemnly. "I want to learn *everything* about the movies."

"Good girl." Mr. Fodor seemed amused but impressed. "In that case, you'd better come with us tonight. After dinner, we're going to see a new movie."

This was 1914, but the war in Europe didn't really touch us. Our interests were confined to the studio. We drove uptown in Mr. Fodor's car, his driver at the wheel and Mr. Fodor beside him, while Peg, Jenny, Mercy and I were squeezed together in the back seat. We were deliciously excited. All the same, I was conscious of not looking my best. Jenny was in a serge dress and matching coat, Peg in a flowered challis with ruffles at the neck and wrists, a dress that was unbecoming. Peg was more comfortable in boy's clothes, but her mother was always making her pretty dresses because Mr. Fodor liked his girls to look feminine. Mercy Brown wore a velvet skirt and a silk shirt she'd bought at Siegel Cooper, but I was in my everyday outfit—skirt, blouse, and topcoat with a velvet collar that made me look as though I were wearing Mama's clothes. Which happened to be a fact. I had grown to my full five feet, six inches; Mama's size and mine were now the same.

Mothers of the Fodor girls didn't worry if we were late coming home. It meant we were either working or having dinner with Mr. Fodor. In either case, they were confident that he'd see to it that we got home safely. Mr. Fodor always made a point of winning the mothers' confidence.

A good table at the Astor, with the waiters hovering. Steaks, and strawberry shortcake for dessert with our milk. While we were eating, Peg held the spotlight. She was teasing Mr. Fodor because her brothers beat him playing ball.

"Next time you better ask *me* to be on your team," she warned him. "I'm the best batter in the family!"

I envied her, seeing how much Mr. Fodor loved her big family. How could I interest him in mine? He was intrigued by Cassie, at least when he first hired her, although he didn't use her all that much and she stayed out of his sight. He liked Mama. But how could she serve a big dinner in our small apartment?

I could only bide my time and pray and occasionally plan.

It may sound like an exaggeration but *Judith of Bethulia* had an extraordinary effect on my life's course. The story was straight out of the Bible: *The Book of Judith* in the *Apocrypha*. Holofernes, Nebuchadnezzar's general, had laid siege to the Israelite city of Bethulia. Forty days' siege and the city was ready to surrender, its inhabitants starved, thirsty, defeated. But they had a savior—Judith, a young widow. She stole into the general's camp during a wild and abandoned night. When he finally collapsed from his excesses, Judith coolly beheaded him. She carried back his bloody head to her people. Inspired by her courage, the Israelites routed the enemy and Bethulia was saved.

Mr. Fodor was raving about Griffith's splendid technique, the authentic flavor of the film and the extraordinarily seductive allure of Blanche Sweet, the star.

What impressed me was the basic idea.

The sexual power of a woman...

I was young in a time when women were little more than slaves, married or not. Now and then a clever woman rose to the heights that made her equal in social and financial stature to a man. Lillian Russell, Lily Langtry, women of their caliber started with fresh good looks, ambition that brought them to lucky encounters, and a subtle but powerful seductive influence on men who could aid in their future. There were other strong women, like Carrie Hull and Marie Stokes and Margaret Sanger, but they weren't my style. I admired their spiritual grace and hoped to learn how to acquire it, but without wasting myself on their peculiar goals.

My future lay where money was. And fame. And power.

For Mama and for Cassie. For my family.

I created my own rules of self-help. Quite by accident, I came upon Dr. Emmet Fox, the precursor of Dr. Norman Vincent Peale, and I initiated my own course of religio-psychiatric training, if you could call it that. When I was alone, apart from the cast, I often found a quiet corner where I could sit and meditate. I wore a string of turquoise beads that Mama had given me for my thirteenth birthday, and I would finger them as I prayed silently. I knew nothing of Oriental "worry beads" or of telling a rosary, but my instincts led me in the same direction. I would close my eyes, let my mind grow blank and then visualize my dreams. It was long before Transcendental Meditation became popular, but whatever it was, I found it helpful. I didn't confide in the girls, knowing they would only make fun. So I kept to myself, although I knew they considered me aloof and preferred Cassie who was warm, cheerful and outgoing.

I had faith in my prayers. I recall that many years later the Bishop of Canterbury answered, when he was asked about prayer, "I only know that when I pray, things happen."

I learned that you must visualize what you want. It's not simple and it's not magical. I also learned a girl mustn't be too available. It reduces her value.

It is better to project Love: *I love you.* Not Sex: *I want you.*
It's the difference between tinsel and gold.
And, more importantly, between failure and success.

THE PAST: VANESSA REMEMBERS:
THE PLEASURE OF THE MALE...

JOSHUA FODOR HAD A PASSION for the Russian novelists, particularly
Dostoevsky. His appreciation of literature was unusual for a director of his time.

"I shall do *Crime and Punishment*," he said in a low voice.

"Is it a book?" I asked timidly. "Should I read it?"

Mr. Fodor took a leatherbound volume from his pocket. "Here
it is."

We were having dinner at Lüchow's, just Mr. Fodor and me.
It was my turn. At last! It was early in December so there was
roast goose on the menu, which Mr. Fodor recommended. The
big menu fascinated me, although I had trouble making out the
names of the delicacies. I read fairly well but new words were
always an obstacle and to save face I turned to my host for advice.
"Will you order for me, please?"

After Mr. Fodor used me in *The Lost Daughter and the Gypsies*,
he began to cast me often, mostly at Hans Rolfsma's suggestion.
Hans told him I was photogenic from all angles, which made his
work easier. And I was learning to emote. Dudley Norton, who
was now in charge of advertising, said I could always produce a
three-handkerchief performance. I was very lucky. The men on
Mr. Fodor's staff all were rooting for me. They had more faith in
me than he had. I understood he didn't have much real hope for
me (which was a challenge). But he thought Cassie had possibilities if she'd only stop clowning.

Well, I'd been doing my utmost to prove myself an actress worthy of his attention. Surely that was the reason for his invitation tonight. Or was it because Peg had been impertinent to him? She seemed to have fallen for one of his junior directors, which was her loss and—hopefully—my gain.

I opened the book to the middle. Mama had taught us reading and arithmetic—the summer I had spent in Muskenaw, Rebecca and I devoured *Anne of Green Gables* and *The Little Colonel* books—but the sentences in Mr. Fodor's book were undecipherable to me.

"What's it about?" I asked.

"It's the story of Raskolnikov, a very poor student who is struggling to stay alive. When he hears his sister will marry for money in order to help him out, he decides instead to murder a mercenary old woman pawnbroker. The woman's sister arrives unexpectedly so he kills her too.

"What follows is his breakdown as the result of his sense of guilt. He begins to act like a suspect. The Police Inspector, Porfiry, plays with him like a cat with a mouse. The inspector is determined to get Raskolnikov to confess. Gradually he builds up his case. Finally the student confesses his guilt to a young prostitute, Sonia, and she suggests that he give himself up. He agrees, and is sentenced to serve eight years in Siberia. Sonia, loyal and loving, follows him into exile. She becomes a mother symbol to the other prisoners as well as Raskolnikov. Her love helps in his regeneration."

It didn't sound very appealing to me.

"Good scenes . . . backgrounds . . ." Mr. Fodor continued. "Shadows of courtyards and cobblestone lanes, canals with dark murky secrets, the crushing poverty of the student. Great possibilities."

I suspected Peg would get the part of Sonia, but I asked, "Will we all be rehearsing Sonia?"

My eagerness amused him. "Jenny may be right for the part."

"Oh, I'm sure she'd be good. But isn't she too healthy, more like a Swedish milkmaid? From what you've said, I see Sonia as frail . . . hungry looking . . ."

He smiled. I was afraid he saw through my attempt but I remained earnest, interested. "It sounds like a part for one of the younger girls." He never cast an older actress as a girl of the streets, which puzzled me.

"Perhaps I'll have Cassie rehearse it." He was watching me intently.

"That would be wonderful, Mr. Fodor. Except, well, how would you *explain* Sonia to Cassie? Cassie doesn't know about such things. And you'd have to warn Mama . . ."

"So I would. And it might embarrass your mother."

He finished his coffee, cut the tip of his cigar with a pen knife and lit it. He paid the bill and left a generous tip. He helped me into my coat and soon we were out on 14th Street, turning east. I prayed that Abel Levy was still working and they'd engage in talk and perhaps I would be free. But no such luck, I thought, trying to keep up with his powerful impatient stride. It was close to nine o'clock and the street looked cold and abandoned. I was shivering.

Mr. Fodor took out his keys, inserted one in the lock and opened the door to the foyer, where a dim light burned. The hall was chilly. I sneezed. Mr. Fodor looked at me abruptly. As though my presence surprised him. Then he smiled. His smile made him look years younger but I was too disturbed to respond.

He stiffened abruptly at a sound coming from the second floor. "Who's there?"

"It's me, sir." Richie Doyle appeared at the top of the curving staircase.

"Richie, what're you doing here at this hour?"

"I promised Abel Levy that I'd come back and clean up his quarters."

"Richie, you don't have to do that. You're not the office boy anymore. You're an actor."

Richie's shyness was one of his assets. He'd developed into an inordinately handsome young man with a well-shaped head, glossy black hair, brilliant blue eyes and high rich color in his cheeks. He was said to resemble his mother, a hypochondriac who ruled her family by terror and tyranny. Still, I really couldn't blame Cassie for her attachment to him, even though I hoped it wouldn't last.

Recently Mr. Fodor had cast Richie as Edgar Allan Poe and Cassie as Virginia, his fifteen-year-old child wife. The result was a stunning picture that *The New York Times* actually mentioned with warm praise. It brought the young pair even closer together. Cassie was simply radiant these days, her darling little breasts emerging, her hips curving out. It was probably time for me to have a little talk with her. And spare Mama the embarrassment.

"Everybody's gone, Mr. Fodor. Mr. Levy and Mr. Ritori finished early tonight; they were all caught up. I left the upstairs lights on." He paused.

"That's all right, Richie," Mr. Fodor answered. "We'll be going up there. I want to check on the day's shooting."

After Richie picked his topcoat off the clothes tree and left, Mr. Fodor locked the front door and bolted it. He motioned me to follow him into his office. He had recently arranged for his secretary's desk to face his. He wanted her present whenever he interviewed professionals or aspirants. Too many girls, coached and prodded by ambitious mothers, were desperate to use any means, including scandal and blackmail, to realize their dreams. Movie executives needed to protect themselves.

The draperies were drawn, only the desk lamp was lit, leaving the rest of the room in darkness. Mr. Fodor removed his hat and his overcoat and his suit jacket and hung them up. Then he loosened his tie and rolled up the sleeves of his shirt.

I remained seated on a straight chair, while he unlocked a closet and brought out a camera, a tripod, and a batch of heavy glass plates.

"Well, little miss . . ." His face was flushed, his eyes amused. "You may undress."

I was numb. It was impossible for me to move. I could only stare at him.

"Do you need help with your buttons?" He put his hands under my arms and raised me to my feet. He was gentle as he unfastened the big pearl buttons on my gray coat and hung it up. Then he unfastened the small pearl-gray buttons on my shirtwaist and pulled it over my head, laughing as he smoothed down my hair. He said, "Turn around, little one," and unfastened my cambric and Irish lace camisole. "You girls . . . how many petticoats do you wear?"

I tried to smile the tremulous smile that he admired when he cast me in a film. I was trembling with tears, not of fear or of shame but tears whose origin I couldn't understand.

He framed my face between his hands. "Your exquisite face. There is no one like you, little miss."

Now I was stripped of serge, cambric, muslin and ruffles. My flesh was white with a rash of goosebumps. Mr. Fodor held out a silk kimono from the closet and bundled me into it.

"We'll take some pictures, and then we'll have our little game, which is all our own. It will remain our secret, do you understand, my dear?"

"Yes, Mr. Fodor, you said so . . . last time."

"And you didn't tell anybody; you kept it all to yourself?"

I nodded. He was in a good mood, so I took a chance.

"Mr. Fodor . . ."

"Yes, my dear?"

"The student . . . when Sonia meets him for the first time, is she afraid of him? Or sorry for him?"

Mr. Fodor was down to his immaculate shirt and trousers. "She has no fear. She's a little saint."

"Mr. Fodor?"

He was waiting.

"Would you show me how to play the first scene between them? I mean, later . . ."

His laughter was rich and exuberant. "So you want to play games, little miss?"

"Oh, no, sir. I want to learn. I want to learn everything about my profession that you can teach me."

"You're a willing student. We'll begin with the photographs again."

He was not in Hans Rolfsma's class as a photographer. He took only stills on 11 by 14 plates, and the first time he used flash powder it scared me nearly out of my wits.

Now he spread a length of rich black velvet on an easy chair. Then he bowed courteously and motioned me to sit. I dropped the kimono and felt the rash of goosebumps again on my skin. I snuggled into the velvet, falling into the poses he suggested, willing myself to carry out his instructions, reminding myself that if I did not pose for him, Peg or Jenny would. He took shots of me with my back to the camera, looking over my shoulders, my

79

eyes downcast, my hands modestly across my breasts. Then straight on, looking into the camera, my legs first crossed, then separated so my private parts were visible. I was too scared to be excited, although I shivered when Mr. Fodor came over to mold my body into a particular pose he wanted. His rough hands stroked my skin as he exposed me in the most intimate way possible.

"What would happen if anyone found these pictures?" I asked.

Mr. Fodor explained he developed these plates himself and the prints were kept under his private lock and key.

I no longer felt cold. There was a strange disturbing heat in my body. I hated his hands and I hungered for them. He touched me in places that made me faint and warm at the same time. I was in a daze; nothing was very clear, although I knew what to anticipate.

He finally tossed aside the velvet drapery and sat down in the armchair. Waiting. I got a towel from his bathroom. When I came back he had loosened his suspenders and they were hanging over the sides of the chair, and his trousers were unfastened at the waist. His white shirt, fresh at dinnertime, was damp under the armpits with a male smell. I opened the buttons of his shirt and touched the pale hair matted in little question marks along his muscular chest. His skin was white but not like a woman's. He leaned toward me. "Come here, dear one. Kneel down."

My heart racing, I obeyed.

He put his hands on my head and drew me toward him. "I now crown thee Princess," he said. And engulfed me in his lap.

I was aware of the enormous bulge between his legs, powerful and demanding.

I knew I must undo the fasteners in his trousers. He liked that, particularly because my fingers were shaking. His smile was benevolent. Did he remember how frightened I was the first time I saw that inflamed, pulsating thing? I groped now through the cloth until I found it, snug in its bushy nest, and coaxed it out for display. The head was smooth but the rest of it was still wrinkled. Almost immediately it developed into a throbbing extension, a long, thick column. It amused him to slap my cheeks with it. But as his breath quickened, he put both of his hands on my head. I felt them like a vise as he guided himself into my mouth. It gagged me and he withdrew slightly and I was grateful for it. I was frightened it would choke me. He was stroking my head now, urging me down, reminding me by touch what he had previously taught me... pausing when I felt his spasms begin, giving him a rest while my quick, moist tongue followed his sex to its roots and below, using my hands to manipulate and squeeze.

He was silent, but his chest was rising. His skin was flushed, his body damp with perspiration. And as I nibbled and licked at him, he pushed it deeper into my mouth until I felt the shudder and the spasms, until I heard his low excruciating moans, and felt the full force of his flow in my mouth. I spit it out as quickly as I could while he was still shuddering.

Then I got up from my knees and hurried into the bathroom and vomited.

I washed my face and brought back a basin filled with water and a towel and I sponged and dried him and he smiled at me with a kind of benevolence and said it was the best he'd ever had.

"The best, Mr. Fodor," I agreed, thinking it was better then we'd had at the hotel in Brooklyn Heights, which was hurtful and exhausting.

"And it's still our little secret," he said, putting his hand under my chin.

"Yes, Mr. Fodor."

"We'll keep it from the others. Promise?"

"I promise, Mr. Fodor."

When we were all dressed and ready to leave, I couldn't believe it had happened. I never could. The best thing was to put it out of my mind as I did before. And as I would again.

Mama had given me a key, so I could let myself in without disturbing her or Cassie. As I hung up my coat in the closet and made for the bathroom, I heard Mama's gentle voice from the bedroom.

"Did you have a pleasant evening, dear?"

"Very pleasant, Mama."

"Get a good night's sleep, dear."

"I will, Mama."

"You sound odd, dear. I hope you haven't caught Cassie's cold."

"I feel all right."

"Well, gargle with hot water and a little salt anyway. Just to be on the safe side."

"I will, Mama."

"Did Mr. Fodor mention his next picture?"

"Yes, he did."

"What sort of picture will it be?"

I explained, standing in the bathroom doorway. "Very tragic. About a young student who murders an old lady and now he finds regeneration through a lovely girl. Sonia is—"

"Sonia?"

"She's the lead."

"Who will play the role? Jenny or Peg?"

"I will, Mama. I shall play Sonia."

"How do you know, dear? He's always changing his mind."

"I can't explain it, Mama. But I'm sure. . . ."

When the film was reviewed, the editor of *Mores*, an intellectual quarterly, wrote: "It is evident now to the world that *Joshua Fodor has a grasp of the psychological motives that drive a man to murder.*

"Vanessa Oxford, that dream child, plays her first important role with a saintly air. She is the exquisite spiritual symbol of the murderer's expiation . . ."

Cassie was difficult.

She didn't like Mr. Fodor and made no effort to hide her dislike. While I often fretted because it was difficult to anticipate Mr. Fodor's plans for the evening, she couldn't have cared less. Not even when I reminded her that he was our bread and butter.

The thought and planning that went into his films were not to be found in his private life. Here he was impulsive. Sometimes on a Saturday night he would take the entire company for dinner and dancing at a Broadway cafe. Cassie was willing to come along, but my problem was to see that she was polite to Mr. Fodor. One evening, when we were all around a large table, talking, smiling, keeping time to the orchestra, Mr. Fodor asked Cassie for a dance.

She refused.

I spoke up. "Now, Cassie mind your manners."

Mr. Fodor didn't seem offended. He said casually, "I never force a young lady."

But I was terrified his feelings were hurt.

"Please, Mr. Fodor, will you dance with me?" I asked.

The wardrobe lady, who was among the quests, told me later that we were beautiful on the dance floor. Mr. Fodor was always so well dressed, so neat, so courteous. He held his partner properly, never too close, like some of his male assistants who tried for a furtive caress. That night I was wearing a rose-print voile with ruffles at the wrists and throat, a dress Mama had finished for me just that afternoon. I wasn't downplaying Mama's talents as a dressmaker, but one day, I resolved, I would be dressed by the designer Lorraine North had patronized.

When Mr. Fodor brought me back to our table, Jenny Mayran's grandmother, who watched over her, said, "Doesn't my Jenny look beautiful? Mr. Fodor bought that dress for her next picture and said she could wear it tonight."

Jenny didn't cause me as much concern as Lorraine had. Jenny's curves were indeed luscious but she was greedy about sweets and it wouldn't be long before she grew plump.

Mr. Fodor hated fat.

Peg was bony. Mr. Fodor said her meager little body was a vessel for her rich feelings. Mr. Fodor said in the presence of all of us, "She is flawless in everything she does." I was afraid I knew what he meant.

He said Cassie also had the spark. Cassie didn't take him seriously; she had little respect for him. Yet after she'd been in the company a few months he began to cast her in parts that I personally thought were much too demanding of her. Sometimes when I stood in the shadow of the set, watching her, I'd think, *If only she would let me show her how to play it right.*

But Cassie remained indifferent to my suggestions. She and Peg would walk off with their jaunty little-boy strides, and I knew that behind my back they were laughing at me.

Little Sister just couldn't grasp the importance of my relationship with Mr. Fodor.

Once she found me kneeling in the first floor bathroom, peering through a knothole into the lower wardrobe room. She pushed me aside rudely to peek. Peg was changing into a pretty dress.

"He's taking her out tonight," I said, dispirited. "Well, let's go home."

Cassie bounced up. "You know something, you're jealous of her!"

"I am not!"

"You are, *you are!*" Cassie was enjoying herself, dancing around me like a wild Indian. Before sprinting to the door, she added, "You know what else? Peg can't stand you either. How about that! And she's a better actress, too."

The feeling was mutual, I wanted to tell Cassie. But I kept silent. I knew all about Peg Dalton and her "acting" talent.

Peg Dalton was the only girl Mr. Fodor saw on Sundays. He often went to church with her family and then stayed on for dinner. He read to the younger children, who adored him. Sometimes, when the older boys were home, he played ball with them.

Since Mr. Fodor enjoyed his visits so much, Mrs. Dalton made sure Peg was home that day. This didn't suit Peg at all—she'd developed a wild crush on one of his assistants. But her mother was firm.

One Friday, as Peg and I were changing into our own clothes, I said, "Gosh, I don't know what I'm going to do Sunday. It'll be a long day."

Peg was all sympathy. Sometimes she was really warm-hearted. "Why's that? What about your mother and Cassie?"

"They're going to visit a friend of Mama's who was on tour with her once. Poor thing, she's really very sick."

"Well, then, come to my house for the day."

"Peg, do you really mean that?"

"Of course, it won't be much—the family mostly—" She hesitated, as though remembering something, but I answered quickly.

"I'd love it. You're really very kind, Peg. No wonder everybody loves you."

As it turned out, the Dalton kids made me welcome, but it seemed to me that Peg's mother was rather distant, even after I thanked her profusely for saving me from a solitary day. Then Peg and I went up to her bedroom in the rambling old house and had a confidential girl-talk session in which she confided with a giggle that she was crazy about Thomas, Mr. Fodor's new assistant. "Don't tell anybody, Vanessa. Promise!"

"I promise," I said with a light heart.

When we returned from church, Mr. Fodor was sitting in a rocker on the front porch, his wide-brimmed hat pushed up over his forehead, his topcoat unfastened as he enjoyed the noonday sun.

"Mr. Fodor!" Mrs. Dalton practically surrounded him, so pleased that he was there, so anxious to make him welcome. "When you weren't here for church, we gave up hope."

"I was detained." He stood up, smiling at Peg and her five younger brothers and two sisters, all handsome and dressed up in their Sunday clothes. When he saw me he was visibly surprised. I felt suddenly the chill of his subtle disapproval, but I cheerily explained that the Daltons had taken pity on me today and wasn't I lucky to share in their Sunday!

During dinner—a delicious spicy pot roast made with crushed gingersnaps and served with hot applesauce—Mr. Fodor's good spirits seemed restored. He teased the younger children, played the cavalier to the little girls, who responded with giggles and kisses. He ignored Peg and me, but since spirits were high I didn't feel exactly left out. It was clear to me that he was happy here with Peg and her family. Peg had clearly made a place for herself in his life. Why?

Curiosity didn't ruin my appetite. I'd learned to eat whenever I had the opportunity. Too many times on our travels we were forced to skip meals. Or eat dry unpalatable sandwiches. Finally Mr. Fodor pushed back his plate.

"Mrs. Dalton, Charles Dickens should've had the pleasure of your company." He took out his Havana cigar and one of the small girls begged for the colorful band, which she put on her finger. She ran around the table showing it off.

"Mr. Fodor's gonna marry me."

His laughter was loud and hearty. "How can I choose from all of you?"

The sister, younger than Peg, said, "And will you make us all actresses like Peg?"

"I wish I could. But there's only one Peg."

Afterward, Mr. Fodor got up and went to the window, looking out at the yard, already winter-seared but with a golden cast from the sun. Beyond stretched the woods, marked with silver birch and scrub oak, their leaves still clinging stubbornly.

"What a lovely day," Mrs. Dalton said.

"Nice day for a stroll," Mr. Fodor said. "I need to walk off that pot roast."

Peg looked uncertain. "But I have to clear the table."

"Vanessa will help me," Mrs. Dalton said. "Run along, Peg."

In no time the room was empty. The younger children ran down the hill to play with friends, the others scattered, and finally Mrs. Dalton and I were left to clean up.

As I dried the dishes, I looked out of the window at the yard and beyond it at the old two-story barn. "I love this house," I said. "Peg's so lucky to live here."

"Without Peg's help, we couldn't stay here." Mrs. Dalton's voice was suddenly somber. "That's why I remember Mr. Fodor in my prayers." Then, abruptly, she was brisk. "Why don't you sit in the parlor or take a little nap."

"Oh, don't worry about me, please. I'm used to being by myself."

"Then I'll go up and take a little rest. My feet bother me if I stand too long."

I wandered around the parlor, looking at the chromo pictures of the girls in their communion dresses, until I heard her heavy step overhead. Then I went softly to the hall closet, got my coat and let myself out of the front door. I'd take an after-dinner constitutional myself. Maybe follow the cowpath that went beyond the barn into the woods.

Where had Mr. Fodor gone with Peg? Down this path, leading to the woods? What were they talking about? Just laughing and enjoying the day, with Mr. Fodor teasing Peg and Peg returning his banter?

There were no leaves on the path, the winds had long since wiped it clean and I walked softly.

I heard them before I saw them. Beyond the silver birches there was an outcropping of rock, three times a man's height, and there, sitting on a shelf of rock, was Mr. Fodor. He was motioning to Peg, who had climbed to the low branch of a nearby tree and was swinging like a boy, laughing. Mr. Fodor got up, strode across the short distance, caught her by the waist and pulled her with such force that they both tumbled to the earth. Mr. Fodor didn't get up, his strong arms locked themselves around Peg's shoulders and he pulled her down on him so her face was in line with his hips. She had stopped struggling, her laughter had died as she watched him unfasten his trousers. I saw his piece of reddish flesh, upright, throbbing, and I saw Peg raise herself and open her mouth to take it in.

I could stand no more. I felt myself gulping air and knew I was having dry heaves and knew I had to get away quickly. Not that there was any danger of their seeing me. But I was taken with a sickness that threatened a blackout.

I longed to black out, to wipe away this awful vision, to forget I ever saw it. Yet I knew I must get back to the house, make some hasty excuse and take the trolley back home. I was sick and shaken. The sight of them together on the ground, with Peg choking on his huge thing, was something I'd never forget. Did her own *mother* know what they did together? Was that the reason she never let Peg see anyone else Sundays?

Did he do it with Lorraine North? And Jenny Mayran?

And Cassie? Oh, my God, not Cassie! I put *that* image right out of my mind.

I had thought I was the *only one* of his little girls he had picked to please him *that way*. Once he had said to me, "You're the only one, Little Miss. The only one."

He was a liar. Mr. Fodor wanted the same thing probably from all his little girls.

Well, he was a man. Men didn't care about what girls did for love. They just wanted any pleasure they could find from *any* little girl.

I couldn't change him. I knew it instinctively even then. There was only one thing I could do—please him better than any of the other little girls. I would use my mouth so cleverly that he would never want any other girl to do it for him. And soon he wouldn't need Peg, or Lorraine or Jenny ... for *that*. And he'd remember who he would have to choose to please him. And that girl would be rewarded.

That girl would be me.

I swore to it.

And I always kept my promises. Especially to myself.

Three:

THE PRESENT: HOW SUE BECAME INVOLVED WITH THE MADONNA OF THE SILENTS

VANESSA OXFORD CAME into Sue Palmer's life at precisely the right moment.

Earlier Sue might have accorded the legend too much reverence and awe.

Later she might have undervalued the perfection and concentrated heavily on the shortcomings.

Celebrities weren't rare in Sue's life. Her father, Elliott Palmer, the distinguished professor of economics at Williams, a disciple of John Keynes, often commuted from Williamstown to Washington to San Diego. He was an advisor to presidents and a consultant to a think tank in California. In the past year at the Film

Wing, Sue came into contact with the conservative rich, the jet-set millionaires and the film stars, so she didn't impress easily.

She was also an only child, a fact of life that generated special problems. She was twelve when her mother died of leukemia, and her adjustment to life was a testimony to her father's loving concern.

He was a wise man of few pretensions. For two summers after her mother's death he took Sue to a ranch in Wyoming where they shared togetherness with other single-parent families. However nature in the raw triggered allergic attacks of sneezing and flooded tear ducts. The following summer he sent her to Europe with a group of overprivileged "underprivileged" teenagers.

Sue was a product of social change that she accepted without question.

Many of her friends, the girls from Wykeham Rise, the boys from Choate, had been fragmented by divorce. The original set of parents, the source of the primal security and love, had split, the result being parents in duplicate, guardian uncles, surrogate mommies, nannies recalled from retirement, and tutors.

Whenever she saw her friends playing musical houses during vacations, deciding which parents to favor and to blackmail with their presence, she became more reconciled to the loss of her mother. Fortunately, her father, despite academic pressures, had a talent for parenting. He allowed her to stretch her horizons and he always stood by, tolerant and sympathetic whenever she needed him.

In the mid-'60s she was too young for violence on the campus, although she saw indications of unrest that frightened her whenever she came home weekends. In her junior year at Wykeham Rise she was attracted to a local boy who'd switched from Andover to the nearby high school. His family discovered his problem when he overdosed at a party. Sue and another of his friends walked him in a survival marathon until his breathing was no longer depressed and his mind was somewhat in control. He was shipped off to a private hospital in Westport.

Still, Sue felt her friends were adjusting reasonably well to the world. It was, after all, the only world they knew.

Her father disagreed. He said they were outrunning their feelings. Blocking out. "They're terrified of any one-to-one feelings for fear it will cause some genuine emotional involvement. They're a hit-and-run generation."

Sue's encounters with young men from Dartmouth and Williams seemed to verify his statement. Self-centered and hardly able to relate to anyone, they took but could not give.

Her mother had set assumed goals for Sue—the continuity of marriage, children, the nurturing role of the woman. The price of happiness was taken for granted by her mother's generation.

Once when she was at home during spring vacation Sue sat by her bedroom window overlooking the Clarke Museum and really tried to think of her parents as people. She had come across a photo album with prints of her parents on their honeymoon, and in the pictures her father was always looking at her mother but her mother was staring into the camera. She'd overheard one of the great-aunts comment not long ago that her mother had envied her father his achievements; that marriage, home and child had not been enough for her. Unfortunately her mother had died before they could try to solve the differences between parent and adolescent and meld their feelings into some kind of familial truce. But Sue understood one thing.

Her mother had been an unfulfilled, unhappy woman....

"Sue, you're too much in control," her counselor at Mount Holyoke had suggested. "What I'd like to see is a good gut reaction."

How could she explain what was a puzzle to herself? Had her mother really wanted her to marry and raise children? Or did she want her to set out on a voyage of self-discovery, no matter where it led her?

Her father was disturbed when she dropped out of Mount Holyoke, but he at least offered some honest questions: What would she like to do? Where would she want to live?

"A safe neighborhood is more important than a good address," Sue's father advised her when she decided to test life in New York City. "I doubt that you'd be happy in a nunnery like the Barbizon Hotel for Girls. Still, I want to be assured that you're safe."

He wrote his younger brother, Sheldon, who promised to look after her. And Sue went to live with her uncle and aunt in a distinguished old apartment house on East 63rd Street off Fifth Avenue. Her uncle had been obliged to curtail his extravagant life style, so the staff had been reduced to one full-time maid and a weekly cleaning woman and laundress. This left available one of the servants' rooms on the second floor. It was fairly spacious, but since it looked out on the airshaft Sue kept the colorful blinds drawn. It had a kind of Art Deco charm, furnished with duplex leftovers from the time her uncle had had money and her aunt had bought taste. The daybed, once quilted in white satin, had a sturdy denim cover, bright patchwork pillows, and a blue ombre afghan Sue inherited from her mother. The Biedermeyer chest and chairs were more valuable than her Aunt Harriet estimated. She added a Picasso lithograph and straw baskets filled with spider and schefflera plants.

Whenever her father sent her a check, she replenished her small larder at Bloomingdale's food department. She was generous with the goodies, so her neighbors, often bored, hungry or thirsty, knocked on her door at odd hours. Her most frequent visitor was a girl who looked like Liv Ulmann. "Liv" as she called herself, was the granddaughter of the baron who'd been the hero of the Mannerheim Line in World War I, and she apparently simply couldn't understand that what she wanted wasn't hers for the taking—having been asked to leave Bloomingdale's without an ostrich boa she'd attached to the mink lining of her raincoat. She often stopped by to borrow taxi money from Sue. . . .

The New England Palmers' blood, often inbred, was gloriously diluted in the '30s when a Palmer married the daughter of a Portuguese fisherman on Cape Cod. This genetic fusion produced her father, who enjoyed individuality without excess, and her Uncle Sheldon, who was a mathematical genius and, inevitably during the wild '60s, a Wall Street operator.

As the wonderboy of the Hedge Funds, he was celebrated in *Fortune* magazine's pages. Like many brilliant men, Sheldon's disabling flaw was his taste in women. After he sampled the showgirls and the models, he settled on a Brooklyn born psychologist, who was now Sue's Aunt Harriet.

For a while Sue worked at Saks Fifth Avenue but was quickly bored. Then she decided to take a film course at NYU, and there she met a very intriguing young man named Charlie Bryson. She found she had a real interest in films, especially their history, and so her Uncle Sheldon found an opening for her at the Museum's Film Wing.

Which was where she met Vanessa Oxford.

After which Sue Palmer was never the same again.

THE PRESENT: WHAT SUE DISCOVERED IN THE CELLULOID ARCHIVES

IT WAS MRS. ELSBERG, a handsome Viking who resembled Ingrid Bergman, who singled Sue out for the Fodor project.

Sue had been at the Film Wing for three months, concentrating mainly in the ground-floor bookshop where she sold film posters, glossy prints of actors and film scenes, and books on the art of the cinema.

Mrs. Elsberg, searching through the bookshelves one morning as Sue came over to help her, saw a young girl of medium height with dark brown hair in center part pulled away in a chignon that outlined her small beautifully shaped head. She had glowing dark eyes, a good nose saved from prettiness by a small bump in the cartilage and a full mouth, bare of lipstick. The effect was casual, disarming, with a kind of throw-away sex appeal.

"Can I be of help?" Sue asked.

Mrs. Elsberg straightened up. "We're planning a Joshua Fodor retrospective in October," she said. "Do we have a biography of him?"

Sue glanced down the shelves, where posters lay in horizontal display, and over the scattering of books on film people—biographies of Charlie Chaplin, Mary Pickford, Mabel Normand, Cecile B. de Mille, the Gish sisters. The pickings were lean.

"The early days of the movies are 'in,'" Sue said. "We can't keep the books in stock."

"Have we *anything* on Joshua Fodor?"

"Not unless Mrs. Block has material in her files." Sue checked the catalogue. "He didn't live long enough to write his memoirs. But there is something on him in *The Rise of the International Film* and also in *Hollywood: The Ultimate Fantasy*.

"We'll need information on Fodor for the souvenir booklet."

"Would you like me to photocopy whatever I can find?"

"Will you, please?"

When Sue brought her the scanty material, Mrs. Elsberg said, "Normally, this would be in Mrs. Block's department. She's our authority on Fodor. But she's out of town so often, tracking down old films that she simply hasn't the time. I checked with her. She's agreeable to let you do the souvenir booklet; that is, if you'd like to."

"I'd love it! It sounds exciting!"

"Actually, it should be simple. We'll need the chronology of Joshua Fodor's films, dates of release, names of the cast and production notes. Some information was supplied when the films were first released; we have those. Others may be lost. Mrs. Block tells me Fodor's possessions were scattered, but she has some leads on his files for *Jesus Christ—Son and Savior*. Your job, Sue, will be to research and collate, beginning with Fodor's first film. It may involve a good deal of legwork."

"I have a friend who'll give me leads," Sue said, thinking of Charlie.

The following day Mrs. Elsberg arranged to have her transferred to the Film Library, which pleased Sue no end. Except for the hours devoted to the bookshop, she was a floater, filling in wherever she was needed, sometimes helping out Mr. Friedlander, the Film Wing curator, when his secretary was out, although her shorthand wasn't up to his hectic dictation. She helped out in Mrs. Block's department, mostly to file the great mass of material on the early silent movies. Mrs. Block had just returned the previous week from her latest foraging trip to Russia, reporting that negotiations were difficult but she had finally traded a fragment of a Serge Eisenstein film for Joshua Fodor's first one-reeler starring Vanessa Oxford, *The Lost Daughter and the Gypsies*. Sue was working in Mrs. Block's office on Wednesday when Mr. Friedlander entered, offering Mrs. Block his excited congratulations.

"I thought there wasn't a copy left," he said. "I understand Fodor hated the picture and tried to buy up and destroy all negatives."

"He was probably offended when a few critics said he was plagiarizing Griffith," Mrs. Block replied. She was a slight, attractive woman whose LaCoste knit dress, earth shoes and short haircut suggested energy and no nonsense. Her walnut-brown, prematurely wrinkled face was beaming with the satisfaction of an anthropologist after a rare find. "Of course, he was deeply influenced by Griffith; he worked with him for a couple of years."

"Joshua Fodor was less an innovator than an adapter." Mr. Friedlander's voice was the rich, pontifical one he used for his seminars on The Early Giants of the Silents. "Practically every director in the nickelodeon days stole from Griffith. But then, the old boy wasn't above a bit of larceny himself—Griffith borrowed from Dickens and Browning and Poe, among others.

"Most directors who stole from Griffith were clods. But Joshua Fodor understood what Griffith was aiming for. And, as often happens, he outranked his teacher. He took greater chances than his master. As a matter of fact, Fodor was ahead of the German surrealists."

"Now that the format for the retrospective is taking shape," Mrs. Block said, raking her fingers through her short tousled hair, "we'll lead off with *The Lost Daughter and the Gypsies*, include *The Land of the Free*, about the immigrants on Ellis Island, and *The Rivals—Daughter and Mother*. He really had an instinct about psychiatry, d'you suppose he was Oedipal? We'll focus on his masterpiece, *Jesus Christ—Son and Savior*, and end with *Confession of a Woman of Pleasure*."

"That was his last film," Mr. Friedlander said. "The final picture he and Vanessa Oxford did together."

"Yes, she's giving the Wing her uncut reels of the film."

"Great! She actually finished the film after he died. Vanessa Oxford's a remarkable woman, a truly remarkable woman! . . ."

Plans for the Joshua Fodor retrospective, which would include a kickoff gala for Film Wing funds, were initiated in May. Six weeks before the event the staff began to live from crisis to crisis.

As usual, each member thought another had done a specific job, so the plans were in chaos. By Labor Day, however, they proved their ability to function best on adrenaline and deadlines.

Sue was behind, but then her assignment had come quite late. George Freedly at Lincoln Center had plenty of material on Griffith, but little on Fodor. Fortunately some Joshua Fodor files had been rescued from dead storage by a film buff who donated them to the Film Wing in exchange for a tax deduction. No one had bothered to sort the material. Sue was allergic to dust but, fortified with antihistamines, she went to work on the boxes that were stored in the Wing's basement.

"I feel like an anthropologist," she reported to Mrs. Block. "The only important information I've uncovered is that he was big on personal publicity."

"Well, yes." Mrs. Block was tolerant. "Genius and conceit are natural bedfellows."

Sue's first three days had also uncovered a record of Joshua Fodor's expenditures for 1919. He'd spent $200,000 on personal publicity. *Impossible*, she thought. According to Mrs. Block he was a man of modest tastes. Except for his well-tailored clothes and his foreign motorcars, he had no extravagances. Sue tried to form an image of the man, of his background, his talent, his relationship to his staff and players, but he stayed an enigma.

What intrigued her more was the record of Vanessa Oxford's salary. Five hundred dollars a week, plus five percent of the film's gross. This wasn't much, considering the actress had captured the world with her fresh, original interpretation of Mary and Mary Magdalene in *Jesus Christ—Son and Savior*.

"The virgin is always a smash as the whore," Mrs. Elsberg said when Sue brought her the file.

"There's an article in an old issue of *Theatre Magazine* that says the world laughed with Chaplin, wept with Gish and was inspired by Vanessa Oxford."

"Quite true. Vanessa is the symbol of pure, undefiled love. We must, of course, include her in the souvenir booklet, but it's practically impossible to get any personal information about her past, except where it concerns Fodor."

"Well, she's the sole survivor of Fodor's great years. My friend Charlie says she knows where all the bodies are buried."

"I'm not sure it's worth talking to her," Mrs. Elsberg said, handing back the file. "She never gives you a direct answer to a direct question. She tells you only what she wants you to know."

"Difficult?"

"Complex. And fascinating."

"Was she Fodor's mistress?"

Mrs. Elsberg shrugged eloquently. "Everyone in the industry has speculated for years and never uncovered the truth. He's dead, and she just smiles her ethereal smile. She's got some dangerous secrets locked in her heart, I'd wager. And I suspect they'll be buried with her." Mrs. Elsberg walked Sue to the corridor. "I wouldn't dig too deeply. All we need, essentially, is a Fodor chronology."

In other words, Sue thought, returning to the cave of files, *keep your nose out of what is none of your business.*

"Vanessa Oxford," people were apt to say, "I thought she was dead!"

Although she had faded into legend, Vanessa was very much alive. Though she was associated with the early "flicks" when they were regarded with scorn—pap for immigrants, on a level with the cartoon strips—and no legitimate actor would sully his reputation or diminish his ego by appearing in these flickering monstrosities, she had surpassed her beginnings. Critics today mentioned her with respect: she was a great lady of the theater, right up there with the likes of Katharine Cornell or Helen Hayes. Nothing in Vanessa's public behavior suggested an over-the-hill movie queen, feeding her demented ego on the narcotic of former glory like the actress Gloria Swanson played in *Sunset Boulevard.* Nor like the obsessed neurotic superstars who transformed their hangups into Oscar performances.

Vanessa was revered by the New Directors, those street-smart boys from N.Y.U. classes who believed the director was all. They envied her for having been there when it all began. And for having inspired emotions in the great Joshua Fodor that went beyond his respect for a fine actress and made him a great artist.

"Vanessa's life is the history of films made personal," Friedlander said in a *New York Times* interview. He was prejudiced. It was through Vanessa's unflagging efforts that the Film Wing acquired the rare early Joshua Fodor films. But there was more than a little truth in his statement.

In order to get a rounded picture of Fodor films, Sue leafed through Mrs. Block's files on Vanessa and, as she read interviews and articles, she began to grasp the range of Vanessa's influence, not only as an international film star but as a personality. While most of her contemporaries concentrated primarily on their careers, leaving the selling of World War I Liberty Bonds to Mary Pickford and Douglas Fairbanks and the championing of America First to Lillian Gish, Vanessa worked for a national theater and, in later years, for the release of artists imprisoned behind the Iron Curtain and for world peace and disarmament. That she wasn't forgotten was evident in her consistent inclusion in the magazine polls of outstanding women, along with Rose and Ethel Kennedy. At a dinner in her honor at The Players club, she was saluted as the American Duse.

Film buffs and students, studying early film memorabilia, discovered that while D. W. Griffith was associated with Mary Pickford, Blanche Sweet, Marion Leonard, Gertrude Robinson, Mae Marsh, Lillian Gish and Carol Dempster, Joshua Fodor was mainly linked with Vanessa Oxford.

If Griffith's *Birth of a Nation* transformed the nickelodeon into an art form, Fodor's *Jesus Christ—Son and Savior* guaranteed the American films' international reputation. And now the Film Wing was launching its retrospective of Joshua Fodor (1880–1934) in a dedicated effort to rescue the forgotten giant from obscurity.

Vanessa Oxford would be the guest of honor at the gala, which would include officers of the Film Wing, members of the board of the adjacent museum, the influential rich and powerful of the city. . . .

Sue was helping Mrs. Elsberg and her secretary mail invitations on thick, creamy Tiffany stationery when Mrs. Elsberg said, "I see Miss Vanessa will be accompanied by Dann Houston."

Sue looked up from the pile of envelopes. "Who's he?"

"Oklahoma oil. Very attractive."

"Young?" Sue asked, surprised.

"Quite. These actresses start out as little girls with old men and finish as old ladies with young boys."

"Why not? It should work both ways," Sue said. Vanessa

Oxford was shaping up in her imagination not as a film relic but as a fascinating woman.

"Most females are born losers," Mrs. Elsberg said, parceling out more envelopes. "A few are self-made winners. Vanessa's in that category."

"Are you inviting any other old-timers?" Sue asked.

"We're sending invitations, but few of the old stars are available. Vanessa's sister, Cassandra, is in town. But I understand she'll have nothing to do with her film past."

Early stars like Blanche Sweet, Colleen Moore and Miriam Cooper had retired to their private worlds. Others were in the Rest Home for Retired Actors or the Motion Picture Hospital or were vegetating in warm climates for the good of their bodies if not their minds.

When Mrs. Elsberg consulted Vanessa about tracking down some of Joshua Fodor's favorite players, the actress firmly vetoed the suggestion.

"Many of them have bitter memories of Mr. Fodor. After he made them famous he often let them go. He felt he couldn't hold them back. But the sad thing is that they never achieved equal fame under other directors. Some never forgave him."

This made sense, so Mrs. Elsberg didn't persist. Vanessa was so knowledgeable about the pioneers who'd launched the American film that few would dare question her statements or contradict her. "After all," Mrs. Elsberg said, "she was there when it all happened."

Vanessa also agreed to make a little speech at the gala, to include anecdotes that would illuminate Joshua Fodor the man as well as the creator.

"Vanessa appears to have an intuitive feeling about what people would like to see and hear," Mrs. Elsberg added, gathering a batch of envelopes for the "out" basket. "She was telling me most of her fan mail now comes from young people. They're obsessed with the early films."

She reminded Sue that copy for the souvenir booklet should go to the printer in four weeks. "You'll want to sort stills and write captions. And see the Fodor films in sequence, so I'll have Thomas run them for you whenever the screening room is free."

Mr. Friedlander, Mrs. Elsberg and Sue sat in the screening

room, a small theater with deep comfortable plush seats. Mr. Friedlander turned to Sue on his right. "The best way to analyze Fodor's talents is to compare him to Griffith, so we'll run a film by each on the same subject. In both cases it's the first film. We'll see what Griffith did with his. And how, just a few years later, Fodor improved on it. The plot for the Griffith one-reeler, *The Adventures of Dollie*, is simple. Gypsies kidnap a child, they hide her in a barrel that they pile on their wagon, then take off. As they cross a rough bridge, the barrel topples off and falls into the river. It floats toward shore where a couple of boys rescue it. Dollie is set free and united with her parents."

He explained that Griffith found the location for *The Adventures of Dollie* in Greenwich, Connecticut. Arthur Johnson, one of Griffith's favorite players, was the father; Lionel Barrymore was the kidnapper. Griffith, with one day to complete the film, had little time for preparation. He told Barrymore to drive his wagon down the road, pause before the wealthy home where a young child was playing on the lawn, snatch the youngster and hold her for ransom. The child's parents were in the rear of the house when the gypsy struck.

"Until he began directing," Mr. Friedlander explained, his voice excited at Griffith's innovation that Fodor improved on, "all movies were photographed like stage plays. Griffith decided to try something new. He switched the camera from one character in one scene to another character in another scene, then back to the first one. By doing this he was able to show the audience what was going on simultaneously in two places.

"Sue, notice how Griffith brings out the dramatic feeling in his very first attempt. Pay attention to his sensitivity to rural scenes, which would identify many of his future films and which greatly influenced Joshua Fodor. This film was released in July 1908, and it made Griffith immensely valuable to his bosses at Biograph."

Silents and piano players went together. Thomas, a distinguished white-haired gentleman recently retired from the staff at Juilliard, was playing for the screening. But even with sound, the Griffith film seemed ludicrous to Sue. Movements were exaggerated, emotions raw. She could scarcely control her amusement.

"Don't judge it by today's standards," Mr. Friedlander reprimanded her. "Think of its impact sixty years ago. Remember the nickelodeon, which was the original movie house, played to audiences who didn't know the English language or the American culture. What they did understand was emotion: the girl's fright, the vicious gypsy, the terror of her abduction, the relief at her rescue. The film brought audiences communication and suggested to them a code of morality and behavior. This was important for a melting pot. Griffith was the first to appreciate the film's value as a universal language. And Joshua Fodor wasn't far behind."

"When did Joshua Fodor turn out *his* gypsy films?" Sue asked.

"Three years later. As you watch, you'll see how shrewdly he refined Griffith's technique. If you please, Thomas."

The Lost Daughter and the Gypsies. A Joshua Fodor Production. Written and Directed by Joshua Fodor.

The opening shot was a gypsy encampment. Sunlight was filtering through the leaves of the tall trees. The heroine was carrying a bucket of water from the river. She was no more than thirteen, her thick, fair hair was too heavy for her head and spindly neck and her shabby garments hung on her thin boy's frame. She had a scar on her cheek near her right eye. As she joined the Romany girls, the contrast between her and them was noticeable not only in coloring but in attitude. Where they were bold and aggressive, she was shy and timid. Where they flaunted their early sexuality, she was childishly virginal.

Her father, the gypsy king, was displeased because she had rejected the young man he'd chosen for her mate. After scolding her, he briefed all the girls on their duties in the nearby village. Gypsy women were taught to tell fortunes, to steal, to use their wits for evil ends. The other girls listened. Only the heroine refused to obey the king, and as a result he gave her a vicious beating with his whip.

"You'll notice the first suggestion of sadism we see in practically all later Fodor films," Mr. Friedlander said, sounding not quite comfortable. "His heroines were invariably the helpless victims of cruel men."

Sue was fascinated. The heroine's fright was so vivid. She was terrorized by the gypsy, who was ostensibly her father. There was a suggestion of incest in the gypsy's grappling with her. She ran away from him and escaped. He ordered the chosen bridegroom to follow her and bring her back for punishment. Meanwhile the girl had something of a head start, but the audience knew her flight was hopeless, that she would be captured and subjected to degradation. She ran, her terror giving her speed. She fell into gullies, brambles tore at her flesh. The audience feared that the brute pursuing her would not wait until the bridal night to take his pleasure with her. At last, utterly spent, she reached an isolated house. Sanctuary. But her way was barred by a vicious dog guarding the place. Desperation gave her the spurt of courage to dash past the animal, who began barking. The front door opened. An elderly man called off the dog. The woman behind him stepped out in time to catch the heroine, who collapsed in her arms. The man and woman looked at her. There was a moment of recognition—the scar on her cheek. . . . She was their long-lost daughter stolen years ago, the daughter whose disappearance they had so deeply mourned.

The girl stared at them. Fear gave way to understanding. And finally to joy. Reunion.

The girl was Vanessa Oxford and she was magnificent.

"How old was she when the film was made?" Sue asked.

"Thirteen," Mrs. Elsberg said. "Those early Cooper-Hewitt lights were so bad that anyone over sixteen looked like a hag."

"Now that you've seen both films," Mr. Friedlander said, "you can appreciate the difference between Griffith and Fodor. Griffith had an instinct for suspense, which he often belabored. Fodor was more sensitive. The contrast between the heroine and the gypsy girls was shown not only in appearance but in morality and ethics. Notice also how he suggested incest but rendered it harmless. We realize the heroine isn't one of the clan. The king's lust for her is evident even though he has betrothed her to the young brute. We are titillated but not offended because we sense she's not his real daughter."

He paused. "Joshua Fodor was remarkable even in his first film."

"Yes," Mrs. Elsberg reminded hm, "but we mustn't forget he was refining Griffith's work."

"They all plagiarized each other, but few had Griffith's talent. Fodor did. Later, he even surpassed the master. Fodor went to the same sources for his material: the poets, Dickens, Shakespeare, the Bible. And he did what Griffith did, developed a theme in a one-reeler and then later expanded it in longer films. Actually

Griffith plagiarized himself when he refined some of his early one-reelers, and they appeared as scenes in *The Birth of a Nation*.

Mrs. Elsberg smiled. "Now that we've given each man his due, let's concentrate on Vanessa."

Most of the Film Wing staff were dedicated silent film buffs, but Sue gathered that Mrs. Elsberg was less given to reverence. A mature, sophisticated woman, fortified by the realism of her Swedish culture, she was objective about the girl-child who gave the original films the image of the heroine as a love object. "The first flicker actresses were illiterate," she said, "mostly unworldly and motivated by calculating mothers and innocent greed. Their shrewd mothers were in constant attendance, programming their careers and their loves."

Thomas switched on the overhead lights. Mr. Friedlander, Mrs. Elsberg and Sue stood up and as they moved up the aisle to the door, they saw two women seated in the last row.

"Why, it's Miss Vanessa!" Mr. Friedlander exclaimed, suddenly regretting his frank dissection of Joshua Fodor. He held out his hand. "It's *good* to see you! I wasn't told you were here."

Vanessa Oxford answered gently, "I came by to leave a print of Mr. Fodor playing with his dog. You may want some informal pictures for the souvenir booklet." She turned to her companion. "My agent, Mrs. Kramer."

Even in her seat, the middle-aged woman seemed taller than Vanessa, broad-boned, imposing in a gray tweed Chanel suit and a wide-brimmed black felt hat that covered her dark bangs, which touched the upper rims of her blue-tinted glasses. She hovered protectively over her client.

"Did you see the entire film?" Mr. Friedlander asked.

"Oh, yes." Vanessa's voice was soft, tender. "What memories it brought up for me. I remember his coming to dinner one Sunday—he was very fond of Mother and Cassie, you know—and talking about the gypsy film. 'If I could only remake it,' he said. He explained how he'd have heightened the suspense . . . 'Suppose her mother was dying and only the return of her daughter could prolong her life. The gypsies remembered suddenly it was in this neighborhood that they'd abducted the girl. So they decide to push on, taking the girl with them. A fierce storm comes up and they daren't move.' He wrote a short story about it, but it was never published. He often wrote stories based on his films. His early dream was to be a successful writer, you know..."

"Well, he wrote on celluloid instead of in print," Mr. Friedlander said. "But even his first film holds up remarkably, don't you think?"

"I never fail to marvel at his genius"—Mrs. Kramer's voice was deep and husky with a suggestion of a Russian accent—"and personally I have always considered him Griffith's superior."

"Oh, but we can't say that, can we?" Vanessa put her gloved hand to her cheek in visible anxiety. "We'd be cruelly criticized. But if the Sunday *Times* suggested it in a story ... Do you think Vincent Canby might write a piece on Fodor? Rediscover him?"

"I'm sure he'll do an article after the retrospective," Mr. Friedlander said. "I'll be in touch with him."

"That's very kind of you, Mr. Friedlander. Those of us who remember Joshua Fodor will appreciate it."

Sue thought, surprised, that Vanessa had an old-fashioned way of speaking. It seemed a contradiction to her smart blue suede suit and the Yves St. Laurent silk scarf knotted under her chin. She looked taller than she was because of her narrow bones. The effect was astonishingly youthful. Her hair, an artful strawberry blonde, was brushed off her high, smooth forehead and rolled into a pageboy curl. Her small face was shaped like a candy valentine and her eyes were altogether arresting. Sue recalled her art teacher saying that if a woman's eyes were too wide-spaced the effect was either like that of an animal or a Mongoloid. Vanessa's eyes were properly spaced, large with the luminous prominence of a hyperthyroid person, the irises a pure blue, the lashes still thick and carefully darkened with mascara. Whatever cosmetic surgery she may have had was hidden by the blue penciling of the lower lashes.

She can't be over seventy-five, Sue thought. *It's not possible! Only the sag of her chin and her hands betray her years. Otherwise she could pass for fifty. What is her secret?*

"Some of my material is stored in the basement of Dann Houston's house," Vanessa said. "I will sort it out soon and send you whatever memorabilia is pertinent to the Fodor exhibition. Some of the Fodor packing cases have disappeared.... I believe they were auctioned for delinquent storage fees. I don't know who bought them. I hope what I have is ample."

Her oddly formal manner of speaking fascinated Sue. It was as though each word was carefully weighed in her mind before it was released by her voice.

"Miss Vanessa, we'll be needing your introduction to the souvenir booklet by the end of the week."

"You'll have it," Mrs. Kramer interrupted. "Miss Vanessa is meticulous about her obligations."

"And Sue will be in touch with you about the Fodor chronology," Mrs. Elsberg added.

Vanessa nodded, a gentle gracious smile in the direction of Sue. "By all means, call me. I want to help in every way I can."

"We must double-check the facts," Mr. Friedlander said.

"Definitely." Mrs. Kramer was emphatic. "There have been such distortions about the early actors. Some stories were true. We know that Mabel Normand and Wally Reid took drugs and that poor girl in the Fatty Arbuckle case was allegedly raped with a soda bottle. But these were the exceptions. Most of the players lived quiet, decent, circumspect lives. Like Vanessa and Cassie and their mother. But one biographer conjures up a wild story and others, using him as a supposed source, compound the lies."

"We must tell the truth." Vanessa sounded determined "Joshua Fodor has been branded with too many cruel untruths."

"Suppose Sue came to you for source material," Mrs. Kramer suggested. "Miss Vanessa knows more about that period than any other living soul."

Vanessa laughed with pleasure. She looked at the moment quite different from any photograph Sue had ever seen of her. There wasn't a single picture of her laughing.

"Most of my contemporaries are gone"—Vanessa's voice was abruptly sad—"as a matter of fact, most people are surprised to hear I'm still among the living."

While they chatted they moved out into the hall, where the walls were backgrounds for huge grainy blowups of early motion picture scenes. Next to the elevator was the famous scene from *Jesus Christ—Son and Savior:* Mary Magdalene kneeling at the feet of Jesus. The man who was Jesus had long since been reduced to a set of yellowed clippings in the newspaper morgues, but Mary Magdalene was alive and present here on the third floor of the Film Wing, looking scarcely older than the fragile exquisite creature draped in veils and bowed in reverence, and lust, before the Savior.

Vanessa ignored her likeness as she pressed the elevator button and stood there, smiling at Sue.

Behind them, Mrs. Kramer's husky voice was clearly heard. "Mr. Friedlander, we must take care not to mention Griffith during the retrospective. Comparisons would be unfair to both men. Fodor has been in Griffith's shadow too long. This is something we must correct."

"We'll do our best, but we can't control the critics."

"We must try. It's only fair to Miss Vanessa. She's giving not only her vast collection of film material to the retrospective but her time as well. You appreciate how much it means to her."

"I do, Mrs. Kramer," acknowledging her subtle threat.

"She refused an offer for a new film from Paramount because it would interfere with the timing of the retrospective."

"We're aware of it. The trustees appreciate her generosity, they'll do anything for her."

"She wants only recognition for Joshua Fodor."

"We'll do our best," he repeated.

The ladies stepped into the elevator. Miss Vanessa's smile was gentle and ethereal, as though she were listening to an inner voice.

In the corridor Mrs. Elsberg turned to the curator. "Why doesn't she speak for herself?"

"Miss Vanessa?" Mr. Friedlander said. "She is too sensitive, she's afraid of hurting. Hers is a rare character, you know."

He returned to his office, and Sue looked at Mrs. Elsberg, who was smiling faintly.

"Mrs. Elsberg, is Mr. Friedlander married?"

"No, as a matter of fact, he's not married."

"Does he live with his mother?"

"Yes, he does. Why do you ask?"

"My friend Charlie Bryson says that many of the men who adore Miss Vanessa are gentle middle-aged bachelors who live with their mothers."

"Middle-aged bachelors are a fact of life, Sue, and the lady's made the most of it. Those men made her one of the greatest stars the movies have ever had."

Gossip was common at the Film Wing and it was inevitable, considering that the people the staff dealt with, either from yesterday or today, were *personalities*. With the forthcoming retrospective it was natural that the talk should concentrate on Vanessa Oxford and Joshua Fodor. Even now, a half-century after their liaison and his great, tragic failure, *Jesus Christ—Son and Savior*, there were survivors who remembered stories about the pair that never saw publication.

One of the Wing office workers, Madge Korman, had been a bit player in the early days of the movies and she was there when Vanessa and Mr. Fodor were inseparable. Sometimes during coffee break Madge would reminisce, her wrinkled face flushing with importance.

"She was lovely as long as she had her own way," Madge said, "and she was sweet and kind to just about everybody, especially those who could help her career."

"But she never married?" Sue asked.

"There was talk about them getting married, but it never happened. There was talk that she had a child by him. But nobody could ever prove it. For a nice girl, she certainly inspired a good deal of gossip."

"It must've been tough on girls in those days," Sue reflected. "No pill, no contraceptive advice, no abortion clinics." She couldn't imagine Vanessa Oxford becoming a mother. Vanessa was too virginal.

Four:

THE PRESENT: SUE AND THE DEVIL'S ADVOCATE

EVEN AS SHE confided in Charlie, Sue suspected it was a mistake.

"I take a dim view of any living legend, particularly Vanessa Oxford," Charlie said.

"All she's doing is helping me with the chronology of Fodor films. The only thing I have to do is make up a fact sheet."

"Then what d'you need her for? The archives at Lincoln Center can supply all the material you'll need."

"We can't do a tribute to Joshua Fodor without including Miss Vanessa. Mr. Friedlander insists on it, he says they made history together."

Sue wrapped her fingers around the coffee mug. The fountain in the center of the fourth-floor restaurant was scattering a rainbow spray. Under previous ownership, when Will Wattenberg used it for any number of cultural events, the fountain was disconnected after Labor Day, its tiled rim then set with fresh potted plants. But since the building now belonged to the Film Wing, Mr. Friedlander decided to keep it active until the October gala that would launch the Joshua Fodor retrospective with a dinner and reception honoring Miss Vanessa Oxford and the Board of Trustees.

Workmen were rearranging lush indoor plants in strategic corners under blowups of Joshua Fodor films. Charlie had stopped by the Wing to have lunch with Sue and to leave with her the galleys of a soon-to-be-published novel. She would read them, prepare a brief outline and evaluate the story's screen potential. She enjoyed this freelance work and was flattered that he trusted her judgment.

Charlie was really very dear, she thought, and quite attractive. His long, strong face, blue eyes, short blunt nose and wide mouth with strong, regular teeth made him very masculine—and very sexy. But how he could appear scrubbed and sloppy at the same time never failed to surprise her. His suit was old, probably from his college days, and needed pressing. He held himself with the unconscious pride of one maybe too smart for his own good, yet Sue found him gentle and considerate, except for outbursts when his clients drove him up the wall.

Charlie didn't approve of her new assignment. Could it be that he'd heard something about Miss Oxford, she wondered. Charlie felt Sue already carried too big a workload. The Film Wing was understaffed and its people, comprising mostly the younger sons and daughters of the rich or the talented, were underpaid. "It's supposed to be an honor to work here," she commented.

"Big deal," said Charlie. "I suppose the trustees think if they do homage to the lady she'll eventually divide her millions between the Wing and the American Academy of Dramatic Art."

"Well, the Wing does owe Fodor recognition."

"It owes *all* the old-timers recognition. If not for them, where would all those big-deal *auteur* directors be, and especially Bogdanovitch, who lives on sending up the oldies?" He drained his coffee. "I still wish you'd say no."

"Mrs. Elsberg is depending on me, Charlie."

"Let me tell you what happened to a friend of mine who wrote a television script for her. She had the right to make revisions and after the sixth rewrite he realized what they were doing was collaborating. You know Bloomingdale's?"

"Sure, I shop there every Saturday."

"Not the store, love. The sanitorium. He spent six months there. First he fell madly in love with her, then he tried to kill her."

"Charlie, you're blowing this all out of proportion. I only have to prepare this souvenir booklet."

"You won't take a pal's advice?"

" 'Fraid not."

"When you're hanging on a cliff, I'll come to the rescue."

"Spoken like a true film buff."

Sue felt comfortable with Charlie. She appreciated his warm, concerned interest and even though at times she wondered if he were using her, he was always generous and dependable. She knew that if she turned to him for help while preparing the souvenir booklet he'd give her everything she needed.

Charlie was a publicist for an established, once profitable film company that, in the midst of financial upheavals, was saved and then swallowed by a conglomerate. He dealt with the new actors who, in spite of shrinks and reality consciousness, were mostly temperamental, irresponsible and infantile. His sessions in the film department of N.Y.U. did not encourage awe for the people he worked with, including the New Wave directors who took their cues from early individualistic geniuses like D. W. Griffith and Joshua Fodor.

Charlie's pad was a walkup off Gramercy Park on Irving Place. His job encouraged insomnia, so when he wasn't hacking around with his friends in the business or the press or escorting starlets with greasy hair and patched jeans, he holed up with a six-pack of beer and watched movies on the Late Show. Or if he were restless, he'd track down an early silent in an art house. As for herself, Sue admitted her fascination with family pictures of the '40s, even the Andy Hardy series, probably came from her hunger for a big gregarious family.

She'd first met Charlie Bryson when she signed up at Washington Square for some film courses given in the evening and attended by people who had daytime jobs. They got in the habit of meeting before class in a delicatessen on Mulberry Street to share hero sandwiches and Cokes; and after class, if the weather was good, they'd walk up Fifth Avenue, during one of which strolls he offered her freelance reading jobs and became impressed by her sensible instincts about books and scripts.

Now, as she walked him to the elevator, he kissed her lightly on the cheek and said, "If you need help, holler," and went off to retain a pair of studs for the delicate, sweet-voiced English star whose matinees were incomplete without a threesome.

Ars gratia artis.

THE PRESENT: SUE—AND SIBLING RIVALRY IN THE OXFORD GIRLS?

FRIENDSHIP WITH CHARLIE BRYSON had intensified Sue's enthusiasm for the old films. But until she met Vanessa Oxford her interest had been general and rather abstract. Working with her, collecting material on the late Joshua Fodor, quickly changed that. Vanessa fascinated Sue, and her admiration for the old star grew with each working session. Despite suggestions to the contrary, she found Vanessa gentle and considerate. Whatever her behavior in her heyday, she couldn't, Sue decided, have been like, say, a Joan Crawford, always so aware of her stature and making very certain everyone else was too. Whenever Sue worked in her apartment, Vanessa asked her to stay for lunch or, if it were a late afternoon session, for dinner. She worried about Sue when she came down with a cold from the stuffy heat in the radiators and fed her fruit juices and carloads of vitamin C. She disapproved of her usual breakfast of coffee and a toasted English muffin, and brought her gifts of whole wheat muffins from the health shop she patronized. Sue had the impression Vanessa really liked her, and although she told herself it was probably just the usual Oxford charm, it was nevertheless flattering and very pleasant.

One morning Sue opened a cardboard box of clippings and pamphlets, mostly about Vanessa but also a few about Joshua Fodor. While she spread them out on the living room rug, Vanessa took the slantboard out of the utility closet, set it up and stretched out on it, head lower than her feet, her blue robe snug around her flat hips, her arms at her side, hands folded, eyes closed. "I must take care of my body," she said, "it is the instrument of my work." There was something about her that Sue could not possibly define in words, but it was as though the space around her somehow glowed. She remembered reading somewhere that everybody has an aura that gives off rays unseen to the naked eye, and wondered if Vanessa was just possibly tuned in to some mysterious charges of energy that were denied to the less sensitive beings. Lying there, so quiet, Vanessa's breathing seemed suspended, and it reminded Sue of the Indian fakirs who were buried alive and then resurrected, with suspended animation substituting for death. Perhaps it was the child in herself, Sue thought, that was responding to Vanessa, the child still wanting to believe in magic. *Was* she in touch with inner sources that triggered her extraordinary vitality and power? She recalled that Mrs. Elsberg had included Vanessa among the group of women who managed through fate, contingency and sheer will to bring favorable circumstances into their lives and then to make the very most of them.

A clever, extraordinary woman, Vanessa Oxford. A woman who had made her own history.

Was there a reason why she was brought into Vanessa Oxford's life? Sue asked herself. *Should she be clever and resourceful and take advantage of the situation?*

Am I perhaps about to be part of her future, Sue wondered? *And she of mine?*

Among the material Sue now pored over was a folder that seemed to have no bearing on Joshua Fodor, a collection of notes headed by *Sisters*. The pages weren't typed, but handwritten in a clear, undistinguished Palmer Method script. While Vanessa remained lying in her near-trance on the slantboard Sue scanned the notes:

"*Sisters. The subject fascinates me endlessly. Are there strands of rivalry in the love that binds them? Jealousy? Hate? Vindictiveness? In the successful Sister Acts, what is the genesis of their power? Are the seeds in their genes, even if they are unalike, since they share a common source, and as siblings are prone to the emotions that charge them with drive and survival, as well as a need to surpass each other?*

"*Sisters in history share qualities that make them unforgettable. The Brontes, the Peabody Sisters of Salem, the von Richthofen Sisters of Germany, the Gish Sisters of the movies, the Langhorne Sisters of Virginia, the Cushing Sisters of Massachusetts, the Gabor Sisters of Hungary, the Dolly Sisters . . .*

"*And Vanessa and Cassandra Oxford . . .*

"*Why did they make it? And how? There have been more beautiful women, more sexually alluring women, yet these are the ones we link with rich and famous men.*

"*Is it the mystique of the ambitious mother?*

"*The mother who indoctrinates them early: You deserve fame, success, money and the power they bring. And you will get them!*

"*They are mostly girls without fathers.*

"*Even when the father is physically present, he seems to be parent without portfolio.*

"*Beside the ambitious mother, these girls seem fired by the search for the beloved, for identification with the father, for loving acceptance by the father.*

"*Not surprising that Louis B. Mayer was the father image for so many stars, even poor ill-fated Judy Garland.*

"*Before that, there was D. W. Griffith, the good father for Seena Owen, Blanche Sweet, Mae Marsh, Miriam Cooper, Lillian and Dorothy Gish and Carol Dempster.*

"*And for Vanessa Oxford, Joshua Fodor was the Good Father.*

"*It was not the mother's ambition that drove Vanessa to her success. Just the opposite; Vanessa's need to take care of her mother and her sister . . .*

"*There is a script in one of these Sister Acts. I must write it for Vanessa and Cassie. Before it is too late for poor Cassie."*

The initials of the writer: R.K.

Vanessa opened her eyes. She rose from the slantboard with surprising grace. "Flossie," she called, "will you fetch us some camomile tea."

Sue showed Vanessa the notes.

"Oh, those are my best friend Rebecca's. Rebecca Kahn. She was doing some research for an independent producer. I agreed to play in the film for Cassie's sake, but by the time Mrs. Kramer arranged for the contracts Cassie was too sick to play in anything."

"Have you done many films together?"

"No, not really. What I did mostly was to advise Cassie about what offers to accept. As I told you, her forte was comedy, and few films had roles for both a tragedienne and a comedienne. And poor Cassie was so high-strung that the few times we did play together I was a wreck." Vanessa sipped her herb tea. "As children, we did a kind of vaudeville act. Later, Mr. Fodor cast us both in a single film. Cassie nearly stole the film from me, which delighted me, of course, because both Mama and I worried so much about her. But Cassie, poor dear, was never suited for the life of an actress. She needed roots and stability from childhood on, and by the time we were able to give them to her, I'm afraid it was too late."

Sue was moved by the unspoken pain she sensed in Vanessa's account, and by her gentle yet stoic acceptance of it. Sue would make, she resolved, the souvenir booklet something much more than a mere fact sheet. She wanted to please Vanessa. Very much. If she had ever needed a model of a truly feminine woman, Vanessa surely was it.

Sue had not yet, of course, heard Cassie's straight-faced comment on her sister's on-and-off-screen image of perfection: "Vanessa is a saint; everybody says so. I'm the only one who knows she's too good to be true."

THE PRESENT: SUE—A LANDMARK AS A WOMAN?

LET US NOW REFLECT *on my love life, or rather lack of it,* Sue thought as she returned to Mrs. Elsberg's office for work on the Fodor material. Case in question: Charlie Bryson, and what went wrong.

Charlie was fond of her in his fashion. He'd said as much. But mostly it came out in affectionate carpings such as, "Why the devil do you wear such baggy sweaters with a body like yours?"

And her devastating reply was something on the order of "I want men to desire me for my soul."

"A girl should use all her resources. If those Hollywood turkeys had your body, they'd be right on top . . . or maybe under . . ."

"Which reminds me," she said, "we were discussing some of the Washington women Vanessa knows and she said, 'I judge a woman by the man she lies under.'"

Charlie laughed. "She should know."

"Charlie, I'm sure she's still faithful to Fodor's memory."

"At her age what does it matter? But she was a swinger in her time."

Sue didn't believe him. You had only to look at Miss Vanessa's serene, innocent, almost transported face to know different. Poor Charlie. His cynicism cut him off from seeing old-world virtue when it was right in front of his nose.

But now as she sorted through glossy prints of early Fodor films, Sue's head was focused on her own problem. Also known as sex . . . love?

Sue was, and she wasn't, a child of her times. She would use the Pill if she needed it. She was tolerant of the girls at Wykeham

Rise and Mount Holyoke who had a reference file of the gyne-cologists who did abortions. She knew "Liv" had a live-in lover, and at times she definitely envied her. But marriage also appealed to Sue, despite acceptance of affairs. There was in her still the uncertain little girl, the little girl who was still searching for the comfort of an absent mother. She was so aware of her yearning that at times it was a real physical ache—a genuine yearning to belong, to share . . . "Arrangements" such as her friends often had seemed to her impossible unless a girl was strong-minded and emotionally independent, and if, on the surface, Sue had those traits, underneath she felt a need, a hunger for some kind of roots that, hopefully, marriage would give her. One night stands . . . she just couldn't face that. She was sure she'd end up feeling rejected, demeaned.

Were you just born old-fashioned? Sue asked herself, *or could you get over this feeling—fear—after a few affairs? Could you meet a man for the first time and go to bed with him for sex? Nothing more?*

And suppose you do hold out for marriage? Do you get a lasting union? There were, of course, no guarantees, but she knew she craved a one-to-one kind of relationship. Maybe such expectations in her world were unrealistic. And she did feel intuitively that although in any close relationship she'd be loving and tender, she'd also be too passive—in Vanessa's day they'd have called it being the victim. It was a pity, too, because part of her *was* fiercely independent, reluctant to be put in any such vulnerable position. . . .

She and Charlie shared a rather silly joke. Whenever they left the classroom or the movie or the screening room, he would turn to her and say lightly, "Your place or mine?"

And she would answer flippantly, "Your place for you. Mine for me."

Next time, Charlie, she decided, I'll change the words.
And she did.

Sunday was a day for pairing, a time for lovers.
Most of the time Sue told herself she didn't mind being alone.
This Sunday she called Charlie.
It was noon and he was working in his apartment on press

releases for a new film. The sound of her voice seemed to cheer him. "How about lunch?" he suggested.

Lunch at the Plaza, eggs Benedict and white wine and a view of the park, where families and couples were strolling about in spite of the early autumn weather.

"Want to try the zoo?" he asked

"Not particularly."

"You off your animal kick?"

"No"—with a shrug—"I'm just not in the mood."

"What's up, Sue?"

She shrugged. "Nothing."

"Something. Definitely."

"Oh, I'm just practicing being a complete woman."

He laughed briefly, then leaned across the table and his eyes deepened. "Don't be a cockteaser, sweetie. Your place or mine?"

"Mine," she said.

She gave him the key and he opened the door to the color and warmth of her room. The bed was made up with fresh scented sheets, the blanket turned down. Charlie looked at the bed and then his glance returned to her. He seemed different from the man she usually knew, who teased her, who was often blunt and critical. More like the Charles who was sometimes also tender and understanding when she came to him, raw with the hurt of criticism or a rejection. She was aware of new feelings, gratitude, perhaps even a surge of something close to love. She turned away so he wouldn't see the gathering of tears.

"Come here, Sue." No waiting. No pretense. His hands began to undress her, the jacket, the soft white turtleneck pulled over her head, the camel tweed skirt dropping to her ankles, the bra, the pantyhose. She felt docile, pliant, under his hands, and when he kissed her dark hair tumbling over her face and then gently her lips, she felt a growing response that bewildered her. She wondered if her hunger was stronger than her shyness and she wondered if other girls would react as she did. Her friends had always been casual about sex, discussing their experiences without modesty or reticence. There was always one girl more experienced than the others, a source of advice on what to expect, how to behave ... she had taught the younger girls how to use their vaginal muscles to enhance sex. "You milk him with your muscles," the girl had counseled, "and he'll come. It drives them crazy." So all of them had practiced. Tighten. Hold. Relax. Vaginal isometrics.

Those images were in her mind now.

"You seem far away," Charlie said.

She was floating, breathless. She was eager, ready for him to make love to her. Now it was only her own performance that worried her. She couldn't bear for him to recognize her innocence. She felt untouched, truly naked.

She stood in front of him, trembling, and as he looked at her she felt weak. His hand ran over her shoulder, down her breast, which he cupped as though it were infinitely fragile, precious.

"Now it's your turn," he said, and she undressed him, divided between shyness and pleasure, concentrating on each garment. In a way she felt it was like a ritual, in which they were actors rather than the participants. She felt an enormous gratitude toward him for overlooking her inexperience. When he was stripped, she blushed at the sight of him, at his thick, long, erect penis, impatient, somehow frightening.

"Come," he said, and led her into the bathroom, where he turned on the shower. This too seemed part of the ritual, and was a welcome leitmotif, more a game. Still, when he soaped her pubic hair, she felt herself tighten, knowing that he expected her to do the same for him. He brought her hand to his penis. She pulled away, but he held her firm and then brought her close to him and their wet soapy bodies began to move in instinctive rhythm. He was kissing her face and her breasts and she imagined his lips shaping words of pleasure and tenderness.

He dried her body with the thick white towel, and then she dried his body. He was smiling at her, an intimate smile, the smile of a man who is pleased, she thought, and she responded, feeling a new warmth, a swelling tenderness. He was lovely, he would make it easy for her. Yet at that same moment the thought of his experiences sent a shudder through her. All the women he'd made love to, those eager, knowing women. And how ridiculous, she thought, that I should be jealous of the women Charlie has slept with . . . I never minded before.

Except this was a special moment; she wanted it to mean as

much to him as it would surely to her. She hoped it would be very special for them both.

He put her gently on the bed and spread himself over her. The heat of their bodies made up for the chill in the room. He kissed her gently at first, and then, as his tongue explored hers, he said, "Hold me, Sue, raise your legs, straddle me."

She obeyed, instinctively tightening herself around him, and as his hands drew down her body, reached under her hips to lift her, he said, abruptly, "You're on the Pill . . . ?"

She was aroused from her trance. "No, Charlie, I'm not."

He looked incredulous, sat up, swung his muscled legs over the bed and went to the chair where his clothes lay. He tried the inner pocket of his jacket and came out with a small packet of Trojans.

"Emergency rations," he said, and shrugged.

He opened the pack, took out a condom and handed it to her. She stared at it.

"You roll it on me," he said.

She sat up against the pillows, her hair tumbled over her face and shoulders. She held it gingerly.

"The problems of deflowering a virgin, I suppose," she said.

He squatted above her.

"Sue! You're kidding. Yes?"

"Yes. I mean, no. *No!* I'm *not* kidding."

"A virgin. Good lord, I didn't know there were any left."

"That's because of the company you keep."

"But why?" He was genuinely puzzled.

"Because I wanted the first time to mean something."

"And it does? With me?"

"It does, Charlie. It means a great deal."

"God . . . this makes it a first for me too. I'm not sure I can handle it. . . ."

His penis, full-veined, throbbing, was slowly losing its strength. She watched, shocked, as it shriveled and became flaccid. He pushed her gently back on the sheet, and his mouth began to arouse her. She felt the juices of her body respond. His mouth moved down her throat and breasts, sucking at her pink-brown nipples, continued in a near-frenzy, as he attempted to work himself up, to her flat little belly, and then to her bud, hidden in the nest of silky hair. He was laboring now, willing himself to regain his strength, his fingers stiff, demanding a probing substitute for his penis. She cried out in pain. But nothing helped, nothing restored him. After a while, his face grim, his body wet with sweat, he gave up.

"I'm sorry, Sue. We'll try again if you like...a virgin..." This last was said more to himself than to her.

To laugh or cry. She couldn't decide.

They never spoke of it again, and they stayed close friends. For which she was grateful. As was he. Sue Palmer, he decided, was a remarkably generous woman.

THE PRESENT: SUE: BOYS AND GIRLS TOGETHER

Two WEEKS LATER, Charlie took Sue to lunch again.

They were given a choice table at the Italian Pavilion, where the headwaiter was reasonably civil to them and the lunch was on the expense account. The Italian Pavilion was selected so Charlie could meet casually an editor from an important publishing house. She had an air of excitement about her. The activities at the Wing for the past week had given her a sustained high. She slipped her arms out of her beige suede coat, saying, "I'm sorry, Charlie. I haven't finished the galleys."

Charlie looked surprised and disappointed. Despite their sexual fiasco, Sue was the one person in his life whom he always counted on. Now she'd let him down. All because of that damned retrospective and that overage virgin, La Belle Vanessa, tying Sue up so she'd have no time for anyone else.

"It's been a wild week," Sue apologized. "The souvenir book has been redone three times. The printer is furious, the overtime charges are awful! But Vanessa wants it letter perfect—"

"Couldn't she have done that on the first go-round?"

"Well, she's been rechecking—she says her memory is faulty so she's been in touch with people who knew Fodor. We've added a few recollections and anecdotes. We don't want it dry and factual."

"Say, how much time are you spending with her?"

"All day. Every day."

"What about your boss at the Wing?"

"It's okay with Mr. Friedlander. Vanessa's asked me to spend several days a week helping her. The film archives in Hollywood have inquired about her memorabilia. I'll spend two days and weekends with her and three days at the Wing."

"How much will she pay you?"

"We haven't got that far. I'd like to do it for free, if I could afford it. I doubt if she has much money."

"Think of yourself, kid. You've got to eat."

"Well, if you keep taking me to expense-account lunches, I'll survive."

The most recent set of galleys he'd sent her were part of his future. Two of the earlier ones she'd read for him were distinct possibilities for films. But the final bidding had gone far beyond his limits. Now Charlie hoped to come on a property that could be optioned cheaply, and turn out to be a sleeper success of the year.

"I understand paperback rights on the one I just gave you are hot," Charlie said, his voice low. Sue could hardly hear him. There wasn't a person in the room who didn't have a third ear tuned in on nearby tables. But Sue was giving him only half her attention and he was aware of it.

"Look, sweet, you're getting compulsive about Vanessa and Fodor. Whenever I try to reach you, you're either in the basement or the files."

"Well, there's been so much to sort out. I'm really very much into the Fodor files even with the souvenir booklet finished—"

"You going to work late tomorrow?"

"I'm 'fraid so. Last minute details."

"Can you get away by six or seven? I'll spring for dinner."

"Two days in succession! Charlie, what's the deal?"

"Does there have to be one?"

"With you—*yes!*"

"Okay, I'll level with you. We'll be going to the Dakota. Friend of mine is holding auditions for investors. It's an English comedy. The *Times* man saw it in London and went bananas for it."

"What do I know about plays, Charlie?"

"Not much. But I bank on your feminine intuition."

"I can't decide whether to be flattered or annoyed. Why don't you consult my quote-unquote intuition when you're playing the horses or shooting craps?"

"This is different. This play is for matinee and theater parties, where the audience is three-fourths female. And since you're superfemale..." He screwed his face into a leer as he surveyed the curve of her sweater, which was a body hugger.

Sue was aware of the lapse in her attention. She was back in Vanessa's apartment, listening to Vanessa relate incidents from the filming of *Jesus Christ—Son and Savior*, how she had timidly given Fodor a suggestion for the character of Mary Magdalene. The whore had been a blind spot with Fodor. He saw the shell, not the essence. After a long argument Fodor had turned to his cameraman. "Let her try it her way," he'd agreed. "She's a flighty, ignorant little thing, but she knows how a woman would react...." Sue couldn't get that last out of her mind.

Charlie signed for the check and, as the waiter helped Sue with her coat, he took a final look around the room. The man he'd hoped to meet accidentally hadn't shown today. Well, that meant a call to the fellow. His mind was busy with plans so he wasn't listening to Sue as they came out on the street.

"So you'll meet me in my office tomorrow? Sixish," he said.

"Charlie, I *told* you. I can't make it."

"Why not?"

"Charlie, you have the invitation. The preview of the retrospective.

"Tomorrow night?"

"Tomorrow night."

"Well, so be it. I'll go off to the Dakota alone." He slouched down and kissed her on the cheek. He seemed to have forgotten his recent failure with her. "Just watch it, baby. My new secretary has the hots for me."

"Well," Sue said, "good luck to her, and to you too," and immediately began an apology, which Charlie waved off.

"Touché, my dear. But maybe better luck to us . . . next time."

They parted on that.

THE PRESENT: SUE: A GIRL CAN DREAM

THE DAY BEFORE the retrospective, Vanessa inspected her wardrobe: dresses on scented, padded hangers, sterile in their plastic shells; the designer clothes from Paris; the suits by her dear friend Mainbocher; the flowing gowns of Vionnet, reminiscent of Isadora Duncan's chiffons. None seemed quite right for the great day. She wanted something extra-special, a gown not easily overshadowed by the costumes of younger, more fashionably dressed guests.

She was wearing a caftan of soft blue wool, an accessory she'd adopted long before caftans were universally accepted. At home, out of the public eye, she had no vanity about her appearance. Her long hair, still thick, hung to her shoulders in an oddly youthful style. Her pale face shone with oil. The dear man who looked after her complexion didn't believe in loading the pores with heavy creams. She slept with her face naked, and after getting up, washed it meticulously, splashing water on her face thirty times as he'd ordered. Self-care was a ritual with her.

In the dinning room she found Sue, back from lunch and working at the table sorting out mail. Sue was well organized, Vanessa noted. There were three piles: bills, personal correspondence and fan letters. The fourth-class mail sat on a chair. Vanessa glanced briefly at Sue's face, at the flawless bone structure, the flush of youth on her fresh skin that, she reflected sadly, could not be duplicated by any creams or oils.

"Sue, I'm going to call Dann Houston. Some of my trunks are stored in his basement. There's a big Vuitton with a tag. The year, I think, is 1937. I want the black velvet gown. Will you go over to his house and get it? Flossie will steam it. Later, please go to Tiffany's. I left my pearls to be restrung and they should be ready."

Sue carefully controlled the pleasure Vanessa's request gave her. Vanessa was going out for several hours and Sue knew she had an appointment with Miss Klinger for a facial, although Vanessa never admitted having any treatments.

Sue grabbed her heavy-knit brown cardigan and her handbag. The prospect of seeing Dann Houston was also exciting and she strode down Second Avenue feeling light-headed. Some instinct had cautioned her not to apply fresh lipstick while she was still in the apartment, but now she stopped at a drugstore, ostensibly to have a cup of tea at the food counter but actually to apply lipstick and straighten her unruly hair, which allowed her a few minutes to compose herself so she could meet Dann without totally betraying her sense of excitement.

She'd met him for the first time only last week. She'd been going over bills with Vanessa when the doorbell in the apartment chimed. Vanessa stirred herself, a luminous smile on her face, made a soft cooing sound and went swiftly to the door.

"Oh, *Dann!*" Her greeting was intimate and loving and her expression reminded Sue of those exquisite closeups in her most romantic films.

The young man kissed her on the lips and took her in his arms. Then hand in hand they came into the living room.

"Sue"—Vanessa was radiant—"this is my dear, dear Dann Houston."

"Hello, Sue." His hand covered hers, and Sue reacted to him immediately and powerfully in a way she never had with her casual dates or even that time in bed with Charlie Bryson.

The male models for Esquire or Playboy men's fashions, striking rather than virile, never impressed her. Men caught up with the latest styles in clothes, hair and automobiles left her indifferent. And as for men in Edwardian suits . . .

Yet here was a tan Edwardian suit on a young man who looked as though he should be wearing jeans and a Stetson and herding cattle. His rough, sunstreaked brown hair refused to conform to his well-shaped head. His body was lithe, young; his face weathered by the sun, with premature lines on his forehead and around his big, well-modeled mouth. The nose was bold, prominent; the chin well shaped but sharply defined at the jawline. And the eyes, rather narrow, as though he were accustomed to squinting in the sun, were blue. She found the rough-smooth contrast of him instantly exciting. . . .

Dann's home was one of the townhouses that protected the communal gardens of Turtle Bay from intruders. The beige stucco was set off by the black iron grillwork over the French windows on the second floor. Sue paused on the step, thinking of the lovely song "On the Street Where You Live." And she wasn't the least embarrassed by it.

She went down three steps to the entrance, protected by an iron grille. Round tubs of greens brought an accent of color to the stucco. Sue pressed the bell.

The door opened on a young black man in jeans and a T-shirt, a heavy gold chain around his neck weighed down by a rough-cut piece of malachite. He was astonishingly handsome.

"Come in, Miss Palmer. Dann is expecting you."

From the small foyer she had a glimpse of the dining room ahead and beyond it a terrace and a stretch of garden. Dann was coming up from the basement.

"I've been developing film," he said, shaking hands with Sue. "Come upstairs and I'll make you a drink."

"Are you a photographer?" she asked. There was so little she knew about him.

"I'm trying. It's quite an art, although people say most photographers are failed painters."

"What does it matter, if they're good at it."

"That's kind of you. Would you like a drink or tea?"

"Tea, if it isn't too much trouble."

"Tea, it is." He nodded to the young black man. "See if you

can dig up some cakes, Jeff." He added, "Jeff's a great cook, but since Vanessa's been indoctrinating him he's stopped baking anything but wheat bread. We're revoltingly healthy." He smiled at Sue and Jeff, turned to lead her up the stairs, then to the left into a room whose walls were tapestried with books. A small camel loveseat and two black leather chairs framed the fireplace. Whatever space was free of books was taken up by framed photographs.

"Are these yours?" Sue asked.

"Yes. I haven't been at it long, so they're rather amateurish."

"Don't belittle yourself. They're great." She looked at a triptych of tigers, black-and-white shots of animal beauty but suggestive of potential violence. "I'd love to hold him. He's so cuddly," she said of another shot, a baby lion.

"That 'cuddly' creature weighed forty pounds, and I felt as you did until he left me a memento." Dann pushed up the sleeve of his knit shirt and exposed an ugly welt. "I've since settled for the domesticated kind." He nodded toward the shorthair cat, tiger-striped, who had slunk into the room, glaring at Sue, obviously marking her as an intruder.

Well, Sue thought, *a man who loves animals can't be all bad.*

He asked, "What're you grinning about?"

She repeated her thought out loud.

"Why should I be all bad?" He was amused.

"Because you've got too much going for you. You'd have to be a saint to remain uncorrupted."

"I'm not a saint." Jeff, who appeared with a tray, joined in their laughter. "But does that make me a heel?"

"Perhaps, where women are concerned. The girls probably stalk you the way you go after those magnificent animals."

"An exaggeration, but go ahead. I love it."

Jeff set the tray on a low table and poured. The tea was full-bodied and fragrant and Sue told him so.

"Vanessa taught me about tea," Dann said. "She's taught me how to appreciate the good things in life. My family is third-generation oil. Their idea of a cup of tea, which they consider an effete drink, is a Lipton tea bag."

"You're making up for it."

"I try," he said. "How is Vanessa holding up?"

"Beautifully. She's completely nerveless."

"Not so." He put down the cup and a look of concern shadowed his handsomely structured face. "She's a master of self-control. I can tell you, though, that she's very worried about Cassie. You know, Vanessa lives for her sister. And I'm afraid Cassie is going downhill fast."

"Can't something be done for her?"

"She needs a psychiatrist," Dann said. "I've suggested it to her several times, but she laughs it off. 'Why should I pay a doctor,' she always says, 'when my friends will listen to me for free.' " He paused. "Cassie has always been witty and freewheeling, and Vanessa has always worried because she's such a maverick. Well, it's allowed in the theatrical profession.... Vanessa told me about an incident that happened years ago, when she was auditioning for one of the great old-timers; I think she said it was David Belasco. They were talking about the emotional demands of the profession. He showed her the dressing room of his star—a woman at the peak of her career. What'd you think she had on the shelves?"

She shrugged.

"Dolls. Toys. Teddy bears. This great star was off her rocker except when she appeared in front of the footlights. It made a deep impression on Vanessa. She's always been worried about Cassie. Their father died in an institution, you know."

"A mental hospital?"

Dann nodded. "Vanessa never speaks of it, so don't let on I told you. But the fear haunts her, lives with her. She's always watching Cassie for any signs of irrational behavior..."

Sue was astonished at his candor. And touched. He must have had good feelings about her to have shared this confidence.

"I don't have the impression that Cassie is irrational," she said. "Only on the defensive, like a child who's been ordered around too much. But of course I haven't met her yet."

"You will. She's something special, our Cassie."

Jeff had left them alone. They finished their tea, and then Dann guided her down the staircase, through the foyer and left into the basement, which was opposite the kitchen wing. In the basement the smell of acetic acid was strong, coming from the darkroom at the front. Dann explained, "I took some pictures of

Vanessa at the Wing last week and I posed her against the blow-ups of Mary Magdalene and Jesus. She looked like a nun who had just taken off her habit."

"Does she still photograph well?"

"Magnificently. From any angle. And she can sit quietly for several minutes without moving. I suppose this comes from the early days when they had no stand-ins and had to pose while the lights were arranged around her."

"Sometimes she sits just as quietly in her living room," Sue said. "I often wonder if she's meditating. Once I asked her and she said No, she was just breathing peacefully, minute to minute."

"That's important to her." Dann's voice was sympathetic. "She's had a rough life."

In the rear, big theatrical trunks were staggered, their exteriors tattooed with reminders of the Oxford travels: The *Ile de France*, the Ritz in Paris, the Savoy in London, the Beverly Hills Hotel in Los Angeles.

"I warn you"—Dann switched on more lights to illuminate the dark corners of the basement—"going through Vanessa's trunks is an ordeal. She insists they are all carefully marked as to date and contents, but she goes through them and forgets to put things back where they're supposed to be."

"I don't mind at all. I'm the kind who likes exploring an old attic on a rainy day."

"Some of these costumes are earmarked for the Museum of the City of New York," Dann said. "Others are going out to the West Coast. The new film museum out there has asked for Oxford mementoes."

"She's got plenty to give," Sue said, looking around at the trunks in big, medium and small sizes. Among them were files, packing cases and, leaning against the wall, a large flat package secure in mummylike brown-paper wrapping, tied with rope and marked *"Do Not Open."*

"Cassie is always losing things," Dann said, "but Vanessa's a magpie about possessions."

He peered at the tags, trying to find the right trunk. Sue was watching him almost covertly—his straight spine, muscular shoulders and small flanks. He is beautiful, she thought. But very much a man.

As Dann expected, the trunk Vanessa had mentioned didn't have the velvet dress but it did contain some beautiful costumes that Charles James had designed for Vanessa and that she'd worn in one of her early Broadway plays.

"These would be in keeping," Sue said. "I wonder if she'd settle for one?"

Dann shook his head. "If she wants the black velvet, we've got to find it." He grinned. "What Vanessa wants, Vanessa gets."

One hour and three trunks later, they found the gown. Meanwhile Sue had absorbed another aspect of Vanessa Oxford's life through her collection of costumes and personal clothes designed by the great fashion names of the early '20s and '30s—Poiret, Vionnet, Patou, Valentina. And an awesome collection of photographs that ranged from the silents to Vanessa's last Broadway appearance as an aging English lady who murders her young husband and goes free.

"Are there any photographs of Joshua Fodor?" Sue asked. "I'm curious to see what he was like in his early years."

"If we start looking through the portraits, we'll be here forever," Dann said, closing a trunk. "There must be some. Fodor didn't consider himself a photographer; he had this genius, Hans Rolfsma. But he did take pictures of Vanessa. Some have been lost. Or misplaced."

"What maybe should be done," Sue suggested, "is to file all material in chronological sequence."

"That's an idea! We've got a date for a rainy day." He picked up the handsome black velvet gown and led the way to the front of the basement. "Next time you're here, I'll show you the darkroom."

"No etchings?" She laughed.

"No. But how about nudes?" His eyes appreciatively followed the curve of her sweater. "At the moment I have some fine ones of African tribal royalty. I would be pleased, though, to diversify— and, you know, even a relative beginner like myself can look awfully good with a subject as marvelous as the female body. It takes a butcher's eye to ruin a beautiful nude woman." He looked steadily at her as he spoke.

Sue was ecstatic. Dann appreciated her as a woman . . . perhaps a beautiful woman ...? She felt a glow that showed in her eyes. It didn't leave as Dann helped her with her sweatercoat and carried the dress, wrapped in tissue paper and glassine, to a taxi that drew up to the curb.

From: Sue Palmer
    The Film Wing
    Tel: 232-1234, ext. 441

For release October 25, 1977.

FILM WING TO OPEN WITH A RETROSPECTIVE
OF THE FILMS OF JOSHUA FODOR

In a tribute to the late Joshua Fodor, the Film Wing will mark its opening with a retrospective of the film master's works on Thursday, October 27th.

Miss Vanessa Oxford, who made her film debut at the age of thirteen in Fodor's *The Lost Daughter and the Gypsies,* will be guest of honor. Miss Cassandra Oxford, her sister, is also expected to attend this gala evening.

Joshua Fodor is considered second only to D. W. Griffith as an innovator and creator in the early days of the films, according to Samuel Friedlander, Curator of the Film Wing and noted film historian.

"Joshua Fodor often turned out one-reel films within a day's shooting," Mr. Friedlander said. "In these films character was quickly defined and plot was tight. The first films already showed Fodor's passionate interest in freedom, his pity for the downtrodden and his encouragement for those who longed to break out of their milieu. Produced in the World War I days, they reflect a sociologist's grasp and a poet's compassion."

Actors of the early years who participated in his efforts to refine the crude "flickers" into an art form, making him one of the most imitated of directors, are expected to join the Oxford sisters in paying tribute to this film pioneer.

The by-invitation-only gala for friends and associates of the Film Wing, as well as the Board of Directors and critics, will include a screening of Joshua Fodor's early one-reel films, as well as a reception and buffet.

The second program, open to the public, will begin Thursday evening, October 28, at 8:30 P.M. and will include Fodor's films of social protest, among them his series of Indian pictures that, according to film historians, were years ahead of their time.

131

The retrospective has been arranged by Mr. Friedlander, with Mrs. Ilona Elsberg, Director, and Mrs. Denise Block, Chief of the Joshua Fodor Section.

NOTES FROM VANESSA OXFORD
FOR THE JOSHUA FODOR SOUVENIR
BOOKLET:

"I THINK Mr. Fodor listened to me with increasing attention because my generation was a link between the 19th century and the 20th century.

"When my sister, Cassandra, and I were children, there was no radio or television or movies.

"Our minds and our bodies were wrapped in swaddling clothes. We dressed in suffocating layers. We wore long, ribbed-cotton stockings called Ironclad. We took Cod Liver Oil (usually rancid) for strength and Fletcher's Castoria for anything that ailed us. We were conventional in our morality and our aspirations.

"Only scarlet women used makeup.

"We believed that God Helps Him Who Helps Himself. We believed Honesty is the Best Policy.

"We believed in the Golden Rule, in a girl's virtue, in a mother's love.

"We believed what Joshua Fodor did so magnificently was to catch our beliefs, our dreams, our hopes on film.

"If you want to know life in the early 20th century, you'll see it all in the retrospective."

THE PRESENT: VANESSA AND
THE INFERNO

A MOAN.

Low, rising in crescendo, splintering the night's peace. Night
terrors unreel before her eyes, unending, a film without end ...

*Dear God, they've found my hiding place! I flee through endless
barren streets and dark crooked alleys of a bombed-out village,
trying to save myself from pits, boulders, ditches, ruts, my breath
spent, my heart pounding, too large for my small empty chest,
oxygen cut off, my mouth open, gasping for air before a blackout
envelops me. They are gaining on me, these men, two of them,
monstrous in their dark suits, faceless, each with a knife in hand,
a knife held like a saber. I stumble trying to escape them, but
they are swift, these two ogres. One catches me by my hair, long,
fair hair reaching to my waist, uses it as a rope to drag me along,
then lifts me to my feet again. A burning in my head, I have
been scalped. They lash out with their knives, playing some crazy
kind of tic-tac-toe on my flesh. Blood, hot, sticky, is pouring down
my thighs.*

*Why are my legs sheathed in white? Do I wear ribbed knee
socks or bandages? They are stained with the blood draining out
of my body. What is left? More suffering, more agony? I am dying
but I know with a horrifying certainty that death will not release
me, that these monstrous men will follow me to purgatory.*

"Please ... oh, please ..." I am on my knees, embracing the leg

*of the monster, clinging like a child. "Please help me . . . save me
. . . don't let them kill me, please!"*

*Am I crazy? Begging these creatures to save me when it is they
who are murdering me? They are slashing my legs, hacking me to
pieces. And knowing what they are doing, I am still begging for
their protection—*

*The assault has left me deranged. Surely it is the madness of
pain, unbearable pain, that impels me to turn to them, pretending
ignorance of their villainy. Some strange instincts, what Rebecca
calls my "voices," suggest that if I pretend not to recognize them
as murderers they might allow me to escape—*

Pain brings fresh cries, and tears.

Yet I cling to consciousness.

*Because once darkness takes hold, I lose the safety . . . they will
do away with me completely. How much more can I endure? The
blood spurts, the burning engulfs me.*

I scream, begging for the savior.

A knock. Sharp, persistent. A voice other than her own.

"Miss Vanessa, you all right?"

Flossie spoke through the inch-opening of the door. Cautious.
Flossie, Jamaica-born, English-trained, discreet. The screams
erupted often, sometimes waking Flossie if she happened to be
staying over in the maid's room. But never, she noted, when
there was a man sharing Miss Vanessa's bed.

"Was I screaming, Flossie?"

"Yes, Miss Vanessa. You have a bad dream?"

"One of my famous nightmares." Vanessa's voice, feather light,
suggested her night vapors should be honored with no more than
laughter.

"You ready for breakfast, Miss Vanessa?"

"Later. I'll rest a bit longer."

She never admitted, even to her dear friend Rebecca Kahn,
that recently the nightmares had perpetuated themselves and,
although she rarely recalled their content, the resulting depression
dogged her through the day and clouded the evening.

Only those close to her knew of her troubled dreams. Mrs.

Kramer, her agent, Jack Foley, her sometime manager, and of course Rebecca.

To divert her mind, she recalled a weekend visit the previous May to Rebecca's recently restored New England farmhouse at Easton Corners. They ate breakfast on the terrace and afterward they just sat there and rocked gently in the cool spring sunshine. Rebecca had brought the pine rockers, rush seated, from North Carolina. For Rebecca they were a symbol of her youth in Muskenaw, where she and Vanessa first met. They often sat on the front-porch rockers at Rebecca's house, eating fresh *challah*, the braided white bread Rebecca's mother baked for the Sabbath, its slices thick and fragrant with sweet home-churned butter and brown sugar. Vanessa loved the taste. And she loved those memories of her youth. She reveled in the hot morning sun, the cool wind blowing in from Lake Michigan, the sense of well-being. And the wonderful peace she never found in later years. Those two adolescent girls in their checked ginghams were so different: Rebecca, dark, sallow, with enormous eyes as black as Greek olives and a bony nose much too big for her small face, just as her head was much too big for her spindly body; and Vanessa, like the Victorian darlings on the Valentine cards, thick blonde hair (not naturally curly but rolled up in rags every night and brushed into a nimbus of golden strands), enormous blue eyes with that marvelous freak of nature, a double row of lashes, her body small-boned, slender, an expression of nunlike serenity on her perfect little face.

The guestroom and the master bedroom in Rebecca's country house were separated by a luxurious bathroom, and whenever Vanessa visited there she asked that the connecting door remain open all night.

"If you hear me cry out at night, be sure and wake me," she told Rebecca.

The reason Rebecca took her friend's nightmares seriously was because Cassie had spoken of them.

"Having trouble falling asleep?" Rebecca's voice was sympathetic. She was a night person. She worked at her typewriter until long after midnight and then was too stimulated to fall asleep.

"Oh, I have no trouble"—Vanessa was as emphatic as when

she denied ever having had a sick day in her life—"but I do often have these silly nightmares. I wouldn't want to frighten your housekeeper with a scream in the night."

Rebecca had nodded and said casually, "The heroine of my new book is giving me trouble. She won't listen to me. I can't convince her that a dream is a message from within a person."

Vanessa said, "Isn't that what you're always telling me? That I don't listen?"

Rebecca broke into a grin, the effect of which, since she'd had her teeth capped, was stunning in her strong homely face. She followed up quickly, "Won't you believe that your mind, the sleeping part of your mind, is trying to tell you something?"

"What can it tell me that I don't already know?"

"Plenty. You know it as well as I do."

When Rebecca went on probing her secrets that way, Vanessa simply shut out her voice and concentrated on her own private thoughts.

"Vanessa, something really should be done about your night terrors," Rebecca persisted.

"Everybody has nightmares."

"Night *terrors*, Vanessa. There's a difference between nightmares and night terrors."

"Nonsense. I'm certain I must just be reliving some of those early films. You know, Mr. Fodor put us through so much . . . just like *The Perils of Pauline*."

Rebecca wasn't giving an inch. "Night terrors are the result of deep anxiety, Vanessa—"

"I'm not the *least* anxious. *Or* depressed. You should know, Rebecca, I've always looked on the positive side of life."

Rebecca decided to risk probing further. "Would they possibly have anything to do with the wreck of the yacht . . . ?"

"I doubt it."

". . . Or perhaps with the summer in Muskenaw? . . . with Eric . . . ?"

Vanessa's face remained serene. "Not at all." Her voice lacked conviction. She added quickly, "Let's not talk about it any more, Rebecca. Tell me about your new heroine? Could I play her in a film or on the stage?"

Rebecca took the hint and didn't mention Eric again.

She knew why Vanessa could not bear to talk about Eric. He was the one love in her life that was pure and totally unselfish. And if she had stayed with him, had not lied to him, her life would have been very different.

Perhaps happier.

Perhaps not.

But certainly different.

Did Vanessa ever look back at what might have been, Rebecca wondered.

She knew she would never know the answer. Eric was a wound in Vanessa's life that would never, ever heal.

That Rebecca did know. To her sorrow.

THE PAST: REBECCA REMEMBERS: FROM HER PRIVATE DIARY LOCKED IN HER SAFE DEPOSIT VAULT

I HAVE NEVER been able to write dispassionately about Vanessa. She and Cassie are not only my friends but the sisters I never had. It doesn't matter that when we first met as girls in Muskenaw they too were outcasts in that Dutch Reform town. Or that this rejection brought us together and forged the links of a lifetime's friendship, which might not have survived so strongly had any of us married.

What might she have been like if she'd stayed in Muskenaw, gone to high school there, given up acting for the routine of the insulated little community, and married that fine boy, Eric?

She was so beautiful that summer she spent there, so ravishingly lovely, although she played herself down. She seemed a fairy tale creature compared to the sturdy, plodding girls of Dutch descent whom Eric knew.

It was an idyllic summer. Picnics at the beach. Walks along the quiet moonlit streets at night. Boys and girls on porch swings, singing in harmony. The band concerts in the park and the little popcorn wagon with the smell of fresh buttered corn. God, how sweet, how innocent it was ... even in their fantasies the young men didn't dare transgress.

To Eric, she seemed unreal, unearthly, a dream that had come to life. When I saw the way he looked at Vanessa, I thought I'd give anything in the world if a boy looked at me like that.

He had a touch of the poet, young as he was, and he was handsome—tall and narrowly put together, a face with good bones, dark blue eyes ... girls yearned over him as they never yearned even over the football captains.

Everybody knew Vanessa was Eric's girl. In a crowd, they always paired off. Cassie and I were usually together; even then there weren't enough boys to go around. Cassie sometimes told me what Vanessa and Eric talked about; she eavesdropped shamelessly. "He wants her to wait until he's a doctor like his father, and then they'll marry. She promised him."

"You mean, she'll stay in Muskenaw?" I was delighted—imagine having that lovely friend here for good.

"I wouldn't count on it," Cassie said.

She was right. In a baffling way Cassie was always astute about her big sister.

When Mrs. Oxford and Vanessa decided to return to New York in the fall, I was terribly upset, with a sense of almost traumatic loss. Vanessa, with her beauty, her sweetness, her serene manner, was a talisman I clung to. And so did Eric. I never knew how she broke the news to him. But Cassie did and confided to me. "He kept saying, 'But you promised. You *promised*. How can you break your promise? Don't you love me?'

"And she just said, 'I want to be an actress, a great actress. I want it more than anything in the whole world.'

" 'Why didn't you say so? Why did you lead me on? *Vanessa*—' "

None of us believed the Oxfords would soon be leaving town. Not the cousins, Aunt Annie's children, nor Eric, nor I.

But they left.

Eric didn't see them off at the station, although I know Vanessa was looking for him.

That night, Eric went for a swim at the lake.

They found his clothes in a neat little pile on the sand dune. They never found his body.

I ask myself, what did she already have, this young girl, only an adolescent? What was it, an endowment from fate, a genetic pattern that led her to the destiny she set out for herself? Determination? Discipline? What her friends later called her blinders, her voices, her visions?

What raises a woman above her peers?

Beauty helps, of course. But much of Vanessa's beauty was in the *quality* of loveliness she projected. *And* the blessings of thick golden hair, *and* the slightly prominent glowing eyes that she had trained to project the emotions *she* wanted to project.

God, if I ever return to this earth, give me a beautiful face combined with a will to be adored, worshipped. Give me a chance to be Vanessa Oxford. But Vanessa with a heart.

Five:

THE PRESENT: VANESSA'S PRIVATE THOUGHTS BEFORE HER PUBLIC APPEARANCE

WHAT REALLY BOTHERED Vanessa was that once she came awake, she never remembered her dreams.

Only the terrors.

But on the morning of the retrospective she remembered more than she cared to.

She had never followed up Rebecca's suggestions about seeing a psychiatrist . . . Rebecca rather overdid the *subconscious* aspect, Vanessa thought. Rebecca was an admirer of Freud even back in the '20s, and she used what she learned from him to sharpen her fictional characters. She also thought analysis might help her friend, but Vanessa closed her ears. She hated it when Rebecca got so analytical. . . .

The truth probably was that, in some ways, for all her affectionate feelings, Rebecca didn't really understand Vanessa—Rebecca, intense, orthodox Jewish, unmarried; Vanessa, "quintessential WASP, . . ." unmarried but hardly untouched. Yet their goals were similar—both wanted fame and success.

Rebecca, though, was an intellectual who, in Vanessa's eyes, made everything seem complicated.

Vanessa's dreams were quite simple: to take care of Mama and Cassie, to be internationally recognized, admired, worshipped.

And now in both goals she'd been successful. Mama had lived a good life, loved, respected, cherished, her every wish fulfilled. As the mother of two great film stars she had been honored as the Mother of the Year. Cassie was still remembered by film buffs as the finest comedienne of the silents. Her private income would suffice for her life. She had accepted the end of her career as a film actress with astonishing good humor.

I paid a price to keep Mama and Cassie content, Vanessa reflected. Her youth was gone, her beauty faded, as though seen through an old mirror. But, thank heaven, fame, money, adulation were still hers. Whenever she appeared on Broadway or in films, through the good will of her dear friends and ex-lovers, she was accorded the reverence appropriate to a living legend. Chase Manhattan had handled her money wisely, and her capital had increased most gratifyingly. Even in the current depressed market she was richer than she'd ever dreamed possible in the days when Joshua Fodor paid her five dollars a day as an extra in his flickers.

Joshua's image—his rangy body, his deep, sad eyes, his mouth, passionate but capable of discipline and cold anger—was always in her mind, an image that would not dissolve or fade out. In her nightmare she'd seen him beaten, blood pouring in crimson streams from the orifices of his body.

What was the essence of this dream? Not the murder of herself, but the murder of one whom she dared not even contemplate as her victim.

The murder of Joshua Fodor?

Joshua . . . teacher, lover, master. Destroyer.

The furnishings of Vanessa's bedroom were made for her in

Paris, and the room, spacious and tranquil with muted colors, gave her the sense of peace a cell might afford a nun. Elegance and luxury, but in a low, subdued key, a climate that encouraged beauty and serenity.

Vanessa dismissed the dream and closed her mind to its implications. She had a talent for focusing on the business at hand, shutting out all else. Concentration was the secret of her success. She lay in her bed, with its headboard of painted nymphs and courtiers, lying still, legs together, thighs touching, arms crossed on her chest. *Relax. It is important to show the best of yourself today.* She was trying to put the pieces back together in her head and to ignore the ache at the base of her skull.

Morning was drifting through the filmy curtains, offering the soft northern exposure Joshua loved.

"You belong to the Renaissance," Joshua Fodor had once complimented her . . . "the small pointed face with its high beautiful dome . . . a noble forehead." Of all the girls in his company, she was the only one whose forehead didn't require shaving to increase its span. She'd always detested her forehead, so like a child's, prominent; but a liability in life proved an asset on the screen. "Your architecture cannot be duplicated," he'd added. "Never allow American designers to dress you. Your garments should flow."

Vanessa sat up in bed completely naked and swung her legs to the floor, reaching for the short crêpe de chine sleepcoat. Her figure was barely marked by her life experiences. The small breasts, the gently sloping shoulders, the narrow ribcage and flat abdomen belonged to a young woman. Her hairdresser kept her thick, glossy hair strawberry blonde. She refused hormone therapy from her American physician, though she had availed herself of the services of dear Dr. Niehans and Dr. Aslan and had profited from their youth-restoring miracles. From the distance between her and the carved gilt mirror over the chest of drawers, her face appeared flawless.

She unfolded the exercise mat and arranged it on the Aubusson rug. Over it lay a heavy bath towel. As she got down on her knees, the resilience, the play of muscles verified her belief that her body was her instrument of life and, as such, deserved loving attention.

The Yoga exercises she learned a generation ago from a Hollywood *guru* were performed with the same application and intensity she gave a theatrical role even after its thousandth performance. Now the deep breathing, the stretches and twists and, finally, the headstand, for which she moved close to the wall. Energy charged through her cells; she had to be especially alert these days. She was in good shape except for her failing memory.

Her bath water was tepid. She worked energetically with her Swedish mitt and soap until her skin turned pink. Then she drained the water, replenishing it with cold, and finally stepped out and dried herself with a rough towel. Enveloped in a white terry burnoose, she sat before the triple mirror on her dressing table, flooded with lights similar to those in a theatrical dressing room. Her glance was as impersonal as a surgeon's as she measured the assault of the years. The puffs under her eyes were noticeable again. But no more surgery. Once skin began to lose its elasticity, the surgeon couldn't repeat his magic. Skillful makeup was the best disguise.

She went into the kitchen for ice cubes to apply before the moisturizing cream. Flossie was preparing her tray.

By the time Flossie carried it into the bedroom, Vanessa was relaxing on the chaise, the *Daily News* on her lap. She moistened her thumb as she turned the pages, a habit carried over from her childhood.

Flossie waited for her to remove the paper, which was now turned to Liz Smith's column, then placed the wicker tray on her lap. Vanessa's breakfast seldom varied: Hot water with lemon, a health muffin and the single cup of coffee she allowed herself each day.

As she ate, Vanessa watched the interviewers on television. She had been, in her time, a guest of all of them. She made a good subject, since her shyness and simplicity reinforced her fans' conviction that she was indeed a diamond among cheap glass.

"Possessions bore me," she would say on TV. "Perhaps because I had so few when I was growing up. All I really care about are books."

Often after an interview, Cassie made fun of her. "All I really care about are books . . ." she would mimic, adding, "*and* jewels, *and* furs, *and* real estate."

"I couldn't very well discuss such things on television," Vanessa would answer her tartly.

"I know," Cassie would say. "And you always believe the last things you've said, especially the lies."

Cassie always teased Vanessa for being so frugal—she'd call her a miser—and sometimes Vanessa said gently, but with reproach, "Just where do you think we'd be if I were a spendthrift like you, Sister? Who would have paid for all of Mama's medical bills?"

It took Vanessa a lifetime to acquire the security she'd dreamed of. In Hollywood, during the '20s, her money was invested in real estate, including a parcel on Wilshire Boulevard, but then it all was lost during the Depression. Whenever she bemoaned those great losses, the executive of the bank that took care of her portfolio quickly reassured her.

"You needn't be concerned, Miss Oxford. Your income is ample to cover your needs even if you decide never to work again."

Still, memory of the hardships and hungers of childhood always stayed with her. She regarded each assignment as her final one. As a result she had squirreled away a great portion of her salary and allowed income from her investments to stockpile, always pretending the money was salary and therefore to be partly saved.

She'd bought her East Side cooperative for ten thousand dollars in the Depression, and even today the monthly charges were minuscule compared to the rent Cassie paid for two rooms at an East Side hotel.

She had the money to go wherever she wanted. The summers in Italy, for instance. People wondered why she didn't stay home summers and appear in summer stock at the prestige playhouses, like Westport. She never made up any excuses. She lived by the principle that Elsie de Wolfe had once suggested to her . . . "Never complain, never explain."

And those summers in Italy were vital to her.

They helped keep her young, alive and sane.

Only she and a few close friends knew why she went there—where she went and what she did within its privacy.

She was determined to keep it that way.

THE PRESENT: THE MADONNA AND
THE MYTH—VANESSA REMEMBERS

"WE LIVE out our old myths," my friend Rebecca once said to me. "And your myth, dear Vanessa, is the Little Match Girl."

I didn't always understand Rebecca, although she is as close to me as my own sister. She had an oblique way of talking, even when we were very young. "Vanessa is always listening to her inner voices," she used to tell our friends.

Which is rather high-flown and ridiculous. I had no inner voices. All of my life I weighed each crucial moment, asked advice of those who were smarter, more educated and more powerful than I, and, using this knowledge, I have created my future.

Or rather, Mama's and Cassie's futures as well as mine.

Mine has always come last.

"Cassie needs our care," Mama usually reminded me. "We must look after Cassie, decide what is best for her. We must use reason."

"Between reason and emotion," Joshua Fodor often said, "we must choose emotion in our work. The public will forgive us our lack of rational motivation if they are captivated by each emotional scene. If they suffer or love or laugh with the images on the screen, we have achieved success. Films are catharsis for the masses."

He was so right. In those early days of the silents he listened to his emotions, he probed the feelings of his troupe, and he triumphed. But when awful reality took over, when the films portrayed life in the '20s with a cruel dissecting eye, he lost touch with himself. He was ignored. And forgotten.

But *now* is his time.

It usually takes me only an hour at my dressing table in the morning. But the scheduled television interview demands my utmost in looks, charm and acting skills. Carefully I thicken my lashes with the German mascara, rub my cheeks with the crême rouge from France, and an application of deeper color to hide the loose muscles under my chin.

I debate whether to wear a silk scarf. Loosely tied, a scarf was a lifesaver for sagging muscles; every middle-aged actress included it among her beautifiers. But would it go with the Fortuny gown?

The silver-framed photograph of Joshua Fodor stands on my dressing table, apart from the porcelain and silver cosmetic jars. This is how he looked when I first came to him, a head-and-shoulders picture, his face in three-quarters view so you appreciated the fine head, the wide forehead, the light hair with a center part, the deep, sad eyes under their bony arches, the big flat nose, the wide sensual mouth. Flesh and bones suggested an obstinate strength; his eyes admitted a sensitivity that the mouth denied. Such contradictions! You never knew how he would react—he was so withdrawn, so distant, except while directing. Sometimes he'd pass you by without acknowledging you.

"He has so much on his mind." Mama always made excuses for him. But then Joshua was always his most thoughtful, his most courteous with Mama and the elderly actresses in the company. "Now don't you or Cassie bother him."

She knew she didn't need to warn Cassie . . . Sister made it clear she wouldn't go within a mile of Joshua. She hated him.

I touch the silver frame with my fingers, wishing with an unbearable longing that he were here, that he could enjoy his belated glory.

Dear one, you served such a painful apprenticeship to life. You never spoke of the sufferings of your youth, but Rebecca always said that it was all written in your films. Hunger, humiliation, defeat, failure, and out of them came those inspired peaks of greatness.... Well, your time has come. The spotlight again, so richly deserved but too long denied. The praise, medals, citations, Oscars, the international adulation so rightfully yours and so unfairly denied you by the Hollywood pirates, all will be acknowledged through the retrospective.

Your place in the history of the films will be recognized. You will stand beside D. W. Griffith, your mentor and friend, as the men who developed the "flickers" into an art form, America's only art form. Those thieves who manipulated the studios and money managed to bypass you. Now Griffith is studied in college film departments, his techniques admired, analyzed and imitated by young film directors, while you, dear heart, have been nearly forgotten.

But no longer.

I am waiting in my bedroom to make my entrance for the interview.

A half hour ago, when the BBC crew arrived, I came out to greet them briefly. I was wrapped in a Japanese Kimono sent to me by one of my devoted fans, my hair piled carelessly on top of my head. It was an effect that Joshua often used in his early films, when I was made up to suggest innocent passion, and it is still impressive.

The taped interview will be shown in conjunction with the retrospective. There are four young men from the BBC staff—so young, in their mid-twenties, longish hair, beards, T-shirts, jeans, suede safari boots. Casual, pleasant.

To Joshua, they would have appeared sloppy. He was so health-conscious and immaculate—the needle-sharp cold showers, the jogging, the boxing workouts at Philadelphia Jack O'Brian's; and his clothes, faultless as an Englishman's. He demanded cleanliness and proper attire from his troupe. His young actresses were obliged to wash their hair before each day's filming so the camera could catch the fresh golden luster. All of his girls, except Mercy Brown, were almost albino fair. . . .

Unwanted images have a habit of dogging my mind. Mostly, I can turn them off. But now, in a kind of replay, I am in another land, which is Hollywood, the land of make-believe, more real to me than reality. The primitive set is a wooden platform, the kind used for outdoor dance floors, with flaps of canvas for walls. The carpenter is working on the set, and I am perched on a kitchen chair watching him. Everything connected with making a "flicker" concerns me. I must know. *I must know everything so that I will become indispensable.* I am sitting on a wooden kitchen chair—the one Mr. Fodor often uses when he is directing—and I am drying my freshly washed hair. Beside me on a wooden crate is a small basket of the cotton strips I use to roll up my hair for curls.

Mr. Fodor passes by (never at that time did I think of him as anything but *Mr. Fodor*). He is lost in his thoughts, but he abruptly pauses and turns back to me. My prayers are answered! He lifts a strand of my damp hair and looks at it as though it were gold.

"Beautiful. So beautiful. Let it hang straight..."—his voice is low, it has an hypnotic effect on me—"...like a page boy's."

He resumes his stride and as he reaches the spot where the camera is set up, Peg Dalton runs out to greet him. Peg, lively as a cricket, all teasing and laughter, with no respect for his age and station, treating him like one of her contemporaries. She is the only girl in our troupe who isn't beautiful. But she has something I lack.

Mr. Fodor smiles at her and tousles her hair, light like mine but not nearly as thick and glossy. She is freckled, all angles, a tomboy. He puts his hand to Peg's chin, cups it, smiles, listens, then breaks into laughter at her impudent response.

She can make him laugh, I remember thinking. He likes a girl who can make him laugh.

A lot of good it did her in the end.

Where is she now? Is she dead or alive?

And who is there to care? ...

"Whenever you are ready, Miss Vanessa." Jamison the young English director had offered her the deference that pleased her.

Vanessa hesitated. This was always the bad time, before she made an entrance, whether it was for a film, a play or a social event. Earlier, Jamison had supplied her with a list of questions—this was always a requisite when she agreed to an interview. She knew the questions and their answers by heart.

1) HOW DID YOU FIRST MEET JOSHUA FODOR?

The truth would do. It was simple and effective, it would generate sympathy for the image she evoked of the scrawny, frightened youngster, scarcely in her teens, who was the provider for the family.

2) ABOUT THE EARLY DAYS OF THE SILENTS:

Here, too, she was letter perfect. Nobody alive knew as much about those early days as she. In spite of her professed bad memory, the images were still vivid, photographic. Critics and film buffs were dying to hear some of the true tales, waiting for her to talk. But she knew what to say, what to suggest, when to retreat in winsome, pensive silence.

3) DID HE REALIZE THE SPLENDOR OF HIS MAJOR FILM WHILE HE WAS MAKING IT? WE REFER, OF COURSE, TO *JESUS CHRIST—SON AND SAVIOR.*

If she told the truth about this one the myth would collapse. Fodor was jealous when Griffith produced *The Birth of a Nation.* He was jealous when the Italians produced the first great spectacles, *Quo Vadis,* made by Enrico Guazzoni, and followed by *Mark Antony and Cleopatra.* When he heard about the Griffith epic *Intolerance,* it was the Crucifixion that moved him and sparked his enthusiasm. He decided to make the story of Christ, not as a religious epic or a myth but as a kind of documentary.

She could speak effectively about Joshua Fodor's unique vision of Jesus Christ. She might stress how far ahead of his time he was and even mention the rock opera on Broadway a few seasons ago: *Jesus Christ, Superstar.*

But the question about his last film ... Vanessa was cautious. It could be a trap. Yes, he died before it was completed. It was safe to make that statement. She'd rehearsed it last night in the privacy of her bedroom.

Jamison would no doubt ask, "He died in an accident?"

And she would say sadly, "Yes, that is true."

"How long ago was it?"

"Dear Mr. Jamison, I'm not good at dates."

"Wasn't he in the midst of a new film?"

"Yes, he was."

He might ask, "Who finished the film?"

And she would answer, "I did."

"That was *The Confessions of a Woman of Pleasure?*"

"Yes, have you seen it?" She knew he had.

"Mr. Friedlander arranged a screening for us. It's a fantastic film. How did you manage to direct and play in it at the same time?"

"I simply thought, 'How would Mr. Fodor have done this?' and I followed what I thought would be his ideas. He taught me everything I know."

Poised, gracious, confident, she knew the questions and could arrange answers to her liking. She moved around the living room, slender, willowy, a wistful smile on her lips. The young men watched her, somewhat awed by her presence.

The living room had the serenity of sun and space, with thick ivory silk draperies at the tall windows facing East 53rd Street. The walls, paintings and furniture were a blend of pastels, mostly blues with a touch of apricot. The camera, portable lights and snaked cables were a threat to a careless step.

"Careful." Young Jamison put out a hand to guide her.

"Thank you." A delicate smile barely touched her lips as she looked directly into his eyes. With her gift for intimacy, she asked, "Where do you want me?"

"On the sofa, perhaps?"

"The sofa will be excellent." Her voice was low with the gentle formality that intrigued strangers.

She sat at the end of the sofa, its tufted blue silk in contrast to the lavender, celadon and silver of her Fortuny dress. Supported by needlepoint pillows, gifts from devoted fans, she was erect but not straight on, to avoid a suggestion of a thickened waistline—the camera added ten pounds, which would be unfortunate even to her thin figure. She kept her legs close together, the Fortuny pleats covering her ankles, never her best feature.

"We'll set up the lights quickly," the director apologized.

"Oh, I'm accustomed to sitting under lights."

"I wish we had a stand-in."

"Goodness, don't worry about *me*." She put him at his ease. "In the beginning, we worked mostly in daylight. Sunlight, to be exact. That's why Mr. Fodor moved us out to California. In New York, we finally got electricity on the set—it was about 1914, I believe. We had to sit under the lights for hours while the cameraman fussed to get just what Mr. Fodor wanted. What Mr. Fodor was trying to do was paint with lights."

"I wish I'd been there." Admiration and envy in young Jamison's voice. "Those first steps . . ."

She nodded. "Yes, in a way we were like children in a nursery. We were involved in a new form of communication but we had no perspective on our work. Only Griffith and Mr. Fodor and a few other directors recognized the fantastic potential—"

"It was all so primitive," the man at the lights said. "All of our equipment is so superb now it's hard to believe it was never like this."

"It's the difference between a Conestoga wagon and a Rolls-Royce," she said, pleased with her analogy. "We improvised as we went along. Mr. Fodor wore a dozen hats—producer, director, set designer, writer, casting director.... He directed during the day and every night he'd check the day's rushes and put the rough cuts together with Abel Levy, his cutter, who spliced the film for him. Then the actors were allowed to inspect the scenes to see how the story was taking shape. He was always pleased when we showed an interest in the mechanics of film making."

"I understand you know a good deal about making films," the director said, looking through the ground glass.

"Well, it happened naturally. I always stayed to see the day's rushes. The other girls weren't so interested. After the filming was done, I'd go into the lab and watch and listen to Mr. Fodor and Abel, and pretty soon I knew how to develop film and to read it."

The BBC boys were listening, entranced. In England they had filmed many well-known people, but she was unique. She was there at the beginning. She knew them all, the masters of the silents, the pioneers, the innovators.

But Jamison was afraid this rich, warm anecdotal flow would be lost. "Shall we save it for the interview?"

"Oh, I'll remember. This is so much a part of my life, I couldn't possibly forget any of it." She smiled and went on. "Later I had a one-picture deal with Metro but I found a big company utterly confusing. That dreadful man who ran it terrified me. He was all threats and temper tantrums. I was concerned about the day's rushes, but my new director refused to let me see them. It seemed that none of the other actresses, not even Garbo, showed the faintest interest in the day's results. When Mr. Fodor saw my enthusiasm, he always invited me to see the screenings. We'd discuss the scenes and how they could have been improved. Unfortunately, he couldn't afford retakes. Film was very expensive, you know. But he was a great teacher. Everything I know about films, I learned from him."

Her voice softened to an introspective whisper; she closed her eyes against the barrage of powerful lights and summoned strength from depths that never failed her. "The camera filters into the soul," Joshua had once told her. "Everything hidden or secret comes to the surface. You are what the camera eye sees." ... *Oh, Joshua, if only I could see that brilliance in your face once more, the spark of excitement ... the tension just before the wild release, and the relief that came afterward. ...*

Exaggerate, intensify, pour your deep love into the polished glass eye.

Jamison said in an undertone to his assistant, "She's far away." To interview Vanessa Oxford, he reflected, was like being in church on Easter Sunday.

But Vanessa's hearing was acute, particularly with her eyes closed. She took a break from her memories and bestirred herself. Now she was all attention and gentle smiles as she looked down at her hands folded in her lap.

"Shall I put makeup on my hand?" she asked.

"Not unless you prefer to. I notice you keep your palms up, so it won't show."

She looked down at the right hand that hadn't healed properly. "It happened during the filming of *Jesus Christ—Son and Savior*. We had no stunt men in those days; we did whatever was necessary ourselves. Mr. Fodor never spared us, and we never thought to refuse what he asked. It happened in the mob scene, my hand was crushed ..."

Jamison nodded, turned to his staff and signaled the man at the camera. He introduced Vanessa, who looked into the lens, head raised, smile tentative, shyly pleading for forbearance and sympathy.

After the introduction, Jamison, sitting in the wing chair opposite her, said, "Miss Vanessa, before we discuss Joshua Fodor, can we talk a bit about you and your sister?"

"Certainly, Mr. Jamison."

"You and your sister were known as the beautiful Oxford sisters. You were usually photographed together."

"We were extremely close. Almost like Siamese twins. There is only a year's difference between us." Vanessa was gentle with memories. "Mama dressed us alike. Yet we were totally different."

"You mean in the type of films you did?"

"Yes, but primarily in nature."

"That's interesting. I understand that even in the early films you were known as 'My Lady of the Sorrows.'"

"I'm afraid so. Mr. Fodor called me that during the filming of a tragedy. It had to do with the effect of a social disease on a man's wife and children. At fifteen I was playing the wife who was infected by her husband. She murdered her children and killed herself. Mr. Fodor was always warning us of the dangers of such disease, and I'm sure this fear he instilled added to my performance. We lived in an age of innocence." She looked directly into the camera as she said it.

"Your sister, Cassandra, was a comedienne?"

"From the very first time she appeared on film, even before she was a teenager. Yes, Cassie was a natural clown. I should add that she wasn't at all like some women comics today who distort their appearance in order to arouse laughter."

"She was more like Carole Lombard?"

"Yes, you might say that. She was born with a certain style. She was saucy, too. I know that's an old-fashioned word, but it describes her perfectly. Mr. Fodor expected his young actresses to act like ladies at all times. But Cassie, while very feminine, was a tomboy. She was a great trial to Mr. Fodor."

"She was a natural, though. I saw one of her films, the *Anne of Cleves* she made in Holland, and I thought she played Anne most effectively, arousing complete sympathy for the poor ungainly queen."

"Wasn't she wonderful! She's the only actress I ever knew who could transform an ugly woman into a sexual object that even Henry the Eighth could respond to. And as she developed, all the leading men played opposite her. John Barrymore; he wasn't drinking so badly then. Fredric March and Ronald Colman. And Neil Hamilton, that beautiful man . . ."

"You admire your sister, I see."

"Oh, yes! Immensely! Both as an actress and a woman." Vanessa smiled. Her small white teeth were uniform, healthy and all her own. "She has many virtues that nature left out in me."

Did it sound too much like *Photoplay?* Vanessa asked herself. She was sensitive to Jamison's reactions; these young men were very sharp. Sure enough, he hit her with a tough question.

"Do you ever disagree?"

"You mean did we fight? Goodness, yes, all the time. We still do! Cassie was a star, but she was my kid sister. That's how I thought of her—Little Sister. You must understand something about Cassie—" She leaned forward, confiding not in Jamison but in the camera, her eyes lustrous with the suggestion of unshed tears that was her trademark in films. "My sister was a generation ahead of her time, perhaps even more. She was the original Flower Child. It doesn't surprise me that today's young people adore her films. She communicates with them."

Vanessa added with candor, "When we were in pictures, some fans imitated me. But most girls of our time adored Cassie and wanted to be like her."

"She's retired?"

"Yes, she hasn't made a film or performed on Broadway for some years."

"What does she do with her time?"

The tears in Vanessa's soulful, expressive eyes were brimming over now. She confessed with a kind of controlled anguish, "She sits before the television set all day. Watching soap operas."

"Are soap operas much different from the first one-reelers you made?"

"Not really. Which is why, I imagine, she enjoys them so much. We also dealt with simple elemental emotions."

It was going well. Vanessa was relieved, conscious of the pastel of her mother framed in antique gold on the opposite wall. It had been executed in the last year of her mother's life, when her heart couldn't pump enough energy into her clogged arteries, and the result was evident in the pallor and the shadows under the deep-set blue eyes. It will turn out well, Mama, not as Cassie feared ...

Vanessa was the optimist of the family, always had been, even in the days of hunger and cold. She'd been down, but never crushed. "Vanessa has the strength of ten," her friend Rebecca often said, her tone partly admiration, partly annoyance. But it was true, Vanessa thought, facing her polite inquisitor with a serene smile. These young men were all speculating about her private life, wondering who were her lovers and if Joshua Fodor was among them. Fortunately the truth was known to only a few in the industry, never got to such rumormongers as Louella

Parsons or Hedda Hopper who could use their columns for blackmail and revenge.

I hired publicity men to keep my name *out* of the papers,
Vanessa reminded herself. And I need not fear these pleasant
courteous young men. I won't slip.

"Miss Vanessa, you've often been compared to Eleanora Duse,
the great Italian tragedienne," said Jamison. The coffee break
over, they were taping again.

"Critics have been kind enough to suggest a resemblance in our
acting styles." Modest, eyes down, a deprecating note in her
voice. "Oddly enough, our backgrounds were similar."

"I believe that in her youth Eleanora Duse traveled with a
troupe in Italy."

"Just as my sister and I toured America. When I was in my
early teens, I already had years of experience behind me. I already
understood the importance of discipline and I was quick to accept
direction. All of us obeyed the code of behavior of the day. We
were taught to believe in respect, morality, honesty, hard work.
The fact that my sister and I were children didn't lessen our
respect for our craft. But I was also often cold, hungry and home-
less like Madame Duse."

"Duse married."

"Unhappily. I believe she was always exploited in love."

"And you, Miss Vanessa, you were, of course, an object of
worship for so many men. Why didn't *you* marry?"

"You mustn't ask me that, Mr. Jamison."

"Sorry. Duse had D'Annunzio. And you had Joshua Fodor?"

"Joshua Fodor was my director." Her voice was prim.

"Wasn't there a rumor that you were to marry?"

"Mr. Fodor already had a wife. Now let's talk about the retrospective, shall we?"

"Right you are. We've been digressing. But it isn't often that
you allow yourself to be interviewed, Miss Vanessa."

"I'm happy to do this interview, Mr. Jamison, since it's on behalf of a nearly forgotten genius."

"I understand you're responsible for the renewed interest in
Fodor's work."

"It's been my dream for years that the film world would recognize one of its great pioneers."

"I understand Mr. Fodor had a passion for America?"

"Oh, yes! Fortunately, in his day, it wasn't chic to criticize our great country. His parents were immigrants, you know. Intellectuals, who fled from Austria. . . . He would have appreciated Thomas Wolfe. I wish he could have filmed *Look Homeward, Angel*. He had a heroic concept of our country. He would have filmed it with what he called 'the Remembering Eye,' the camera, which he prophesied would be a vital force in shaping our future. And he was right."

"He had no such grand concepts when he first went into films—"

"Of course not. Actually the flickers were merely a means of putting bread on the table. It had always been his secret desire to succeed as a novelist, but his failure with the pen was sublimated into success with the camera. Once he grasped the potential of this new medium, his vision soared."

"I understand Fodor gave many young actors a break."

"Yes. For one thing, he liked to train his people his way. For another, the accent was very much on youth. Lights and cameras in those days were cruel. Anyone over sixteen looked like an old lady." Vanessa was smiling, sharing intimate memories with the camera.

"The result was that we girls were expected to interpret parts far beyond our comprehension. Mr. Fodor's parents were Viennese, and he sometimes added touches of sophistication that were beyond the simple medium. The bosses were always criticizing him for trying new ideas. The Biograph Company was equally rough on Griffith for his adventurous spirit, and Mr. Fodor often used to consult with Mr. Griffith. I think he gained courage from the fact that Griffith wouldn't listen to the front office and he did likewise."

"What was the source of Fodor one-reelers before he went on to his more important works?"

Her shrug was eloquent.

"A kind of group improvisation, you might call it. In those years, he'd listen to all of us. He'd throw out an idea while we were having our box lunches, and we'd all chime in. 'Let's exercise our brain cells,' he'd say. 'A girl is running away.'

"Then someone would ask, 'Why is she running away?' And another would suggest, 'Maybe she's looking for the man who seduced her and then disappeared.' 'Or perhaps because her father threatens her with a beating.' I remember once Cassie piped up, 'Because she wants to scare her mother.'

"Then Mr. Fodor would develop the story. 'Her reckless act causes trouble. It's a summer night. She decides to sleep in the field, although she is uneasy. Clouds gather. An electric storm streaks the sky with lightning. A downpour. She is drenched, shivering. She huddles, terrified, under a tree until lightning strikes nearby. She thinks of home, the warm kitchen, her kitten on the rocking chair, the cooking smells and her dear parents.'

" 'Why doesn't she go home?' I ask, upset for her and for her mother, who must've been so worried.

" 'She wants to. But she's lost her way.' Mr. Fodor always made the suspense unbearable, even when he told a story. But something always happened when he tried to write it down. The story somehow became stiff and unwieldy. Old-fashioned. What a pity we didn't have tape recorders in those days."

"How did he finish that film?" Jamison asked, caught in spite of himself.

"The poor girl is stumbling, ready to collapse. A flash of lightning shows a nearby hayloft. Ah, she is saved! She turns toward it, not knowing that a vicious tramp is hiding there."

"Go on—"

Vanessa's sound was between a laugh and a giggle, which would have sounded absurd in anyone but her.

"You'll have to wait to see the ending during the retrospective."

"Miss Vanessa! You're a bit of a tease."

"It was a happy ending—most of the early one-reelers had happy endings. We all needed the good fairy tales."

"This was long before he did *Jesus Christ—Son and Savior?*"

"Yes. The film on Christ was the climax of his career, although even before that he'd been concerned with important themes. He admired Zola as well as Dickens. He had an instinct for what people wanted, though it's true his choices sometimes made us anxious. He'd lay out great sums for books or plays we didn't

think too much of. 'You aren't going to buy that old turkey,' we'd
say when he showed interest in some cheap thriller. 'You're as bad
as Griffith.' And he'd say, 'Trust me.' And of course we did. He
began turning out one great film after another."

It was going well. Vanessa was reassured by the attention of the
Englishmen. She hadn't lost them once in this long interview.
But she was beginning to tire and was afraid that she wasn't
quite so alert and that Jamison might hit her with an embarrassing question.

"About his last film . . ." the director began.

Here it was, just as she'd anticipated. Be careful now. "You
mean *The Confessions of a Woman of Pleasure?*"

"Yes, the picture half-completed at his death."

Under her serene manner, her pulse was racing. "That was
one I advised against."

"Yet after his death you completed the picture. Is that right?"

She nodded, her luminous eyes sad as she faced Jamison. She
looked smaller suddenly, frail and forlorn as the camera eye
cruelly searched out the shadows under her eyes, the downward
lines at the corners of her tiny, prim mouth.

"True. I took over and finished the picture."

"Wasn't this to be his comeback film after a series of failures?"

"It turned out a success. For both critics and public."

"Because of Joshua Fodor—or you?"

"Because of Joshua Fodor." Her lips tightened to a thin line,
her face lost its pallor and her cheeks flushed. "I simply completed
what he'd begun."

"I understand you scrapped everything and started fresh?"

"What utter nonsense!" She made a gesture that signified the
end of the interview. "I built on his structure."

"One more question, Miss Vanessa. Was his body ever found?"

Her head drooped. She was speechless, overcome, but her eyes,
exquisite reflections of her emotions, gazed sorrowfully into the
camera lens. Their expression was more effective than any words
she could have uttered.

Jamison went along. "I'm sorry, Miss Vanessa. But it must be
gratifying to know you have rescued him from obscurity."

He concluded with: "A retrospective of Joshua Fodor's films
is opening at the Film Wing in New York City. We have been

159

talking with Miss Vanessa Oxford, the star of Fodor's finest films, who is responsible for the retrospective.

"And now, thank you, Miss Vanessa."

"Thank *you*, Mr. Jamison."

I can breathe again, Vanessa thought gratefully.

"It went very well, Miss Vanessa," Jamison said, blotting his damp forehead with a Kleenex. The men were busy with the camera, lights and yards of snake-black cable.

"I hope this interview will stir up some interest in England," she said. "It would be nice if a retrospective could be arranged in London. Mr. Fodor was immensely popular over there as well...."

Oh, Joshua, if you only knew! If there were only some way to communicate ...

And then, chiding herself, she brought her attention back to matters at hand. "Flossie is preparing sandwiches and drinks," she told them, and, as the maid entered bearing the salver, Vanessa gave her hand to Jamison and his crew, excused herself and disappeared.

Jamison shook his head. Unbelievable. He had interviewed many great ladies of the British stage—Gladys Cooper, Edith Evans, Beatrice Lillie, Gertrude Lawrence. But this was an interview he'd not be likely to forget.

Especially since he'd once heard Noel Coward's astonishing account of the story behind the story of her life.

While Vanessa was enchanting the British Broadcasting Company staff with her memories, Sue was preparing to visit the lady for dinner. In the spacious restroom for women employees of the Film Wing, Sue changed from a beige to a black shift, a copy of a Halston, added an Indian silver and turquoise squash blossom necklace her father had sent her from a Scottsdale vacation, and her all-weather gabardine coat.

When she reached East 53rd Street her pace slowed. It was one of her favorite cross streets, reminding her of what she loved in Paris—restaurants, hairdressers, upholsterers, artisans, dressmakers, small galleries in the ground floors of the fine old townhouses. Toward the end of the street, near the East River was a white stone structure, larger than a townhouse, smaller than an apartment house, with elegant architectural lines, occupied by families whose incomes came from blue chip investments. Vanessa Oxford owned an apartment on the top floor of this cooperative, just under the penthouse.

An elderly doorman in blue tails, gilt epaulettes and black trousers smiled and opened the front door.

"Miss Vanessa Oxford's apartment."

"Is she expecting you?"

"Yes. She is."

Nevertheless, he checked at the switchboard before he escorted her to the elevator. As the elevator rose, Sue wondered—does she value her privacy as much now as when she was overwhelmed by her fans? Mrs. Elsberg said she used to receive fantastic fan mail, thousands of letters and gifts every day.

The elevator stopped at the top floor and the operator waited until Sue rang the bell. The door was opened by an elderly black woman in a shapeless housedress and heavy sweater.

"For Miss Oxford," the elevator man said.

Flossie recognized Sue and stepped aside so she could enter the foyer. Silently, she put her fingers to her lips.

"Miss Vanessa is on camera."

Directly ahead was the living room, cluttered with lights, camera, cables. Vanessa's voice, though small, was clear and rounded. Sue paused; the maid touched her arm and led her to the butler's pantry and from there into a small room crowded with a bed, a nondescript chest of drawers and an armchair. The space near the window, looking out on a drab, blank adjacent wall, was filled by a color television set. Propped in front of it, sitting on a straight-backed chair, was a woman dressed in black, wearing a white straw hat with a stiff brim and a white ostrich boa draped around her neck. Near the door was an ironing board with a steam iron, where the maid had evidently been working. Velvet-padded hangers were hooked to the top of the door and several silk garments hung freshly pressed, their sleeves stuffed with tissue paper. The fragrance of Bal à Versailles was overpowering.

"Please wait here until Miss Vanessa is finished." Flossie lifted an unpressed wool dress from the armchair so Sue could sit down. "Would you like coffee?"

"No, thanks."

Flossie took her coat and hung it in the closet. The woman in front of the television concentrated on the actors going through their overwrought paces, quavering voices accented by the moan of the background organ.

"Miss Cassandra, will you *please* turn down the volume?" Flossie asked. "That nice sound man asked you nicely, remember? You don't want to make Miss Vanessa mad—"

"I certainly do. I want to make her *furious!*" The voice was high, clear and oddly youthful. "Flossie, I should drown her out and do her a favor. All that malarky she's giving them won't do her any good. Won't do *me* any good. As for *him,* she's just driving another nail in his coffin—"

"Miss Cassandra, *please!* You know how upset she gets when you talk like that. We have a guest here. This young lady is Miss Palmer. She's from the Film Wing."

As the last mournful strains of organ music signaled the end of the TV drama, Miss Cassandra turned around and Sue saw her clearly. So *this* was the younger sister! Her features resembled Vanessa's but were more vivid. She wore heavy bifocals that slipped down her nose, and she returned them to the bridge with an abrupt movement that dislodged her summer hat and revealed her thick curly hair. She restored the hat with a blithe slap of her palm on its crown. It was a comic gesture.

Sue thought, surprised and a little awed, *This is the comedienne who was the equal of Mabel Normand and Constance Talmadge.* How often Sue and Charlie Bryson had seen her early films in cinema houses and marveled at her effortless, ingratiating clowning. Sue felt herself in the presence of history; it was ridiculous but that was exactly how she felt.

"So you're from the Film Wing?"

Sue nodded. Flossie, working on a long blue silk dress, lifted the steam iron, reminded Cassandra that Sue was staying for dinner. Her manner with Cassie was loving and indulgent, as though she were talking to a difficult child.

"Flossie, make us some sandwiches and tea," Cassandra said.

"Dinner is early t'night. Soon as the gentlemen leave."

"Then bring us cookies and tea. This poor girl needs some pre-dinner nourishment. I bet this is a night for steamed onions and mashed turnips. Ugh."

I like her, Sue thought.

"Flossie, you heard some of the interview. Did they treat Sister like a *personage?*" Cassie turned to Sue. "Sister has outlived all her critics and their criticism. She has now been designated an international landmark."

She paused as Vanessa looked into the room. Vanessa was unbelievable, Sue thought. TV makeup erased years. It was impossible to think of her as "old"; she was ageless, so serene and lovely in that fragile pleated silk. Sue knew she was being carried away, that her feelings were more suited to a teenager, but she couldn't help it. She stood up and took Vanessa's hand. To her surprise, the great lady kissed her on the cheek.

"How'd it go, Sister?" Cassandra asked slyly.

Vanessa ignored her question. "Cassie, take off that ridiculous hat and boa!"

Cassandra stared at her in silence.

Vanessa turned to Sue. "I'm sorry the taping took so long. They seemed very pleased with the results. Mr. Jamison thought they might break it up into two interviews."

"That's marvelous publicity," Sue said enthusiastically.

"Didn't you know? . . . Sister *loathes* publicity," Cassandra put in.

"It's true. I used to pay a press agent to keep my name *out* of the papers," said Vanessa. It was one of her pet phrases.

Cassandra smiled. "With good reason, I'd say."

Vanessa ignored her. "Sue, how is everything at the Wing?"

"Making progress. All the blowups have been hung in the café and the Board Room and corridors. They're very effective."

"I presume Mrs. Elsberg has checked the press list. I do hope she bars the *National Enquirer.*"

"It's no longer just a scandal sheet," Sue said. "It runs some rather interesting articles—"

"No matter. I don't want them represented."

"Okay, I'll check with Mrs. Elsberg."

"Sister, dear, your private files would certainly supply them with some terrific material."

"Cassie, don't be tiresome. And *will* you remove that ridiculous hat?"

"Does it look familiar, Sister? It's the boater from *The Ad-*

venturous Heart. I was supposed to play the part *you* played. Remember? All these years I've kept it—*and* the boa."

Vanessa looked significantly at Flossie. Her voice was patient, however, with Cassie. "Come along, Sister, I want to talk to you. Sue, will you make yourself comfortable in the living room. Flossie will get you a drink."

Seated in the Queen Anne wingchair, Sue looked around her. The French furniture, the heavy cream-silk draperies with their elaborate swags, the delicate pastels of the chairs and sofa, the Aubusson rug, the antique harp and music stand before the wall of books...it was a room that appealed to the eye and the senses, beautiful and sensuous. It was surely not a room for a prim, self-controlled Victorian lady. Obviously, Sue decided, Vanessa Oxford must have another side to her.

The sisters were fascinating, Sue reflected, fascinating, baffling, living history. They came from another age; yet Cassandra, Cassie, with her antique clothes would be right at home in the East Village. And Vanessa, for all her elegance and propriety, seemed also very much of today, as though she knew the world that was really important for her to relate to.

She's more like a mother to Cassandra than an older sister, Sue decided, a bit sharp, impatient, but concerned the way a mother would be. And in a way Cassie behaved with her rather like a small girl, willful, obstinate. But there was also something enormously likable about Cassandra Oxford.

The air conditioner in the spacious room kept the street noises out but cooled the air too much. An afternoon in late October needed heat rather than cold. Sue was uncomfortable and wondered if it would be tactful to go back to the other room, where Flossie's steam iron had warmed the air somewhat.

But suddenly voices that had blurred with the air conditioner now grew louder and decipherable. They came from the master bedroom, where the sisters were. The door was slightly open.

"He's gone. Why don't you let him die in peace?" Cassie was saying.

"I'm doing it in his memory. I owe him that. I'm going to repay him..."

"Such selfless virtue doesn't become you, Sister. You're riding on his coattails, just as you did for years. You hope that by reviving him, you'll revive your own career. Age hasn't changed you a bit. You're still totally selfish—"

"*Cassie!*"

"How long do you thing you can manipulate the facts before the truth comes out?"

"I'm doing what's best for his memory."

"His memory! *Shit!*"

"Cassie, hold your tongue!"

"You're encouraging people to ask questions! To dig! I wish Mama was here—not that you ever listened to her, either—"

"Cassie, don't get carried away. And don't worry, dear. Everything will be all right."

"Your favorite slogan. 'Everything will be all right. I'll make it all right.' Maybe it used to be like that, but not anymore. You can't manipulate men now, Vanessa. *You're an old woman.* I always suspected you were crazy. Taking such risks! What does it matter if he's forgotten? Greater men than Joshua Fodor have been lost in the past. Who cares? But your ego can't let him rest! The world must remember Joshua Fodor and Vanessa—like D'Annunzio and Duse. You never give up, do you?"

"I never give up." Vanessa was strangely calm, her voice scarcely audible. "And I never will."

"You don't give a damn about the consequences—"

"The consequences will be to the good, Cassie."

"That's what you say. Just because you always had your way, you think it'll go on forever. Well, sister mine, you can't seduce men any more. Your looks are gone, in spite of Dr. Niehans and Dr. Aslan. You've only got Dann now—and that's only because he's a decent guy who appreciates what you've done for him—"

"Cassie, I know what I'm doing."

"Like hell you do! You're an old woman. Look at yourself, *face it.* Even Joshua Fodor would turn away from you. He detested age. He loved youth, remember?"

"Cassie, you're working up a case of hysteria. Now stop it. Do you hear me! You lie down and I'll call the doctor. You need a shot."

"I don't need anything. I'm in perfect control—"

"Dear, trust me. Haven't I always done what's best for you?" . . .

Sue was embarrassed, she felt like a voyeur. The bedroom door couldn't possibly have been left open by intent. The sisters were so absorbed in themselves that they'd forgotten their guest. Just then Flossie walked through the living room and headed in the direction of the bedroom. Five minutes of quiet passed and finally Vanessa emerged, her face lovely and serene, without a shadow of anxiety. She sat down on the sofa, which had been moved back to the wall. She had changed into a long flowing robe, medieval in cut, deepening the blue of her eyes.

"Sue, I hope you weren't disturbed . . ."

"I tried not to listen"—she decided it would be ridiculous to pretend she'd not heard them—"but short of earplugs, I couldn't help it. I'm sorry."

"I'm the one who should apologize. But since you will be with us, I must tell you. Poor Cassie is often out of control these days."

Flossie came out of the corridor from the bedroom, muttering to herself.

"Flossie, Miss Cassie will have a light supper on a tray in my room."

"Baby wants to go to her apartment."

"I don't think it's wise, Flossie."

"I'll take her after dinner."

"Flossie, I'll worry about her all night. She's so helpless. What will become of her when I'm gone?"

"There's me, Miss Vanessa. I'll never leave Miss Cassie. Poor baby."

Vanessa was silent until Flossie disappeared. Now she leaned over the cocktail table, stroking the tea roses misted with baby's breath in a Lalique bowl. "People think of us as twins . . ." She seemed to be thinking out loud. "There are eleven months between us but no two sisters could be more totally unlike. Years ago, one of my beaux once gave me a book by Sabatini. It began, 'He was born with a gift of laughter and a sense that the world was mad.' Well, change the gender and you have my sister. Cassie was already crawling at two months. You couldn't keep her down. She was a laughing child, sweet-natured, full of mischief . . ." Vanessa moved to the small table by the window and picked up a photograph in an oval frame. "Here we are together. I was five, Cassie four."

"You look very much alike."

"It's the curls. Mother used to put up our hair in rags every night so that we had sausage curls like Mary Pickford. I was already so serious, see how my lips are pressed together, while Cassie was all smiles and dimples. Mama used to say, 'Cassie is such a *delicious* child.'" Her voice vibrated with affection. "I was always organized, Cassie was always irresponsible without a care in the world. But everybody loved her—" She corrected herself quickly, . . . "*loves* her."

Vanessa touched Sue's hand, as though in an appeal for understanding. "We must be forbearing. She isn't well. So difficult for a woman who was beautiful and talented to come to a dead end. It's so much worse for her than for most women . . ."

"But you've accepted the change so gracefully," Sue said in a burst of sympathy.

"Only because I'm a realist. And I learned long ago not to look at myself in the mirror."

Vanessa grew silent. She had a strange way of retreating into her private world and, although the smile was still gentle, the eyes were remote, the irises curiously vacant.

Sue sat politely waiting for Vanessa to go on, and realized she had never seriously thought of age. But right here in this house was what growing old was about. *It will eventually happen to me. I wonder if it's something I will accept as a defeat, like Cassandra? Or as a challenge, like Vanessa . . . ?*

Dann's arrival for dinner was a welcome interruption to her thoughts. Sue was delighted to see him again. And a bit alarmed. He was an overwhelmingly attractive young male and very much aware of his sexual appeal.

Vanessa clearly responded to his masculinity. She used special mannerisms for men; they brought out a flowering of her feminine charm and grace, and just a hint of the well-bred coquette.

Seated now at the head of the table, with Dann on her right and Sue on her left, Vanessa was transformed. No longer was she the reserved, gentle, older woman; she had become mysterious, seductive.

Flossie served the food: wholesome, deliciously herbed roast chicken, creamed onions, mashed turnips, a green salad bathed in oil and lemon juice. Vanessa ate without apparent appetite, but Sue noted that she finished all the food on her plate. As she ate, she paid rapt attention to Dann, her small chin lowered, her huge eyes glowing, nodding with interest, until a curl came loose and tumbled over her round, gleaming forehead.

Flossie cleared the crumbs from the table and set it with the crystal dessert plates and the finger bowls, in which a few rose petals drifted.

"We're having melon with ice cream," Vanessa said. "They're the last of the season. We used to call them muskmelons in Michigan, that's where we were brought up, you know. Sister is quite mad for them. Flossie, ask Miss Cassandra to join us."

"She's sleeping," Flossie said quickly.

"I hear the television," Vanessa said. "Flossie, get her to put on that white lace robe I bought her. She'll listen to you."

The maid finally left the room. Vanessa's expression was resigned. "Poor Flossie, she's getting a bit senile, I fear. But Cassie loves her. Cassie would be *lost* without her."

"The only thing Cassie would be lost without is television," Dann said, sounding indulgent rather than critical. "She knows every soap opera by heart."

After a short wait, Vanessa said anxiously, "Flossie may be having problems. Dann, would you check, please?"

"Of course." He pushed back his chair and headed for the smaller bedroom.

"She's in my room, Dann." After he left, she confided to Sue, "He's such a comfort to me. I don't know how I'd manage without him."

Dann returned in five minutes, his arm around Cassie's shoulder as he guided her into the room. She wasn't wearing the robe Vanessa had suggested. Her emaciated body was lost in billowing turquoise Chinese silk pajamas, her long, full hair, gray streaked with blonde, was caught back with an Alice-in-Wonderland ribbon. Tense and nervous, she still somehow exuded an air of casual elegance.

Sue was impressed. *No matter how many years the Oxford girls had racked up*, she thought, *they were still unique.*

Vanessa left her chair and went over to Cassandra. "Does my little sister feel better?" Her voice was low, almost crooning.

Cassandra looked at her, wordless, blank-eyed.

"Sit down, dear. You must have some goodies, even though you're on that absurd diet again. Here, dear, sit beside Sue."

Dann helped Cassandra into her chair. She sat rigid, silent, withdrawn. The soft overhead chandelier was kind to aging women's faces, but the contrast between Cassandra's face and the Alice-in-Wonderland hair style was cruel. She kept her eyes down until Flossie brought her melon and ice cream, then turned her head, as though to speak to the maid, but abruptly again seemed lost in her own thoughts. Flossie passed a crystal plate filled with petit fours. Cassandra suddenly grabbed a handful and spilled them on her place mat. Several fell to the floor, and Dann retrieved them.

"Dear, you mustn't be greedy," Vanessa chided her patiently.

"Then why the devil did you ask me out here? You give with one hand and take away with the other—as usual!" The wildness of Cassandra's face was echoed in her shrill voice, now almost out of control.

Vanessa seemed stunned. She tapped her breast with her scarred hand. *"Mea culpa,* Sister. I'm torn between making you happy— and food *does* make you happy, Sister—and worrying about your blood sugar."

Sue was uncomfortable. Cassandra appeared to be slipping more and more away from reality. Dann, she saw, took no special notice of the encounter, reacting to it as though it were an everyday occurence. But these weren't ordinary sisters, Sue thought. They were world-famous women . . . and she recalled how Charlie Bryson had once said, "These superstars, baby, have super hangups that would boggle the imagination of poor mortals like thee and me." And Charlie was no slouch on hangups himself . . . well, one, anyway . . .

Flossie brought in a pot of herb tea for Vanessa, Dann and Sue. And hot chocolate for Cassandra.

"Sue has brought over some old stills we should go through," Vanessa said, turning to her sister. "They're to be used for publicity during the retrospective. Would you like to see them?"

"What for? I paid homage to the master while I worked for him. There's nothing left in me for him."

"But you *will* show up for the retrospective?"

"The Rockefellers and the Whitneys will have to do without me. You know how I detest crowds."

"So do I, Sister. But I do what I must."

"Oh, come off it, Vanessa! It may be *his* retrospective but it'll be *your* big day. You'll be better off without me."

An expression, stern and steely, froze Vanessa's features. The small, prim Victorian mouth tightened, and she thought to herself, *Perhaps I'd always have been better off without you, but I promised Mama* ... And then she, Dann and Sue finally moved into the living room, Cassie remaining at the table, as though frozen.

Vanessa called over her shoulder, "Flossie, put her to bed. See that she doesn't leave. I'll fetch her some hot milk and honey later."

It was time for Sue to leave. Vanessa had leafed through the stills of Fodor's old films. Sue hoped she would reminisce, but even Dann's efforts couldn't coax her to talk about the past. She was obviously disturbed by her sister's behavior. When they came across a glossy print of Cassie, slim and stunning in jodhpurs and a hacking jacket, Vanessa cried out abruptly, "Oh, Dann, I feel so *helpless*."

"Just hang in there, Vanessa." His touch on her arm was gentle and reassuring. "She needs you, even while she's rejecting you."

"Her doctor's giving her Valium again. She eats them like candy."

"He must know what he's doing."

"D'you think we should have a consultation?"

"Let's wait a bit," he suggested.

Sue sat and waited, feeling invisible. Dann wasn't the least bit aware of her; he was completely absorbed in Vanessa's problem. Which was natural, of course, since Vanessa was his friend of long standing. . . . But Sue was aware of her growing interest in him, though she felt he wasn't really interested in her. Still, she wanted to see him again, and wondered how she could manage it.

The musical chimes of the clock reminded them of the late hour. Sue closed the portfolio of prints.

"Sue, can you come tomorrow morning?" Vanessa asked. The dark circles under her eyes betrayed her fatigue and anxiety. "I've got some scripts and photographs to add to the display of memorabilia."

"I'll be here early."

She kissed Sue warmly. "I hope you weren't embarrassed by Sister. She means well."

"I understand. And I do like her," Sue said with a sense of conviction that surprised even herself.

"Thank you, dear. Goodnight. Dann will see you to a cab."

Vanessa remained at the door, waiting with them for the elevator. Her farewell smile was like a blessing. Sue was star-struck, hopelessly fascinated by this living monument of film history. What grace and courage Vanessa had, coping with her sister's illness, showing such patience with Cassie's snide tongue. Never having had a sister herself, Sue felt envious. How lovely it would be to have had a blood relationhip with a woman like Vanessa!

In the elevator, Dann was silent. There were few cabs cruising at this hour. The theaters on the West Side had just let out. The doorman used his whistle, but no success. He was about to set off for First Avenue when Dann stopped him.

"We'll walk until we find a taxi," he said, sparing the old man the effort.

Although she was a walker, Sue could scarcely keep up with him. As they waited for traffic lights to change, he spotted a cab going north, flagged it and helped her in.

"Where do you live?" he asked, and repeated her address to the driver, giving the man some bills as he did so.

Sue wet her lips. Was *this* how it was going to end? "Can I drop you off?" she said.

"No, thanks. I'll walk."

"Good night, Dann."

"Good night."

He began walking with that long, impatient stride. Settling back in the seat, Sue felt empty. She saw a young couple walking down the street, practically making love in public. *He's probably going back to Vanessa's,* she thought. She had seen the sadness in Vanessa's farewell smile. And the invitation.

Was Dann her lover? Sue wondered, thinking about the difference in Dann's and Vanessa's ages.

Or was he only her friend?

Just what was their relationship all about?

Sue thought about it as she fell asleep. But her dreams gave her no clues. They were of Dann and herself.

And in them Vanessa was nowhere to be seen.

Six:

THE PRESENT: HOMAGE TO JOSHUA FODOR

Film Wing Celebrates Opening with Cocktails, Dinner and a Night of the Silents

PERSONNEL RESPONSIBLE FOR TONIGHT'S GALA:

Mr. Friedlander, Curator of the Film Wing. Authority on Joshua Fodor's films. Friend and admirer of Vanessa Oxford.

Mrs. Elsberg, Director of the Film Wing. She was thinking, *If Friedlander bugs me once more, I'll scream!* She opened the lowest drawer of her desk, took out two aspirins and a Valium and handed them to Mr. Friedlander. The poor man was in a bad way. Tonight must be a success, not only because of Joshua Fodor, Miss Vanessa and hundreds of long-forgotten actors of the silents, but because Mr. Friedlander was counting on the event to add stature—and space—to the Wing. He meant to use all his persuasive powers on Mrs. Stephen Marsh, president of the Film Wing. The future held great promise. He was determined to convince her and the directors that Miss Vanessa should be invited to sit on the board. Surely a film luminary was needed on the board of a film institute that consisted entirely of bankers, stockbrokers, real estate tycoons and political figures.

He anticipated Vanessa's gratitude, her gentle voice saying, "Oh, Mr. Friedlander, how *kind* of you . . ."

Mrs. Block was thinking, *This is my day!* After all the running down of leads, negotiating, frustration and disappointments, digging like an archeologist who spends months searching for another lost fragment, success at last!

Not that the collection of Joshua Fodor films was anywhere near complete. Of his three hundred one-reelers, many were lost. Somewhere in packing cases she hadn't tracked down there were others, but the old negatives had probably disintegrated. Mrs. Block consoled herself with the thought that the Film Wing had his major films, and Miss Vanessa was giving them her own reels of *The Confessions of a Woman of Pleasure*.

Technically, *Confessions* didn't really belong in the retrospective. "It's actually Miss Vanessa's picture," Mrs. Block said. "She tossed out the reels Mr. Fodor had done, recast the film and directed it herself."

"We must include it." Mr. Friedlander was unyielding on that point.

Sue Palmer: The souvenir booklet had arrived from the printers and Sue looked at it with satisfaction. Her baby. She brought a copy into the office and Mr. Friedlander snatched it from her hand. The cover was deep royal purple, the letters in gold script.

"Purple was Mr. Fodor's favorite color," Miss Vanessa had said. "The color of kings."

The frontispiece was a photograph on the steps of the White House, President Harding and Joshua Fodor after *Jesus Christ— Son and Savior* had been screened privately for the President.

"A new, compassionate insight into the life of Christ," the President was quoted as saying. He was unaware of the barrage of anger his ghostwritten words would set off. There were many photographs from the Wing and from Miss Vanessa's private collection, stills from the early films and later features, including *Jesus Christ—Son and Savior*. Everyone at the Wing praised Sue's work on the booklet.

"Miss Vanessa must be delighted," Mrs. Block said.

"She didn't say very much when I brought her the proof," Sue said. "I'd hoped for a little more reaction."

"Well, it was probably traumatic for her," Mr. Friedlander suggested, "bringing the past to life."

Mrs. Stephen Marsh: The President of the Film Wing, Mrs. Marsh was the wife of the second of the four Marsh brothers, whose money and political savvy had created, through philanthropy and public service, the substructure upon which the city's cultural life had blossomed.

Vanessa Oxford fascinated Mrs. Marsh. How could an elderly woman remain so beautiful and fascinating? Mrs. Marsh thought it would be a good idea to show Fodor films at charity matinees with Miss Vanessa as guest of honor. Mrs. Marsh's mother was of Vanessa's generation and she was thrilled to hear her daughter would be meeting Vanessa.

"You've never seen anything like Vanessa Oxford in *The Passion of a Portuguese Nun*," her mother had said. "I don't believe Bernhardt or Duse or Ellen Terry—and I saw them all—could equal her. Of course at that time she was involved with Van Cleave here and I suppose there's nothing like a great romance to give fire to a performance."

WHY IS THE STAFF SO NERVOUS?

In Mrs. Elsberg's office the telephones were going mad. So was the staff. People demanded tickets, callers who said they were old friends of Joshua Fodor, dear friends of Miss Vanessa Oxford, and why couldn't they come, if not to the dinner at least to the screening?

A group of women, "Mothers for Christ," planned to picket the Film Wing. Announcement of the retrospective in the press had included the story of what happened more than forty years before when *Jesus Christ—Son and Savior* first played the Capitol Theater in New York City. Many people considered it anti-Christ and there were angry threats as well as glowing praise for the film.

"Not to worry," Mrs. Elsberg soothed the curator. "I don't think we'll run into any trouble. We aren't screening *Jesus Christ* tonight. Besides, we've invited the Cardinal. His presence ought to calm everybody."

FOCUS ON SUE:

Sue felt like a monkey on a string. She was supposed to be in three places at the same time. How would she get off in time to bathe, dress and appear at Vanessa's by six o'clock for an early dinner?

"Aren't you going to have dinner at the Wing? They're expecting you," she'd said to Vanessa the previous night.

"I shall sit at the table," Miss Vanessa replied, "but I never eat in public. It makes me nervous. I always eat lightly before leaving home."

She'd explained the habit was a carry-over from the early days when she and Cassie were beginning to make public appearances to convince their audiences they were flesh and blood.

"At first audiences couldn't believe that the images on the screen were living people. They thought of us as creatures from another world. I must say, Mr. Fodor encouraged that idea. He was convinced that if they knew too much about our private lives, and if our private lives couldn't bear scrutiny, they would become disillusioned and lose interest in us."

Vanessa would make her entrance at 7:30. Sue regretted that Charlie wasn't coming. The postmortems would be delicious with him. Still, perhaps it was better that he didn't show. Dann Houston was escorting Vanessa, and Sue admitted wryly to herself that she couldn't wait to see Dann again.

REPORTER FROM *THE NEW YORK TIMES*, SUPPLIED WITH GUEST LIST, DESCRIPTION OF LADIES FASHIONS, MENUS, FILMS TO BE SHOWN, ETC., ETC., PLANNING HER LEAD FOR TONIGHT'S STORY:

Tonight in the screening room of the newly refurbished Film Wing, two hundred guests will recapture the fantasies of their youth. Many of them will be transported back to long delicious Saturdays in movie houses, when the magic on the screen took them into strange new worlds, where they were exposed to unfamiliar and fascinating emotions.

They will view a series of one reelers starring Vanessa Oxford, angelic, virginal Vanessa, exposed to all the horrors of life that her director Joshua Fodor can inflict on her. They will suffer with her, marveling that this frail creature can withstand such horrible abuse, but knowing that in the end, this delicate flower of Victorian virtue will triumph.

Oh, shit! The reporter tore the paper out of the typewriter, crumpled it, lit a cigarette, inserted fresh paper into the roller and started again.

"Vanessa Oxford, the Madonna of the Silents, will be honored tonight at a dinner celebrating the works of the late great film director Joshua Fodor.

"The guests, seated at charmingly decorated tables in the café, will dine on poached salmon, tournedos of beef, and chocolate mousse. The ladies will be wearing gowns in keeping with the era of the silents ..."

In Vanessa's dining room, she, Dann and Sue were eating rare roast beef (to reinforce the platelets in Vanessa's blood) on Limoges plates and drinking Zinfandel from fine Venetian glass. Vanessa looked radiant in black velvet with big romantic medieval sleeves, her hair piled high with a curl falling over her shoulder. Her triple strand of pearls reflected the luster in her artlessly made-up face. She was too much, Sue reflected, in awe. No one her age had the right to such beauty.

Dann Houston, in conservative dinner jacket, was polite to Sue but attentive to Vanessa, who was distressed because the Film Wing had not included one of Fodor's early films, *Second Sight*, in the retrospective.

"It wasn't one of Fodor's successes," she said, "but it was such an *honest* film!" She didn't add that it was about the effect of a parent's syphilis on his daughter ... the daughter played by sweet, virginal Vanessa.

Dinner over, they prepared to leave. Vanessa wore a chinchilla stole over her bare shoulders, her hands hidden in an artful muff of pale pink camellias that Dann had sent her. Sue was wearing her good black broadcloth coat, which she wore only for the theater or church, over a double-breasted white jersey dress with gold buttons. Excitement had put color into her cheeks and her dark eyes were flashing. Dann's interest, though, as he helped her into her coat, was polite but distant. He seemed to have forgotten the lovely afternoon they'd shared at his house.

A black Cadillac was waiting in a "No Parking" zone near the apartment. The chauffeur, a tall powerful-looking man, more like a bodyguard than a driver, stepped out of the car and opened the door.

"You get in first, Sue," Vanessa said, and as Sue slid across the leather seat to the farthest corner, Vanessa stepped in with extraordinary grace and Dann spread a mink laprobe over her knees. Her camellia muff rested on the dark, silky fur. He took the jump seat facing her. The interior was rich with the fragrance of her Bal à Versailles.

"What a shame Cassie wouldn't come," he said. "She'll be missed."

"I know." Vanessa sounded upset. "But she's in one of her moods. It's best to leave her alone."

Sue could appreciate Vanessa's concern. At the same time she found Cassandra an endless source of interest, partly, she admitted, because the threshold of approaching madness held a mixture of fascination and fear all its own.

"Don't let Cassie spoil your evening." Dann put his hand over Vanessa's, offering her comfort and support. "She's just being contrary."

"Dann, she's getting worse."

"Perhaps she needs a change of climate."

"You remember what happened last time, Dann."

"Let's not think of it now. This is your big evening, Vanessa. You've worked so hard for it. Enjoy it."

JOSHUA FODOR REVISITED
AND RESURRECTED

THE CHAUFFEUR guided the Cadillac cautiously through the traffic, crowded not only with other private limousines, cars and taxis, but with pedestrians who ignored the sidewalks for the easier mobility of the street. A canopy protected the bare heads of the invited guests from the night wind. The red carpet underfoot bore the imprint of the rich and the famous as they left their limousines for the entrance, beyond which a representative of the Wing stood beside the announcer from Channel 9 who was doing a commentary for the television audience while the crowds gaped.

As the chauffeur ushered them out of the car, Vanessa walked on ahead and Dann whispered to Sue, "Stay close to Miss Vanessa. Crowds bother her."

Sue responded warmly as he pressed her arm. She was ridiculously grateful for his touch and for making her feel like a close friend of his and Vanessa's.

The crowd seemed to part for Vanessa as she walked quickly toward the entrance, eyes straight ahead, gaze unwavering. Sue hoped she missed the pickets who were trying to catch her attention as they waved their placards: *FODOR DESECRATED CHRIST. MOTHERS AGAINST "JESUS CHRIST—SON AND SAVIOR."*

The guests overflowed the foyer and spilled onto the sidewalk, surrounded by reporters, photographers, young fans who did not recognize many of those attending but were impressed by their elegance. The women were dressed in the fashions of the silent movie era, their dresses rescued from family wardrobes, gowns originally designed for their mothers and grandmothers by the great French houses of Poiret, Worth, Patou.

Delegates from families that controlled the city's money and politics, as well as the power brokers in society, fashion and show business ascended the curving staircase to the spacious reception room on the second floor. The Hollywood contingent wore creations from Edith Head, Helen Rose, Adrian, and Travis Banton. The wife of a rock singer, who looked very much like her husband and was always being singled out for her styles of the future, had regressed in a copy of the black satin dress worn by Rita Hayworth in *Gilda*. Even Garbo was expected to attend because she was an admirer of Vanessa, but so far she had not appeared. Streisand was expected too because a producer wanted to interest her in a film about the nickelodeon days, but she hadn't arrived either. The elegant Mrs. Henry Ford was there, though, as was Mrs. William Paley and Lena Horne and the Joshua Logans and Marisa and Berry Berenson (who were invited to be photographed with Vanessa and Cassandra, as a kind of sisters' act for *Vogue*). And a scattering of bright young directors, whose work a half-century hence would be collected in the Film Wing's archives.

Kleig lights from the entrance shone into the windows. On the walls were showcases and blowups of Joshua Fodor's films. Among the characters in the blowups were those Joshua Fodor used often in his early flickers, faces unfamiliar to all but film buffs and the elderly guests: Francis X. Bushman, Wallace Reid, Lionel Barrymore, Mary Pickford, Anna Q. Nillson, Seena Owen, Blanche Sweet, Theda Bara.

Mrs. Stephen Marsh stood at the head of the staircase greeting guests in an understated black crêpe with a matching scarf, graying hair combed back in a knot, her tanned, corded neck bare of jewels. When you were as rich as the Marshes, you listened to your public relations man, who stressed quiet elegance.

Vanessa stood beside her, very erect, the black velvet a frame for her swan neck, her small face artfully made up, the muff of pink camellias a defense against too much handshaking that might abuse her scarred right hand. Her shining eyes, the pupils dark with belladonna, panned the crowd, searching for any familiar but unwelcome faces. Her smile was reserved for the men in their dinner jackets who carried themselves with authority. She half-smiled at the women, the smile she considered "duty," although she wasn't completely at ease with them, these wives who were the confident products of finishing schools, debutante balls, and Junior Leagues. They wore the mantle of their husbands' power regally. At such moments, it did Vanessa little good to remind herself that *she* was a legend, a symbol, that *she* had sat with kings and that famous men, including President Harding, had courted her. She repeated to herself silently, "I am a beautiful and alluring woman," and prayed that her self-encouragement, which so often had carried her through difficult moments, would work tonight. *Smile, Vanessa. Remember, it is all for Joshua,* she instructed herself.

The guests were too well bred to gape at Vanessa or to surround her. They went to the opposite extreme. Mr. Friedlander and Archer Krandall of the Board escorted Vanessa around the room, introducing her to guests who already knew and adored her through her films. Her presence created a sense of theatrical excitement and continuity and proved more effective than the presence of the Hollywood contingent, who had come to pay her homage. She moved graciously from one group to another, murmuring a few words, always with her delicate, famous, wistful smile.

Sue and Dann watched her as they stood in a corner with Mrs. Elsberg, who was stunning in draped white chiffon with flowing lines.

"Vanessa has such presence," said Sue.

"She says big functions make her nervous, but you'd never guess it," Dann added.

If it weren't for the vast discrepancy in age, Sue would suspect him of being in love with Vanessa. What an obscene thought! And one that had occurred to her more than once.

"She was an actress in her mother's womb," Mrs. Elsberg commented.

Since the screening room was too small to hold all the guests, Mr. Friedlander and the staff had arranged to show the films in the cafeteria. The attention span of their guests was limited so the films they planned to screen were the early flickers. Guests were encouraged to take their cocktails to their tables in the cafeteria while they enjoyed a half-hour of the young Vanessa and the mature Joshua Fodor.

FOCUS ON FODOR

THREE OF HIS early films:

A Loaf of Bread. His first improvisation on social criticism and protest.

"It is astonishing how much Joshua Fodor compressed into one reel," Mr. Friedlander said as he introduced the films, looking ill at ease in his dinner jacket, his tie slightly askew. But his confidence grew as he began to talk.

"A young boy and girl are in love but are too poor to marry. Each has obligations to his family. They have a desperate need for privacy but they are never alone. Finally, one night, they make love. She becomes pregnant. They are desperate. The only choice they have is an abortion. It kills her.

"Economics, Mr. Fodor seems to be saying, can murder as surely as a man with a gun."

The second film was *Man's Weakness*, a forerunner of Marlene Dietrich's *The Blue Angel*.

The final film was *The Fork in the Road*, a charming, idyllic story of a girl who is seduced by a sophisticated villain and then rescued and forgiven for her transgressions by her childhood sweetheart, a young man as naïve and trusting as she. Characters were stereotypes, but the film had the comforting familiarity of a folk myth. The visual beauty of the country landscape, the sympathetic treatment of innocence and faith, and Vanessa's loveliness made a tremendous impact on the audience.

"In these three brief films," the curator said, "the viewers will remember forever the moments of Vanessa's happiness, grief, sorrow. No one has photographed a nubile young girl with such sensitive understanding, such innocent sensuality. Not even Lewis Carroll."

The applause was generous. The guests arranged themselves at their tables covered with wood-violet cloths and centerpieces of the Marsh flowers, yellow and white mums. At each place lay the souvenir booklet. Waiters were stationed at the buffet table with its glittering burden of carved ice, spun-sugar hearts, flowers and a splendid array of foods. Archer Krandall, network president, carried Vanessa's plate to her table like a shy schoolboy.

While the guests were enjoying dinner, reporters were surrounding Vanessa. She was seated near the fountain, her head bowed in a listening pose as she answered questions. Her food remained uneaten. She was gracious, patient, cooperative, posing endlessly for photographs, many of them under the blowup of Mary Magdalene. She tilted her face toward her questioners, gentle yet regal, her eyes raised so that the half-moon whites were visible. It was one of her most successful screen poses, as the guests had just seen in the films.

"Thank you, thank you"—her voice just above a whisper—"you are so kind."

"She's getting tired," Dann said to Sue.

"How can you tell? She looks fine to me."

"I recognize the signs. When she gets tense, you can always tell by the way she holds her mouth. It gets that tight, prim look."

"She still has her speech to give," Sue reminded him.

What they both found singularly touching was the reaction of the younger guests to Vanessa. The young women hovered about Vanessa, joining the circle around her and staring at her with awe. They curtsied as though they were being presented at the Court of St. James. Mr. Friedlander, standing a proud guard, introduced the worshippers to Vanessa. After the youthful contingent had met her, the older admirers congregated, among them a distinguished white-haired couple, the man the president of an industrial empire in Delaware, his wife celebrated for her extraordinary collection of Americana, furniture and art that was on permanent loan to the Metropolitan Museum.

"My dear Miss Oxford, I shall never forget your Mary, Mother of God." The woman's admiration and sincerity gave flavor to her Main Line accent.

"Thank you." Vanessa rewarded her with a gentle smile.

"Nor your Mary Magdalene," the man added. "To have played those two roles in the same film has always seemed to me true genius."

Sue was aware of a change in Vanessa's manner. Her reaction to the man's praise was quite different from her reaction to his wife's. With the woman she was gracious but aloof. With the man, she underwent a kind of transformation. Her smile remained gentle, even shy, but her eyes glowed, their effect hypnotic as she looked at him. She held out her hand, the left, which was unscarred, and he took it between his big hands and pressed it as though it were some precious flower. There was a flow, a vibration between them that did not go unnoticed by his wife.

Mr. Friedlander, watching her reaction, said hastily, "I'm sorry, but it's time, Miss Vanessa, for your personal comments."

THE PRESENT: VANESSA REMEMBERS

"THERE WERE giants at the turn of the century," Vanessa began, her voice faint, "and Joshua Fodor was among them. They pioneered in a new medium ..."

Her voice grew stronger, and Sue suddenly realized better how much this man must have meant to her—and still did!

"Fodor had a strong sense of justice, inherited from his parents ... He revered the likes of Ida Tarbell, Clarence Darrow, and Upton Sinclair. He believed that the most meaningful dramas were shaped by history, but at the same time he satisfied the universal appetite for fairy tales. It's true he retold the classics, but with turns of his own devising. Didn't Emile Zola and Upton

Sinclair and Charles Dickens bend history and sociology to their needs?

"The cry for brotherhood, for understanding, for communication runs through all his films. Even the early flickers demonstrate his ideals.

"Consider the Triangle fire in New York, where the doors were locked and so many young immigrant girls working at their sewing machines were burned to death. I suggest that Fodor's film, based on the tragedy, helped to change the law and prevent future such tragedies.

"His films were so clear, so immediate that his audience, at first mostly immigrants who couldn't read the captions, easily understood their meaning. In his movies they saw reflections of themselves and their own dreams.

"He was on the threshold of ultimate greatness when he was lost aboard a yacht off the Florida coast."

Vanessa paused. Her audiences was attentive, waiting for some revelation that would verify what the world had always suspected.

"I was among the fortunate girls who made up Joshua Fodor's company. We were all very young, unschooled and uneasy. We regarded Mr. Fodor with reverence, respect and devotion. He was not only our director but we felt something in him that was impossible to describe. Later, I realized it was his spirit, hidden except to those of us who worked closely with him. He was always there to help anyone in need, and was embarrassed by vocal appreciation.

"The films he created are still shown all over the world because the motion picture is still the only universal language. Communication, he always said, could convert enemies into friends.

"It is a fitting tribute for the boy whose family escaped tyranny to have become the artist whose every film is a plea for universal love, understanding and justice."

The guests gave her a standing ovation and crowded around her.

Watching, Mrs. Block was thinking of the talk she'd had earlier in the week with Miss Vanessa. "There is something I must ask you."

"Of course, my dear. Has it to do with the retrospective?"

"No, but it does concern Joshua Fodor. Did you know an actress named Lorraine North when she was in Fodor's troupe?"

A faint line shadowed the space between the serene brows. "The name is familiar. She was with Mr. Fodor before my time."

"Was she friendly with him?"

A pause. "I believe so. I recall now that she was southern and beautiful. Why do you ask?"

"She's going to attend the retrospective."

"Oh? How did she happen to be invited?"

"Well, she really invited herself. She called and said she was one of the remaining Fodor stars and also . . ."—Mrs. Block paused—". . . his good friend."

Vanessa had remained serene.

But she was prepared. . . .

The guest line was thinning. The press and photographers were gone, and Vanessa was free. As Sue and Dann approached her, they paused to give way to an old woman. Her unfashionable black crêpe dress was too big for her frail body. Her white hair was marcelled in deep scallops and set in a thick bun at the nape of her neck. Her face was heavily powdered. She used an old-fashioned crutch to support the weakness of her right leg.

"I presume," she addressed herself to Vanessa, "that this is a moment for congratulations."

Vanessa was puzzled, the woman's voice seemed to strike some chord in her memory, yet she wasn't quite certain. Suddenly her eyes widened, the muscles of her long neck stood out.

"I didn't expect you to recognize me, Vanessa. The change is more apparent in me than in you. But then, we always knew you would outlast and outdistance us all."

Sue could not help but overhear, the woman made no attempt to lower her voice. There was something deeper here than the meeting of two old friends, or enemies. Reproach, threat, what was there in the woman's smile, so like a clown's in that heavy white makeup?

Vanessa glanced over her shoulder as though looking for an escape. Her smile was fixed, more a perfunctory grimace. Her question was tentative. "I'm sorry. You are . . . ?"

"Lorraine North."

"Oh, Lorraine, it's been so *long!*"

"How appropriate that Mr. Fodor should bring us together again. A pity the press didn't ask *me* about the Master."

"Well . . . it's wonderful to see you again, Lorraine . . ." Vanessa was at her quiet, most formal—"...but if you'll forgive me, it's really been a very long evening—"

"Of course. But now that we've met again ..."

But Vanessa had taken Dann's arm as he led her off to the exit. Sue watched them leave, unsure whether to join them or take a taxi home. Vanessa was not only fatigued but visibly upset. The small mouth was a tight line.

"I think I will call on my old friend again," Lorraine North was saying. But nobody was listening.

THE PRESENT: REBECCA KAHN'S NOTES FOR A NOVEL SHE'LL NEVER WRITE

THE SVENGALI SYNDROME.

The master-slave relationship.

Cleopatra and Caesar. D. W. Griffith and Lillian Gish. Josef von Sternberg and Marlene Dietrich. Maurice Stiller and Greta Garbo.

Joshua Fodor and Vanessa Oxford.

Rebecca was working in the study of her Connecticut farmhouse, her leg raised on an ottoman to ease the stabbing pain of the arthritis that had kept her from attending the retrospective.

Dear Vanessa, she thought, this was your night and I hope all went well. What does it matter whether you did this to restore Fodor to his pedestal or to revive your own career?

Sometimes you've driven me up the wall, tested our friendship to the extreme, and yet, in the worst moments of my life, you always stood by. Just as you did with your mother and with Cassie, and with Joshua Fodor and the men who have loved you.

187

You have done good for so many people, the world adores you, and rightly, and yet there are some who detest you. Do you know why they do? Can you understand the hurt you've done them?

No matter . . . I still feel blessed for having known you. And it is not merely the worship of an ugly girl for a great beauty.

Five hours of sleep weren't enough for Sue, but the excitement of the previous night had given her a sustained high. She bathed, dressed in pants and a bulky sweater and took the elevator to her Uncle Sheldon's apartment to tell them all about the retrospective.

Her aunt and uncle were having breakfast at the small Chippendale table by the window rather than the oblong dining room table with its ornate silver candelabra and epergnes filled with dime-store artificial fruits. The duplex was a hodgepodge of good taste (her uncle's) and banality (her aunt's). Harriet's sharp intellectual insights had earned her a Ph.D. in psychology but her decorative tastes derived from Bensonhurst.

"Morning, Sue." Harriet motioned toward the empty chair opposite her. She was wearing a gray jersey jumper, offsetting the white turtleneck that added a bit of fullness to her pointed chin. Her face was sharp, intent. The gray jersey was illuminated by a fine gold-and-pearl brooch, a gift from Sheldon, who was always giving her jewels in the hope of adding a feminine touch. He often said that his wife wasn't born with a silver spoon but a doctoral degree.

Yet they complemented each other. She was organized and disciplined. He had a careless attitude toward life except where his Fund was concerned.

"How'd it go?" Sheldon asked. Where his wife was all lines and angles, Sheldon was soft under the body-hugging shirt. Sue remembered when his bones and muscle made him resemble her father. Now, at forty, he was growing fleshy.

"The press was generous," Harriet said, glancing at the *Times* coverage of the event.

"It was a fabulous evening," Sue said. "She is still a beauty . . . I can't understand why she never married."

"She probably had more opportunities for affairs than matrimony," Harriet observed. "When she was young, actresses were on a par with hookers."

Sue was startled. "She hardly seems one for affairs. She's so ... proper, almost prim."

"Perhaps that was the secret of her allure?" Harriet said. "People always mentioned Marilyn Monroe's availability as the secret of her hold on the male population. But Vanessa Oxford had something better going for her. Men like a challenge. They need to conquer a woman who's turned down other men ... Sue, you be careful. All stars are narcissists and overage film stars are mostly bloodsuckers."

Why was everyone so uptight about Vanessa? First Charlie, now Harriet.

"Well, all I can say is she's very nice to work for—"

"Superficially she may be," Harriet conceded. "But to succeed as she has, a woman has to be tough, and hard. I'll wager she devours people ... with loving kindness, of course."

"Wasn't she involved in some scandal years ago?" Sheldon asked. "I think I remember reading about it somewhere."

"Probably. That meek quiet beauty ... skin deep, I tell you ..." and with that Harriet picked up her briefcase, her severe gray topcoat and, nodding, disappeared.

"Our loss is Hunter College's gain." Sheldon looked relieved. "But you might well pay attention, Sue. Harriet is pretty sharp."

FROM A NEWSPAPER INTERVIEW WITH VANESSA THE DAY AFTER THE RETROSPECTIVE

"PEG DALTON was the only actress I was jealous of in those early days. She could project poignant wistfulness, and she could break your heart with a simple gesture. It's a pity her career fizzled after she left Mr. Fodor. Louis B. Mayer offered her four thousand dollars a week, which was thirty-five hundred more than she was getting from Mr. Fodor.

"But her first film for Metro was a flop.

"Yes . . . well, it's a pity she couldn't join us in paying homage to Mr. Fodor's memory. I believe she's in a nursing home. I don't know whether it's a heart condition or senility. But it's very sad."

WHAT VANESSA DID NOT MENTION IN THE INTERVIEW:

I had made a promise to myself about Peg Dalton, and I kept it.

Oh, I didn't expose her *or* Mr. Fodor. Nothing so obvious as that. Or as dangerous.

I simply showed more eagerness for our "private moments" with Mr. Fodor. I let him know that I was always available to him and that I *enjoyed* pleasing him. And I thought of new ways to please and excite him, always showing my fear and innocence, allowing him to believe he almost had to force me to do it. How he loved being the master, feeling he was subjugating me to his desires. I acted the innocent, using all the gestures and mannerisms he taught me for my roles as the virgin waif before the camera.

And all the while I made subtle comments about Peg—her limited range as an actress, her questionable dedication to her work, her unsatisfactory clothes and makeup. And I dropped hints to *her* that Mr. Fodor was increasingly unhappy with her work. He used her less and less frequently, both in front of the camera . . . and elsewhere.

She was chosen less and less frequently for the choice parts. Mr. Fodor stopped coming to her house every Sunday afternoon.

Finally she quit. Just walked out on him. Mr. Fodor was upset at first, but I pointed out that Cassie could play Peg's hoydenish roles just as well, probably even better.

Cassie was happy.

I was happy for her.

Mr. Fodor didn't seem to mind at all.

After all, he soon realized Peg wasn't essential, as long as I was there, available to him.

In any way he wished.

At any time he wished.

I was his special little girl.

Seven:

THE PRESENT: SUE FINDS OUT ALL ABOUT DANN

Two DAYS AFTER the retrospective Rebecca Kahn appeared at Vanessa's apartment. Vanessa was not expecting her. Not even Rebecca was encouraged to drop in unexpectedly and Vanessa had gone to meet with Dann Houston. Sue was working at the dining room table trying to catch up with correspondence and to make some chronological order out of the A's in Vanessa's filing cabinets, which were lodged in an unused closet of the master bedroom.

The smog sat motionless over the city and the *Daily News* reported the day's air was acceptable. The dining room with its windows facing the blank stone walls of other buildings was gloomy. Sue switched on the chandelier and felt guilty.

Vanessa believed in conservation—and economy.

Flossie was out marketing, so Sue answered the doorbell. She was surprised at the sight of Rebecca, who looked small and shrunken in her tan storm coat, a heavy ribbed stocking cap pulled over her big head, her face pinched with cold.

"Come in," Sue said warmly and Rebecca followed her, using a cane to give herself balance. Helping her remove her coat, Sue asked, "What's wrong?"

"Damned arthritis. My childhood in Michigan. We lived in the second coldest town in the country."

"Rheumatoid arthritis?"

"No, just the good old osteo. We grow old and our joints start creaking. Drives me crazy. But it hasn't touched Vanessa. All her joints are well lubricated." Rebecca eased herself gingerly onto the wing chair.

"I'll get you some coffee," Sue said, and pushed up a footstool so Rebecca could stretch out her leg. "Have you had lunch?"

"Thank you, yes. I stopped at the Women's Exchange for a sandwich after I left the rheumatologist's." Rebecca lit a cigarette, and her hand, flexible still with only small nodules on the hinges, trembled with fatigue. "Where's Vanessa?"

"Dann Houston took her to a luncheon at the Waldorf. They're giving awards to outstanding women and they asked her to attend, even though she wasn't chosen."

"Don't worry, next year she will be. Did you see the press on the retrospective?"

"Wasn't it fabulous?"

"Fabulous. I'm sure everyone in the profession will be touched by Vanessa's loyalty to the master's memory."

Sue brought her coffee, a health muffin, honey and safflower margarine on the English bone china. Rebecca's visit was a delightful interlude. Sue was charmed by her often outrageous comments, especially in Vanessa's absence. Rebecca had the writer's eye that went laser-deep. And while her primary devotion was to Vanessa, she had tender feelings for Cassie too. She must know them so well. And Dann Houston, too.

"Dann's very thoughtful," Sue said. "He'll do anything for Vanessa."

"He owes her a good deal," Rebecca said, rubbing her palm

over her swollen knee. "She opened a new world for him when she took him under her wing. She's been a rabbit's foot for a good many young people. And, of course, Vanessa needs a handsome man around her, even if just as an escort. It keeps her young."

"What's his background?" Sue tried to sound casual but Rebecca wasn't fooled.

"Dirt farmers, scratching for a living until oil was found on their farm. Dann pretends to be first generation, but he's third. His family never grew into their money. They were plain unpretentious people who'd let their money accumulate in banks and trusts because they didn't know how to spend it. His grandfather, who owned the land, was elected to the U.S. Senate as a Populist. He's endowed wings for several colleges. I suppose that's how Dann got sent to an Ivy League college. He told us his grandfather hired tutors for the whole family, but they wanted no part of it. Can you imagine it? A McDonald's-and-Coke generation riding around in a Rolls!"

"I suppose you see a lot of that in Oklahoma."

"It's the mix that makes Dann so damned attractive. And complex. The English strain, and then a touch of the Indian ... his grandmother, a Comanche. The Anglo-Saxon effete and the Indian savage. I wish I'd met his grandmother, she'd have made quite a character for a novel."

"I'm surprised you haven't used Vanessa for one of your heroines," Sue said.

Rebecca smiled. "Who'd believe it?" she asked.

THE PRESENT: VANESSA: IN THE
BEGINNING WAS THE SEEING EYE

THE RETROSPECTIVE had a great press. While it focused on Joshua Fodor, Vanessa benefited greatly. She was in the limelight again. People who had seen her on the screen when they were children were filled with renewed sentiment and curiosity. What was Vanessa like today, the frail, exquisite creature once known as the Madonna of the Sorrows? Mrs. Kramer, her agent, was besieged with calls, invitations for Vanessa to appear on talk shows, to be interviewed, to lecture.

A fortnight after the retrospective Vanessa agreed to speak to a class at the New School on the genesis of the film. She asked Sue to accompany her. For all her independence, Vanessa disliked going alone. She said with a little smile that she had been spoiled. When she was at her peak in films, wherever she went, she was accompanied by her secretary and a press agent from the studio. "Mr. Fodor kept us on a short leash," she confided. "He disapproved of any publicity for us. But after I left him, the big studios treated me royally. It took some getting used to."

"Why did Mr. Fodor object to publicity for his stars?" Sue asked.

Vanessa's gaze turned inward. "Why ... I really don't know. Except that perhaps he felt, particularly after *Jesus Christ—Son and Savior*, that everything in the film was rightfully his. Well, I suppose we were all his puppets, so to speak ... Oh, *he* didn't say that, of course. And there was his feeling that if the actors received too much personal publicity, the audience would realize they had lives of their own. He didn't want reality to spoil the image."

They took a cab down Fifth Avenue. Indian summer had retreated before the early November cold, but the air was crisp and exhilarating with no sign of smog. Vanessa was quiet, leaning back in her seat. She was nervous, Sue sensed. Sue was growing accustomed to Vanessa's sudden withdrawals into her private world. She understood better what a noted critic meant when he suggested that Vanessa's personality was as elusive as smoke.

Vanessa rehearsed the lecture meticulously in her mind. She took all public appearances seriously. How to begin? she wondered. With how the movies were born? She could tell them how in 1894 the first Edison Kinetoscope appeared in a penny arcade. Such excitement! You squinted through a glass and what a miracle —images of scantily clad soubrettes, baggy pants comedians taking pratfalls, bathing beauties. Unbelievable! And they moved!

She'd go on to say that the next step in the development of what turned out to be the movies was the nickelodeon. Here was an improvement on the Kinetoscope, but still mostly images without continuity—a comedy skit, a dance team, a lady snake charmer... No, too factual, dull. These were people who'd cut their eye teeth on television. They were accustomed to The Teaser... Start with a raid. Policemen looked like Mack Sennett cops would look a few years later. They raided the nickelodeons. Yes, raids. Reformers and church groups got after the nickelodeon owners who were showing pictures the Bluenoses didn't approve of —No, no! Instinct reminded her that personality counted most. Hers and Joshua Fodor's. She wanted those brash young students to appreciate who The Master was. And that she was still a great actress and surely somewhere there must be a part for Vanessa Oxford, who wasn't dead, as some of her enemies often suggested, but was very alive and could show these beginners what art was really like....

"Let me tell you about my introduction to the nickelodeon; I was about seven, my sister a year younger. Our mother was working in a dry goods store to support us that summer. Nearby there was a nickelodeon. Mother sent us off to see our first "flicker." What an odd pair we were. Looking less like children than grown women. Children in the early years of the 1900s were dressed like miniature adults. We were burdened with muslin dresses trimmed with lace, ribbon sashes around our hips, long ribbed white stockings and patent leather Mary Jane slippers, and we wore brimmed leghorn hats that made us look top-heavy. All females from infancy on looked top-heavy in those days. Pompadours. Big satin hair ribbons. Enormous hats ..."

And then she would give them a graphic description of herself, standing on tiptoe, to pay admissions. And leading Cassie into the store, finding two chairs and sitting there, hunched up, frightened but excited, waiting for the white sheet to cast its magic spell.

She was nearly ready now, but there was often one particular question that people aimed at her, and no doubt these young people would include it.

Was Joshua Fodor a lovable sort of man?

Vanessa knew how to answer, she'd schooled herself. Lovable? What genius was lovable? Joshua Fodor was kind to his staff but never sentimental. And at a distance. They looked up to him. They revered him. But lovable?

No, it was too dangerous ground ... Best to end with a note of optimism for these young would-be directors.

"If Fodor were directing today," she'd conclude, "I am confident he would be one of you." ...

There were nine young men in the room, with shoulder-length hair, Jesus beards, jeans and boots. And three young women in T-shirts and pants, their hair cropped short, their faces bare of cosmetics. Bill Anderson, the regular lecturer, introduced Vanessa and Sue to each one. Vanessa's handclasp was warm and gracious, her eyes trusting, sending out vibrations of love and concern.

Make it simple, she told herself as she began. And humble ... these budding *auteur* directors don't want a movie queen posturing about past glories. ...

"Because it is so far in the past, it is necessary to explain what a nickelodeon looked like, it's equipment, how it functioned. First a man would scout a location, deciding on one where pedestrian traffic was heavy. Then he rented an empty store, painted the front windows black, hired a carpenter to tear down the front entrance and replace it with a sheltered ticket booth. He'd leave plenty of open space on either side for gaudy posters to lure in customers.

"Next he'd build a wooden projection booth on the inside.

This was at the front of the store and directly above the rows of folding chairs, which he'd rented by the day or week from the local undertaker. Where the rear of the store once was, he'd erect a wooden square on which he tacked a white bedsheet. This was the screen.

"The next step was to rent a projector, which was set up in the booth. The operator was expected to crank that projector twelve hours a day, which meant, I assure you, that he needed the muscles of a blacksmith. He had to keep the film in focus on that white bedsheet. He had to learn how to improvise. He often made his own rheostats, the coils of wire that were always placed at a good distance from the projector and film.

"Film was the hazard of the nickelodeon.... Water couldn't extinguish burning celluloid. Edison projectors used carbons. Power lines were unpredictable. Too much power and the carbons would overheat and burn out. Too often the man in the booth would stop cranking his machine, climb out of the booth and announce to the audience, 'Projection machine's gone dead. Please vacate the building. Quickly. Get your refund at the box office.' Which meant a fire.

"The nickelodeon owner was always in need of new film, which he rented from the new film exchanges that were set up to meet the voracious needs of the audience. He'd rent a piano, usually in need of tuning, and hire a player, usually a woman, to accompany the action on the screen. Sometimes her interest wandered and her music was at odds with the action on the screen. Outside a woman sat in the booth selling tickets and sometimes there was even a barker to lure in customers, just like in a circus or carnival.

"The nickelodeon brought windfall riches to men who ordinarily would hardly have dared dream of them. Many of them were immigrants. In America, as in England during that period, there were the very rich, a very small middle class and an enormous working class. The Horatio Alger hero was so popular because he was so rare. People were born into a class and stayed there. But if a young fellow was dissatisfied enough with his lot in life—the factory or the mill or clerking in a store—but lacked the special gumption to strike out for the west, he might latch onto something new that made few demands on his brains, or his pocketbook.

197

"So a new breed of men were made rich by the lowly nickel-odeons. To own a nickelodeon was socially on a par with running a saloon. But there was more money to be made on a nickel admission ticket than a nickel glass of beer. The average nickelodeon in a good location stayed open twelve hours a day. Each performance ran a half hour and used up about one thousand feet of film—news, vaudeville and sketches. Each performance played to about fifty customers at a nickel apiece. Film rentals came to fifteen dollars a week, and the staff's pay didn't amount to much. The nickelodeons were licensed for $25, while vaudeville acts or stage plays were performed in theaters that were required to pay $500 for a license. The Aitken Brothers, who later backed *The Birth of a Nation*, made a profit of $300 the first week in their first nickelodeon, and this was in a time when fifteen dollars a week was pretty good pay."

Her spirits were lifting now. She felt more at ease with Bill Anderson's eager, oh-so-serious young men. So far so good. She described the people waiting outside a nickelodeon—men in shabby suits and caps, women in heavy skirts and shawls, holding babies in their arms, immigrants recently out of Ellis Island. Nobody today, she said, could imagine the effect the "flickers" had on that first generation of moviegoers. Working in sweat shops or at pushcarts, hungry, frightened in an alien land, they found in the nickelodeon a friend, an introduction to this baffling new world. Joshua Fodor said that "flickers," not religion, were the opiate of the masses.

What the audience shared with the figures on the screen, she told them, was emotion, elemental feelings. People at first couldn't believe that the images on the screen were real. And when they did, they believed the actors were playing out their own life stories. Fantasy and reality blurred. "Why, the first time I saw myself on the screen, I couldn't believe it was me. . . ."

The neighborhood saloon, of course, was the meeting place for men, but now their women no longer had to remain at home. They crowded the nickelodeons, which were soon transformed into movie houses, and the fantasies on the screen acted out their own hunger for Love and Romance and the Good Things In Life. . . .

"And so, I suppose you might say, the movie fan was born.

Audiences singled out certain players for absolute worship—little Mary Pickford with her incredible golden sausage curls, and Florence Turner, the Biograph Girl. They devoured information about their favorites, and the fan magazines were born to provide it. As were, I'm afraid, publicity men, who began to feed newspapers and magazines a steady stream of glamorous, exaggerated *mis*information.

"At any rate, as nickelodeons with their flickers developed into moving picture houses, the infant industry so recently born began to boom. The nickelodeons ate up film, needed constant replenishment, but the film exchanges that bought film from the few producers couldn't keep up with the voracious demand. So nickelodeon owners bypassed the exchanges and became producers themselves. It didn't matter that they lacked knowledge about making films. It was fresh territory. There were no roadmaps. So they improvised. And out of improvisation came a fresh if perhaps clumsy technique.

"Theater people, of course, would have nothing to do with the flickers. The new producers were obliged to hire actors who were nonentities. But this handful of producers, mostly ignorant, ruthless men, grew in power as the magic of movies took hold across the nation and then the whole world."

How clumsy it all was, how chaotic. How uninspired... until D. W. Griffith came along. And shortly after him, Joshua Fodor.

"The Model T was ready to develop into a Rolls Royce...."

She had them now, and like the experienced trouper that she was, she knew enough to get off stage when she was ahead. And she did.

After her talk the young people gathered around her, obviously taken with her. Here was the gracious, modest, beautiful lady who'd played such a significant role in the development of America's greatest art form. In their film courses they'd seen the Fodor films she'd played in—such a fragile, exquisite girl-child then, her enormous eyes filled with sorrow, always on the verge of tears, with that irresistible, virginal innocence. And the girl had been fulfilled in this luminous woman.

A young man took her hand and kissed it. "Thank you," he said, and spoke for them all.

Later that evening Sue was telling her aunt and uncle, "You

know, she really is a woman of contradictions. I mean, here she was surrounded by these young, bright people who obviously revered her—and they're not impressed all that easily. At least not usually. I had the feeling that they were ready to carry her out on their shoulders. And then, on the way home, she had the cab stop at one of those health stores on Madison Avenue and she popped right out and bought bran and date muffins. For *me*. She's always saying white bread isn't fit for human consumption."

"Maybe she does miss never having had a child of her own," Aunt Harriet said. "Though I understand her sister is like a daughter to her."

And what is she to her sister, Sue thought, and said nothing.

Eight:

THE PRESENT: DANGER! A LITTLE KNOWLEDGE

AFTER A MONTH with Vanessa, Sue began to discover events in the private lives of the Oxford sisters that didn't appear in press releases or fan magazines.

She'd gathered from Charlie's wry comments that most stars managed along the way to rid themselves of people who helped them get to the top.

Not so with Vanessa.

Her files were crowded with letters from people she'd known on the Fodor lot, and with whom she'd kept in touch over the years. There were also canceled checks for sums ranging from ten dollars to thousands, made out to names unfamiliar to Sue. When she mentioned them, Vanessa explained, "Oh, he was a manager when we were on the road with *East Lynne*. His wife had a cancer operation and he was hard pressed." Or, "She was a friend of mother's, they played together on the Keith Circuit." Or, when Sue held out a faded check for fifty thousand dollars, Vanessa said, "It was a loan to Mr. Fodor. For his last picture."

Sue risked the question, "Was it ever repaid?"

Vanessa didn't answer. She sat silent, immobile, her emotions masked.

A number of checks for small sums, usually a hundred dollars apiece, were made out to Rebecca Kahn. All carried dates in the early 1930s. "It was a difficult time," Vanessa said, "particularly bad for Rebecca. She was struggling to exist as a freelance writer in New York. This was just before Ray Long, the editor of *Cosmopolitan*, discovered her."

She stared at a pile of faded checks. She picked them up, riffled through them. "Doctors. Hospitals. Poor Mama's life is written in those scraps of paper. Her poor tired heart."

Sue was baffled. Vanessa's generosity was also mixed with stinginess. Sue received from her not much more than Vanessa paid Flossie, which was not much more than the minimum hourly wage.

Mrs. Elsberg had warned Sue, "Miss Oxford is asking us to share you. You'll divide the week between her and us. She'll pay you for the time you spend with her, she expects us to take care of the rest. Frankly I think it's rather chintzy of her, but Sue, we're asking you to stay along with her and of course we'll make up the difference in your salary. We understand she plans to divide all her memorabilia between us, the Archives in Hollywood and the American Academy of Dramatic Art. With you working with her, we're hoping we won't be shortchanged. Her possessions are priceless. And whenever you're at her place and she speaks of the past, not only about Fodor but other producers and directors she later worked with, jot down notes. She is the last of the great stars of the silent screen. When she dies, the source will have dried up and we'll get totally inaccurate versions of the past."

One morning, the third week in November, Sue was working in Vanessa's dining room among cardboard boxes and cartons brought over from Dann Houston's basement. Vanessa was preparing to visit her hairdresser and from there her doctor.

"I'll be back for lunch," she said. "I'm expecting some people. By the way, did you meet Will Wattenburg at the retrospective?"

"Was he the tall scarecrow in jeans?" Sue asked. "The photographers were making a great fuss over him."

"Well, he donated the building to the Wing, you know. I invited him. He was delighted to come. His grandmother"—her smile was wry—"is a great fan of mine. Look through my file of photographs, Sue, and find a glossy of me in the habit of a nun. It should be among the stills for *The Passions of a Portuguese Nun.*"

"That film wasn't done with Mr. Fodor, was it? I didn't see any record of it in his file—"

"No, it came much later. After..." Vanessa, without completing her thought, shrugged. "Piers van Cleave was the producer. While I was filming it Mr. Fodor came up with an idea for a movie tracing the development of the human mind over the ages, from the cave man to the man of today. He called it *Man Alive* and he cashed his insurance to underwrite it." She paused. "*The Portuguese Nun* made millions. Mr. Fodor lost everything."

"And you lent him money?"

"For his last film, *The Confessions of a Woman of Pleasure.*"

"Did you ever get your money back?" Sue risked the question again, with surprising results—Vanessa, ever the unpredictable.

"Yes, after the film was released."

"But that wasn't the only money you lent him?"

"No...he went through a terrible dry period when his *friends* and the film world forgot about him. He desperately needed help."

From other canceled checks, Sue realized Vanessa had been practically an annuity for the director. She was matter of fact about it; as though she couldn't have done otherwise. How much he must have meant to her!

"As I'm going through all this material, I'd like to build continuity," Sue explained. "So people who will come to the Archives or the Wing for research will have the sequences of your life. So much is undated, you know."

"My memory is awful," Vanessa said. "If you need material that you can't find in interviews or press releases, you might ask Rebecca. She knows me better than I know myself. Just one thing—don't use the date of my birth. I loathe dates."

The history of the Oxford girls was on the round table draped in striped eggshell satin. In their silver and turquoise frames, the photographs were yellow with time and the imperfections of old-fashioned fixing solution. Some photographs, daguerreotypes nearly a century old, were of their maternal grandparents. There was no picture of the father's family.

The photograph with the most meaning for the sisters was of their parents, taken shortly after their marriage. They were a singularly handsome couple, the young man with deep-set eyes, a rakish tilt to his dark head; the young woman with her innocent face, her thick, pale hair in a topknot. Sue glanced at those two whenever she passed by, thinking they were two innocent children in the 1890s, gullible, naïve, cast adrift in the world they couldn't cope with. How could they have parented Vanessa? Vanessa, who sat with kings, who was worshipped, adored, the first international film star, the great lady. It was possible, even natural, for a great man to emerge from modest beginnings. But for a woman to achieve greatness, particularly in the first quarter of the twentieth century! How she'd have loved to have known them ... what were the girls like as infants, as children? Vanessa was obviously concerned about Cassie's welfare. Yet there must've been rivalry, it wouldn't be natural otherwise. . . .

The photographs of Vanessa and Cassandra: the large heads, framed by fat sausage curls, each little girl with a big taffeta bow anchored to her hair. They were the epitome of the Victorian children, Sue thought. Lewis Carroll would have loved them.

In the hall between Vanessa's bedroom and the living room the walls were hung with an extension of the girls' history—photographs and reproductions of paintings set in simple old-fashioned gilt frames. The photographs included the men whom Vanessa had been close to. In the upper corner, the large sepia photograph was of the master himself, Joshua Fodor, when *Jesus Christ—Son and Savior* echoed throughout the world with its new insights and interpretation of the Gospel. By no means a conventionally handsome man, he was undeniably imposing, even distinguished, the head of thick hair growing rather long, the

sideburns full like an opera tenor's. The face had the bone
structure of his Austrian heritage, the high cheekbones of the
Slav, with a broad mouth ready for good humor or sudden fury.
He looked immaculate; Sue remembered Vanessa speaking of his
compulsive cleanliness. There was also photography of Sir James
Barrie, who had wanted Vanessa for *Peter Pan*, a deal that somehow fell through. And of Max Reinhardt, the great European
director, who had thought of her first for the nun in *The Miracle*,
but that too hadn't come off. And of Sean O'Casey, who'd hoped
to write a play especially for her but died before he could fulfill
his promise. And a costume picture of Cassie as a circus clown,
looking all poignant and roguish, and a closeup of Vanessa taking
her vows in *The Passions of a Portuguese Nun* with a purity of
expression that could fit her for sainthood.

What is Vanessa really like, Sue asked herself.

"The most reckless person I've ever known," Rebecca had once
said.

Whatever, the lady had gotten under her skin. Aunt Harriet
would have warned her to beware. But Aunt Harriet didn't know
how *kind*, how *selfless* Vanessa was.

Later that morning Sue and Rebecca Kahn were seated on the
sofa in Vanessa's living room, drinking coffee and nibbling on
Vanessa's prescribed raisin-bran muffins. The china was fragile,
the napkins of fine linen artfully embroidered by nuns in a
convent in Italy.

Sue was asking Rebecca about Vanessa's first appearance with
Cassandra in road companies and on the vaudeville stage.

"Their very early experiences were before my time. They used
to visit their aunt in Muskenaw, but I didn't really get to know
them until Vanessa and I were thirteen and they were taking a
forced hiatus from the stage."

"Can you tell me anything about those years? Just enough so
I at least can get the chronology right. Mrs. Elsberg thought I
should include some human-interest material—interviews, personal
anecdotes."

"We'd just be wasting our time, unless you want some choice
tidbits for your private information. Whatever I tell you, she'll
deny anyway."

Sue looked startled. The older woman's smile emphasized the lines in her cheeks. Her iron-gray hair was cut short, curls falling around her overly large head. A ruffled white silk shirt highlighted her navy blue knit suit. The result was spare and fresh. The scent of her perfume, Jungle Gardenia, was totally incongruous but attractive. Out of an ungainly girl Rebecca had made herself into a woman of style and elegance. Of course the Pulitzer prize didn't hurt her image. She had achieved status on her own, though it was hardly of Vanessa's star quality.

"Vanessa computerized herself for success," Rebecca said, not without admiration. "She had and still has a passionate, single-minded way of attacking life. She's hypnotized herself to see only success, while Cass"—a shadow flickered over the strong, bony face—"Cass sees only failure."

"But Cassandra's been successful too," Sue said. "I've been going through the list of her films and plays. She's done almost as much as Vanessa."

"Perhaps even more," Rebecca agreed, "but she never got to Vanessa's stature as a star. You see, Cass didn't really care about a career. Vanessa often got exasperated with her about that. Cass once even refused an offer to do a film with Korda because she wanted to go to Vermont with a lover, for the blooming of the New England spring. Vanessa took over the part and played it superbly, but she was awfully upset about Cass' unprofessional behavior. When she complained about it to Mr. Fodor, he said, 'Cassie's a rebel. You've never accepted it, Vanessa, but it would be wiser if you could. You cannot make your sister over in your image. She's a special person.' "

"But Vanessa seems devoted to Cassie—"

"Oh, she *is*. Definitely!" Rebecca drained her coffee. "Vanessa's world remains unchanged, you know. It's still the world she used to see from the window of a coach car while a train carried her from one dreary town to another. I often think of that little girl stitting there, staring out at the speeding landscape, and wonder what her thoughts really were. You know, it was her duty to keep Cass quiet so the adults wouldn't be annoyed. In those days children were seen but not heard. I feel so sorry for that child. . . ."

Sue was surprised at the emotion in Rebecca's voice. Usually she kept herself aloof, unwilling to disclose her feelings, perhaps the result of *her* youthful training. When women of her generation were young they were expected to speak only in polite, superficial terms. True feelings were never admitted, were blocked or at the least severely screened. And for Vanessa, such rigid containment must have been worse than for most, because it was based on fear.

"Vanessa lived in a world where you had to work to survive," Rebecca said. "A world of adults. She adored her mother and wanted to look after her. Cassie was her special responsibility. She took her responsibilities seriously at too early an age." Rebecca lit a fresh cigarette. "Such a background doesn't exactly make for a whole, well-adjusted person. It *can* create a criminal, a master-mind or a *femme fatale.* Take your choice."

And then she added something Sue would never forget.

"One day you'll learn, Sue, no one can save us from our-selves." . . .

Sue and Rebecca were finishing coffee when the door opened and Cassandra entered. She held her apricot poodle, somewhat larger than a miniature, on her hip the way a peasant woman carries a child. The brisk prewinter air had given color to her cheeks. Unlike Vanessa, whose skin was buttermilk white, Cassandra had a healthy color. She was endowed with the kind of skin that has a natural luster, which made her unusually photogenic. Today, from a distance of a dozen feet, she seemed to Sue no more than a woman in her late forties, considerably better than the first time she'd met her at that awful dinner party. In her man-tailored stormcoat, her jaunty brimmed hat, her foulard ascot, she seemed quite modern.

"Hello. Where's Sister?" she asked, depositing the poodle on the sofa. Rebecca picked up the dog, petted him and set him on the rug. "Better the Aubusson than the quilted satin," she suggested. "His kidneys aren't in the best condition."

"Oh, Vanessa loves him," Cassie said, stripping off her coat and scarf.

"Not to the extent of cleaning bills. You know how it disturbs her—"

"Now, Rebecca," Cassie said, "don't *you* go making me feel guilty."

Talk, which had been brisk between Rebecca, and Sue, now lagged. Flossie brought Cassandra a health muffin and tea, and

Cassie said airily, "Take that crap away. Bring me some real food, Flossie. What have you got stashed away out of Sister's sight?"

"Well, Miss Cassie, I have a pecan pie I was fixin' to take home with me—"

"Bring it out, Flossie!"

"You'll ruin your appetite. Lunch is in half an hour. An' you know how mad Miss Vanessa gets if you don't eat."

"Okay, *okay*." The sofa was faced by two bergeres. Cassandra snuggled into one, accommodating her small bones to its limited space. A delicate porcelain plate perched on her knees as she fed bits of Rebecca's muffin to her poodle.

"It's probably got bran in it," she said, wrinkling her nose. "And that crap makes the little guy run."

"No doubt," Rebecca said drily, "but it'd better not happen here. Why don't you park him in the bathroom until you leave?"

"He'd be lonesome there." Cassie's voice betrayed a quaver that surprised Sue. It was abruptly a child's voice, hurt, indignant. "How would *you* like to be shut up in the bathroom? All by yourself? For hours . . ."

Rebecca asked with sudden gentleness, "Did that ever happen to you, Cass?"

And Cassie's voice shifted to its usual tone and humor. "Yeh. Back in Muskenaw. At a party. I got locked in the bathroom and they had to call the fire department to get me out. Vanessa was furious because they were fussing about me. It was *her* birthday. . . . Of course Sister was very forgiving about it, even though it spoiled her party. She said, 'You're my clumsy little sister, but I love you.' " . . .

Vanessa returned at noon, the small gilt-and-porcelain clock on the center bookshelf chiming the hour. She was compulsively prompt. Her key was in the door before Flossie could attend to it. She wore a Mainbocher tweed wool, copied in Italy from the original, in a becoming blue, with her coral necklaces and bracelets and a small turban flat to her ears and high above her prominent forehead. She put her white gloves and purse on the chest in the hall, which held the morning's mail, and came toward them, smiling winsomely.

"Oh, Sue," her voice was affectionate, indulgent. Sue offered her cheek, but Vanessa kissed her lightly on the mouth. As she did Rebecca and Cassandra.

She sat down in the other bergere opposite Cassandra. Seen together, Sue thought, they were quite dissimilar. When they were youngsters, the curly fair hair, the enormous eyes, the Victorian rosebud mouths gave them a marked resemblance. Cassie ignored time's erosion. But when Vanessa loosened her signature silk scarf, the sagging muscles under her chin were obvious.

"Did you have your shot?" Cassie asked.

"Oh, yes." Vanessa placed her hand gingerly on her neck. "It's rather painful, and one must rest at the doctor's office for a half-hour. But I wish you'd reconsider, Sister. They'd do you good."

"Sister has discovered the elixir of youth," Cassie announced lightly. "Whenever she comes on some new marvel, she insists on sharing it with her family and friends."

"What's the latest, Vanessa?" Rebecca asked, lighting a fresh cigarette.

"K-3." The poodle returned from inspecting the room and settled at Cassie's feet. "It's this marvelous serum by Dr. Ana Aslan, the Rumanian doctor. It's really a miracle drug."

"Oh," Rebecca said, "I thought it wasn't allowed in the country."

"Vanessa has ways," said Cassie tartly. "She smuggles in anything from jewels to Perrugina chocolates to Dr. Aslan's serum. You're kidding yourself, Vannie. It's nothing but novocaine."

Vanessa flushed, and for a moment it seeemd to Sue that she was on the threshold of a display of temper. But she merely smiled and said, "If you'd listen to me, Cassandra, you'd be far better off. I mean the best for you, after all . . ."

"No shots. No happy pills, either."

Vanessa's brow lifted. *Happy pills*, Sue thought. *Was Cassie on uppers?*

At lunch Cassie complained that, "Sister neutralizes everything with soya extender or wheat germ, it's all so *bland.*"

"But very good for you, Cassie." Vanessa was stern, as though speaking to a stubborn child.

Cassie's eyes became blue sparks of mischief. "I think I'll repair to McDonald's. Anybody care to join me?"

Vanessa blinked, then elected to join in the general laughter.

The mood lightened, the talk ranged from fashions to the theater to inflation, all on a superficial level. They had coffee in the living room, helping themselves to delicate chocolates from Plumbridge's, although Vanessa was vehemently against sugar in any form.

"Sue is working on the chronology of my films today," Vanessa said. "Cassie, do you have yours?"

Her sister shrugged. "I don't know where to find them."

Vanessa chided her sternly, "You should keep them in a cabinet. They're *important*."

"Oh, for heaven's sake, who cares about what film came first! They were all one-reelers and perfectly ghastly. You were fifteen and I was fourteen and we looked like old hags."

"Only because of those Cooper-Hewitt lights ... but let's not get distracted. To start at the beginning—"

Rebecca inhaled luxuriously, hoarded the smoke and finally exhaled. "Chronology begins in the womb," she commented. "It's the only time you're a free soul. The minute you emerge from the birth canal, screaming bloody murder, you're never again free. No one can fight the destiny of his umbilical cord!"

"Oh, Rebecca, that's not so—"

"Certainly it is. Consider yourself, my dear. Had your mother continued in an unhappy marriage, wouldn't *your* life have been different? You might have settled for good in Muskenaw. Married there—"

"A perfectly nice boy. Like Eric ..." Cassandra interrupted.

Vanessa remained calm, ignoring her. "Mother was delicate and unprepared for the hazards of the life that was forced on her. But she showed remarkable fortitude."

"A trait that she passed on to you and Cass," Rebecca said, and nodded emphatically.

"Mother had the courage to walk out on a difficult marriage," Vanessa explained to Sue. "It was a time when divorce was unthinkable. She had two small daughters to support and no profession. But she managed—"

Before she could continue, the doorbell chimed and Flossie opened the door to admit two men, one youngish, lanky, redheaded, freckled, looking like a farmhand in his faded jeans and suede jacket; the other middle-aged, portly, his gray cropped hair and heavy face reflecting the dignity of his gray suit and topcoat.

"Miss Oxford is expecting us," the older man said.

"Oh, yes." Vanessa came toward them, her hands outstretched in welcome. "Will," she said to the younger man in a low, intimate voice, "how *good* of you." She waited until the other took off his topcoat and then guided both into the living room and made the introductions.

"Will Wattenburg, you know, he was at the retrospective. And this is his friend, Sidney Nathan. Mr. Nathan is a builder. He is responsible for the new building on West 56th Street that has already won all sorts of awards. Now, if you'll excuse us, we'll work in the dining room. Mr. Nathan has some ideas for me . . ."

After the dining room door was closed, Rebecca asked, "What's that all about?"

"Sister never confides in *me*." Cassie shrugged. "But I'll bet anything it has something to do with the Master," she said, biting into a chocolate.

Twenty minutes passed before the door opened and Vanessa led the men out and directed them to her picture gallery. "This is my favorite portrait of Joshua Fodor," she told her guests. "The combination of dreamer and doer . . ."

"Wait till my kids hear who I was visiting today," Sidney Nathan said. "Will they be impressed!"

"Are they interested in film?" Vanessa asked.

"What kid isn't today?"

"Then they have seen *Jesus Christ—Son and Savior?*"

"They sure have! They like to remind me that Jesus was a rebel too."

"Perhaps you'll bring them here for tea? I could tell them how *Jesus* was filmed."

"That'd be great, Miss Oxford. I'll go up in their estimation. And don't worry, Miss Oxford. I'll take care of everything."

They left and Vanessa returned to the living room. She suddenly looked drained.

"The Joshua Fodor Cinema will be in Mr. Nathan's new building." She sounded as though she were making an announcement to the press. "And periodically, I'm glad to say, they will screen

Mr. Fodor's films along with foreign contemporary films. There's a world, especially of young people, waiting to admire his genius. I am very pleased."

"The Year of Joshua Fodor," Cassie said.

Vanessa held the stage with her plans for the Joshua Fodor Cinema. Afterward Cassie remained with her; Sue and Rebecca left.

Rebecca called a cab. "Can I give you a lift?"

"No, thanks. I'll walk."

"You sound like you have something on your mind ... can I help?"

Sue smiled. "Well, nothing serious. But it was interesting that when Vanessa was just with us, it was all so ... well, almost like a girls' dormitory, you know, chummy and relaxed. But when the men came, there was such a change in her. It was as though an electric current were switched on."

"It was. Something happens to her in a man's presence. A switch *does* seem to go on.... Take a lesson from her, Sue. I didn't, which was foolish of me. Vanessa, as they say, knows where it's at. She always did ... even sixty years ago. She's never forgotten it. And she never will."

THE PRESENT: SUE WANDERS DOWN MEMORY LANE

MORE THAN SIX MONTHS had passed since Sue began work on the Fodor chronology, and with Vanessa loathing dates so, Sue felt a marvelous sense of discovery whenever she stumbled on a clue that put Vanessa and Cassie in the right historical context. Among them:

In *The Lost Daughter and the Gypsies,* Vanessa Oxford appeared for the first time in a leading part. She appeared in many pictures of that period in small roles. . . .

and:

The Transformed Tomboy: Was the first picture in which Peg Dalton had the lead and Vanessa a secondary role. . . .

The Woman Thou Gavest Me: With Lorraine North, henceforth to be known as the New World Girl, the logo for Joshua Fodor Pictures. . . .

Lorraine North . . . wasn't she at the retrospective? The elderly woman using a cane. Vanessa was courteous to her but rather short. Lorraine North was in *The Weaker Sex?,* with Vanessa as the betrayed girl, Richie Doyle as the man, and Lorraine as the seductress. Strange, Sue thought, Vanessa never spoke of Lorraine.

Sue also found memoranda in the boxes from Fodor to himself or his secretary, voluminous notes, and photographs from newspapers and magazines that he evidently used to create his backgrounds.

The photographs showed a lower Fifth Avenue certainly different from the one Sue knew. Handsome townhouses of French architecture, walks with abundant trees, horse-drawn omnibuses. And young men in blazers, flat caps and side whiskers. And the lords of creation—the Vanderbilts, the Astors, the van Cleaves, the Schuylers, the Goelets.

There were notes in a man's handwriting . . . Fodor's!

Must try to sign Vernon and Irene Castle for a film. She was foolish to have her hair cut, even though the "bob" is sweeping the country. A woman's crowning glory is her hair. (Idea for a two-reeler?) . . . .

Saw Frances Starr in *The Easiest Way,* about prostitution. Audiences accept it as long as the prostitute is punished or seeks expiation. The whore and the preacher, sure-fire theme. . . .

Marie Dressler appearing in a film *Tillie's Nightmare.* She has the face of a young bulldog. Good for a boarding house owner. . . .

An advertisement for a book called *The Rosary* had a notation: Make heroine somewhat older but beautiful. Lorraine? A photograph of John and Ethel Barrymore, both incredibly handsome, playing in the theater in James M. Barrie's *A Slice of Life*. Underneath, Fodor had penciled, "Griffith has their older brother, Lionel, working for him. I may be able to use the power of persuasion on John." ...

Another note:

This child has extraordinary feeling. Deserves attention. Should be developed. Superior to her sister. . . .

It was a picture of Cassandra Oxford. All purity and innocence before life had bruised her.

And the war with her sister was launched, presided over by The Master.

In Vanessa's bulging files Sue discovered a bonanza: Rebecca's thoughts on the first generation of movie stars and their Svengalis. . . .

"The first stars of the silents sprang from a long line of *no fathers*. Especially Joshua Fodor's little actresses. Fodor was partial to the nubile girls who were the support of their mothers. All pretty, breastless, enormous eyes and fair complexions, scarcely out of childhood, favored by the innocent sexuality of girls on the brink of maturity.

"Girls flooded his offices, and if they appealed to him, they were hired. They didn't know the first thing about screen acting, but then who did? Since Joshua Fodor was refining technique while he ground out hundreds of short films, he and his players were learning together.

"The little girls started life poor and anonymous—underprivileged, although that wasn't a word in popular use in 1915. Vanessa often referred to herself as 'Little Orphan Annie.'

"Three years and X number of films later, coached and molded by Fodor, these Fodor heroines were known all over the country. And soon after all over the world.

"From two rooms and a Murphy bed to a spacious house looking over Hollywoods Hills. From doing the dishes and laundry to a staff of cook, chauffeur, butler, upstairs maid, laundress, personal maid.

"No wonder they lost all sense of proportion.

"Consider this: girls of small education, mostly provincial, unfamiliar with their own tongue, lacking manners, background, polish to give them poise and self-assurance.

"In their wake came along a new breed of humanity—movie fans—who elevated these young girls to the level of goddesses, endowing them with every possible virtue. The older character actresses were obliged to look after the younger ones. Girls were expected to keep regular hours, to have enough sleep so they would be fresh for an early morning call.

"No man ever swore in a girl's presence. No drinking was allowed. Yet the studio was Fodor's saloon, his locker room, the retreat where all-night sessions of poker took place. His male staff were his pals.

"Several of the staff once told me that Fodor was essentially a loner. That for all his generosity and kindness there was something that set him apart. A kind of isolation that made you feel sorry for him.

"During the summer of 1914 that Vanessa and Cassie spent in Muskenaw, just before World War I, we would save all our nickels for visits to the local movie house. This was before the Oxford sisters had any prospect of ever getting into the movies. As a matter of fact, they looked down on films—*they* were, as they liked to say, 'of the legitimate theater.' But that didn't keep them from loving films. How they admired the images that flitted across the screen! They couldn't believe they were real people.

"Later, fans would say the same thing to them. 'We never believed you were real!' "

Among several memos to Vanessa: "A love affair can be as constricting as a joyless marriage."

And another, which Rebecca evidently sent after Vanessa appeared in *The Passions of a Portuguese Nun:* "Do you have the feeling that we don't allow ourselves to see the obstacles in our lives until we are ready to overcome them?"

And Sue found more notes—these on the birth of the movies:

"From the very beginning, it was dog eat dog.

"At first the action was centered in and around New York City.

"Both Vitagraph and Biograph were turning out first-rate products, which gave Joshua Fodor something to aim for. There was already a superior motion picture of *The Life of Moses*. A three-reel version of *A Tale of Two Cities*. Essanay promoted the first cowboy idol, Bronco Billy Anderson. Along came Tom Mix (happily married) and William S. Hart (who lived with his sister).

"Griffith had little patience with Mack Sennett's obsession with comedies about the police. But Fodor, who'd remained friends with Sennett, even after leaving Griffith, understood and applauded. To slip on a banana peel, to be clobbered in the face with a pie, to cringe behind the wheel of a Model-T Ford hanging on a cliff, to participate in the wild chases of the Keystone Cops— these intrigued Fodor. Vanessa told me he said that Sennett had a great talent for deflating stuffed shirts. And his audiences loved him for it. But Fodor also used to chide Sennett for two-timing Mabel Normand, who drowned her sorrows in drugs and death. Which, I confess, sounds like one of Fodor's more florid subtitles.

"According to Vanessa the director Fodor most admired wasn't Griffith but a Frenchman, Maurice Tourneur, who he said had a gift for bringing out the best talents in his players. *Alias Jimmy Valentine* was his, and later, *The Bluebird*. Tourneur, though, lacked the sense of cruelty and latent sadism that Fodor was to use in creating suspense, which related him to Erich von Stroheim, whom he also, not surprisingly, greatly admired."

And then more on the early business side:

"As early as 1913 Jesse Lasky and Samuel Goldfish founded the Jesse L. Lasky Feature Play Company. Their studio was an old barn on Vine and Sunset Boulevard, which was where they produced *The Squaw Man*. And Paramount Company was born.

"The trek west came about by accident.

"In 1910 Thomas A. Edison was constantly threatening suits for patent infringements. Some of the film companies escaped lawsuits by going to California. Besides safety from Edison's lawyers, they found a good climate, much sun, little rain, the ocean, the mountains, the desert. Hollywood, in the foothills of the Santa Monica Mountains, was a glorious stretch of fragrant orange groves and farmland.

"Fodor denied it, but he knew the time would come when he'd

migrate to Hollywood, for at least part of the year. Meanwhile, he was strongly attuned to movie activity in Europe, where film companies were also proliferating.

"Producers in a frantic search for stories took published material without giving credit to their sources or even thinking of paying for them. Audiences were hungry for new faces as well as those they were familiar with. Actually the great stage stars were faring badly on the screen. When Sarah Bernhardt played Queen Elizabeth, her style, so powerful on the stage, became overblown and comic before the camera. The exception was Eleanora Duse, who displayed her customary restraint.

"Fodor was slavishly admiring of Dr. Robert Wiene's German film, *The Cabinet of Dr. Caligari*, possibly the first film to examine madness, and a film that influenced many innovative directors.

"Most Italian productions emphasized staging and camera work. But he learned from them a spectacle was not a movie. A movie had to *move*.

"Fodor amused his audiences. He inspired them. He taught them.

"He never played it safe. Which was his glory. And his downfall."

Sue began seeing a good deal of Rebecca Kahn.

Originally it was at Vanessa's suggestion. Whenever Sue prodded her about various incidents in her life, Vanessa would say, "My memory is awful. Ask Rebecca. She'll remember even if she wasn't there . . . we were always in touch."

What Vanessa did discuss was her background . . . Aunt Annie and the cousins in Michigan, relatives on her mother's side. Her father evidently left no kin, she knew practically nothing about his people . . . she longed for roots. . . .

"Sometimes she inflates her family way out of proportion to the facts," Rebecca told her. "They were good people, a step above blue collar. But Vanessa has always cherished her fantasies."

"In so many ways, she isn't what people think she is," Sue said.

Sue and Rebecca were having tea at the Women's Exchange, sitting in a corner enjoying the fresh strong brew and slices of a rich Lady Baltimore cake. "Can you believe it, when I came in yesterday morning she was standing on a chair ladder in the middle of the kitchen, screwing in the fixture that Flossie couldn't reach."

"She's a bundle of complex emotions, all right," Rebecca said. "Sometimes she's fussy and spinsterish and right out of *Ethan Frome*. Other times she's remote, sort of other-worldly, especially when she just sits quietly staring into space. She has a strong spiritual streak, but her idea of God is rather childish. She's always asking Him for favors, and she's constantly making bargains with Him. The odd thing is"—Rebecca laughed—"that for her, it seems to work."

The creamy coconut frosting left a little white rim on her wide upper lip. "After all, God was good to her, steering her into the path of Joshua Fodor."

"Did Vanessa appreciate her fantastic effect on men?" Sue wondered.

"She certainly did, as I've already told you, from the time she was scarcely more than a child. From the time she traveled with those shabby troupes and the favorite "uncle" held her on his knee. From the time she spent a summer in Muskenaw and Eric, the doctor's son, fell wildly in love with her." Rebecca's voice was divided between admiration and asperity. "She was very young, innocent, wide-eyed and proper, but she already had a talent for leading a man on, promising whatever he wanted and then drawing back. She was elusive. Men were crazy about her, they wanted to conquer her—what benighted male doesn't want the unattainable? She had what Dietrich and Garbo had, an appeal that fascinated *both* men and women." She looked closely at Sue. "Do you think I'm disloyal?"

Sue didn't know how to answer.

"I'm not, Sue. Not at all. I love her dearly. Not as much as I love Cassie, but enough. Still, I've always been aware of the woman behind the film image. I understand her wheels within wheels." And sometimes she wished she didn't.

"The true story of her life and its effect on those close to her will be told only *after* she dies. But by then there won't be anyone to tell it."

"You . . . ?" Sue was tentative.

Rebecca shook her iron-gray hair and the curls tumbled over her prominent eyes, shutting out the pain.

"She will go down in film history as the first great legend. She will be remembered as an American Eleanora Duse, which is what she has been longing for. But the secrets in her heart—and there are many—will die with her."

Rebecca leaned toward Sue, carried away by the moment. "She knows the truth about what happened to Joshua Fodor. She was on the yacht the last day of his life."

Wide-eyed, Sue wanted to hear more. But Rebecca suddenly stopped reminiscing, as though she had accidentally wandered too close to an abyss of pain and suffering.

Seeing that Rebecca was determined to say no more, Sue paid the bill and left the restaurant with her.

Rebecca took the first taxi that passed and left Sue without even saying goodbye. She was lost in her thoughts, lost in the long-ago world of Joshua Fodor's and Vanessa Oxford's greatest years together.

THE PAST: VANESSA REMEMBERS: EAST SIDE, WEST SIDE, AND WHY MR. FODOR WENT TO HOLLYWOOD—THE *REAL* REASON

MY LIFE has spanned nearly eight decades. They can be sectioned into compartments, starting with the Age of Innocence.

America as I first knew it was rural and credulous, but decent and kindly. True, we were gullible because of a lack of experience. This was especially true for women.

Rebecca said there wasn't much difference between us and women in purdah, except that we didn't wear the veil.

While working on a newspaper, she began writing her first

stories of the independent woman, a woman who sold insurance and real estate and was on a business level with men in her profession. Women readers devoured the stories in *Cosmopolitan*. Rebecca then went beyond fiction. She wrote crusading articles about Mrs. August Belmont and Carrie Chapman Catt who were in the vanguard fighting for women's rights.

"The way it is now, a woman has no right to her body," Rebecca was always fuming. "It's her husband's property and for his pleasure, and if babies come forth every year, well, that's *her* problem."

Rebecca said the Melting Pot hadn't blended. To be a Jew was a hazard, to be Irish was a threat, to be Italian was hopeless. It was indeed the time of power for the White Anglo-Saxon Protestant.

But I must say I wasn't particularly sympathetic to Rebecca's cries of social injustice.

Once our finances were in better shape, Mama, Cassie and I were enjoying our lives in New York before Mr. Fodor sent us off to California for six months of the year. Fifth Avenue was already the most elegant avenue in the world. Where the Empire State skyscraper stands today there was a magnificent scattering of Astor townhouses.

The section of the city between 42nd Street and Madison Square was known as *The Rialto*.

Mama, Cassie and I often walked after dinner along the beautiful streets, pausing to admire the new luxury hotels, the theater lobbies, the sense of elegance and glitter. Sidewalks were always crowded before curtain time with guests emerging from hotel lobbies, carriages and even a few motorcars.

It was not a time of great acting, but rather of great professional beauties who drew people to the theater. Their "cabinet size" photographs were collected by their fans. This period saw the birth of the press agent, who thought up scandalous stories about them.

I knew all about Lily Langtry, known as the Jersey Lily, who had been courted in New York by a rich socialite, Frederick Gebhart. The wardrobe lady loved to gossip about his extravagant courtship, the flowers, furs, jewels. It was rumored that he'd set her up in a handsome townhouse. Everyone was scandalized and longed to hear more and more.

In contrast, there was the American actress Mary Anderson, innocent and virginal. She was called "Our Mary," long before Mary Pickford became America's sweetheart.

I was torn between dreams of being the Jersey Lily and Our Mary.

Mama never allowed me to enjoy my appearance; she never said I was beautiful. I knew it only from the way I looked on film and the way men acted in my presence.

Yet the fact that Mama was chary with compliments had a curiously positive effect on me. I was never, never quite sure of myself. I had to fight a lack of confidence and I did it so successfully that nobody ever suspected how insecure I really was.

Mama sent me to study the Delsarte method of acquiring grace. But it never overcame my rather sturdy peasant walk.

Yet within no more than three years my name was included among the great beauties. It was all so unreal. I never believed it. Was it possible that the fragile, wistful girl with sorrowful eyes and masses of fair hair moving on the screen was really me?

It was surprising how quickly our images became familiar to audiences. Carl Laemmle was the first to understand the value of film personalities. If someone proved popular and attracted the patronage of audiences, he would use that individual again and again. Which is how the star system began. It's never changed. Even Samuel Goldwyn couldn't break down audience resistance with the millions he spent trying to make a star out of Anna Sten.

The fan magazines were an answer to the audiences' need to know more about their new idols. But when the magazines called the Fodor Studios to set up interviews or arrange for sittings for the players, Mr. Fodor was usually uncooperative.

"An actress' private life should be cloaked in mystery," he insisted.

But Dudley Norton, who had recently been put in charge of advertising, thought such pictures and stories were good for the company. Whenever he approached me, wanting to arrange for interviews, I refused, quite terrified. To have my words misinterpreted or misquoted by some writer terrified me. Then, too, I was afraid of the inevitable question . . . "Are you and Mr. Fodor in love? Is it true that you are going to get married?"

The only one who actually dared to comment was Louella Parsons, who was forecasting our marriage at least once a month.

"No one seems to remember that Mr. Fodor is married," I told a columnist who wrote for King Features about the film people. "No, I don't know his wife. She never comes to the studio."

Mr. Fodor was one of the last film pioneers to leave New York for Los Angeles.

The *truth* was that he was leaving because his wife was beginning to be a nuisance.

He once told me about her. She was a Russian girl, an immigrant to whom he taught English at fifty cents a lesson when he was very poor. She was small and delicately made, with rich, dark hair and the dark, enormous eyes of a waif. Sometimes she went hungry but she always had her fifty cents to pay for her lesson. She was all alone and he was sorry for her. He married her but they never really lived together. He supported her and told me that she refused to give him a divorce.

Which was just as well. He was not good husband material.

The pretty little girls of Hollywood were more his style.

THE PAST: VANESSA REMEMBERS: HOLLYWOOD WAS WHERE MOVIE QUEENS WERE MADE—NOT BORN

It took eight days by train to get to Hollywood in the early days. There were no sleepers. We sat up in day coaches, eating box lunches, bedding down cramped and jackknifed on the seats. Cassie and I didn't complain. Our childhood experiences had prepared us for discomforts.

In 1914 Los Angeles was a sprawling city with no particular charm.

Hollywood was a tranquil sleepy village on its outskirts, with big rambling houses framed by lawns and gardens.

You traveled from Los Angeles station to Hollywood by way of Hollywood Boulevard, which was colorful with palms and fresh bright flowers. You used streetcars for transportation. Or the jitney, a big open automobile, the forerunner of the bus.

Beverly Hills was country.

San Fernando Valley was a desert.

The air was golden and fresh, fragrant with the overwhelming scent of orange blossoms.

The Hollywood Hotel, a yellow wooden building with a front veranda filled with rocking chairs, was home to the more affluent actors. Mr. Fodor stayed at the Alexandria Hotel in Los Angeles. Most of us found rooming houses or small light-housekeeping apartments.

Mr. Fodor admitted, though reluctantly, that Los Angeles had the ideal climate and topography for making movies, with its nearby locations to fill every need.

We were in its primitive stage, pioneers gathered together at an outpost.

Mr. Fodor met with his backers, Lambros and Delos Boyar, in Los Angeles to decide on a property to be used for a studio. We caught a glimpse of them, two big, dark-haired, attractive men who seemed to be deferring to him. Shortly afterward we heard they had bought a sprawling frame house on an acre of land. Soon carpenters were building a stage and dressing rooms for men and women, and the house itself was reconverted into a darkroom, a room for cutting and splicing and a projection room. Downstairs were the business offices. Mr. Fodor now had a half-dozen rehearsal rooms and he arranged for a commissary where food would be sold at cost to the company. A dime for a sandwich, a nickel for milk or dessert, which was usually apple pie.

While the stages were in preparation there wasn't much for us to do. But Mr. Fodor didn't approve of our wandering away from the studio. So Richie and Cassie had ample time together and they were ecstatically happy. Mr. Fodor didn't seem to notice them.

Mr. Fodor's reputation had arrived in Los Angeles before him.

He was already a major figure in our infant industry. When he had dinner at the Alexandria or in one of the well-known cafes, people would point him out, saying, "There is Joshua Fodor, the director."

The wardrobe lady, who'd come with us and claimed the sun was easing her arthritis, told me that Mr. Fodor was making loads of money because his contract with the Boyar brothers gave him a royalty on every picture he made for them.

He didn't act like a rich man, though, except for his room at the Alexandria and his automobile and chauffeur. He was too busy supervising the building of the studio to pay much attention to any of us girls. Me included. Which worried me a good deal. Our secret little meetings had decreased in frequency over the past six months. Well, I decided, I must increase my interest in picture-making, which I did and which pleased him. Sometimes when I timidly asked a question, he would consider it before answering and smile. "You know, little miss, that's something to think about."

In front of others he called me Miss Vanessa or Little Miss.

During our precious moments, he called me Dear One.

Mr. Fodor was now obsessed with his work. Dudley Norton said, "I hope he doesn't run dry. He's beginning to repeat himself."

No. His preoccupation with his work didn't disturb me.

My jealousy of Peg was lessening, too. Because I was beginning to feel a sense of power. What pleasures he had time for me to give him left him completely satisfied and happy.

A foundation on which I could build a future. Of course, here in Los Angeles, there were more girls than Peg to be concerned about.

I resolved to:

Work at creating a kind of beauty and personality that would make me unique among his girls.

Be strong, for he demanded much of his performers.

Use my beauty for my profit.

I cannot remember how much of my resolve was conscious or otherwise. But I had my plan (what Rebecca calls my visions), and I steadfastly adhered to it.

The first time Mr. Fodor took me for an evening's drive in his car, his chauffeur waited while we walked along the quiet sleepy outskirts of the city. And when we found a quiet spot and lay down on the robe he'd brought with him, I felt a wildness, a recklessness that coursed through my blood. He'd remember this night, I vowed, using my tongue and my cheeks and my fingers in places they had never explored before, overcome by the scent of his male body, the violence of his response, his cry, like some wild animal.

"My God," he said later. "You little animal. You little animal."

I don't need a psychiatrist to tell me when my night terrors began.

THE PAST: VANESSA REMEMBERS: REBECCA SAYS, HOLLYWOOD IS WHERE YOU STRIP THE TINSEL TO SEE THE TINSEL UNDERNEATH

THE PRESSURE to go commercial began early.

The battles between the director-producer and the Front Office were endless, although the Boyar brothers were tolerant of Mr. Fodor's mounting expenses for each new film because the finished products were profitable and lauded by the press, which was now taking films seriously.

Adolph Zukor presented the great Sarah Bernhardt in *Queen Elizabeth*, thus establishing his Famous Players. Other producers were signing up famous stage and operatic stars, who received endless columns of newspaper publicity and failed with embarrassing regularity before the camera.

Mr. Fodor made no overtures to established players. He still enjoyed discovering and developing talent. His troupe of girl actresses might all seem similar, but his choice of male performers was more catholic. His leading men were virile and earthy without being brutal. And they were beautiful men, particularly Neil Bradshaw, whom Mr. Fodor discovered when Neil was out at the coast during his summer vacation. Neil was a junior at Princeton, a superb swimmer and tennis player. He had the rangy good looks that made Gary Cooper a top box office star some years later. All the Fodor girls were captivated by him.

Not that Mr. Fodor had time or interest to give to anything outside of his films. As Fodor Productions grew in popularity, the Boyar brothers pressured him to turn out larger and more important movies. Which pleased him, but at the same time demanded all of his resources.

"A good director is a god." Mr. Fodor was not being blasphemous during an interview for *Photoplay*, but he had developed a tendency to pontificate. "He breathes life into his characters. He sets up obstacles his characters must overcome. He satisfies his audiences' need for escape from reality. And also gives them insight into their emotions."

Movies were no longer solely the entertainment of the early immigrants crowding the ghettos. They were now accepted by the middle classes. The early entrepreneurs were children of the ghetto and their films reflected their cultural dreams and orthodox morality. The whore and the madonna—these were the two extremes of womanhood they understood. Their mothers remained their guiding light long after they were mature men.

As witness, Louis B. Mayer, who chased his little actresses around his desk.

Mr. Fodor took his little actresses for a walk in the woods.

Rebecca is funny. I love her humor when it isn't directed at me.

"Hollywood is a burgeoning orphanage in search of the father," she said. All those little girls and their ambitious mothers. And all the gross, earthy men with their casting couches (originally started, it is said, by Mr. Fodor's old friend Mack Sennett).

Whatever. When we arrived in Los Angeles on our first trip, we were in the midst of a Children's Crusade. Children, propelled by their ambitious mothers, migrated here in hordes, feeding hunger on hope. Studios were besieged. Acting schools with no validity preyed on the naïve. Girls who ran away from home ended up in brothels over the Mexican border. Young talent went wild on money, drink and drugs.

The press set aside columns devoted mainly to building up already inflated egos.

As far as the Los Angeles natives were concerned, film people were pariahs. Excesses among the actors were blown up by the newspapers and condemned in the pulpits. The movie colony was considered The Untouchables.

Naturally, the movie people clung together. Sometimes they gathered at the Country Club in Vernon, a suburb of Los Angeles.

We had no social life, except when Mr. Fodor took us out for dinner and dancing. Even Cassie didn't see Richie away from the studio. Our small three-room apartment was a half-mile from the studio and sometimes the girls in the company met there for cocoa and cookies and gossip, which was their only form of conversation.

Because I never joined them, they considered me odd. But I was conscious not only of our good fortune but the fact that it might not last. I was always terrified of some unknown disaster ruining us.

Perhaps I'd always been a loner. Unlike Cassie, who was always bubbling over with high spirits, I could show the world only a serious sober nature. And because of my nature I found it difficult to accept our good fortune, whereas the other girls in the company took fame and money as a natural course of events.

Cassie and I were not much different from the other girls who came to work for Mr. Fodor as extras and bit players. Yet with each film, our reputations were growing. We were celebrities. Strangers wrote us the most personal and intimate letters. We were beginning to be recognized when we went shopping. It was unbelievable.

I was unprepared for what was happening. I couldn't handle it. Cassie was insouciant about it She was always clowning with her friend Ronnie Terhune, or she was off mooning with Richie. Nothing of this mad new reality seemed to touch her.

I knew there was a lifetime of intense work ahead of me. The girls used to laugh when they saw me off the set, reading a book. "Look at Vanessa, putting on airs," they said.

Well, I was a provincial at heart, which was perhaps a saving grace. I was friendly with everyone on the lot; I was merely following Mr. Fodor's advice to be polite and kind to everyone because you never knew when today's office boy would become tomorrow's executive.

I knew I must become a Personality, perhaps even a Star, before Mr. Fodor tired of me. So many girls sought his approval. Of course, he never saw one without his secretary being present. He was cautious. And busy. But suppose one drifted in who attracted him.

I had to devise some form of insurance.

Joshua Fodor was my destiny. I absorbed what was best for me. My strength was my devotion to him. I wanted only to serve him. In order to do so, I often had to tell him what he wanted to hear.

I had staying power, which pleased him. I was always at the studio, in case I was needed or could substitute for another. If he didn't ask me out for an evening, either for dinner or to come back to the studio for work, or pleasure, I never showed anxiety or anger the way Lorraine North had so foolishly done. I'd learned from that experience. A man detests *reproaches.* If he's uncomfortable or guilty, he will avoid you.

Meanwhile, my education was progressing.

I admired his power of concentration and tried to emulate it. He generously taught me the art of the motion picture as he had devised it. He taught me how to make a character come alive before the camera. He showed me how to move, how to use my hands, how to express feelings with facial expressions.

"Remember, your eyes are the mirror of your soul," he said. The statement wasn't original with him, but he had a talent for making it sound fresh. When we were having dinner in a restaurant, he would analyze the people at nearby tables. He was always watching people, picking up little traits that would be useful to develop a character.

As a result of all this I was closer to him than the other girls on the lot. We were developing a marvelous working relationship.

I even learned to cut film, which demanded patience and a dramatic sense, and Mr. Fodor was pleased with the results. He often
talked over a new film idea with me, and he paid attention to my
reactions. Because, as he said, women were his greatest fans.

I was so woefully ignorant.

There was no school for us on the Fodor lot. Years later, MGM
had a teacher and classes for their young talent like Judy Garland,
Mickey Rooney and Elizabeth Taylor. I was so inhibited by my
ignorance that I was too self-conscious to utter a word in front of
strangers. Instead I devised sign language. Using the expressive
facial expressions Mr. Fodor had taught me, I listened, rapt, like
a mute. At first I was terrified that my behavior would bore men.
But on the contrary they all seemed fascinated.

Sometimes when she was discussing my admirers, Rebecca
would say I had an elusive quality that drove them crazy.

She would say, "The very quality that illuminates Vanessa's art,
limits it."

Or, "Vanessa is the fantasy of every boy's adolescent dreams."

Sometimes, if she thought I played badly in a film, she
would say, "Madame One Note. How long do you intend playing
the innocent virginal girl who is wronged by the villain?"

"As long as Mr. Fodor wants me to," I'd answer.

She meant it for my good and I understood this.

But I attached more importance to the critic from the *Times*
who wrote, "Fodor's finest moments are the poetic insights he
brings to the bruised long-suffering Vanessa Oxford. He has discovered what she does in her flawless best . . . to suffer and suffer
and suffer."

Off the set, I lived by my own self-imposed private time table.
Work, preparation for work, rest after work.

I had so much to learn! Everything from writing in the back-
hand slanting script of the fashionable eastern preparatory schools,
to peeling a ripe fig or a peach at the dinner table, to enjoying
the right wines, to murmuring a few French phrases, enough to
convince a waiter I was knowledgeable.

Parties made me feel wretched. I always felt like a wallflower
and probably was one, even when Neil Bradshaw squired me. As
a matter of fact he invited me to a dance given by friends of his

family, Californians who ignored most of the film colony, and because I found him so very attractive I went. I'm afraid I was a dud.

I had no instinct for clothes so, as my salary increased, I bought a few designer clothes in Paris and had them copied in Italy. But my hair, which was long and thick, was never properly styled. I rolled the ends under in a kind of modified pageboy secured by an invisible hairnet.

I met Harry Kellogg at lunch one day at Lady Mendl's. He was not a doctor of nutrition then, but he was already preaching the importance of health-giving foods, and we became good friends. I learned from him the importance of help to nourish the thyroid gland and step up metabolism, and the value of good nutrition.

"Your body is your means to fame and fortune. Treat it like the precious commodity it is," he said.

I listened and I learned. From everybody.

From the night Mr. Fodor had chosen me as his Dearly Beloved, I had no real interest in anyone else. My intensity was concentrated on him. In the second and third years of our relationship, however, he often was interested in new young actresses, though briefly.

At such times a strange feeling took over, though I tried to deny it. To this day I cannot quite analyze it, because it wasn't really desire, or even jealousy. It was an inner burning, a craving, a restlessness that wouldn't be appeased.

Richie was the young man I was most comfortable with. But of course he was captivated by Cassie and I knew they were planning eventually to marry. To be honest, I was very attracted to him but I tried not to think about it.

Perhaps I was too tied up with Mama and Cassie, I thought. Perhaps I should be out on my own. It would be better for them as well....

When I sounded out Cassie about my taking a separate apartment, she looked at me with that cute lopsided smile.

"I need to be alone more," I said. "I want to study scripts."

"Quit your kidding." Cassie was laughing at me. "Nobody studies scripts. Mr. Fodor tells you what to do and that's it."

"I need to be alone."

"I won't tell Mama. But we all know that you're starting an affair with Neil Bradshaw."

Mr. Fodor always came back to me, even when another girl caught his temporary interest. As I said, I could usually lure him back with questions about his work. And my special skills. He loved to talk and I was a perfect listener.

I was helpful, dedicated, totally loyal to him. He appreciated these qualities in me.

I brought several young men to his attention, as well as a handsome character actress, much older than myself.

I remember reading at that time about the mistress of a French king, a clever woman who kept her influence on him long after he'd ceased to desire her. She was his friend and his confidante; he knew that of all his court it was she alone whom he could trust. She even chose the young girls for his bed. She had power.

I used to dream about her.

I began to understand something that has guided my life ever since:

You judge a woman by the man she lies under.

THE PAST: REBECCA'S NOTES: VANESSA OXFORD AS LIZZIE BORDEN?

THE DELICATE, fragile, spiritual Vanessa playing a murderess, a demented epileptic creature who hacked her father and her stepmother into bloody pieces of flesh?

It was a miracle of casting.

Who indeed *but* Vanessa? Vanessa as Lizzie, the frustrated spinster who adored her father, whose feelings for him came from a Greek drama. *Thou shalt have no love but thy father.*

Lizzie lost her mother when she was three years old. Vanessa could understand the loss. She had herself become her sister's—and her own—mother at an early, if not quite so tender, age. Or perhaps it was the early loss of her father, or her own instinctive sense—and appearance—of waifdom . . . Whatever, throughout the tense moments of Lizzie's trial, Vanessa was able to bring to the image of Lizzie, seated in the courthouse awaiting her verdict, the bewilderment of a lost, frightened child.

Vanessa believed that Lizzie endured through her fantasies—her love for her father went beyond the range of conventional filial sensibilities . . . there were symbols that, in the time of innocence, were ignored . . . Papa gave Lizzie a diamond ring that she wore on her ring finger; Lizzie in turn gave Papa a ring that he always wore.

How then could he betray her with another woman, her hated stepmother? To think this despicable creature could share the moments in papa's bedroom that were forbidden to Lizzie!

She wasn't stable. Epilepsy may have caused the blackouts and the crazed child reached out, irrational with anger and frustration. Could Lizzie have bludgeoned them to death during one of her seizures? She was given to odd behavior. A kleptomaniac, although her father was a rich man. The night she sat with the body of a friend's mother, and after she left the mortician discovered the corpse's underwear was missing. Lizzie's father was originally an undertaker. Such a strange raveled thread.

The Fall River legend was still alive when Vanessa and Cassandra were children. Women in the troupes were always discussing it. The truth remained a question mark. Lizzie went free but curiosity about her never died.

Fodor had been considering the idea of filming the Borden murder, and her friends were astonished when Vanessa agreed to play Lizzie. They tried to dissuade her. It would ruin her image. It did nothing of the kind. Lizzie remained one of her finest characterizations.

And those who saw the final scene, where she recalled the happy days with her dear papa, never forgot it.

In the productive rewarding years, both in money and acclaim, Fodor and Vanessa shared in the glory of a half-dozen major films.

Gradually, as I recall it, there was a change in their relationship. The delicate balance of power began to swing toward Vanessa. She was utterly dedicated to Fodor and his work, and even when she played a small part in a production, she was always there, his shadow, listening, absorbing like a sponge, so that when they discussed the project over dinner she had *constructive* ideas to offer.

She manipulated him with infinite tact. More than once when I visited the set I heard her say in her gentle, soft voice, "Mr. Fodor, you suggested this the other day—" And he believed her, or perhaps it was a way of saving face for him ... in any case, he let her get away with it.

But there may have been arguments and quarrels when they were alone. I remember her saying, "Sometimes Mr. Fodor is like a judge who has already condemned the victim without hearing all the facts because he's in a rush to get on to the next defendant."

I'm not sure whether she was thinking of his little actresses or his films. Perhaps both. His artistic attention span was considerable during those years, but his interest in a new girlish face was often short-lived.

He didn't believe in the star system, which other studios were cultivating. He was confident of his power to create a good actress out of commonplace clay.

After all, despite the fact that he'd originally been dubious of Vanessa's ability, he had developed her talents so artfully that she was one of the silent screen's legendary stars. The sad thing was that the emotions he taught Vanessa to portray were the only ones she understood and accepted as reality. Her life away from the studio, her experiences with other lovers (even when she was emotionally faithful to her Mr. Fodor) were part of a fantasy.

She drifted through what was reality to most of us, deploying her emotions, reacting to life's crises as though Mr. Fodor were at a megaphone, shouting directions. To cower, terrified of the world, crushed, weeping, the outcast, the orphan—and then in the end to be rescued by the knight who came riding in at the last moment.

This was her life style in the best years of *his* life.

233

Once, many years ago, when we were discussing woman's self-fulfillment, she said impulsively, for her, "A woman cannot be free as long as she is afraid of losing her man."

Which was the foundation of her attitude toward all men.

She set her own standards in her private life. For her public, she wore the straightjacket of propriety.

It must've taken the most fantastic self-control for her to keep her wild impulses in check. I remember when she was in Paris with Piers van Cleave. He took her to an international brothel, and the next day she gave me all the details of every form of erotica she had seen (and in which she may have participated, although she never confided this to me).

I was startled. "You, Vanessa, at an orgy?"

Her expression was prim. "An actress must experience everything in order to interpret whatever she's called on to do."

Many of the films during the last years of their relationship were the most sensitive of her career. Her Heloise in *Heloise and Abelard* was exquisite, with no indelicate suggestion of the castration, which was fantasized by and through Hans' camera. . . .

Fodor's *Joan of Arc* was the first film to represent Joan as a puzzled, frightened young girl who listened to her Voices against her will, and her death at the stake was so realistic that critics warned parents not to take their children to see it. Vanessa actually had to be treated for scorch burns.

The greater his reputation, the more demanding Fodor was of himself and his company.

More than ever, he created competitive jealousy among his people, believing it gave him the best results. He made each person understand that unless he did his best, he would be replaced.

He was never satisfied, he was always cutting, changing, trying variations. Did this work? Would it be better another way? Is the suspense *unbearable*?

Just before he embarked on his film *Jesus Christ—Son and Savior*, Vanessa said to me that he was becoming vain, that he was withdrawing from constructive criticism, that he became impatient with her when she made the most tactful suggestions.

She added sadly, "He believes in truth and justice. But his *audiences* want entertainment." We were both afraid for him.

Afraid that his passion for truth, combined with his need to be a success, would be too great a burden . . . would destroy him. . . .

We were both right and wrong.

He believed it was the greatest film he had ever made and that his public would agree.

He was both right and wrong.

Fifty years was a long time to wait to be properly recognized, to have one's vindication.

But Vanessa was determined he, and she, would have it.

And Vanessa had the *patience* of a saint.

After all, Fodor had taught her well.

Nine:

THE PAST: REBECCA REMEMBERS: *JESUS CHRIST—SON AND SAVIOR*

How I happened to become involved:

I'D TAKEN A leave of absence from my job as a reporter to work on a new book, but my funds were running low and the characters in my novel, especially the heroines, were balking my direction and going their own way, leaving me frustrated and unsure of myself and the worth of the project.

Vanessa offered me money to carry on until the book was finished. I refused her offer with thanks but that didn't quiet her anxiety, and the next thing I knew there was a call from Joshua Fodor. He was in New York for meetings with the Boyar brothers.

"I understand your father was an orthodox rabbi," he said.

"Yes, in a small town." I don't know why I felt it necessary to elaborate. Perhaps because of my childhood memories of when the little boys at school pelted me with snowballs and called me "dirty sheeny." "There were only five Jewish families."

"But you know something about the Jewish culture?"

"As much as an orthodox Jew allows his daughter to know, which is how to bless the candles, how to shave her head after her marriage and wear a wig so no other man will look at her, how often to go to the ritual bath so she is *clean* for her husband after her period, how to cook and wash and bring up her daughters in her image—"

"I'm about to start a film about the beginning of Christianity, which of course starts with the birth of Christ. I shall need someone who is familiar with the Jewish faith and can do research for me."

He hired me by telephone for a generous weekly sum. I was glad to put aside my manuscript and looked forward to working with Mr. Fodor and his company. Vanessa had confided she was to play two roles: the Virgin Mary *and* Mary Magdalene (reflecting Fodor's own conflict about women?).

Vanessa had arranged for me to come out on the Twentieth Century Limited, which left Grand Central at six in the evening. I still remember walking down the long red carpet that was spread the length of the platform and thinking of the three-day trip by coach over a bumpy track that marked my departure from Muskenaw to seek a reporter's career in New York. I suspect that was also in Vanessa's mind when she booked me for a drawing room. With the ticket she had enclosed an extravagantly generous check for what she called incidentals.

My first trip in style had a most therapeutic effect on my self-confidence. When we arrived in the Chicago station the following morning, I was already in better spirits. As the Pullman was attached to the Sante Fe Chief, I began to feel like a wanderer who sees the vision of El Dorado. Two days later, when I arrived in Los Angeles' Union Station, I was ready to work with Mr. Fodor, finish my novel, tackle any project. It had been a three-day rest cure, and when I saw Vanessa waiting for me in the station my gratitude was stronger than my usual self-defense of irony and sarcasm. I burst into tears as we hugged each other.

"I have the car parked outside," she said, nodding toward a redcap. Porters seemed to appear miraculously whenever she needed them, and one now took care of my meager baggage.

I wondered uneasily if she were going to take the wheel. Both Oxford sisters drove cars early. Cassie was an expert, she handled a car effortlessly with an air of confidence and you always felt safe with her. Vanessa, however, was a reckless driver. She seemed to feel obligated to pass everybody on the road, intersections meant nothing to her, she always felt she had the right of way. Perhaps there was indeed some truth, I thought, in the notion that a person's style of driving reflected his attitude toward life.

A chauffeur was standing at the door of her Packard, and on the way she told me she expected me to stay in her house in Los Angeles. We hadn't seen each other for several years, but had kept in touch by letter. I'd read about her, of course, in the papers and magazines, and even allowing for the exaggeration of the publicity men and the fan magazines, I could imagine the considerable change in her life style. Still, I was startled when I saw it.

The house Vanessa had bought for her mother was a charming French Provincial, white brick with a courtyard, espaliered fruit trees and tubs of specimen shrubs and flowers.

Mrs. Oxford greeted me affectionately, and Cassie, who happened to be home, was exuberant.

"It's like old times!" she said, hugging me. "Like Muskenaw!"

At home, the girls certainly didn't play the role of the fabulous film stars the world admired. They were simply the Oxford sisters who brought a cozy small-town ambience to their private life. The house was exquisite. Knowing how much her mother appreciated beauty and knowing too how stoically she'd suffered in their years of deprivation, Vanessa surrounded her with exquisite fabrics in soft pastels, fine French furniture, inlaid rosewood for her bed and dressing room (Directoire pieces for her own bedroom and Cassie's). Vanessa told me that she'd planned Cassie's bedroom, even to the generous closets. Not that it helped. Cassie was as disorderly as ever.

But she looked marvelous. They both did. I assumed it was the sun and the sea, because neither of them was addicted to the cosmetics that most film players used, obsessed as they were with the terror of age. Cassie ignored the whole subject, but Vanessa, with her usual concentration, attacked it through health.

Already a nutrition nut, she had found a Japanese farmer who grew specimen vegetables and twice a week drove in from the Valley to leave baskets of fresh produce that looked like paintings. Mrs. Oxford no longer had to prepare meals over a gas plate. There were four in help: a cook, a chauffeur who also served dinner, a maid and a gardener. Meals were served formally in the handsome dining room, set with old English silver, Royal Worcester china and Venetian glass that Vanessa had ordered from abroad. And yet, despite their splendid home, the Oxford girls seemed ill at ease. I had the feeling they resented playing roles expected of them as public figures. After all, they were now part of the upper movie strata, dominated by Mary Pickford and Douglas Fairbanks, who were already entertaining English nobility to enhance their social position. The foreign actors, whom American producers were importing to lend their films "class," created their own small exclusive colony in Hollywood, where Cassie was accepted more warmly than Vanessa.

Not that it mattered to Vanessa. She was still party shy. Whenever she was free from the studio, she devoted herself to her mother. Mrs. Oxford, a warm friendly woman, took pride in her daughters' achievements without allowing their egos to become inflated. She was the center of the household and many of the young stars who were Cassie's friends sought from her the mothering they'd missed in their lives.

Cassie had many admirers, but she didn't take any of them seriously. She usually, and casually, dated the leading man of her most recent film.

Vanessa concentrated exclusively on Joshua Fodor. She left for the studio early in the morning and seldom came home until just before dinner. Often Mr. Fodor returned with her. After they had eaten together from trays served in the sunroom, they discussed the new film in production or a future one. Vanessa was clearly an integral part of Mr. Fodor's life, and Mrs. Oxford said with innocent pride, "He depends so *much* on her."

Cassie merely looked pained.

"Does he come here often?" My curiosity was stronger than discretion.

"Several evenings a week. Vanessa usually accompanies him to screenings and many times even to business meetings with the Boyar brothers. Sometimes they get annoyed because Mr. Fodor has no idea of the value of money and he often overspends on a production. But when Vanessa sits in they know she'll do her best to control his extravagances. I really don't see how he could ever manage without her.

"And he never will," Cassie added lightly, "if Sister has anything to do with it."

Rebecca and Joshua Fodor:

I met Joshua Fodor again the second night after my arrival in Los Angeles. I was familiar with him from the sisters' early days on East 14th Street, but the few times I had met him were casual enough, and I doubted that he would have shown an interest in me except for Vanessa. She was always generous with her contacts and did her best to help her friends. That is, after she had cemented her own relationship—of course this is quite understandable. That is, you can't very well help others before you have entrenched yourself. Now can you?

Joshua Fodor must have been in his quite late thirties at the time. He was still lean, erect, and sunburned now, his leathery skin contrasting with his light hair, which lay clipped short to his skull. He had evidently had some work done on his nose. (Vanessa told me later the surgery was to correct a deviated septum, the result of a blow.) He certainly made a distinguished appearance. His suits now came from London, as well as his shoes and shirts. His manner was equally distinguished. He was more like a visiting professor of English literature on a sabbatical in the world of vulgar commerce.

Dinner was served by the butler and the maid, both in uniform, both wearing white gloves, a habit that Vanessa had adopted for her staff after a brief first visit to Italy.

Mrs. Oxford sat at the head of the table, Fodor opposite her with me at his right, Cassie next to me and Vanessa at his left. Flowers from the cutting gardens, heavy silver, English bone china, vintage wine, on a beautiful cloth embroidered by the nuns in a convent near Harold Kellogg's small castle, once the private lodge of an Italian king in upper Italy near the Swiss border. Kellogg had taste and shared it with his friend Vanessa.

Mrs. Oxford, small, exquisite, dressed in a fine Chinese robe, was bright and lively during the meal. Most of her talk was directed to Mr. Fodor but often it included me. I thought how fortunate she was to have daughters. And how fortunate the girls were to have her. She was every girl's dream of the ideal mother, gentle, compliant, suggesting tactfully but never ordering. So different from my own mother, who considered a day lost unless she could goad my father into verbal battle.

Dinner, impeccably served, was dedicated to Vanessa's health theories. No meat, but seafood steamed in a court bouillion and certainly the most succulent collection of fresh vegetables I'd ever seen. And, to top it, a sinfully rich chocolate mousse. Vanessa passed it up, so Cassie finished her portion too, licking the spoon with the unashamed pleasure of a child. Mr. Fodor found her performance amusing, his laughter deep and unrestrained. When Vanessa frowned, Cassie quieted down, blotting her mouth with her napkin.

I thought, Vanessa is afraid of his disapproval for *any* reason, no matter how trivial. He is security for her and her family; not the loving sort she might have had with young Eric, the lovesick boy in Muskenaw, but the support of a man who could make her the object of adulation by millions. She had made her choice, apparently without regret.

For Vanessa, working with Joshua Fodor meant a daily form of rebirth. How else could she justify it to herself . . . ?

For Cassie, it was easier to drift; power and adulation meant little to her. Of the two, it was Cassie who needed love the way people need oxygen. . . .

I was to stay in Hollywood through the entire filming of *Jesus Christ—Son and Savior,* and during those exhausting weeks the Oxfords insisted that I continue to live with them rather than move to the Château Montmartre.

The Oxford girls were no longer a part of a family of players. The days of a kind of boarding school friendship that linked the young actresses five years earlier were finished. Each actress lived apart from the others now, in comfort if not in elegance. They were now film luminaries, each much more jealous of the others than in the early days when Fodor often kept them in line by playing on their insecurities.

(Later, when Vanessa was so badly shaken by his treatment of her, I wondered why she hadn't understood his fear of permanent commitments.)

I wondered, too, how Vanessa had learned to give him direction, to further his work without deflating his ballooning ego.

"We have to keep him from preaching," Vanessa told me again, "or his fans will desert him."

Often before going to bed, Vanessa and I would sit reminiscing over a cup of herb tea.

"You know what surprises me," I said. "You earn a weekly salary that would have been unbelievable half a dozen years ago. You live in an elegant house. You have furs your fans have given you and jewels from Mr. Fodor. And you still think of yourself as a helpless waif."

She put down her cup and sat up on the chaise, her filmy robe falling in soft folds around her. Her hair was down around her shoulders and her face was clean of makeup and she reminded me of the small exquisite girl I had first met in Muskenaw ten years before.

And then, without dramatics, she told me of their squalid days on the road in third-rate touring companies. And of the time she saw a man fondle her mother. She knew that she had to be a success as an actress and earn enough so Mama wouldn't have to allow gross men like "Uncle" Ed to do those awful things to her.

"Vanessa"—I was moved by her account but it was so pitifully childish, surely it was time she faced facts—"has it occurred to you that your mother was a healthy young woman and quite possibly she *liked* what the man was doing to her?"

"I don't believe it!" and then she said something that I always remembered when gossip linked her with many men in Hollywood.

"Mama? Oh no!" She shuddered. "Sex is so unsanitary." ...

How did Vanessa develop into a woman so fascinating that men created fantasies about her? To begin with she was born beautiful. Her madonna smile was gentle, her eyes were brilliant with enchanting promises. She learned to establish an immediate rapport between a man and herself. She brought her talent for concentration to each man, stranger or lover, and offered it to him as a generous gift. *You are the sole object of my interest,* her glowing eyes suggested. *I am here only for you, no one else exists for me. I will care for you. Are you lonely? Do you need understanding? I am here ... do with me what you will....*

So much for her image. Let me tell you the truth about her as a woman.

Vanessa is frigid. She has always been frigid. She has always searched for the man who could excite her so the tension in her muscles would relax into ecstasy.

But she hates orgasm. She has always fought it.

Because she is utterly terrified of losing control. Over herself. And others.

It is a terror that fills her nights.

And she's aware of it every lonely day and night of her long life.

THE PAST: REBECCA—IN MY FATHER'S HOUSE, AND THE MAKING OF THE CHRIST STORY

"MR. FODOR, I'm not sure you picked the right person as a consultant to your film. As a child of an orthodox family, I'm painfully aware of the millions of Jews who've been slaughtered in the name of Jesus."

We were sitting on the sunporch of Vanessa's house, with night falling though there was still the bright sun. Fodor, Vanessa and I were in the first of many conferences. He tried to soothe me, but I felt it necessary to explain myself.

"In my home during childhood the name Jesus was never

uttered; indeed it was forbidden, as though its very mention might bring down pogroms on our little midwestern community. I had to pass the Catholic church on my way to school each day and I'd hurry by, terrified that they'd snatch me up and I'd be put to the wheel like the girls in the tales of the Inquisition my father used to read to us. Once I saw something glittery on the sidewalk near the church. I picked it up and immediately threw it away as though it were a flaming coal—it was a crucifix. This was my childhood"— I was aware of Fodor's intense gaze—"and if I suggest certain scenes, or write them, I am apt to be biased."

"Many of His people were biased against Christ in His time. But He taught a small percentage of them to *see*. And they spread His Gospel," Fodor answered, his voice sincere.

Vanessa was quiet as she looked at each of us. I knew she wanted me to succeed with Fodor, to bring me into her professional family, guaranteeing that I wouldn't go through another near-starvation period ... it was for this kind of generosity, which she'd shown often before, that I loved her dearly. At the same time, I worried that Mr. Fodor, and she, would find me a disappointment.

"I don't see Jesus as a statue in a long flowing robe and with a halo around His head." Fodor crossed his legs, leaned back in his easy chair and speculated aloud. His voice was resonant, with a hypnotic quality as he elaborated his point of view. "He was a true Jew and in His character and outlook, He was totally committed to the Jewishness of His heritage. But He was also a rebel. He was an angry young man. He spoke out against the injustices around Him. He was an idealist, especially compassionate toward the poor and illiterate, although they didn't understand His preachings. He was furious at the venality and stupidity around Him. He was a dreamer who dreamed of doing. He challenged those in authority, and, of course, they began to fear Him. . . . I see Him as poor, His clothes dirty and ragged, I see Him as a man who cannot find enough listeners for what He knows to be true—"

"But that isn't how we've been taught to see Jesus," Vanessa said, disturbed.

"Exactly." Her protest seemed to feed Fodor's enthusiasm. "My Jesus will be a man of the people. He will have rough edges that the rich do not have. His fishermen will be big-bearded, rude men who are inspired to follow Him. They too are rebels in search of a leader and they band together, with Jesus at their head, with the dream of freeing their country from the Romans."

Vanessa was unsure, but I found his concept exciting. It seemed to me that Fodor's approach would give the story of Jesus Christ a realistic, factual aspect that would help make it understandable to average people.

Understandable? Maybe. Acceptable? A hundred times *no!*

But we didn't realize it in the beginning.

Or that Fodor was carried away by his legitimate reason to preach.

Still, the closer I worked with Fodor, the more I developed respect for him. I began to understand better Vanessa's awe of him: his patience with the research, which he went over himself; his work with Hans Rolfsma and the electricians in planning the lighting for the scenes; his conferences about authenticity with the new wardrobe woman. Sketches that filled huge scrapbooks taken from Biblical references were the source books. He was everywhere, no detail escaped him, and slowly the illusion he was creating took over and the company seemed touched by a kind of religious fervor. Vanessa took to carrying a small leatherbound New Testament with her. Others discussed the Birth, the Crucifixion, the Resurrection. There were art books available to the actors containing some of the great Renaissance paintings of the Italian masters; Fodor wanted them for their authentic backgrounds. He was spending more extravagantly than ever before. I knew Vanessa was concerned because of the Boyar brothers. . . . "This picture must be a success or they'll never trust him again," she told me nervously. "He's so deeply involved that he's lost all perspective."

Each set turned into a small masterpiece of realism. He had progressed far since the days of the first studio set, which was nothing but a floor with canvas sides. Other directors often asked to come around to watch him filming, but Fodor discouraged them. They were, after all, forever stealing ideas from him.

Vanessa was to play two roles: the Virgin Mary and Mary Magdalene. It was the most creative stroke of casting in his career.

Joshua Fodor had great reverence for the Virgin Mary. And Mary Magdalene held a powerful fascination for him.

He hoped, among other things, to suggest that in Christ's time women were feared and therefore subjugated. Their sexuality had to be controlled. The high value placed on virginity gave men an additional weapon against them.

He intended to include ritual prostitution, human sacrifices and orgies common among the conquerors. Although he refused to use the Bible for sex exploitation, as de Mille did, his film nonetheless justified pictures of the licentiousness and the cruel superstitions of the times.

The company was, as always, in suspense until Fodor made his final casting choices. Except for Jesus. Fodor didn't choose this player from his company but went scouting for the right man, and found him, actually living in the hills like a young hermit. He was, appropriately, a Jesuit who had left his order for the wisdom of Eastern philosophies. Fodor didn't even screen-test him but, when we first met Christopher, a tall, angular young man with fair hair and a beard and haunted, searing eyes, we knew Mr. Fodor's choice was right.

"Christianity was founded on the concepts of the Old Testament," he said, "so it's basically not a Gentile religion." His words coincided with Fodor's belief that Jesus was a true Jew of his time and place, that Jesus accepted his Jewishness. His family was Jewish, he attended the synagogue to worship, he adhered to Jewish rituals, respected Jewish festivals and participated in the sanctity of the Temple, which he called "My Father's House." And when those in power feared Him, He said, "Think not that I have come to abolish the laws and the prophets . . . but to fulfill them."

Of all its many stunningly visual scenes, I remember most vividly the Birth in the stable.

It was in this scene that Hans Rolfsma showed his extraordinary talent. Vanessa had naturally dark circles under her prominent eyes. Hans usually washed them out with lights and then he retouched with additional lights to achieve the smooth facial effect. He had discovered that if he lit Vanessa's hair too much the result made her eyes glassy, so he used a back light that created the effect of a halo. As she lay on the floor of the stable, he used a white diffuser six inches off the ground, arranged the camera five feet off the floor, tried a yellow baby spot, then the Cooper-Hewitt two feet off the floor.

The Virgin Mary giving birth to the Christ child. On film!

Nobody had ever thought of her labor pains or how she had managed to deliver the child herself and cut the umbilical cord and bathe and wrap him in his swaddling clothes. Fodor concentrated on the ritual of the childbirth. The camera caught her agony, her heavy breathing, her instinctive pushing, the way she held her legs up. He had a gynecologist on the set to tell him the reactions of a woman in labor. He arranged to photograph a woman in labor, paying her handsomely for it, and then used that in his film. (Vanessa later told me that when Fodor's parents first came to America his mother was a midwife in the ghetto, and that he'd actually gone with her a few times and never forgot the screams he heard as he waited for her outside the bedrooms.)

The last close-up of this scene, really the prologue, showed Mary, serene and lovely, the Child in her arms, looking like the classic madonna.

Vanessa disapproved of it. "Mary was human. She was young and frightened. She was in labor a long time. First babies don't come that easily. If you're making it realistic, she should be exhausted, unkempt, her hair damp from sweat."

Fodor was angry with her. "She *has* been shown human. Now she must become the Virgin Mary."

In the rest of the film, he combined reality with a certain spiritual beauty. You saw the boy Jesus and the young rabbi Jesus, to whom so few paid heed. You saw him with Mary Magdalene. If Vanessa was the essence of spirituality as the Virgin Mary, she was the incarnation of physical love as Mary Magdalene. The madonna and the whore.

The Crucifixion, too, was extraordinary. I cannot write about it even now without my imagination hearing screams of the Christ as the nails were hammered through His flesh.

Jesus Christ—Son and Savior was hailed by agnostics and atheists as a work of art. And condemned by the Church. It opened to crowds, to mobs, to police lines.

The bottom line, as they say, was: it lost money. The Boyars, devout Greek Christians, cut their ties with Joshua Fodor.

A half-century later, today, in the theater named for Joshua Fodor, it has been playing to standees for six months and hailed as a masterpiece of realism.

THE PAST: REBECCA REMEMBERS:
AFTER THE FALL

THE SHOWING of *Jesus Christ—Son and Savior* marked a change in Vanessa's career.

It would be, in retrospect, her finest hour. An "hour" that dragged out for days, months, years, during which time she dedicated herself to the task of seeing that the film received recognition. It didn't matter to her that many critics disliked it, that the Catholic world seemed dedicated to its failure and banishment. That those players whose reputations as Fodor players would have guaranteed them generous contracts with other companies suddenly found themselves unemployable.

It was the first blacklist in Hollywood.

Vanessa joined Fodor, defending him, standing by him, accompanying him to cities where he made pleas for fair assessment of his film. He spoke out strongly against censorship. He met with priests, bishops, even cardinals to explain his position in telling the story of Christ not as a glorified myth but as a factual revelation. He suggested that the Lord did not intend to deck His Son with myths but with humanity, that the film was concerned with a man's reactions to his time and place.

His beliefs were considered blasphemy.

During one meeting in a Missouri town hall, while Fodor and Vanessa were trying to explain the essence of the film, they were actually stoned. Not by the tough kids of the town but by "respectable" middle-aged men and women. They escaped with the help of police by way of the rear entrance, but not before Fodor suffered a bruise on his head and Vanessa bled from a pebble cut on her cheek. Her right hand, crushed during the stoning scene in the film, was still weak. She told me later that in the car driving to the station he took her hand in his and lifted it to his lips. "My friend, my love, forever."

She was touched. He was so chary about showing any feelings. His gesture began another phase in their relationship. She was bound to him forever.

He listened to her. This stubborn, arrogant, generous man leaned on her, became dependent on her. She took this as his respect for her judgment. I suspected it was also his panic. He was learning that he was not always right. That he could even be wrong.

Newspapers refused advertisements for the film. Parents demanded the film be banned in every state, even where censorship didn't exist. Almost worst of all, the *Russians* loved it, or said they did. . . .

"No one mentioned the marvelous technical effects," Vanessa complained angrily to me. She meant Fodor's use of half- and quarter-screens, the breathtaking iris opening on Jerusalem, the fade-in and fade-out to indicate the hours Mary was in labor. And the best photography Fodor and Hans had ever devised: the clarity when it was necessary; the soft focus when he suggested miracles; the close-ups of Jesus with the people, performing His miracles; the close-up of Mary Magdalene—a commingling of lust and expiation in her painted lips and spiritual love.

"We are not punishing Fodor, who has a great reputation, but we are protecting ourselves from his defamation of our Lord," wrote a famous Protestant minister.

"What they're protecting is the status quo," said Fodor. "The Romans, not the Jews, killed Jesus. It was Pontius Pilate who was responsible for the Crucifixion."

It didn't matter. Joshua Fodor lost. He was stripped of his power if not his fame, now turned to notoriety.

Cassie saw it again recently, just before she was committed to Sunset Hill Inn.

"Vanessa plays Mary Magdalene like a virgin who's been assaulted in a gang rape," was her comment.

The Boyar brothers withdrew their backing. No other money men came forward to underwrite his future projects. Joshua Fodor had already exhausted his own funds in defending his film. He could borrow no more. He could not, would not, produce a movie without having absolute control, and the studio moguls would not give him money without *their* having absolute control.

"The money men!" Vanessa exploded to me. "They'll destroy anybody who stands in their way! They've forgotten all the money Mr. Fodor made for them."

She was seeing a good deal of Mr. Fodor. Sometimes his new manager, John Kinney, joined them at lunch or dinner at the Oxfords'. Kinney, a small wrinkled man with protuberant eyes behind thick glasses, a flat nose and an adding-machine mind, had great respect for Vanessa. Like every man who dealt superficially with her, he soon became her devoted slave.

"She looks so . . . so ethereal," he said, "but she's the most practical woman. She knows every side of making films and she's saved the boss from some bad mistakes. If he'd listened to her while he was making *Jesus Christ* he wouldn't have gone so far off the track. He's offended everybody for his so-called work of art."

I told him I felt guilty, that I was afraid I'd contributed to its failure.

He shook his head. "Fodor is an artist and a gentleman. But he's surrounded now by people who feed his ego. Except Vanessa. She gives him the truth, even though she sugarcoats it. And even then he gets annoyed with her sometimes. He loves to surprise and shock his audiences. Well, this time he went too far."

"What will this do to Vanessa's future? She's had no offers from other companies." It seemed incredible. Vanessa a has-been at twenty-one?

"Oh, it'll die down after a while. Unless she marries him."

"You think that's a possibility?" I was divided between hope for her—after all her tie to him was *so* powerful—and fear it would harm her.

"His wife died recently." John Kinney suddenly looked anxious, as though he'd talked out of turn. "It wasn't in the papers."

"What was wrong with her?"

"TB. I guess she picked it up when she was a young girl. Fodor says it was all over the tenements."

"How did he take it?"

Kinney shrugged. "They'd never been close. I think he was sorry for her. That's why he married her. He's got too much on his mind these days to grieve about a wife he didn't really love."

It sounded heartless to me, but then I had always been aware of a cruel streak in Fodor's nature that was in contrast to his usual kindness and consideration. He also sat in judgment on himself and didn't like what he saw. This great man did not have respect for himself. He did not love himself. I knew it without knowing why.

I knew Vanessa, too. I knew all her little tricks of self-advancement. I knew that the men who admired her were no match for her (except Joshua Fodor, who was her fatal weakness). I knew she could be gentle and submissive until she realized her power, and then in a gentle, submissive way she would manipulate that power without seeming to care what it did to others. I knew nobody could make her do what she didn't want to do.

But I also knew the other side of her.

I thought of her many kindnesses, her generosity not only to her mother, Cassie and me, and Fodor, but to whoever turned to her for help. Her stinginess disappeared in the face of a friend's or co-worker's needs. I knew she was paying for the support of the original wardrobe lady in the company, who was now helpless after a series of small strokes and needed around-the-clock care. I knew she'd set up a trust fund for her mother and Cassie, in case anything happened to her. (The fact that Cassie didn't need it, earning nearly as much as Vanessa, is beside the point.)

Admiration and envy, that was my bag. But admiration was always stronger than envy. I never imagined the time would come when I'd feel pity for Vanessa.

It did.

She was having a great deal of discomfort, although she never complained, from the injury to her hand she'd suffered during the filming of *Jesus Christ*. Her mother told me that Vanessa often couldn't sleep because of the pain, but refused to take any medication to ease it.

Shortly thereafter the press carried in its movie columns a notice that Miss Vanessa Oxford was leaving for Germany "to secure treatment for her injured hand. Her sister, Cassandra, will accompany her, although it means turning down a starring role in a new Paramount film. . . ."

The girls were to sail unobtrusively from Canada. Before their departure Vanessa asked me to lunch with her and she told me, without going into details, that this was the most terrible moment in all her life. It startled me.

I had never seen her cry before.

How kind of Cassie, I thought to stand by her.

It was only years later that she finally told me the truth.

The girls were gone for nearly a year.

"This is their first vacation," Mrs. Oxford said. "I hope they make the most of it."

She didn't join them because of her health, which wasn't stable. However, they kept in touch, and she read their letters to me. They spent time in Italy with Vanessa's friend, Harold Kellogg, the health nut, who was now an authority on nutrition and included among his new friends royalty as well as film stars.

Whenever I was in Los Angeles on business—when a story or a book of mine was bought by a film company—I stayed with Mrs. Oxford and wrote almost daily reports to the girls.

One evening while Mrs. Oxford and I were having dinner, the doorbell chimed. A moment later the butler returned.

"Mr. Fodor is here, madame." He sounded disapproving. Almost immediately I saw the reason for it. Joshua Fodor had followed him into the dining room. The tall, distinguished man was not at all distinguished at the moment. He was visibly drunk.

"Where is she?" His voice was blurred. "*Why did she leave me?*"

It was a scene worthy of one of his melodramas and I must say we responded. The butler helped Fodor to a sofa on the sunporch and the downstairs maid brought him hot coffee. Mrs. Oxford was so upset by his behavior that I persuaded her to go and lie down in her room. When she was in bed, with her pill and a glass of warm milk, I hurried downstairs to the sunporch. The butler had helped Fodor take off his jacket, loosen his tie and unfasten the buttons of his starched shirt. He had tried to refurbish himself. His light hair, turning gray, was now a dark brown. The cartilage in his nose was built up. He *looked* like a handsome middle-aged man. He was still groggy with liquor but he recognized me and he shook his head, half apology, half in humor, implying, and accurately, *How the mighty have fallen. . . .*

"I've made an ass of myself," he said. "I never hid behind a drink before. It's a poor time to start."

What could I say? I was sorry for him, embarrassed for him. Failure shouldn't work such indignity on such a man.

"When is she coming home?" he asked.

I hesitated, wondering whether an honest answer would do him, or her, any good.

"You must know, Rebecca," he insisted. "You're like a sister to them."

"Next month, I believe. They're in London right now. Cassie is signing a contract with an Austrian producer for a series of comedies made in England—"

"The English won't know how to take her."

"Evidently she doesn't want to return home for a while." And I thought it was a sound idea. Cassie had never been allowed to set her own course—either as a woman or an actress. It would be good for her to be on her own.

What a joke all my ponderous thoughts would turn out to be when I discovered the true reason for her trip.

Shortly afterward *Photoplay* carried a story on Joshua Fodor's plans for a new film based on the life of Marie Antoinette. He was upset about war and peace these days because he felt that, two years before, President Wilson had been an innocent lamb among the wolves in Versailles.

Peace in 1918 certainly hadn't brought serenity. There was an aftermath of violence—bombings on Wall Street, the Chicago race riots, bloody strikes, a resurgence of the Ku Klux Klan. I wasn't convinced the public was ready just now for Marie Antoinette and the excesses of the French Revolution. But Fodor was. And as Vanessa said, he'd go ahead and do what he believed right, and public opinion could go hang.

Anyway, Vanessa would be marvelous as the young queen who lost her head.

THE PRESENT: VANESSA: REUNION
AT LÜCHOW'S

VANESSA SAT at the dining room table piled high with Christmas
cards and presents from friends and fans who had never forgotten
her.

Christmas Eve. Lüchow's for dinner, of course. And with whom?

Rebecca, of course, since Cassie refused to travel to her place
in Connecticut. And Sue, who was not keen about spending her
holiday with her aunt and uncle. Yes, definitely Sue. She was
growing very fond of her. Such a nice girl, dependable, devoted,
and doing such a fine job.

And Dann. How could she analyze her feelings about Dann?
He was such a beautiful, virile man, so dear and so grateful that
she had accepted him into her little circle. And he was so young;
he made her feel young just being with him; he made her feel
desirable again.

Rebecca, Sue, Dann and Cassie. Family. If only Cassie would
behave it could be a memorable evening.

And it was, in a way Vanessa could never have imagined even
in the grip of her most frightening "night terrors."

Roast goose, crisp skin like bacon cracklings, and the delicious
smell of sage and apple stuffing.

Vanessa licked her lips in anticipation like a greedy child. She
remembered Christmas at Lüchow's with Mr. Fodor, Mama and
Cassie, and a few members of the Fodor company, mostly elderly
ladies. Mr. Fodor was gallant to the older women, courteous,
thoughtful, almost like a son. How they all revered him! Joshua
Fodor could do no wrong, and if he did—well, the company
loyalty brooked no criticism nor gossip about him. Thank the Lord

there was no *Confidential* magazine in those days! Or Mr. Fodor might not have gone on to greatness.

No reason for poor spirits this Christmas, Vanessa reminded herself. She no longer had the shimmer of youth, no longer had the irresistible charm that attracted a certain type of male, but still she was healthy and vigorous. She looked better than women twenty or thirty years her junior. Nor was it actually necessary for her to celebrate Christmas with just Cassie and a few friends. Many young actresses who'd played with her were now married to rich, influential men and they sent her warm invitations each Christmas to spend the holidays with them. As godmother to their offspring she dutifully shopped for the children and sent off packages from F.A.O. Schwartz.

And Rebecca was always to be counted on. "Come out for the holiday weekend," her letter read. "We'll celebrate Christmas and Chanukah together. Persuade Cassie to join us. She's too addicted to her soap operas, anyway."

Rebecca was concerned. She knew the mood swings of Cassie's nature. Still, Vanessa was reluctant to tell her about the recent problems . . . *Cassie, you're so pale. Have you had a blood count? If you'd eat regular meals instead of snacking on those awful potato chips and ice cream. You are what you eat, Cassie. You know this. Heaven knows, I've told you enough times! Look what good care has done for me. I was always weaker than you. My heavens, Cassie, you were strong as a young ox—and now look at me—and look at you. Cassie, listen to me!*

Vanessa was rehearsing a dialogue with Cassie. Not that it would be a dialogue. Cassie would just listen, or pretend to.

Vanessa, so strong in her fragile way, suddenly felt drained of energy. Thinking about Cassie made her body ache. But why shouldn't she be upset, with Cassie being a problem again?

Of course Cassie had been a problem from the time of birth. Unlike Vanessa, she wasn't old in her mother's womb. She was always gay and irresponsible and frivolous, and now she was heading for disaster and Mama wasn't here to help. It was all on Vanessa's shoulders. Again.

A shower of snow, melting to rain as it made contact with the pavements, but snow nevertheless and gentle as it lightly touched the people rushing by, intent on last-minute chores. On 14th Street the stores were open Christmas Eve, traffic was congested and the holiday trimmings gleamed in the artificial light.

The Christmas tree at Lüchow's was memorable, glowing with precious baubles. The headwaiter recognized Vanessa and led her party to a table where they could enjoy the beauty of the tree and the brass band and the surrounding tables filled with three generations of families. Vanessa was touched by the pervading sense of family and continuity. She took the chair the waiter had pulled out for her and, once seated, looked as if she was posing for her portrait in the black velvet she'd worn at the retrospective. The triple strand of pearls added luster to her carefully made-up face. Her hair was piled high, in the style Howard Chandler Christy had admired when she'd posed for him.

"Cassie"—she pointed to a seat—"there, dear. Opposite me."

Cassie was wrapped in a tired mink cape and wore a mink beret perched on her thick graying hair. Cassie's once flawless face was heavily made up in deference to Vanessa's request that she look her best. Cassie had no patience with Vanessa's cosmetic ammunition. What the hell, let nature take its course! Who did Vanessa think she was fooling anyway?

Cassie looked at Sue. Sue was wearing a red pants suit with a black-and-silver ribbed sweater over a white silk shirt. Vanessa was right when she considered Sue "good goods," which was the highest praise Vanessa gave. And Dann looked so handsome, except that he always reminded Cassie of Tom Sawyer in Edwardian clothes. Dann was *such* a contradiction. But that was a great part of his charm. *They spark each other*, Cassie thought. *If only Vanessa doesn't spoil it.*

And Vanessa was thinking, *Sue is attracted to Dann. I hope the poor girl doesn't get ideas.*

Rebecca, like Cassie, was obviously admiring Dann and Sue. Vanessa always noticed a hunger in Rebecca's eyes when she was with young people. Did she suffer for what she'd missed? In her early novels Rebecca wrote with a passionate yet rather clinical intensity about her heroines' sex drives. Her editors had vigorously blue-penciled her candor. Indeed Rebecca used to complain that her editors hardly acknowledged the existence of women's insides, and if they did, only as receptacles waiting to be filled. They were shocked when she drew her women with warm vital strokes, full of needs and longings that demanded satisfaction.

But Rebecca looked happy tonight. *My family*, Vanessa thought, with a rush of pride.

There were no appetizers to dull the taste of the feast Vanessa had ordered. The goose arrived in splendor, rich brown in color, tempting the nostrils, and Vanessa put her palms to her cheeks in an expression of girlish delight.

Expression Number One, Cassandra thought. *Joshua taught her that one, palms to cheeks, eyes on the verge of joyous tears. Oh the beauty of her! Always on stage. Even with family.*

"Beautiful," Vanessa whispered to the headwaiter, who was her instant slave.

Cassandra was watching Vanessa closely. Lüchow's had strong memories for them both, but particularly for Vannie. *What was she thinking? What was she feeling?*

Sue was enchanted. It was a holiday feast worthy of an 18th-century novel: the warm, old-world restaurant, the elderly waiters bustling with pride, the happy families at the tables, the festive glow and cheer. How thoughtful of Vanessa to ask her to share it! Vanessa had said two days before, "Christmas eve can be lonely. My sister and I spent so many lonely holidays when we were young."

Vanessa had also suggested Sue invite a date; she knew about Charlie. But he was committed to dinner at his mother's and later he was squiring a Hollywood actress to a round of parties.

Sue was just as happy that Charlie could not be present. It meant she could respond to Dann if he ever paid any attention to her.

The waiters passed plates of roast goose and red cabbage and individual vegetable dishes; the wine steward opened wine Dann had ordered. Vanessa was radiant with joy, her hands clasped in delight, her eyes sparkling. It was impossible for her guests to look anywhere but at her. The word went around the restaurant: Vanessa Oxford was at that table and wasn't she beautiful! Did you ever see her in *The Passions of a Portuguese Nun?* Do you remember her Mary Magdalene? The most spiritual whore you'll ever see, I guarantee you. . . .

The awed whispers did not include Cassandra. Cassie had much less resemblance to her youthful image.

"Cassie, you aren't eating." Vanessa was so concerned, so maternal. "Please, dear, try the goose. It's *delicious!*"

Cassandra looked through her, then turned her head away. It was Sue and Dann who fascinated her. What were they doing here, paying homage to Sister when they should be having a time together in bed. Cassie had forgotten what it was like to have a man's body enfolding her, the rapture of flesh on flesh, the peak of pleasure so overwhelming it seemed close to dying. It had been a long, long time. Cassie was drifting, her thoughts far away.

These days Vanessa often said in a bored, almost disgusted voice, "Sex is so unsanitary." But Cassie understands her sister ... Who was *last* in the sack with Sister? It couldn't have been much fun for her, or him, what with her ancient vagina. Cassie wanted to scream with laughter. Vanessa looked so young, but she was dried up, and a man's pleasure could give her nothing but pain. She was too frightened of cancer to take hormones to make her soft and elastic. Sex was so unsanitary. *Ha!*

The carolers were bursting with song, and while Vanessa listened raptly Dann put his muscular arm around the back of Sue's chair, not quite touching her shoulder. *Fuck her!* Cassie commanded silently. *Give this lovely girl some pleasure. What're you doing, hanging around a sexless old hag named Vanessa Oxford?*

She was tempted, however, to warn Sue. *Be discreet!* Vanessa didn't like poaching unless *she* was doing the poaching. And Dann was definitely *her* game.

"It came upon a midnight clear ..."

They joined in the singing. All except Rebecca.

Even today, a mature woman with money and respect she'd earned for herself, with world-wide recognition of her talents, Rebecca felt a twinge of guilt on hearing the carols. Her voice box was paralyzed with memories. Vanessa had known her when she was a poor fat, homely little Jewish girl in Muskenaw, but it would never occur to Vanessa that her friend's orthodox upbringing would keep her from participating in the carols.

"We Jews have suffered much because of Jesus Christ,"

Rebecca once explained to her. But it was beyond Vanessa's comprehension. How could anyone suffer because of the dear Christ child? But then, Vanessa was equally obtuse when it came to that boy Eric, dead too early, thanks to her. . . .

Perhaps Cassie understood her best, Rebecca thought. Cassie always said, "Vanessa is equipped with blinders. She sees only what she wants to see."

Which might be the source of her success. And pain for a lot of other people who came into her life.

Vanessa had patterned herself on Eleanora Duse. But Duse was a masochist who suffered at the hands of her lovers. Vanessa more often than not managed to sublimate her feelings into her actor's role—which she pursued on-stage and off.

Vanessa raised her glass now, toasting her old dear friend Rebecca. Her old dear friend Rebecca returned her toast.

Whatever she's up to now, and it has its seed in the Joshua Fodor retrospective, Rebecca reflected, *whatever the results, no matter how catastrophic, I cannot turn away from her. If she has taken from me—and she has, idea-stealer that she is—I have surely gained from her.*

I wouldn't be here at Lüchow's in the year of their Lord 1977, Rebecca Kahn, Pulitzer Prize-winner, if not for Vanessa.

If not for Vanessa, I might have remained an old maid in a little Michigan town (perhaps the librarian, if I didn't have to work Saturdays), eating prunes and bran for breakfast because of constipation.

Rebecca knew she would never discuss the dark parts of Vanessa's life. She owed silence to her. At least that . . .

"Plum pudding!" Vanessa was ecstatic. "I never saw a pudding flamed until I was in London—"

It happened suddenly.

Out of the happy sounds—the laughter, the singing, the brass band—a woman screamed.

"Good God!" Sue pushed back her chair. It was Vanessa who was screaming. Vanessa stood up, her hands gripping the chair's back, her head moving like an animal's, seeking escape.

Then Sue saw him. A man approached their table. This wasn't so unusual, people were forever approaching Vanessa, mostly strangers. But this man was no stranger to Vanessa. He was thin, elderly, with an air of old-fashioned foppish elegance. His white hair was thick and curly, coming down to a vee on his ruddy forehead. His eyes were blue, with the milky color of incipient senility, and there were wattles under his chin. His skin was flushed with holiday spirits and his voice was not quite steady.

"Ah, Vanessa, I always wondered what I'd say to you when we finally met. Now I know—"

Vanessa was staring at him, as though mesmerized. He stood beside her now, his right hand in the pocket of his blazer. Dann was moving toward Vanessa and the headwaiter was moving toward the old man. What was *wrong*? A drunk bothering Miss Oxford...?

"Happy holidays, my precious, my beauty—"

Vanessa came alive. "Stop him!" she cried out to Dann. "He's going to hurt me—"

The headwaiter and a powerful busboy moved toward either side of the white-haired man while Dann quickly took Vanessa out the door, Rebecca and Cassie following. Sue searched for her purse, which had fallen to the floor.

The man stood there, watching Vanessa leave. "I knew she'd come back here one holiday," he said. "She's so sentimental, it was a rendezvous for her and the Master..." His voice was weak, tinged with sadness. Abruptly his face contorted, and Sue, staring at him, couldn't decide whether it was from hatred or sorrow.

"You bitch!" The man began to sob. "All this time... waiting... planning a meeting... and dammit, the sight of you and I'm sunk. I must be crazy... to still love you after what you've done to me?"

His companion stepped forward now. A big blonde woman who looked like a nurse. She took him gently by the arm and gave him a handkerchief.

"I'll take him home now," she said to the headwaiter. "Come, now, Piers."

He went quietly, shaking his head, forming inaudible words. All of them "Vanessa."

In Dann's car, Vanessa was still trembling as Dann tucked the lap robe around her. Rebecca sat to her left, Sue on her right. Cassie was on one jumpseat; Dann on the other, holding Vanessa's hands, trying to rub some life into them.

"He's following me—"

"No," Rebecca reassured her, "it's all over now. They stopped him at the restaurant."

"Oh, dear, I hope the press doesn't hear about it—"

"They must realize you're the object of crazies," Dann said.

"He *is* crazy. He once actually threatened to throw acid in my face—"

"That was a long time ago, Vanessa," Rebecca said.

"Rebecca, he's never forgiven me. And he's vicious! He said that without my looks, I'd be just another woman to him—"

"Who was he, anyway?" Dann asked.

"He was my producer." Vanessa was exhausted, she leaned back against the seat. "Piers van Cleave. He produced *The Passions of a Portuguese Nun.*"

The long car glided to the curb at East 53rd Street. Dann jumped out and assisted Cassie, who gave him a sardonic smile, and then he helped Rebecca, and finally Vanessa. Rebecca stopped him from escorting them upstairs.

"Thanks, Dann. We'll manage," she said.

He was anxious. "You sure she'll be okay?"

"I'm sure Dann. Vanessa has survived worse."

THE PAST: VANESSA REMEMBERS: A TIME WHEN I WAS YOUNG, BEAUTIFUL, AND DESPERATE

THE SHOCK of seeing Piers van Cleave was terrible. Vanessa lay in her darkened bedroom trying to forget what had happened in the restaurant but the past took over, and with it came the events behind what had just happened.

It was after the critical and financial failure of *Jesus Christ —Son and Savior*....

As usual, Rebecca was there to give me courage and strength. She brought me a gift of an illuminated scroll with wise advice from Sara Teasdale's *The Philosopher*:

> I make the most of all that comes,
> And the least of all that goes.

I knew Rebecca would do anything in her power to help me and I knew I would ask her help at the right time.

Meanwhile, I looked deep within myself ...

Item: The career of Vanessa Oxford. At a standstill but not at a dead end. Not a has-been at twenty-one as Louella Parsons dared to suggest.

Resolve: To make a recovery. To achieve greater success. To show Joshua Fodor what I can do without him.

Steps toward my goal: I must disassociate myself from Joshua Fodor. His name is tainted now. The aura of failure is around him.

How do I go about separating my name and reputation from his?

I was alone in a bedroom in our New York hotel suite. Mama was asleep in the master bedroom. She was, at that time, taking medicine for her heart—digitalis, I believe. The trip across country had exhausted her. But I had confidence she would grow stronger. She was concerned about me, but once I was successful again, she would be serene. "Trust me, Mama," I had reassured her, "it will all work out."

I lay on my slantboard (I was one of its first devotees), head down, legs higher, and let my mind wander where it would. I'd found that of all the great thinkers William James was of the most help to me: *"The greatest discovery of my generation is that human beings can alter their lives by altering their attitudes of mind."*

And, of course, the New Testament. Didn't Matthew say, *"If ye have faith, nothing shall be impossible unto you?"*

I had always fed my mind inspirational thoughts. I had always pictured in my mind what I wanted to be and I had achieved it. Yes! Even though Joshua Fodor didn't believe I'd ever compare with Cassie (wasn't that ridiculous; Cassie was talented, true, but only once or at most twice in her career had she proved as good as I consistently was ...).

As my mind roamed I remembered to tighten my stomach muscles, as my friend, Harold Kellogg, suggested. He said taut abdominal muscles were the secret of eternal youth and sex.

My own *Six Steps to Powerful Future:*

(1) Appearance
(2) Money
(3) Resources
(4) People who can help me
(5) An even more successful career
(6) Turn a stumbling block into a stepping-stone

Rebecca always maintained that beauty was power. I had simply not used my looks often enough to my greatest advantage.

I was competing with very young girls. In the camera lens there was a difference between seventeen and twenty-two. A difference ... I was still too young for cosmetic surgery, although the faint pouches under my eyes would soon have to be removed. Hans Rolfsma always blotted them out with clever lighting, but suppose another photographer weren't so knowledgeable? Some surgery? A tuck here and there? Definitely.

As for money, I had enough if I were careful. Memories of cold and hunger had always been with me whenever I deposited my weekly check. The investments I made through my friendship with Otto Kahn, who so admired my art, had laid the groundwork for my future security. He believed the market was rising again, but I was cautious. I wanted only stocks that were safe for widows and orphans.

I had enough resources. During my trips abroad, I made excellent contacts among the press and people in the public eye who might help me. I also had many friends at home. People whom I met when Mr. Fodor took me on trips to introduce his earlier epics. Influential people right up and into the White House. The President would do anything for me. "My darling." That's how he addressed me.

The key to a recovery of my popularity rested entirely on the films I chose and the company that would produce them. How could I gain a voice in the production of my future films? And who could advise me, now that I was no longer dependent on Mr. Fodor?

How could I turn my association with him into something dynamic for the future?

I was linked with his heresy in the production of *Jesus Christ*. How could I undo it?

I wasn't responsible for his making the picture. As far as the world knew I was only involved in acting the Virgin Mary and Mary Magdalene.

If I approached the heads of various newspapers and magazines and told them my side of the story, that I was an innocent victim of Mr. Fodor's determination to film the Christ story as *he* saw it, would they help me? If I confided that my career was ruined and it was not of my doing, and that only the understanding of the press could save me, would that help? . . .

The time was before the Jet Set and the Beautiful People.

In New York, the world that mattered was divided in two: The Round Table at the Algonquin, the intimate hotel managed by Frank Case. And the chic world of Condé Nast, which revolved not only around his magazines (*Vogue*, and *Vanity Fair*) but his fabulous parties.

Rebecca was excited about the Round Table, which was literary. She took me there to lunch one day, but I wasn't impressed. Edna Ferber happened to be present, and Dorothy Parker, and I had no intention of being the victim of Miss Ferber's acid humor or Miss Parker's alcoholic wit. Besides, I wasn't interested in the literary life, unless one of those odd characters wrote a book that could be a film for me.

So gradually I became one of Mr. Nast's pets, the star attraction at his grade-A parties, which included local and visiting celebrities in every field and profession. His interest in me was sparked by stories appearing in various newspapers and magazines, whose publishers I had solicited in my time of trouble. They were all immensely flattering, suggesting that I'd indeed helped almost as much as Mr. Fodor to create the film as art form.

I hoped that through Mr. Nast I would meet outstanding Broadway producers like Gilbert Miller. One successful play and those Hollywood vulgarians would be begging for my return.

Meanwhile, an editor from *Vanity Fair* arranged for me to sit for a new photographic team.

So indirectly it was through Mr. Nast that I met Piers van Cleave.

The photographers, known only by their first names, Nicholas and Benjamin, were young, energetic and wildly innovative. They went beyond Steiglitz and Steichen in their search for new forms of expression and, although the action camera was still in the future, they managed to create an extraordinary sense of movement in their still photographs. They were fashionable and influential.

Their studio was the place to be every Wednesday night, when fencing, food and drinks were dispensed in a bohemian kind of hospitality so characteristic of Greenwich Village in the early '20s. Their studio occupied the second and third floors of a ramshackle old building on MacDougal Street, which they shared with mice, waterbugs and indigent artists. Among their

neighbors was the recently established Provincetown Playhouse.
Their photographs of me didn't live up to my expectations.
I thought they were cruel, showing up what I chose to hide.
But the editors were ecstatic and used a full page in *Vanity Fair*. I doubted it would do me much good in Hollywood, but
the impact on the New York cultural world was startling.

The studio was packed that hot summer night when I walked
in, escorted by a young male editor of *Vanity Fair*. Many of
the famous people they had photographed were present, as well
as a scattering of the Village artists and actors from the Playhouse. Guests were lounging against backdrops or sitting cross-
legged on the floor. The heat was stifling. I stood at the door
and watched the two fencers: one I recognized as Nicholas, the
other was a stranger. He was a rather tall young man with
thick brown hair, a smooth, handsome face, flushed now as he
held his rapier. Nicholas was not particularly attractive in appearance, having bulging eyes, but his voice was nearly as hypnotic as Mr. Fodor's. He was plainly the superior fencer. But
his opponent was light on his feet. He had the grace and assurance that came with good birth and considerable money.

"Piers van Cleave," the editor from *Vanity Fair* introduced
us when we met later over wine and crackers and cheese, "Van-
nessa Oxford."

That introduction laid the groundwork for my best picture,
The Passions of a Portuguese Nun....

Rebecca found the *Nun* for me. She discovered the lyric
tragedy of Marianna Alfocorado, the nubile girl who was both
the heroine and the victim of a love affair that has intrigued
generations of romantics.

"Marianna was not by temperament a suitable candidate for
the sequestered life in a convent," Rebecca said. "But in the
17th century rich families imprisoned their girls in the sanctuary of the convent. Even for a rich, powerful family, it was
the sensible way to deal with superfluous daughters. If, in
Marianna's case, her father, Francisco da Costa, could keep her
from marrying, he could retain her dowry for himself and his
sons."

With her gift for making incidents come alive, Rebecca
dramatized the plight of Marianna Alfocorado, who with her

five-year-old sister, Peregrine, was imprisoned in the Convent of Nossa Senhora da Conceintoa at Beja, outside of Lisbon. "The passions of their Iberian genes were a temptation to the young girls," Rebecca said. "The bloodline was wild, unfettered and considered a hazard to young virgins. The father hoped that discipline of the convent would tame their senses, providing a pious sublimation to keep his daughter from staining the family name.

"But what young girl would accept a permanent ban on the senses? What normal girl could live forever on the stale crumbs of penitence and prayer? Even after a girl had taken her vows, her senses reminded her of all that she had missed.

"The female as cipher," Rebecca said, "with no right to her own life."

I listened, fascinated. Rebecca went on to tell how once Marianna was shut up in the convent, no protest was possible. There was no way she could demand her freedom. Life for Soror Marianna was elemental. She could only submit to the discipline. The prayers. The Mass. The simple cell, like a stone coffin. Heavy walls that retained the bone-chilling dampness. A grille at the small window. A pallet for sleeping. A wooden chair and table. A crucifix. A few religious objects. But she was young, on the verge of awakening. Her body made demands that puzzled and confused her. There was no one to answer her needs, nor was she ever encouraged to venture beyond the boundary of the convent.

Beja was a garrison town, small, dusty, primitive. Soror Marianna had seen the troops riding into Beja with a handsome young officer at the head of the French regiment, the Chevalier de Chamilly, sent to Portugal by Louis the Fourteenth to fight the Spanish aggression. Marianna met the Chevalier in 1666 when her brother Balthazar brought him to the convent for a visit. Rules were somewhat relaxed for new girls like Marianna, especially before the final vows were taken. The Abbess must have allowed the visit. Whether the Chevalier would have singled her out if not for his friendship with Balthazar will never be known, but he was clearly attracted to her dark, mysterious beauty, the contradictions of the wild and the submissive, the promise of unexplored emotions. Her innocence and lack of sophistication must have intrigued him. He was a womanizer who had become bored with the ardors and intrigues of Parisian boudoirs, and doubly bored with the sterile garrison village. To woo the young novice was an aphrodisiac, doubly pleasurable because of the risks attendant on it.

"You must also consider Soror Marianna, conditioned now by long sessions of religious instruction, by days when neither a morsel of food nor a sip of water passed her lips. Conditioned to confession for her sins. Of course, she hadn't yet sinned. Except in her dreams, which were beyond her control, or the church's.

While she wasn't yet judged ready to bestow upon her Lord the gift of herself, she did give it to the Chevalier. But not easily. It was a twelve-month siege before ecstasy overcame self-control and they made love together. It may have happened in her cell; Marianna had no freedom of movement, no clandestine meetings were possible. Never mind, they did meet. And for the Chevalier—was it just a conquest, a diversion? "It was," Rebecca said, "a love affair between an aggressor and his victim. Soror Marianna loved, sinned, suffered, and was purified. A transgression transformed itself into an act of purification."

Then the Chevalier left, departing with his troops for war. Marianna wrote him letters filled with anguish, as well as beautiful and total submission. Evidently the letters left his possession (perhaps he saw them merely as the conquests of a soldier). He never admitted who wrote them. Later they were published anonymously in Paris, where they became famous in the romantic era and inspired Elizabeth Barrett Browning's *Sonnets from the Portuguese.*

Chamilly, the good soldier, returned from the wars and became a Marechal of France. Soror Marianna became one of *les grandes repenties*, as the French called them and, eventually, to honor her for her great suffering and extraordinary piety, she was chosen to be Sister Porteress of the convent, her passions transmuted into devotion for her Sisters.

"*Vous ne trouvier tant l'amour*," she had written her lover. "And all the rest is nothing."

From the Browning poetry, I cherished most the line, "I love thee purely..."

As a matter of fact, I loved the entire story. It cried out for the Fodor touch. Rebecca saw it as a comment on the feminine condition. I saw it as a classic love story, one with passion and purity on the grand scale. The union between the nun and Our Lord appealed to me for its chasteness, its spirit, its freedom from earthly passions.

Rebecca was right. It was perfect for me. In a way Marianna's story was my story. All I needed was the financing for the production. I became an actress in search of a producer.

And Piers van Cleave was an enormously rich, charming, attractive young man in search of a goal to give his life meaning. . . .

"I was a remittance man at twenty-one," Piers van Cleave often said. "My grandfather paid me to stay out of his territory because he was afraid of the competition, but I figured that with a little backing and experience I could beat the old brigand at his own game. And he knew it."

When Piers began to show an interest in me, I asked Rebecca for some of his family background . . . she was particularly good at digging up the story behind the fact, figuring no doubt that it would come in handy sometime. She says that most authors are terrible gossipers anyway, that that's how they earn their bread.

"Well, Piers' grandfather, Abraham van Cleave, was the third-richest man in the country at a time when Ward McAllister said, 'A fortune of only a million is respectable poverty.'"

Abraham van Cleave, cynically branded "Honest Abe" by his contemporaries whom he'd outsmarted, outpirated and outrobbed, came to the United States from the Netherlands. He was a big, robust man, as the result of an overactive pituitary and adrenals that gave him his build and his drive. He exuded a lusty animal magnetism. He had a deliberately foul tongue and the manners of a stablehand. The aristocratic women who refused him a place at their elegant dinner tables often made love with him in secret sessions on his yacht or at his hideaway near Sailors' Snug Harbor. He created his empire in mining, then later in lumber and finally in railroads. He acquired several additional fortunes by wheeling and dealing on Wall Street, simply to remind the snobbish brokers and financiers that he was not only their equal but their superior. Well into his eighties he was hyperactive, too restless to remain quiet for any length of time either in a board room or a brothel.

He also married late, a father for the first time when most were grandfathers for the last time. So, born to Abraham and Mathilde van Cleave, a son, Colin, a gentle, quiet child, no trouble to anyone, which in itself was enough to irritate his hell-raising parent. Colin died young (somehow the sons of overpowering fathers seem to fade away early in life). Colin had married Zoë, the daughter of a socially impeccable family of ministers and philosophers. Socially well-connected, Zoë exercised the power of Abraham's money to establish herself in Ward McAllister's exclusive group and the old man was willing to help her social ambitions in any way she chose... he'd never forgotten the fact that the exclusive clubs had once ignored *him*. Now he used financial and social pressure to bring around the men, and finally their wives, who ruled the new society, to accept Zoë, who was one of them but had, unfortunately, married beneath herself.

Zoë's first and only child, Piers, inherited his grandfather's good looks, his lust for the wrong kind of woman and his genius for taking gambles. By the time he came of age, Piers found that his grandfather's unsavory reputation had been whitewashed by a public relations man who managed to smooth over the memory of a mine massacre where men were killed for going on strike, and who surrounded old Abe with an aura of such generosity that he became known as the first of the great American philanthropists.

It was a period when the grandsons of the great "robber barons" were expected to be playboys, and Piers van Cleave did his best to conform to tradition. To Piers, Yale meant lots of pretty, amiable girls that the musical comedy producers used at the New Haven Shubert Theater for tryouts. When a local girl threatened to sue him in a paternity case, he was sent on a Grand Tour. After his third divorce he'd grown bored with Grand Tours and had exhausted the safaris in Africa; there he'd also shot some film that his friends praised extravagantly. He was cynical about their reaction but, bored and restless as he was, it occurred to him that making a movie might just be the ticket.

He was planning to return to Africa for a possible film project when he met me at the Greenwich Village studio. I confess I found him enormously attractive. Not like Mr. Fodor, but in a clean-cut American way. He could have posed for a Leyendecker painting on a *Saturday Evening Post* cover. Yet his clothes were quiet and unobtrusive, his manner with me shy and tentative. He seemed ill at ease even within his own circle of friends, who were now entrenched in family banking or investment companies.

He also had resources. Although old Abraham's capital was tied up in all kinds of trusts, Piers' mother had certain resources of her own, and he persuaded her to finance our film, *The Passions of a Portuguese Nun.*

THE PAST: REBECCA REMEMBERS: THE MAKING OF A LOVE AFFAIR

PIERS WAS, as they used to say, besotted with love for her. She was like some strange aphrodisiac that burned in his brain, fogging his senses.

Vanessa had never been truly courted before. Plenty of men had admired her, but she was so obsessed by Joshua Fodor and his works that she had carefully created about her an air of remoteness. Oh, she had a *few* brief encounters ... such as the devastating Neil Bradshaw ... but none of the men operated on the level of Piers, who now wooed her as though she were the heir to the British throne.

"You must have the best of everything," Piers said, and money poured out in an endless, golden stream. Vanessa hired some of Joshua Fodor's old staff. John Kinney came along to see that life was made effortless for the star, her director and the staff. The logistics of transporting the company to Spain were staggering, but it was all managed by the staff Vanessa had gathered so quickly. All her experiences with Joshua Fodor were working for her. And so was Piers, who surprised us by his astute sense of organization, his ability to deal with the Spaniards. He assumed responsibility and authority with an expertise none of us had anticipated.

I was in London during the year Vanessa was making *The Passions of a Portuguese Nun* and I often crossed over to Lisbon to visit her.

Again I saw a new and surprising side of Vanessa. There was truly a spiritual quality about the production. Of course there were priests and nuns on the set to give advice to the director and his staff. But it was Vanessa's behavior that was so exemplary. Her standards for the company were extraordinarily high (as were The Master's). No drinking was allowed on the set. No gambling. The director, Herb Gaddis, had been one of Fodor's young assistant directors and this was his big chance. Together he and Vanessa brought numerous Fodor touches to the film, and when I saw the rough cut I felt that there were some remarkable, unforgettable moments.

And Vanessa was exquisite. Her religious fervor in contrast to her passionate response to love was wonderfully moving. I marveled —as always—at her ability to divide herself.

As Piers' mistress, she was living a role that she'd never even dared to dream about.

It was a courtship out of time. He had leased a villa complete with a staff, and she was driven to and from the set every day in a Rolls with a liveried chauffeur. He showed the most imaginative taste in his gifts of jewels. He was always there when she needed him. And Vanessa seemed to respond with gratitude to his gentleness, to the care and protection he gave her. I even began to wonder if this affair might end in marriage. She could certainly take her place as the chatelaine of a great fortune. And when this film was released, I was convinced, her reputation would not only be restored but would reach new heights.

Which is precisely what happened.

The Passions of a Portuguese Nun was a great artistic and financial success. Piers van Cleave was accorded new respect by his friends and the managers of his trust funds. He saw himself as a success on a par with the old brigand, his grandfather. He saw a future as a film producer with his beautiful star as his wife.

Vanessa refused to play out her role. Not the money, the gifts, the genuine love he poured on her could make a dent in her armor. She was running scared. Being completely possessed by one man for long simply was impossible.

Because the man was not Joshua Fodor.

"You're throwing away your future," I pleaded with her.

She smiled pleasantly and made plans to leave.

Of course Piers didn't let her go easily. He begged and cried and cajoled. And finally threatened.

"You said you loved me. You swore you did. For all time, you said. My God, Vanessa, don't you *remember?*" He wasn't ashamed to beg, even in my presence.

"Circumstances change," she said, withdrawing, as she always did when she was frightened. "It's impossible, Piers."

His face became red, and he was, literally, shaking with rage.

"Damn you, I'll let the whole world know what you are—a little tart who plays for money, big money, of course . . . not to mention a rotten little cocksucker."

Whether he also threatened, as she says, to throw acid in her face, I can't say, though it does seem altogether possible.

After *The Passions of a Portuguese Nun*, Vanessa retired for five years. But she was still in the limelight. After all, the film had outplayed and outdrawn any film she'd ever made with Joshua Fodor.

Variety said so. And proved it by publishing the figures.

Cassie said: "Vanessa picks the man who can help her, allows him to seduce her, and discards him when he's done his bit.

"All hail Queen Vanessa. Mistress of 'Off with Their Heads.'"

And then she began to cry.

Ten:

THE PRESENT: SUE—INITIATION RITES

DANN WAS in a state of high excitement. He sat close to Sue in the car, his spine rigid, his hands clenched, his thigh pressed against hers. She sensed his sexual desire—but for whom? The evening was a fiasco. They both were in an emotional mood.

Vanessa's perfume lingered in the limousine, a sensuous reminder of her complex nature.

"D'you think he really meant to harm her?" Sue spoke to ease the tension, but she did not really believe it. There had seemed to be no danger behind Piers van Cleave's confrontation. It had ended in senile tears, without even a threat.

Dann shrugged. "It's hard to tell. If he didn't assault her years ago, it's not likely he would now. Just an old man's fantasies."

"Was he Vanessa's lover?"

"He was her producer."

"I know. Was he also her lover?"

"Are you prying?" he asked coldly.

"Maybe." Her voice was equally frigid. "Curiosity is natural. After all, what we witnessed was an ending. I'd like to know the beginning."

Her frankness relaxed his wary attitude. He wouldn't admit how little he knew, since Sue evidently thought Vanessa confided everything to him. His reply was grudging. "Van Cleave fell in love with her while they were making *The Passions of a Portuguese Nun*. When she rebuffed him, he became vindictive. He made all sorts of threats. She was afraid for her life."

The car turned into Park Avenue, where Christmas trees glistened and traffic lights created blurred ribbons of red and green reflections on the damp pavements.

Dann said abruptly, "Let's walk."

"Okay." At least he wasn't sending her home.

At the curb, he helped her out of the car. He dismissed the chauffeur and took Sue by the arm.

"Park or Fifth?"

"Fifth." She was suddenly happy. "The Christmas windows are so beautiful."

They walked with arms linked, heads close together, with an intimacy that was a carry-over from the incident at Lüchow's. She felt his arm tighten, protecting her, as they paused for red lights, and the pressure sent a tremor through her. How delightful it was to walk with him, heads bare to the damp air, skin glowing, alive, excited! They might be taken for lovers, she thought, celebrating their first Christmas together, marking the beginning of a splendid future. She felt light-headed.

They stopped before Saks' colorful windows, joining the crowds.

"Pity you haven't your camera," she said.

He was pleased that she had mentioned his work. He looked down at her. Their eyes met, sending messages. "It's an idea. Shall we go back and get it?"

She hesitated, confused by her ambivalence. It was so obviously an invitation. She longed to be carried along by circumstances, letting him make the moves, not actually agreeing but permitting herself to be persuaded because it was such a delightful idea. Too shy to look at him, she stared at the Christmas fantasy in the store window.

Was he aware of her hesitation? Offended by it? "Perhaps you'd rather stop for a drink at the Plaza?" he suggested.

"That would be nice." Relieved, yet disappointed, clinging to him, but looking ahead at the bright windows, thinking, *It will happen. I want it to happen . . . don't I?* Her feelings needed sorting out.

In the lobby of the Plaza, he paused. "I'd better call and find out how Vanessa is."

"Of course." His remark brought her back to reality.

She waited, concentrating on the flow of guests—young girls in bright dresses and furs, older couples, still youthful but obviously free of their children, out-of-towners enjoying the holidays. They were all going somewhere to have fun, to be with the person they loved. She was suddenly overcome by loneliness, the sort that often brought on the blues. The imperatives of her life were so simple— to love and be loved. Yet these precious goals always eluded her. She felt so alone on this Christmas night. Why hadn't she agreed to go back to Dann's house? Surely it was better than being stranded. He wasn't merely a warm body; she was violently attracted to him, the thought of lying in his arms . . .

He was coming toward her. "I talked to Rebecca. Vanessa is resting." He seemed relieved, but the crowds at the hotel disturbed him. "D'you mind if we go somewhere quiet?" he said.

"I'd like that." They left by the 58th Street entrance and wandered toward Avenue of the Americas, finally stopping at a bar dim and empty enough to please him. The bar seats were occupied but the booths, empty of guests, were dark enough to encourage confessions and intimacy.

Dann ordered two scotches and lit a cigarette. Sue felt their closeness disrupted, that he'd been lured back to Vanessa's sphere of influence.

"Have you known Vanessa long?" she asked. It sounded like idle talk but she was genuinely curious.

"About ten years."

"How did you happen to meet?"

"She played stock in Oklahoma one summer. My mother was

on one of those charity benefit committees. I met Vanessa through her. Vanessa was very kind to me when she learned I was a movie buff. She told me all about Joshua Fodor and the making of the first silent movies. I wrote her afterward and I always got an answer, even though it sometimes took months. Anyway, I was going to Europe the following summer and she and Cassie were also booked on the new S.S. *France*. I was a seventeen-year-old hayseed. They kind of adopted me. I learned a lot from them. They opened up a whole new world for me and made me feel a part of it."

The Education of Danniel Houston, Sue thought. What a *pleasure* it must have been for the ladies to pass along to a young boy the benefit of the worldliness and sophistication they had acquired from their friendships with the most powerful and famous men and women of the past fifty years.

"I owe Vanessa a great deal," Dann said, obviously meaning it. "I'd do anything for her."

The cigarette smoke curled around his face, blurring it. Sue saw it as the typical face of Vanessa's male admirers . . . young, intense, inclined to extremes in life styles; art movie film critics; assistant professors in university film departments who'd published esoteric books or papers on the silents, with, inevitably, rapturous chapters on Vanessa; young off-Broadway directors and playwrights who asked her to advise, invest or participate in their work.

Dann was an exception. The Turtle Bay townhouse, the society of the rich and the beautiful, inclusion in the city's cultural events, the guidance of an international celebrity lawyer—all this had come about through Vanessa's interest in him. Danniel Houston was one of the most prominent of her young admirers, often mentioned in Suzy's column and recently in Liz Smith's.

No wonder he adored Vanessa. She had made it all possible.

And what did he do for her, Sue wondered.

Dann was on a fresh scotch and a new pack of cigarettes. Liquor softened the lines running from his nose to the corners of his mouth, but the lines around his eyes deepened as he squinted through the smoke. Sue stared at her full glass, wondering what was going on in his mind . . . she worried that he would rather go home . . . alone.

"I'm having a problem with some of Vanessa's old files. Perhaps you can help me," she said casually.

He looked up from his drink. "Oh?"

"I've got most of the material in sequence, from 1913 to 1923. Letters, contracts, bills, memos, scripts, everything. But I can't find a thing about the year 1921. Nothing! It's as though she dropped out of life for that one year."

His voice was soft, slurred. "Take my advice. Don't ask her about it. Don't ask her anything about that year."

"Why not?"

He stared at the cigarette smoke.

"This material is going into archives. A hundred years from now they'll be the only facts about her. They must be accurate," she said somewhat pompously.

"Who says history is accurate?"

"Well, it should try to be!" *What was it,* she wondered, *what did he know . . . ?*

"Listen, Sue, don't, as they say, open up that can of worms."

She was startled. A warning? She wanted to pursue it but he'd signaled for the check. As he helped her on with her coat, she remembered Rebecca saying Vanessa had too many dark secrets hidden in her heart.

"Let's go back to the house," Dann said suddenly, as though he had made an important decision in his life.

On Lexington Avenue, some shabbily dressed people were coming out of a church.

"Who worries about them the day after Christmas?" Dann exploded. "And the next three hundred and sixty-four days to the next Santa Claus?"

She was startled by his comment. Somehow it was more characteristic of Charlie than of Dann. She looked at him with new admiration. It seemed he also had a heart in that fantastic body of his.

As they walked toward his house, Sue was aware of one thought: she was going to be with him, to stay with him. It was decided. They descended the steps, past the tubs of evergreen with their winking red and green holiday lights. Dann fumbled with his keys. The hall was soft with lamplight. They went up the staircase to the second floor. When they reached the landing that divided the drawing room from the library, he jogged her arm. "One more. The bedroom awaits our pleasures." The room was spacious and bare except for a king-sized bed scarcely two feet off the rug, covered with a fur throw. There were no other furnishings. The ceiling was one vast mirror.

Dann stripped off his jacket and shirt, which left his upper body naked.

"Sorry," he muttered. "We should be undressing each other. Right?"

"I don't know," Sue said, admiring his lean, muscled chest.

"We may as well observe the house rules," Dann said, embracing her.

He stripped off her clothes with quick impatient fingers and then waited for her to reciprocate, but she was trembling and too nervous to be good at it. The sight of their nakedness was enough to arouse her to a new and insistent hunger for intimacy.

She had played at sex before, coping with a boy's clumsy aggressions, knowing intuitively that it wasn't her but *it* that excited him, but not caring, not objecting because her aroused feelings demanded an explosive climax, although she didn't really understand what the climax was, except that after a while he stopped his spasmodic rubbing against her panties and they were damp, not only with her secretions but with his, and she was still unsatisfied, nervous, irritable and about to break into tears of frustration.

But that was all in the past. Now she was aware that she was very much a woman and that Dann was a powerful, experienced man who knew how to give and receive sophisticated sexual pleasures.

Sue had grown up innocent after a fashion, perhaps because she had few intimates until she went off to college. Her few encounters with boys her own age had left her embarrassed and unsatisfied; perhaps her self-censoring system had worked too well. Her encounter with Charlie had seemed a rejection. If he'd really wanted me, she thought, my being a virgin wouldn't have mattered to him. She found, though, that his behavior hadn't so much hurt her private emotions, only her image of herself as a desirable female.

It was different with Dann. No man had ever aroused her so deeply and spontaneously; it was, she admitted honestly, somewhat startled by her own needs, a vaginal reaction. She wanted to touch him, to explore every part of his magnificent body shamelessly and hungrily. And she wanted him to be daring and abandoned with her.

Dann was such a beautiful man.

He led her by the hand through the doorway to the bathroom with its dark woods, white porcelain, built-in shower and a rack of thick brown-and-white towels. Unlike the suggestive bedroom, it was austere in its cleanliness.

His hand tightened its grasp on hers, as though his touch would cease her trembling. She was too shy to look directly at him but she met his glance in the mirror over the vanity base and his smile seemed to chase her embarrassment.

"You're cold." When he let go of her hand, she had an inclination to drape her palm over her pubic mound, but her stiffened nipples betrayed the openness of her desire. He switched on a button, bringing a rush of warm air from the ceiling. He busied himself finding a cap for her hair and he put it on her head, tucking her hair under it. "I like the way you wear your hair," he said. He seemed so eager to please her. And she longed to reciprocate by giving him pleasures he'd never had before, devised out of the inventiveness of her feelings for him.

The gush of water from the faucet sent steamy mist through the room, making her feel easier, partly hiding them from each other. Her heart pumped faster. The need in her was growing more demanding.

His penis, she noticed, while long and thick, was not erect. Which confused her . . . surely at that moment he should be ready for lovemaking. Her lack of experience did not help her confidence. . . . He was running his hands down her cheeks, touching her shoulders, her arms, her waist. He paused and explored her slim flat rib cage, then her pubic mound. Down on his knees on the heavy bathmat, he placed his cheek against her pubic bush. He embraced her, his powerful arms around her waist. His tongue flicked at her. It excited her so that her secretions left a touch of moisture on his cheek. The hot water and his male smell were almost unbearably exciting to her.

His eyes half closed, the expression on his face sensuous, almost sleepy, he was throbbing now, stiff, hungrily ready for her. "Just a minute," he said. He stepped out of the shower and padded around the bathroom until he was in control again. "I don't want to be too quick for you," he said.

Back in the glass-enclosed shower, the spray as invigorating as a Finnish massage, he picked up a thick bar of soap and began to lather his chest.

"Let me?" she asked, almost pleading with him.

His thick hair was drenched, the rivulets streaming down his face. He smiled, pleased at her request.

She thought of the Japanese women so adept in making a man feel potent; she wanted more than anything to arouse him to a wild peak. She lathered his chest, her fingers tracing teasing patterns, soaping the hair on his arms, on his chest and flat belly, down to the thick mass of hair around his penis. Her touch was delicate, coaxing, discovering by instinct his pleasure points. His response sent a current of excitement through her body. His hands were everywhere and his mouth explored her body, tasting every delicious crevice. His delight in touching her with his fingers, lips and flesh brought her to near ecstasy. Her old sexual modesty was literally washed away as she responded to him, pouring herself on him, melding herself to him. Her pelvis discovered a rhythm that inspired him to even greater excitement. He said finally, "I can't hold out much longer." As they stepped from the shower he wrapped her in a thick terrycloth towel and led her to the bed.

"The shower. You didn't turn it off."

"First things first." He dried her quickly and pulled off her showercap so that her dark hair tumbled silky and free. She was naked now, but he kept a towel wrapped around his hips. She saw the jutting bulge of his penis thrusting under the towel and she wanted to rip the cloth away from him and see him naked and ready for her.

He lifted her and set her down on the fur coverlet. She lay there, legs spread apart unselfconsciously, an invitation. The animal fur aroused a sensuous response in her; she felt free, sexy and eager to have him at her side.

"You're lovely," he said. "Will you pose for me sometime?"

"Nude?"

"Nude. For my own private collection."

She wanted to ask, "How much of a collection do you have?"

As though reading her thoughts he said, "It's a very small collection. As a matter of fact, it will begin with you."

"Ask me again, when my mind is clear."

Her answer amused him and he lay down beside her, molding her body to his with a mixture of tenderness and need. She felt they had already established the private language of lovers familiar with each other. She smiled at him, lips parted with pleasure. He explored her body again with gentle fingers and a knowing and tireless tongue, a continuous journey of discovery. Her hands, with a life and purpose of their own, searched for the throbbing power of him. She lost herself in his strength, unthinking, her senses wildly alive, not only accepting but demanding, reaching out, to experience the source of their pleasure. His initial probing was gentle, so she felt no pain in her delicious pleasure, but at his first hard thrust into her, she cried out softly and tried instinctively to withdraw. But the force was too powerful, and pain, mixed with pleasure, brought her to the crest to which he'd guided her. She was no longer aware of their bodies as separate beings. Moist with sweat, his breath was rough, like a runner reaching the finishing line, and she found her own peak in the explosion of his fulfillment.

No regrets, she warned her mind, her proper New England Puritan mind.

They lay on the fur cover, their bodies gleaming with sweat, their chests regaining the normal beat of their hearts. The smell of sweat and sperm enfolded them.

The fur reminded her of Theda Bara, the siren of the silents, writhing on a fur rug in the throes of passion. When she told Dann about it he exploded with laughter, scooped her up in his arms and held her so close that they seemed to be joined at the hips.

"Hungry? Thirsty?" he asked. "You rest while I hunt."

She lay there, deliciously relaxed. Suddenly, she realized she was no longer a virgin. She got up on her knees and inspected the fur rug for any telltale signs, and to her relief found none.

Dann came into the room with a tray. Fried chicken, cold champagne, a chocolate mousse.

"Courtesy of Jeff," he said, putting the tray down on the bed.

"Is he your houseboy?" she asked, impressed in spite of herself.

"Not exactly. He's a dancer but he broke his ankle last year and now he's going to Columbia for his master's. He needed a job that would give him time for his classes. He helps me in the darkroom and he's a damned good cook."

Putting the tray aside, he turned to her again, erect, eager. When she praised his vitality, he was pleased. "I've had trouble coming . . . sometimes. The problem isn't really physical. It's more that I don't find it so easy to give everything of myself . . ."

"The girls must appreciate your endurance."

He shrugged and bent down to kiss her nipples. He stroked her, his fingers exploring, his tongue never resting. And this time he made love as though out of control.

Afterward, they began to drift into sleep, in each other's arms.

She heard him ask if it was as wonderful for her as it was for him.

"Yes," she answered. "Wonderful." And would have said more, but she fell into a sleep of delicious exhaustion.

"Stay here with me." He was insatiable, and she was touched, gratified, flattered. He wanted her to move into his house. She was tempted, but then he added soberly, "We'll have to be discreet . . . Vanessa . . ."

She decided to remain at her uncle's apartment.

All the way home in the taxi, she wondered what her decision would have been if he had not mentioned Vanessa's name.

Realizing how important Vanessa was to Dann almost wiped out the pleasure they had shared.

Almost.

But not quite.

Eleven:

PRESENT: CASSIE—MY SISTER, MY LOVE

REBECCA LEFT Vanessa's bedroom to prepare peppermint tea, which Vanessa relied on to calm her whenever she was confronted by a crisis.

In the kitchen, Rebecca found the herb tea, filled the kettle with tap water and placed it on a burner. The breadbox was empty. Cassie, she knew, would want a sweet biscuit. There were health muffins in the refrigerator, but Cassie loathed them. Cassie simply had no vanity; she regarded her body as a nuisance and ignored it. Yet except for her face, she retained a semblance of her former beauty and, at times, a flash of her old marvelous spirit.

Where Vanessa was often dull, a trait disguised effectively by her Mona Lisa smile, Cassie had always been the imp, sparkling with mischief and humor. At a party, Cassie always sought out the quiet ones and brought them forward. They shone under her happy concern.

Cassie, who always said that men and women shouldn't live together, managed without effort to transform her lovers into friends. Vanessa aroused cold fury in the lovers she discarded. Some threatened her, but then, violence was the dark side of passion, wasn't it? It was a miracle Piers hadn't killed her.

All right. What was the secret of Vanessa's silken tentacles? The breathless attention, the helplessness, the gentle, soft voice combined with an elusive quality that men felt necessary to capture and then conquer?

Vanessa never made herself available. A man paid dearly for the privilege of being with her and each man and each film were to enhance her reputation. What man wouldn't respond to the challenge of screwing the most beautiful professional virgin in the world?

The world had always said that Joshua Fodor made Vanessa Oxford a legend.

Rebecca knew better. Carrying the tray back to the bedroom, she thought: *It was the other way around.*

When Joshua ended his affair with Vanessa, something important and vital went out of his work. And his life . . .

In the bedroom, Vanessa was sitting up in her wide bed, leaning against a nest of white lace pillows, her hands folded, her eyes half open. Cassie slouched on the quilted satin pouf nearby. The air was cool—and the scent of Bal à Versailles drifted around Vanessa.

Her near collapse had frightened Cassie.

Cassie was confused, divided between anxiety and anger. Vanessa was vulnerable. Vanessa was old, she was likely to die. Terror froze Cassie's blood. Vanessa dead? Life without Vanessa was unthinkable.

"I never thought I'd see Piers again," Vanessa said, reflective now rather than frightened. In control of herself, she allowed herself to go back over the incident, even to grapple with the possibility that he might confront her again.

"He didn't *look* dangerous." Cassie had to reassure her sister because it also reassured herself. "Maybe he was just surprised to see you."

"Surely you remember his threats?"

"All the same, he was awfully good to you, Vanessa. And to Mama and me." Sometimes she had to jolt Sister's memories.

"Cassie! Whose side are you on?"

How often had Cassie heard those words during Vanessa's long bitter quarrel with Piers! Whose side are you on? His or mine? Not who is right and who is wrong. It was awful for Cassie because she truly liked Piers. He was really so good to them all. But once he'd affronted the fair Vanessa, that was the end of *him!* After that Vanessa found it impossible to recall anything good about him. She remembered only what suited her and what she needed to break free of him. "Vanessa thinks she doesn't need me any more," Piers had said to Cassie (all of Vanessa's suitors confided in Cassie, thinking she was a pipeline to their adored one). "But Vanessa doesn't realize how much she'll *need* me, she isn't as smart as she thinks and one day the way she behaves will catch up with her ... *then* she'll need me ..."

How sad, Cassie thought, that he counted on Vanessa's downfall to bring her back. But he was mistaken. Vanessa sailed along, serene in her sights, ignoring any shoals. Even now, when her position was precarious—what with all the new publicity about Joshua Fodor—she ignored the danger of being exposed. More than once she'd risen from the ashes ...

Tonight, the sight of Piers shocked Cassie. She could not believe this elderly man, trembling with infirmity and frustrated emotions, was the Piers who once courted Vanessa, looking so handsome, so English in his Savile Row clothes. So aristocratic, Mama used to say, linking him with his mother's chateau on Fifth Avenue and the van Cleave fortune in railroads, timberlands and silver mines.

The wild affair between Piers and Vanessa lasted only fifteen months yet produced her greatest film, *The Passions of a Portuguese Nun.* Afterward, she determinedly ignored him as though he were an offensive bill collector. Once the picture was released, and their quarrels threatened to reach court, Vanessa refused even to talk to him, although he telephoned daily. His voice was quite different then, deep and masculine and, Cassie would say, very sexy.

"I'm not home to him," Vanessa would say, her lips tight.

We always did her dirty work. Mama and I were so often shocked, but Vanessa never lost her cool. Whenever there was a threat of trouble, of scandal, like the time Mr. Fodor dumped her or Piers threatened to destroy her beauty, she stayed calm. I had the hysterics. Even Rebecca, who was usually so fearless, suggested getting a guard. But Vanessa went on with her life, outwardly serene. "Don't worry, it will be all right."

And damned if it wasn't!

Rebecca called her an Iron Butterfly and Rebecca was right.

But her Number One priority was always Mama and me. What was good for us was acceptable for her. It wouldn't be fair to downgrade that, Cassie thought. *Few daughters have ever shown more devotion than Vanessa. Few sisters, either, for that matter. . . .*

Looking at Vanessa, lying so still in bed, her eyes closed, Cassie wondered if she was sleeping or meditating. Vanessa had experimented with hypnotism, ESP, the mystic cults. She'd said the mind was master of the body.

Rebecca never took Vanessa's "isms" seriously, Cassie reflected. Until she realized Vanessa had created for herself a life style that gave her the opportunity to control those around her.

Cassie remembered the time she burst into Vanessa's dressing room, while Vanessa was supposed to be dressing for the next take. The room was dim. At first Cassie thought Vanessa was napping. Instead she was sitting before the makeup table, a candle its solitary light. Vanessa was staring so intently into the flame that it gave Cassie the creeps.

"What're you doing?" she demanded.

Vanessa's voice was calm and remote. "Learning to concentrate."

She'd developed strange powers within herself. Discipline. You couldn't get her to drink a Coke for anything in the world. Or eat sweets. Or miss her Yoga exercises every morning.

Whenever she went on tour, even in her peak years, she always carried her own suitcase. And walked so swiftly the others could scarcely keep up with her. Rebecca thought it was a habit of self-reliance from all those years on the road. Often when Vanessa's behavior puzzled her, Cassie turned to Rebecca for enlightenment. You could count on Rebecca. Her childhood, she said, had made her a pragmatist. Which was probably the reason her novels had a sort of documentary feeling. She gave her strong heroines a touch of sentiment, an adolescent reminder of how much hurt and longing love inflicted, but she never underplayed reality.

At the time when Vanessa was so deeply involved with Piers, when he was both her producer and lover, Cassie and Rebecca often discussed the situation.

"D'you realize Vanessa's life has been a series of sexual cliff-hangers?" Rebecca said.

Vanessa's effect on men *was* hypnotic. A delivery boy from Gristede's, a taxi driver, the fitters at Bergdorf's, her hairdresser, all reacted the same to her: with total worship.

Rebecca wondered if her behavior was due to Mr. Fodor's influence. He always reminded his players of their obligation to the staff. But Cassie traced it back to their mother, who was unfailingly gracious to everyone. Whatever, it was impossible to dismiss Vanessa's kindness. Cassie recalled the delivery boy who was going to night school ... Vanessa knew all about his courses and his grades. Her favorite waitress at the Women's Exchange had an elderly arthritic mother ... Vanessa brought her fresh wheat germ from the health food store and a Hydrocolator so she could apply hot wet packs to her mother's painful knees, and she never forgot to ask about the old lady's condition. The driver of the private taxi that she used after selling her car often told her about his pride in his daughter ... when the girl graduated from nursing school Vanessa went out to Brooklyn for the ceremony.

Vanessa inspired love in so many people who had touched her life. What Cassie had never been able to forgive was Vanessa's calculated charm to strangers; it seemed as though she wooed them so that they would become her slaves. And once they were won over, eager to please her, she began taking them for granted. Except Rebecca. She respected Rebecca's intellect, and candor.

Sometimes Vanessa's behavior nauseated Cassie; she could be so insincere. But then Cassie would feel guilty because all of Vanessa's ploys, all her machinations were calculated to protect Sister and Mama.

And protect us she did. Cassie couldn't recall a time when

Vanessa wasn't nearby, being protective, watchful. Strangers might consider her bossy (sometimes Cassie herself thought so), but it was all for their good ... wasn't it? The Three Oxfords ...

The scene that floated into Cassie's memory this Christmas eve could have been one of Joshua Fodor's most effective films, but it had happened in their own lives, leaving a never forgotten trauma.

Mid-January and the little troupe of traveling actors caught in a brutal blizzard in the upper reaches of Massachusetts. Mama playing the lead in a popular melodrama, *The Scarlet Woman*, Vanessa playing her small daughter. Cassie was allowed to come along so that the family wouldn't be separated. Mama was obliged to pay for her rail fare and rooming house bed, but they were so happy to be together, and Cassie, soon to be eight, was ecstatic.

Until the awful incident, with Mama lying in a hospital bed in a women's ward with three other very sick ladies, and the starched top sergeant of a nurse saying, "You can't go in there, little girl."

"But it's my mother." Cassie sobbed. "I want my mother..."

Vanessa stood beside her, clutching her hand, both of them faint. Under their heavy winter coats, they shivered with terror. Mama was their anchor, and Mama was separated from them by the three beds and the nurse who was helping the doctor who was bent over Mama. Children weren't allowed beyond the main lobby. When one of the nurses tried to stop them from coming into the ward, Vanessa said, "Our mother is here, and we are strangers and have no other place to go."

"Poor children," said "Aunt" Laura, the older lady in the company, who'd insisted on calling the doctor when Mama collapsed after the matinee. "We must leave after the performance tonight. What will happen to the little girls?"

Cassie's fear became a silent scream. *Who'll take care of us?* The loneliness that often terrorized her at night gripped her now, and she threw herself into Vanessa's arms, sobbing wildly. The nurse said sternly, "We can't have you children disturbing the patients."

Cassie didn't remember the doctor clearly, but the next thing she knew he was driving them along a snowy road, his horse bucking the gusts of wind, the runners of the cutter finding the road even when it was partially hidden with drifts. Then there was the red brick building looking like a schoolhouse or a prison, except for the cross over the doorway. The woman who opened the door and ushered them in was dressed in a black habit with a white headband. Her steel-rimmed glasses made her plain face even more severe. Across her bosom dangled a silver cross on a narrow chain.

The doctor had found a sanctuary for them at the Convent of the Sisters of St. Joseph. The Sisters welcomed them but Cassie was too frightened to respond to their kindness. She and Vanessa sat in the kitchen eating milktoast and hot chocolate at the oil-cloth table, and Vanessa watched to make sure Cassie didn't spill a drop or disgrace herself (maybe the fact that she was so anxious to be proper in her sister's presence, Cassie sometimes thought, made her tense and she was inclined to stumble or spill food on her dress or dirty herself).

Vanessa wiped Cassie's mouth and nudged her to thank the Sister who fed them and who was now waiting to lead them to the place where they would sleep. They followed her down a long, dark corridor. Cassie remembered the rattle of windows, the smell of damp, the kerosene of the Sister's lamp and the statues of Jesus on his cross with the blood flowing from the wounds. *Mama,* Cassie was crying silently, barely swallowing the sobs, hurting from tight muscles. *Oh, Mama....*

A small room with a narrow bed beneath a crucifix was their shelter. The sheets were rough and clammy, but the blanket was tucked into the bottom of the mattress. After the Sister left them, taking the lamp with her, the tiny room seemed dark and hostile. Cassie huddled on the bed whimpering. "Shhh," Vanessa quieted her. "We must be quiet. If we're a nuisance they'll put us out." But Cassie whimpered even more, imagining them put out into the dark, cold night. They were just like the poor little orphans in one of Mama's plays.

They didn't get into their nightgowns, although "Aunt" Laura had sent their little suitcases. Vanessa helped Cassie take off her dress, petticoat and shoes, but no more. They would sleep in their longsleeved underwear and long ribbed stockings. They slid in be-tween the clammy sheets but Cassie couldn't get warm, she was shaking so hard. Finally Vanessa put her arms around her and kissed her and cuddled her and it was just like having Mama hold her. After her sobs eased, Cassie fell asleep, dreaming it was Mama lying beside her, Mama's arms holding her safe.

Ten days passed before Mama was allowed out of the hospital. Ten days in the convent, and Cassie remembered them clearly.

The Sisters of the convent arose at 5:30, while it was still dark, before the first gray streaks of dawn appeared. After the second day she and Vanessa arose at that hour too—Vanessa wanted to watch the nuns, they fascinated her. But to wake up before ten in the morning was an ordeal for Cassie. She was always a late riser. But now they were dressed and allowed to join the Sisters, who came together early in the morning for community prayer. After lauds, the Sisters remained together for a half hour of mental prayer. Sitting still during this period was an ordeal for Cassie. She stared at the nuns and squirmed until Vanessa pinched her into remaining quiet. After daily mass in the chapel the girls would follow the nuns into the refectory, the common dining room, for a breakfast of bread and cereal with no sugar or condiments. Cassie was starved for sweets but there were never any in sight. Vanessa was watchful to make sure Cassie was silent as the nuns were during breakfast and ate "neat." Afterward the Sisters were assigned to their chores in the house and then left for their apostolic work, either nursing or teaching.

The hours seemed awfully long to Cassie, and she wondered what was happening to Mama and when they would hear how she was feeling. Maybe Mama was dead and they weren't told. She was afraid to ask Vanessa to ask the nuns. Each day dragged until the Sisters came back to the convent in the late afternoon and resumed their house chores.

Cassie welcomed the time they met again for community prayers; she enjoyed the scripture reading, but the half hour of mental prayer made her squirm. She could scarcely wait for vespers, which she thought were lovely . . . all the Sisters chanting the psalms from the Old Testament in their dark gowns and white headbands, making profound bows from the waist, their sleeves covering their hands. What a joyful, heavenly sound . . . it gave Cassie goosebumps. Vanessa always looked transformed afterward. Later they went with the nuns to the refectory for the simple evening meal, which most nights was eaten in silence but on special occasions the Sisters were allowed to talk and socialize.

Evening was the most bearable for Cassie. This was the time of the day when she and Vanessa usually accompanied Mama to the theater. Here in the convent, after the evening chores, the Sisters had an hour of community recreation. Some paired off to play checkers or chess, other mended or knitted. The following hour was devoted to study for the next day's work, then the night prayer, and then at nine o'clock the convent went into the Great Silence. By ten, all lamps were extinguished.

Cassie and Vanessa spent most of the day with the House Sister, a plump middle-aged nun who was the cook. She was enormously kind to them. She walked with them in the yard and let them play in the snow and even rigged up a little swing from the bare branch of an oak. They tagged after her, helping her in the laundry. Cassie never forgot the smell of the hot clothes in the boiler, the yellow Fels Naphtha soap, the zinc washboard.

The nun's garb fascinated Vanessa. She kept asking the House Sister about it—the long black dress, the white linen around the head and face, the double headpiece, which consisted of a short underveil and the long veil over it that fell to the knees, and, for going out, the long black-wool mantle. "Beautiful," Vanessa would murmur with more fervent admiration than she was ever to give, years later, to her dresses by Patou, Chanel and Mainbocher. "Just beautiful . . ."

Cassie was never completely at ease during their ten-day stay with the Sisters, but Vanessa blossomed. When Mama finally was strong enough to leave the hospital, and they made plans to rejoin the company, Vanessa hated to leave the convent. "I wish I could stay here forever," she said, and Cassie, young as she was, realized it was one of the rare times Vanessa had spoken from the heart. . . .

"I imagine Dann took Sue home." Vanessa opened her eyes, evidently rested, quite alert, and interrupting Cassie's reverie.

"I'm sure he did." Rebecca poured fresh tea. Cassie refused a cup, but Vanessa accepted it and thoughtfully sipped. When the telephone rang, Vanessa picked up the receiver from the bedside table.

"Yes, Dann, I am *quite* all right. I *do* appreciate your calling.

Yes, Cassie and Rebecca are with me." Replacing the handpiece in its cradle, she said sadly, "Poor Dann. The evening's ruined for him."

"Where is he now?" Rebecca asked.

"At the Plaza. He took Sue out for a drink, which was very thoughtful of him. I'm afraid her evening was spoiled too."

"He'll make it up to her." Now why, Cassie asked herself, had she said that?

Vanessa appeared distressed. "Oh, dear, she's vulnerable, poor girl. I just hope it doesn't give her ideas."

"Well, I'm going." Cassie felt she had to get away. She carefully gathered her worn mink, her absurd little beret, her scarf and gloves.

"Your bag, Cassie. Where's your bag?"

"How should I know?"

"Did you have it with you when we came in?"

Cassie shrugged, puzzled.

"Did you leave it in Dann's car?" The censuring note hardened Vanessa's voice. "Oh, Cassie, you'd lose your head if it weren't fastened on. I swear it!"

Rebecca went into the living room, searching for the misplaced purse. She retrieved it from the bombé chest in the foyer and as she returned to the bedroom noticed Cassie slumped in the chair, the buttons of her fur jacket unevenly fastened, giving her a tilted look. Rebecca's heart ached. Poor Cassie had never overcome her sense of failure, and it seemed her dejection was always more obvious in Vanessa's presence.

"Cassie, I'm going to the station, I'll drop you at your hotel."

"I thought you were staying with Sister." Suspicion made Cassie wary.

"Well, yes, I'd planned to. But I've changed my mind."

"Because you're worried about how I'll get home?"

"If you want the truth, yes, I am concerned."

"You want to please Sister."

"I want to help *you*, Cassie. You're in no condition to be going *anywhere* alone."

"Cassie, please stay here tonight." Vanessa pleaded, giving the impression that Cassie would be doing her a favor. Cassie gave in, as she usually did when Vanessa was gentle and concerned. At such moments, memories of Vanessa's goodness warmed Cassie, making her feel needed, wanted, protected. She felt guilty for her rebelliousness. If not for Vanessa, she might have ended up behind a counter at Macy's instead of owning a vaultful of bonds. If not for Vanessa, she might never have met Richie.

Or lost him, either.

Guard your tongue, Cassie Oxford. Show your gratitude to Big Sister.

"Oh, shit!" said Cassandra Oxford between thin, stiff lips. . . .

Cassie was in a shocking condition.

Rebecca wondered whether Vanessa was aware of it. True, Cassie had never been at her best around her sister. As a matter of fact, Cassie had always been irritated by Vanessa.

Rebecca accompanied Cassie to the maid's room, where she would sleep. She hung up Cassie's coat and dress and offered her one of Vanessa's nightgowns and robes. Cassie undressed, docile, wordless, while Rebecca sat near the bed, undecided whether to offer help.

"What did you say, Cass?" She aroused herself from her thoughts.

Cassie looked at her, offering her most roguish, endearing little girl smile. "I was saying how nice it would be to have a governess to bathe me and feed me and tell me what to do."

"That's what we'd all like." Rebecca could not control her shiver of apprehension. "But that's all in the past, Cassie."

"Even in the past, I always had to do for myself, running for trains, trying to keep up with grownups who never realized my legs weren't as long as theirs, playing in flickers, acting as my own stand-in and stunt woman for movies. God, what a life!"

"Don't you remember the great things in your life, Cassie? Your great triumphs in Europe . . . in Russia they said you were even superior to Vanessa—"

"Until their critics met her."

"And in England." Rebecca made an effort to bring up all the positives. It had always been important to remind Cassie of her triumphs but never more important than now. Urgent really. Because Rebecca knew that Cassie's self-respect had been pitifully weak since she first joined a theatrical road company. Over a lifetime, her litany had always been, *I'm no good, I can't act, I'm an embarrassment to my sister.* It became a self-fulfilling prophecy.

Cassie was lying curved like a petal, looking graceful because her muscles still responded with grace. In a fetal position.

"Are you all right, Cassie?"

The enormous opal eyes glazed with pain. Her gestures were those of a child begging for relief.

"I hurt, Rebecca. All of me hurts. I feel like I'm tied in knots—"

"Shall I fetch some aspirin?"

"There's Valium in my purse. Valium works better."

"Have you taken many today?"

"I don't know. I can't remember. Rebecca, how can anybody hurt so much?"

Rebecca's hand soothed Cassie's feverish forehead. Rebecca wished she could transfer some of her own strength to her old, cherished friend. *Vanessa has failed Cassie, but I've also failed her,* Rebecca thought. *I've never really given her the attention and devotion that I've given Vanessa, even though she's always needed it more.*

Her sedative taken, Cassie moved to a sitting position against the headrest, and Rebecca was uncertain whether to stay or leave. She had never felt so uneasy about Cassie's state of mind . . . and even at her late age Cassie still suffered from a separation anxiety.

"Are you sleepy? Shall I leave?"

"No, please." Cassie reached out for Rebecca's hand. "Stay with me until I fall asleep."

The room was quiet. No Christmas sounds filtered through the double-hung windows; even the dim lights of the courtyard far below were shut out by the blinds.

It is like a vigil in a sickroom, Rebecca thought, and looking at her friend, recalled the first line of her first book, *Women live to endure their lives. . . .*

Thoughts about the Oxford sisters Rebecca would never dare express:

No film of Cassie's had ever elevated her to the cover of *Time* as *The Passions of a Portuguese Nun* had done for Vanessa. But her bright, lovely face with the opal eyes, the winsome smile, the comic spirit that managed somehow to be sexually alluring had been on fan magazine covers since she and Vanessa both worked for Joshua Fodor.

Cassie had wept bitterly at her masquerade in vaudeville. She hated being a boy, she hated blackface. Her only possible form of rebellion was the clowning.

A decade later, it proved to be star material.

Cassie (she had dropped the formal Cassandra with her first part in a "flicker") was a born comedienne, a madcap irrepressible imp who always said what she thought, but who was also warm, impulsive and loving. Rebecca remembered how desperately she craved love . . . always holding hands with her friends and her lovers, always hugging, fondling, desperately needing body contact.

She was a clown in the tradition of the great early stars like Mabel Normand, Constance Talmadge, Dorothy Gish, and, several decades later, Carole Lombard. You loved their wit, which, unlike some modern female comics, didn't stop them from being pretty and sexy, charming men and women alike.

At the same time the somber side of Cassie's nature contributed a certain poignancy to her acting. You were always sorry for her, you rooted for her to win and you wept when she lost. Joshua Fodor was certainly aware of this and exploited it in one important film—*The Life of the Party*, a story of a good-time girl descending into the depths of alcoholism. After five years of starring in romantic comedies for Fodor, Cassie found herself suddenly taken seriously. The New York critics saluted her emerging talent as a serious actress. Vanessa paid her the greatest possible compliment: "She is nearly as good as me."

Rebecca also remembered when Joshua Fodor contemplated a film on *Anna Karenina*. Anna's punishment appealed to his sense of drama . . . a beautiful woman throwing herself in front of a train, a woman who gave up her children deserved her tragic fate, his audience would agree.

All his young actresses were hoping for the part of Anna and he rehearsed them all impartially. But it was rumored he was favoring Cassie.

Vanessa was disturbed and mentioned her feelings to Fodor.

"Her fans knew her as a comedienne. She has made one dramatic picture but basically she isn't an actress. Mama and I both know it. Cassie is at her best when she is playing herself."

In her next film, Cassie played her customary role of a runaway girl masquerading as a boy. She was shanghaied on a freighter going to China and ended up in the bed and the arms of the fiercely handsome captain.

She lost the critics and kept her fans.

Once, in a moment of misery, Cassie had confided to Rebecca why she had always played the clown. If you made people laugh they were kind. They liked having you around. They bought you sweets. They never left you out in the cold. And being out in the cold to Cassie was the original sin. So she made fun of everyone, including herself.

Vanessa was the exception. You didn't make fun of Vanessa to her face, although many a time Cassie and her pals used to laugh about Vanessa behind her back. She was so serious! So proper! Always walking around the lot with a book under her arm. And more often than not, she never even read it. . . .

"Turn on the television," Cassie was saying.

"I thought you were asleep," Rebecca said.

"It takes a whole handful of pills to knock me out. I don't want to sleep. There's a movie on Channel 9 I want to see."

Rebecca switched on the TV set. The other channels were celebrating Christmas, but Cassie wanted to see *The Red Shoes*, her favorite film. She loved it above all soap operas and all of Vanessa's great films. Moira Shearer, so exquisite in her red ballet slippers, dancing for joy in a celebration of life until the little red slippers take on a mad life of their own and lead her, dancing madly like a whirling dervish, to destruction.

"Whenever I watch it, I think of Richie . . ." Cassie whispered. *Nobody can bring Moira Shearer back from madness. And nobody can bring Richie back to life. Nobody on earth, not even Big Sister.*

Especially not, since she took him away from me.

Twelve:

THE PAST: VANESSA REMEMBERS
RICHIE: A SIMPLE CASE OF RAPE

"How WOULD you act if you were being raped?"

I stared at Mr. Fodor—not startled—*terrified*.

My heart was doing wild, improbable things in my chest. I felt the blood draining from my face. They were watching me: Hans, Dudley Norton, Abel Levy, Jay Ritori, Richie Doyle. It was the first day of rehearsals for a new film. But only I had been summoned from among the young actresses.

We were all wearing heavy sweaters because the morning air was frigid in the rehearsal hall. As usual, Mr. Fodor was seated at the small table that was littered with notes and several medical books. The others were gathered around, standing, as was our habit, like students before a beloved teacher.

He repeated his question: "Miss Vanessa, how would you act in a case of rape? How would you *feel?*"

His voice persisted, his eyes bored into me. My hands had a reaction of their own, palms upraised, taut fingers ready to claw and scratch. I retreated with a feeling of horror.

Sometimes he got cross with me because of my lack of imagination. In this case, imagination wasn't needed. The sheer outrage of the act stirred me as an actress—and as a girl.

He said in his penetrating, sonorous voice, "Rape is an act of violation. Rape is pain. Rape is sometimes the prelude to murder."

The wardrobe lady was reduced to terrible embarrassment. The men were uncomfortable, shifting their feet, not knowing where to look. Mr. Fodor ignored them and continued as though this were a lecture on criminal behavior.

"Every man dreams of exerting complete power over a woman. In the act of rape, a man realizes his wish. He is the violator. She is the helpless victim."

He looked around the group and nodded to Richie. "Richie, come here. If you wanted to rape a girl, how would you go about it?"

Richie, manly but sensitive, looking at nineteen like the young Jesuit his mother hoped he one day would be, stared at Mr. Fodor. His face blanched, then the blood returned, flooding it with shock and horror.

"Well, Richie?"

Mr. Fodor enjoyed contradictions. He said it deepened character delineation. Nobody, said Mr. Fodor, was either good or evil. It was the gradations of character that made a film fascinating.

Richie stammered, "I . . . I don't know, s-sir."

"Haven't you ever thought about it? When you see a pretty girl at the beach . . . or walking alone at night in a dark street? Come on, Richie, you're a normal young man. Aren't you?"

"I . . . I guess so, Mr. Fodor. I . . . I . . . hope so."

Cassie wandered into the rehearsal room. She was never far from Richie and she was watching him now, fascinated. So was Mr. Fodor. But suddenly his attention turned from Richie and me to Cassie.

"Cassie—"

Before he could finish whatever he had wanted to say, I interrupted. "Mr. Fodor?" My voice sounded as though I were strangling. "Mr. Fodor, once when Mama, Cassie and I were on tour, I had to stay late at the theater after a matinee. Mama and Cassie left and I was supposed to go back to the boarding house with a lady in the cast. But she forgot about me. It was dark when I came out of the stage door. I couldn't remember where we were staying. The street was empty. There were no lights on the corners. I cut through a back alley to get to the main street. I walked very softly, scared—but I didn't know what I was scared of. It was like a horrible dream. Then I saw a shadow move and a man came out of a dark house. I started running away. It was slippery under-foot from the mud. I nearly fell, but I saved myself. But not before the man caught up with me and pulled at my arm.

" 'Where're you going, little girl?' he said.

"I struggled to break away. His grip was like iron. I was close to the main street where I would be safe if I only could pull my-self free. I struggled. I knew something awful was about to happen to me. I screamed. I kicked his shin. He slapped me with his other hand. I couldn't see where I was, the tears blurred my eyes and he was trying to cover my mouth but I bit his hand.

"Then suddenly I heard Mama's voice. She was worried about me and had come looking for me. The man let go and I ran down the alley toward her. Mama held me and I started screaming and screaming and couldn't stop—like *this*—:

I uttered a shrill, terrified scream, the scream, I decided, of a girl about to be ravished.

Mr. Fodor moved toward me and put his arm around me.

"All right, Miss Vanessa. You're safe. You're here with us." He dismissed the others, including Cassie.

"Cassie, tell Mama I'll be late," I called. "Tell her not to worry."

She ignored my request. Her eyes were wide. "I didn't know. You never *said* anything . . ."

I asked her not to mention it to Mama, it would only arouse painful memories.

Naturally I couldn't tell her the incident was hatched in my imagination to hook Mr. Fodor's interest. There was no doubt in my mind that the role of the victim would be mine.

Mr. Fodor had asked me to wait. After a while, the studio staff left and finally even Thelma, Mr. Fodor's secretary. I remained in the rehearsal hall, curled up in the old Morris chair, and I was aware of my fright.

I was too good an actress. The scene I'd visualized so realistically for Mr. Fodor's benefit refused to leave my mind. I could even feel the rough male hands on my neck—

"Oh!" My cry was half surprise, half scream, because hands were threatening to strangle me. And then one big palm was clamped over my mouth until the breath left me and a man's body was forcing me to the floor, his knees a wedge between my legs, and I felt the *thing* alive, squirming like a giant snake, and for the moment, I lost consciousness. . . .

"Dear One." It was Mr. Fodor's voice, and he was getting off the floor and pulling me up, his strong hands in my armpits, holding me to him, brushing my hair. "Are you all right?"

I could only nod. Stunned.

"I wanted you really to experience it."

I grew tense. Then he said he suspected my story was for his benefit, to make sure I got the part. Would I ever be able to fool him?

"Did you really think it was a rapist?"

I nodded my head, not trusting myself to speak.

"How did it feel?"

I closed my eyes and my voice was a monotone. "Helpless. Like I was going to be killed."

"Good. Good. Then you'll remember your reactions when you need them."

He was pleased with me, showing that warm, satisfied smile that I both welcomed and dreaded. "Come, Little Miss, we'll go to dinner."

He barely touched his food but I ate ravenously. Afterward, he smoked his cigar and left his customary generous tip and then we took a taxi to the Astor and everything was as always, except for a change of hotels. Mr. Fodor seemed more excited than usual.

Later he told me that he'd been asked by Washington to make a series of propaganda films, of which A *Simple Case of Rape* would be the first. The German brutality in Belgium had given him the idea. In peacetime such a film would be unthinkable, but in view of the times the girl would be a symbol of a ravished country.

Even the other girls agreed I was the logical choice for the victim. In several shots, Mr. Fodor planned to give a madonna mystique to the dying girl as she lay among the branches and thorns in a rough wood. Yet in the final scene he had Hans photograph me with my skirt raised, covering my face. My legs were frozen in death, spread as though to receive the vicious thrust. Blood trickled down my thighs.

After the fadeout, he used his screen titles to plead for spiritual humanity, for the brotherhood of man, which would forbid the slaughter of innocents.

His choice of Richie as the Hun was questioned by the staff until he explained that to make the Hun a monster would be too easy. It was more realistic to take a decent boy and have him brutalized by the war.

As usual Mr. Fodor went into depths with his questions. What was the victim doing in the field at twilight? Searching for a baby lamb that had strayed from its mother. (How he loved symbolism!) How did the women in the village react to her death? Did they have less sympathy because of her beauty and gentle nature than they would have had for an ugly girl?

The atmosphere in the studio was different for this film. Everyone was tense and wound up. Cassie refused to watch either the rehearsals or the filming. She waited for Richie in the dressing room, playing with Tiger, the studio cat.

After the rehearsals of Richie abusing me, he'd go off the set so distressed he was trembling.

"I wish Mr. Fodor'd never started this film," Cassie burst out at supper one night. "Richie hates it! He says it makes him sick!"

When it came to shooting the rape scene, Mr. Fodor cleared the studio. Then he coached Richie, who looked pale and sick. He said, "You aren't Richie Doyle. You are a German boy who's been on the front for months. You have a hunger for something, maybe just to touch the girl, just to be gentle with her as though she were a girl from home. At first, you mean no harm, not until she shows fright. Then something happens, some instinct takes over. You don't know what you're doing; you know only that you must hold her. When she struggles, you hold her tighter and some brute force awakens in you, and you aren't a boy, you are a beast and you conquer her as an animal does in mating." . . .

The film was a sensation.

Women fainted in the movie houses and nurses were on hand to revive them.

It was a film that would never have passed the censors if not for Washington.

Mr. Fodor came to hate the film and would never discuss it.

It made Richie a star. Dudley Norton and Washington arranged for Richie and me to go on tour with the film to sell war bonds, and we nearly equaled the record of Mary Pickford and Douglas Fairbanks, who were also on a bond tour. Dudley also went along with us as director of the tour and a kind of chaperone. Cassie longed to join us but she was busy with a new film, and I had the feeling Richie was just as pleased that she wasn't with us. He was so terribly proper where she was concerned. He disapproved of her wearing lipstick (which she wouldn't have worn anyway), or letting her skirts up too much. But as I pointed out to her, he didn't object to makeup and short skirts in some of the other actresses.

And then one night when we were in Boston, where the film was playing, there was a small riot outside the theater. A group of Catholic women were protesting the showing of the film (as they were later to protest Mr. Fodor's great film *Jesus Christ—Son and Savior*).

After we gave our speech about buying war bonds Dudley Norton got us out of the theater by the back way and over to the quiet hotel in Cambridge where we were staying.

"Don't answer the telephone," he cautioned us. "Or the door. The reporters will be trying to interview you. I've got to get back to New York tonight." He looked at us anxiously. "Will you be all right?"

"Of course," I soothed him.

He turned to Richie. "You'll look after Vanessa?"

"Yes, sir. Sure."

"I'll bring up some sandwiches for you. You can't even take a chance on room service. Just sit tight until morning. I'll call you —after I've talked to the boss."

Richie and I had adjoining rooms but the door between them was bolted. Richie remained in his room and I stayed in mine.

Which seemed awfully silly to me. After all, we were old friends; he would some day probably be my brother-in-law.

I unbolted the door. Richie was lying on the bed in his undershorts. He had a powerful erection, I noticed. The windows were open, but the night air was hot, it moved like a fire across your skin. I felt weak, as though I were swimming under water, unable to take a deep breath.

The sandwiches Dudley had left were lying on the night table. Untouched. I crossed the room aware of Richie's gaze. Beside the bread and meat, there was an apple. I took it up in my hand and smiled at Richie. I felt like Eve at the moment of temptation.

"I suppose Mr. Fodor would do a closeup of it. As a symbol."

He said in a harsh abrupt voice, "Vanessa, come here . . ."

It wasn't necessary for me to move. I was so close to the bed that his hands pulled me toward him and I sat down abruptly beside him. His hands were demanding, his face looked as though he had a fever and his eyes were boring into me. I tried to laugh, even though I didn't want to laugh, because I knew what he was feeling. It was my feeling too, and it was mounting in me, sharp, demanding. My most intimate parts were moist with excitement and desire.

"Vanessa," he said, "I know it's wrong, but I can't get you out of my mind. I'm no good to feel this way, but I've got to have you, my God, Vanessa—"

Absorbed and detached all at the same time, I listened. But then I made the mistake that was to shadow my life forever. I responded as Mr. Fodor had taught me so ingeniously, with my mouth, my lips, my tongue on his strong, handsome penis, playing, teasing, kissing it until it gushed with a magnificent spurt into my mouth. He was young and so beautiful. I wanted him so much. I didn't care that my sister loved him and that he loved her. We made love over and over. And I thought, he's never done this with Cassie. I am his first, and he'll always remember me.

"Oh, my God," he kept moaning. "Oh, my God!" . . .

We went back to New York together. Dudley and Cassie met us at the station, but Richie didn't take her to dinner as she had anticipated. We couldn't trace his whereabouts that afternoon or evening. But sometime that night he registered at the Commodore

Hotel, put a "Do Not Disturb" sign on his door and put a bullet through his head. His brains and fragments of his skull were scattered on the bloody pillow.

Through the intercession of Mr. Fodor's influential friends at the Diocese, he was buried in hallowed ground.

Cassie had a nervous breakdown.

Mr. Fodor blamed it on the film. He said it shook Richie so badly to realize a man could feel such brutish emotions.

Richie was young and sensitive and should have been a Jesuit.

Cassie was young and sensitive and unsuited for the life of a movie star.

Oh, my God.

The night terrors. Reminding me again and again.

THE PRESENT: SUE—PICTURES TELL THE STORY?

ON THE SATURDAY before New Year's Eve, Charlie finished his morning class at NYU's Film Department and stopped in a phone booth to call Sue.

"Free for lunch?"

"Yes." Sue was cordial, although he had been neglecting her. "Can we eat downtown? I'm due at the film archives this afternoon. They've got some more boxes of Fodor material, nobody's gone through them so I've been elected."

"Good, we'll play archeologists together."

"Charlie, I'm so *glad* you called!"

"Then you *did* miss me."

"Of course! I've got lots to tell you."

"I can't wait."

Sue hadn't seen him since before the Christmas Eve dinner at Lüchow's. She hadn't seen Vanessa since that memorable night, either. Rebecca had spirited her friend out to her place in Connecticut.

"It was a jolt for her to see that man," Rebecca reported by telephone. "It brought back ghastly memories. But you're not to worry about her, Sue. However, she is concerned about *you*—"

"About me?"

"Yes. She hates the idea of your being alone on New Year's. D'you have any plans?"

"No. But I really don't mind."

"Vanessa minds. She wonders if you'll join us in the country?"

"That's very thoughtful, Rebecca. But I think I'll just stay in town. I'll be fine."

"In that case, would you look in on Cassie? She refused to come with us. She has loads of friends, of course . . . but sometimes the holiday season can be lonely."

"I'll be in touch with her," Sue promised.

The truth was that Sue was enjoying this brief hiatus away from Vanessa. She felt like a kid unexpectedly let out of school. For all her courtesy, Vanessa was beginning to smother her. She worried about Sue's eating habits, particularly her sweet tooth, about Sue's indifference to makeup and her preference for classic clothes—blazers, pants, T-shirts. She worried because Charlie hadn't made his relationship with Sue more clear and permanent. She had met Charlie several times when he came to pick up Sue for a date, and she liked him. She'd even suggested that he cut down on cigarettes and coffee. She was always asking Sue about him, how often they saw each other, what his future plans were. Sometimes all this concern irritated Sue, who then felt a secret sympathy for the burden Cassie suffered—Vanessa's demanding, smothering love.

The taxi carrying Sue downtown played a game of tag with the other cars, and she was relieved to reach her destination. She hurried into the friendly warmth of the Armenian restaurant, baffled by her eagerness to see Charlie, particularly since her affair with Dann.

She liked Charlie; as a matter of face she *adored* him, and she wondered uncertainly if she was promiscuous—caring for two men at the same time. But her feelings for Charlie, she reminded herself, were different. She was comfortable with him, they shared a zany kind of humor. She could laugh with him over Vanessa's eccentricities. But not with Dann. She could only relate to Dann sexually. Just thinking about it brought a flush to her face.

Charlie got up from his chair to greet her. "You look *great*—"

"Thank you, Charlie." How could she explain what made her glow so excitedly?

They sat side by side on the red vinyl banquette. It was too early for the lunch crowd; they were the only guests. The fragrance of grilled lamb laced with garlic drifted in from the kitchen. Charlie put his arm around her and kissed her cheek.

"You not only look great, you smell great."

"I swiped some of Vanessa's hundred-dollar-an-ounce perfume."

"Very sexy."

"So I thought."

"For my benefit?"

She shrugged and smiled, enormously pleased with herself. Always before, Charlie was in control of their meetings. But now she had a feeling that the balance of power was moving in her direction. It was *delicious!*

She proceeded to tell him about the dinner at Lüchow's. "It was a moment worthy of Joshua Fodor. This Piers van Cleave was really a nice old gentleman. And Charlie, he just looked at her and went to pieces. He started crying. I don't understand it! What *is* her hold on men?"

"Every man yearns to lay a celebrity. Raises his status, not to mention his—"

"All right, Mr. Wiseguy, but it's more than that. Sometimes I think she's a witch."

"You may be right."

"A *good* witch," she corrected him.

"Why so defensive?"

"Because I *like* her, and I've seen so much good in her. But something does bother me. There is, I guess, such a thing as being too good?"

"Sure thing. The old killing with kindness. It has the virtue of being the perfect crime! No weapon but love, no motive but love. Who'd ever suspect a *good* person of being a murderer?"

She started to answer, but he interrupted abruptly, with the real reason for his phone call. "Sue, let's try it again."

She leaned back, startled, then managed to say, "Well, no, Charlie. I don't—I mean things are different . . . well, changed—"

"Maybe it'll go better the next time, even with a virgin—" And then as the significance of her words got through . . . "Hey, you've been had—"

"That's an odd way of putting it."

"Funny. I didn't want to be the first, against my wonderful lofty principles and so forth, but you know something—I'm *sorry*."

Good! she thought, and was immediately startled at her reaction. Had she been hoping to arouse his jealousy? Had his momentary impotence hurt her so badly that she needed to settle a score? Her divided feelings shocked her. She had Dann, so why was she playing footsie with Charlie?

"Charlie"—her smile was so sweet, so beguiling that it sickened her—"you're *very* special to me and I hope you never forget it—"

He glared at her. "Bullshit," he said, looking past her smile into her eyes.

The loft where the Joshua Fodor boxes were stored was leased by the Film Wing and was next to the home of *Movie Star News*. This collection of Fodor memorabilia had been stashed away in a Bronx storage house where Mr. Friedlander had just tracked it down. But a film buff had already made an offer for the material and Mr. Friedlander persuaded the man to donate it to the Film Wing, thereby insuring himself good publicity and a tax deduction.

"I wonder if it'll be worth the trouble," Sue was saying as they climbed the steep, worn stairs and paused on the landing. As they began the next flight, Charlie gave her an encouraging pat on the fanny.

"You can't tell," he said. "A recent Hollywood underground journal suggested the great man was also something of a weirdo."

"I don't buy *that*, Mr. Wiseguy. He was a fine person. I've seen letters Vanessa got after he disappeared and they're simply glowing. He was generous and kind. Everybody felt that way about him."

They reached the fourth floor. The door ahead of them was

sheeted in tin and protected by triple locks. Charlie tapped and, after a pause, tapped again. The door finally opened cautiously, and they were face to face with the custodian of the Fodor legend: an aged man with shaggy gray hair, puffy face, red-rimmed eyes and a stained shirt and baggy trousers. He nodded vaguely to Charlie, opened the door wider and they entered the big chilly loft, a storehouse for packing cases and cardboard boxes. A corner, more squalid than the rest, was the man's living quarters—featuring an unmade cot-bed, a litter of cigarette butts, empty coffee containers and wine bottles. In spite of the space and the cold, the air was rank.

Charlie said in a low voice, "I'm glad you didn't come here alone."

Having pointed to the boxes, the man shuffled back to his bed and Charlie began opening the cartons, cutting rope with his penknife.

No treasures—only letters, telegrams, newspaper clippings, a press book on *Crime and Punishment*, another on *Jesus Christ— Son and Savior.*

"You think this is worth bothering with?" Charlie asked.

"Yes, Mr. Friedlander wants whatever is remotely pertinent. He's hoping there's some old film in the mess—"

"If so, it's turned to dust."

Sue paused to catch her breath. She looked at the press book for *Crime and Punishment*, its corners nibbled by mice. She turned a few pages, and came upon a batch of photographs of Vanessa—young, exquisite, luminous with a purity that was accentuated by soft focus. As she turned another page, she stopped and . . . "What's this . . . ?" and held up an 8 by 10 folder of cardboard.

Inside the folder were sepia photographs of four lovely young girls a step beyond childhood. They were not entirely nude, but draped with chiffon that half-revealed tiny breasts and puffs of pubic hair. The faces were seen only in a fragmented way under locks of abundant curly hair. The backgrounds were movie-set interiors, but scattered around the nubile children were branches of apple blossoms and flowering quince. The little girls were posed unselfconsciously with an innocent air of abandon. . . .

"Charlie, look at *this!*"

Sue held out a photograph of a Victorian girl-child with long, thick, blonde curls, angelic features and enormous eyes turned heavenward. She wore a plaid dress with lace collar and was seated on a Victorian sofa, leaning back, her legs emerging from the full skirts and petticoats to reveal her bare thighs and the little mound of pubic hair.

"The Madonna of the Silents," Charlie said. "In the flesh. Miss Vanessa in all her girlish innocence. Jesus . . ."

"Charlie, Mr. Friedlander mustn't see this . . . but what should we do with them . . . should Vanessa have them?"

"Absolutely not. Sue, she'd never forgive you for finding them. For what it could do to her graven image!" He gathered the pictures and returned them to the folder.

"Yes . . . you're right, it would destroy her. Oh, God . . ."

"Wrap them up and let's go. Something's just occurred to me. There're some bookshops down the street—"

"What do you want?"

"A book I remember a review about in *New York* magazine. Strikes a bell."

The first shop didn't have what he wanted but the second one did. He bought a copy of *Victorian Children*, a recent book of photographs, and they went to a cafeteria where he brought coffee to the table and then opened the book.

"Lewis Carroll was the proper Victorian minister who also made friends of little girls," Charlie said. "He wanted his models undressed because, he said, 'Naked children are so perfectly pure and lovely . . .' "

Sue looked disturbed. "That's odd. I once asked Vanessa if the rumors were true that Mr. Fodor was in love with her. You know her answer? She said he was in love with all his little girls. Because they made him feel young again."

"No doubt."

"Another time she said something I almost forgot. He didn't want his little actresses to wear underpants when they were being filmed. He said they were sexier without them."

"He was apparently in good company," Charlie said as he looked at the photographs of child beggars and prostitutes. "This little item should be a best seller on 42nd Street. The dirty old man's handy bedside companion. And Fodor's ...?"

Sue was upset. How could she ever take Vanessa's royal manner seriously again? Was she always acting? What kind of a woman was the *real* Vanessa Oxford? *Was* there a real Vanessa Oxford— or was everything about her play-acting?

"Look at it this way," Charlie said. "There wouldn't have been an *Alice in Wonderland* without Lewis Carroll's attachment for a little girl. And where would Nabokov be without his Lolita, or Fodor—"

"—without his Vanessa," she finished. "All right, then, but what shall I do with these?"

"Short of stashing them in a locker in Grand Central or destroying them, I suggest you take them home. They may come in handy some time."

"I wish we hadn't found them. I really do, Charlie . . ."

THE PRESENT: CASSIE—NO ONE HER GRIEF CAN TELL

"Cassie's never been equipped to face the emotional necessities of life. And now she's suffering a paralysis of will."

It hurt Rebecca to talk so objectively, so clinically, about Cassie, whom she dearly loved, and pitied. She realized much more than Vanessa that none of them had ever penetrated Cassie's private world, perhaps never would.

"She's so depressed again," Vanessa said, her voice anxious, her eyes misted over with tears.

"What's depression but a fear of helplessness?" Rebecca said, refusing the herb tea Vanessa urged on her. She got up stiffly from the sofa, walked across the room to the small table holding bottles, ice and glasses, and poured herself a stiff scotch. She looked toward Sue, offering a glass, but Sue shook her head.

Vanessa's living room was shadowy in the frigid, pewter-bleak winter twilight. The porcelain lamp on the circular table shed its glow on the family miniatures. Vanessa detested bright lights; they gave her a migraine.

Rebecca carried her drink back to the sofa and plumped the pillows to lend support to her arthritic back. Sue sat beside her, feeling somewhat like a dutiful relative summoned to a family crisis. She was embarrassed by this frank discussion of Cassie's problems, and sympathized very much with Cassie. The change in her in the last four months—since Sue had first met her—was shocking. She was deteriorating, her face gaunt, her voice lifeless.

Vanessa, draped in a rose wool caftan, her hair loose around her shoulders, her face shining with the cold cream she used only during the day, perched at the edge of the bergère beside the low table filled with art books and the fresh roses that had arrived that morning from Dann.

"The last few days she hasn't got out of bed," Vanessa was saying. "Not even to watch her soap operas. She has the doorman walk her poodle and the floor maid feeds him, but the poor little animal senses her condition and he hates to leave her. You'd think she would force herself to be up for the dog's sake."

The city had been hit with a series of violent storms. Now there was a threat of a flu epidemic, and the Department of Health had suggested inoculations for everyone over sixty-five. Vanessa had taken her shot in October, but Cassie refused it until, after New Year's, her doctor had insisted on it. She had a bad reaction. She insisted the virus was breaking down the calcium in her bones and strangling her bronchial tubes. Total misery. Vanessa dispatched Flossie to the hotel to spell the practical nurse. Cassie refused to move to Vanessa's house.

"I don't want you fussing over me," she'd said. . . .

Rebecca now tried to relieve Vanessa's anxiety. "Most of us are depressed at some time or other so we don't take it too seriously, but of course it can be a serious illness."

She voiced what Vanessa wanted to hear . . . Rebecca could always be counted on to supply the necessary information, whether on premenstrual tension, postpartum psychosis or the menopausal syndrome. Much easier than looking for answers in the dull technical books. Besides, Vanessa's attention span for the printed word was daily growing more limited. Even with scripts.

"I suppose we all do have the blues at some time or other," Vanessa conceded.

Rebecca didn't answer but she was thinking that there was a considerable difference between the depressions most people experienced and Cassie's dark, desperate retreats . . . her exhausted body craving sleep that her nerves denied her, her indifference to food, even the sweets she loved, her stomach cramps, chest pains.

Rebecca wondered whether Cassie's condition was the result of environment or genetic factors . . . Cassie never mentioned her rootless childhood. What she seemed to have done was repeat and enlarge on her old feelings of worthlessness, self-blame, helplessness. Ant hills loomed up like mountains. Minor disappointments became major rejections.

"Cassie was such a sunny child," Vanessa recalled, soothing her scarred hand. "She never showed anger. But, of course, Mama taught us to be little ladies."

"Cassie didn't *dare* ever show anger"—Rebecca nodded emphatically—"so she's apparently turned her anger in on herself. That's what depression *is* . . . longstanding unexpressed anger . . . and what it does is make its victim feel rotten, worn out, worthless. Believe me, when Cassie does sometimes strike out, there's a lot of pain and fear that goes with it."

"Isn't there some doctor—" Sue began.

"I wonder . . ." Vanessa lowered her head, rubbing her temple in thought. "Rebecca, what do you think of Sunset Hill?"

"I don't know what to advise you . . . I can't advise you about a sanitarium, Vannie, I'm sorry . . ."

Rebecca finished her scotch and prepared to leave. She went to the foyer closet for her mink coat and cap. Vanessa remained seated, lost in her plans. Sue went to the elevator with Rebecca.

"You know, this isn't Cassie's first breakdown," Rebecca said.

"Oh?"

"It happened before."

"Recently?"

"No, years ago. When she was young. When Richie died."

"Richie?" The name sounded familiar to Sue. He had something to do with their early film career?

"Richie Doyle. He was a Fodor discovery. And he was Cassie's first love. Probably her only one. She's never gotten over his death."

The retreat Vanessa had in mind for Cassie's protection was:

SUNSET HILL INN

(From a brochure circulated by the tax-free Sunset Hill Foundation)

It is the purpose of the staff to diagnose and treat functional nervous disorders. Patients are accepted upon referral by their private physician.

Preston Cooke, M.D., the Director, and his staff keep the referring physician apprised of the patient's progress so that he may take over the care again once the patient has recovered and has returned to his home environment.

Patients who need closed hospital care or who have serious illnesses are not accepted.

Patients are encouraged to lead a normal healthy life, structured, but not stifling.

Most patients spend two months at the Inn and are sometimes encouraged to return for re-evaluation.

Vanessa had always put Cassie's needs before her own.

"My time is Cassie's," she always said.

Except for two months of the year, July and August. The first week in July every year she took the Alitalia night flight out of J. F. Kennedy to Milan and then drove north, with an Italian chauffeur at the wheel of the Fiat, to the spa in Italy near the Swiss border where her dear friend Harold Kellogg opened his villa to a few cherished friends. For Vanessa, the visit with Kellogg meant rejuvenation without the knife or the lamb fetus.

Mid-February, she wrote Harold Kellogg about poor Cassie's condition. Perhaps the protocol Kellogg devised in his best-selling health books could restore Cassie to emotional stability: mega-vitamins, vegetarian diet, biofeedback. Harold used whatever was new and seemed sound. His suggestions for The Good Life, which was to say a long, virile life, had been accepted by the rich, the famous and the powerful. Although Vanessa knew it could be a risky, explosive situation, she asked if it would be wise to put Cassie under Harold Kellogg's care.

315

"*Definitely not*," he replied. "*It might prove, under the circumstances, a disaster. Not because of her treatment, but her presence. To have her here, dear Vanessa, is unthinkable. Just imagine what might happen. What could happen. What will happen.*

"*You know our Cassie.*

"*My suggestion is that you make an arrangement for her to enter a good institution. A quiet place with a competent staff and a loving environment.*"

A Month in the Country:

It was a morning Sue would, in retrospect, long to forget.

They had gathered in Cassie's hotel apartment. Vanessa, Sue and Flossie. Vanessa was dry-eyed, paler than usual, her mouth a determined line. Sue was embarrassed and uncomfortable, as was habitual when they were solving "a Cassie problem." She wished she were anywhere but here in the quiet residential hotel where Cassie had lived for a quarter of a century.

Cassie was sleeping, her body in a fetal curve. The previous night the doctor had given her a shot that kept her in a drugged sleep, and although it was nearly nine in the morning, she hadn't stirred, not even when Vanessa used her latchkey to let the three of them in. Vanessa walked into the bedroom where Cassie slept under rumpled covers. Standing over her, watching her chest rise and fall slightly, Vanessa knelt beside her. Sue turned away, not wanting to look, as though staring might defile the purity of the feeling on Vanessa's face.

After a moment Vanessa stood up and turned to the maid, her voice soft but controlled.

"Flossie, Miss Cassie will need casual clothes—warm ones, mostly, and heavy shoes, and several dinner dresses." Sue looked surprised. "Evidently they dress for dinner Saturday night," Vanessa said, smiling slightly.

Vanessa remembered the many times Flossie had packed for Cassie, for vacations abroad or trips to the coast . . . Cassie loved travel . . ."

Flossie watched Cassie. She saw before the others did the first stirring of her frail body. "Miss Cassie, wake up. It's time to get up."

Cassie made an effort to raise her head. Her eyes were dull. Her delicate hands groped among the covers. "Guy? Where is my baby?"

"We took the little doggie home with us last night, Miss Cassie, so you could get a good night's sleep."

"I want him. Where is he? Flossie. *Where is he?*"

"The poodle is in the car." Vanessa moved toward the bed. "Get up, dear. Flossie will make your breakfast while Sue and I help you dress."

Before Vanessa could fold back the comforter, Cassie had pulled it away from her and burrowed deeper into the warm bedclothes. Strands of her thick graying hair had tumbled over her thin, lined face. Her lips were set tightly in anger. Sue watched uneasily, a sickness in the pit of her stomach . . . pity, anxiety for Cassie, embarrassment at Cassie's helplessness. "The fruits of a shattered childhood," Sue's Aunt Harriet had suggested last night when Sue had confided about Cassie's illness. "Sunset Hill does have a brilliant director. Perhaps he can help her . . . poor old lady . . . this might have happened to her anyway, but I'd bet being a star, maybe against her will, and then being nothing and feeling nothing . . . well, I call her a victim, from way back. Her sister played the role. Cassie seems to have lived it."

Still thinking about her aunt's words, Sue helped Cassie into a blue knit jumper dress with a matching jacket and knotted a bright silk scarf around her neck. It was like dressing a rag doll. Flossie brought in a bowl of oatmeal and cream and sat beside Cassie on a bright chintz loveseat, spooning it into her mouth. Sue stood by, holding a handful of tissues to wipe Cassie's lips after each mouthful. She ached at the indignity that was imposed on this helpless creature. Cassie held the cereal in her mouth. "Swallow it, Miss Cassie." Flossie was loving but firm. "*Swallow. . . .*"

At last they were ready. Cassie fully dressed, protected against the March winds, was led to the elevator. Vanessa, before locking the door, said, "Flossie, after we leave, pack the food that's in the refrigerator and take it to my apartment."

"That means Miss Cassie will be gone a long while?"

"It's too early to tell."

Dann's Cadillac was waiting at the entrance, with Jeff at the wheel. The apricot poodle, Guy, was beside him, excited at the sight of his mistress. As soon as Cassie was made comfortable in the back of the car, the poodle jumped from the front seat into her lap. She gathered him in her arms like a beloved child, while he licked her face with his rough little tongue. Cassie sat in the middle, Sue on the left, Vanessa on her right. Vanessa was erect, in control, every inch her sister's guardian, making it clear she would sacrifice anything or anyone for Sister's good.

Sitting beside Cassie, Sue suddenly smiled and held out her hand. It was an impulsive gesture, a nervous attempt to convey her feelings to Cassie.

Cassie accepted it. "Who are you?" she asked in scarcely more than a whisper.

"I'm your friend." Sue looked into Cassie's eyes, seeking the person, hidden now by layers of pain.

They passed from the Hutchinson River Parkway to the Merritt Parkway and were twenty minutes into Connecticut. Jeff turned off at the proper exit and then left again to the state highway. Vanessa looked straight ahead. Cassie's eyes were closed and she slumped against Sue. As the car braked at the entrance of the big white main house and Jeff stepped out, Cassie opened her eyes, staring as though waking from a dream. She snatched the poodle, her grip so tight that he yelped. "Where are we? What is this place . . . ?"

Vanessa stepped out of the car. "Come, dear."

"I'm not going, you can't make me—"

"Come, dear." For a moment Sue felt there was something faintly ominous in the way Vanessa repeated her command, her face set—whether in determination or pain, Sue could not fathom. "*Please*, Sister, don't make it more difficult than it is—"

Cassie cowered against the upholstery. There was a glint in her wide eyes; her cheeks were flushed. She wrenched herself away from Vanessa's grip.

"Sue, help me." Vanessa grasped Cassie's arm again, leaning into the car's interior and somehow managing to hold her balance.

Sue felt sick. She would not be a partner to this, even though it was supposed to be for Cassie's good. Wasn't there some other way? This was so *demeaning*. And then Cassie shuddered as her first whimper became a shriek. "*Leave me alone*." And she kicked at Vanessa, landing her heel unwittingly on Sue's ankle.

"Cassie, you listen to me," Vanessa said, "if you are wild and disruptive you'll only make it worse for yourself. You know what can happen—"

A man was approaching. Medium height, clean-shaven, graying hair clipped short. In his gray tweed suit and narrow black tie he seemed appropriately anonymous, no sign by his appearance of who he was or what he did.

He introduced himself as the director, shook hands with all of them and said to Cassie, "You're in time for lunch, Miss Oxford. Would you like it on a tray in your room?" He reached into the car's interior, took her by the hand and transferred the poodle to Sue as he helped Cassie out. Vanessa was smiling now, the wonderful luminous smile that suggested her prayers had been answered. And to Sue's amazement, a suggestion of a smile, a feminine, wily smile seemed to touch Cassie's lips, suggesting the sexy madcap of an earlier era. What an effect the presence of a man had on them both! Dr. Preston Cooke looked intently at his patient, who, with his guiding hand under her arm, with his gentle, reaffirming touch, walked calmly up the flagstones to the entrance. Here she was greeted by a tall, attractive woman in her mid-forties, dressed in a blue wool skirt and a layered sweater of blue and brown stripes, looking more like a Fairfield County matron than a psychiatric nurse. She greeted Cassie with a warm smile and held out her hands for the poodle. "Is he friendly?" she asked, and introduced herself as Miss Grovenor.

Cassie nodded. "But I'm his good mommy. He loves me best."

"Of course. Would you like to see your room? We have a little wicker bed for him in case you didn't bring one."

"He won't need it. He sleeps with me," Cassie said and followed her quietly up the staircase.

Sue and Jeff returned to the car to wait for Vanessa, who was now closeted with the director. . . .

"You mustn't think I'm overprotective to my sister."

Vanessa was stiff and anxious; the chintz-and-maple comfort of the director's office had no relaxing effect on her. "She's been so erratic and unpredictable lately that I feel safe only when she's with me. But she refuses to live with me. I'm worried about her being alone."

The doctor was sympathetic. He had read Cassie's charts, which had been sent to him by her internist.

"Did she ever have a drinking problem?"

"Oh, goodness, *no!* She never touches alcohol."

"Drugs?"

"Only Valium, and that isn't a drug, is it?" When he shrugged, she changed tactics. "I know it's much too early to say but what is the usual stay here?"

"A month, six weeks, sometimes longer. It depends on the patient. If a family is understanding and able to have her home—"

"Could you arrange for my sister to stay here indefinitely? Oh, that isn't quite what I mean. Over the next few months, perhaps, until the fall? I have to be away and I'd feel easier, knowing she is properly looked after."

Dr. Cooke was agreeable. In spite of himself, he felt some awe in her presence. A considerable lady as well as a great actress. . . .

When Cassie awakened the next morning in the chintz-and-cherrywood Colonial bedroom, Miss Grovenor was raising the shades to the morning sun and a maid in a blue-and-white-striped uniform was bringing in her breakfast tray.

"Good morning," Miss Grovenor said, patting the poodle lying at the foot of the bed. "What time does he make his first safari?"

"Early."

"Shall I have one of the girls walk him or will you?"

Cassie's head felt clear but she had the very strange feeling that she was in the wings, watching the woman on the bed talk to the woman named Miss Grovenor. The nurse said, "I'll take him—if he'll come with me."

Cassie agreed. Poor little Guy loved her, but he was also accustomed to being walked by doormen and porters.

When the maid and Miss Grovenor had left she lay back, staring with distaste at the tray. *Vanessa has managed it,* she thought. *I am out of the way. She's relieved, because she's afraid I'll talk. Imagine, Vanessa afraid of me! But come to think of it, she has every reason to be afraid of me. I'm the one person who could ruin her life.*

Her memory was playing tricks on Vanessa. She could not sleep the night after she had left Cassie with Dr. Cooke.

The routine she followed so slavishly between films or plays—a routine allowing for exercise, nutrition, rest, practically everything Dr. Cooke had suggested for Cassie—had been disrupted by Cassie's breakdown. Memories rushed out of the hidden crevices in her mind, overwhelming her efforts at self-control. *Listen to us! We must be heard!* Memories of herself and Sister. Fragments too long buried, never expecting to see the light of reality! Cassie. Little Sister.

Your problem, Vanessa. Your obligation. Your love.

"Take care of our Cassie," Mama had said in her hoarse voice when she was in the intensive care unit, her heart's beat artificially strengthened. Vanessa promised, of course. She and Mama were united in looking after Cassie.

But whatever Vanessa did, it was never enough. Or rather, never quite right.

Snatches. Fragments. Joshua Fodor. Richie. Alistair, the Englishman, a younger son who as a film director gave Cassie her greatest success so that she became the darling of Mayfair. Alistair eventually became Lord Something, with a castle in Ireland, another in England, a Georgian house in London. He adored Cassie. . . . Once when she and Cassie were looking through *Country Life* they found a photograph of him, lean, impeccable, riding to the hounds, and she'd asked Cassie, "Are you sorry you didn't marry him?" And Cassie had said, "The English baffle me. I don't have Bea Lillie's class—*or* her wit . . ." So many glittering opportunities wasted or forfeited or ignored because Cassie could love only the ones she pitied, the losers in life . . . What had Cassie done with *her* life, let it dribble away to nothing . . . And she'd labored to get her on the right track, she'd taught, explained, corrected, encouraged. . . .

She tossed sleeplessly.

Dr. Preston Cooke called the next morning and said, "Miss Oxford, would you write out some facts about your sister? It would be very helpful."

"What do you want to know?"

"Whatever has happened that you feel has helped shape her life."

"I'm not sure . . . I mean, how shall I do it?"

"Don't plan it. Write down anything that comes into your

mind. And send it to me. It will help me with Cassie, and it might be helpful to you as well. . . . I'll look forward to whatever you think is of interest."

THE PAST: VANESSA REMEMBERS: FREE ASSOCIATION NOTES FOR DR. COOKE

I ALWAYS listened to Rebecca, my best friend. She had great insight. She once said, "Some children are born so sensitive, so delicately attuned that it's difficult for them to cope with the problems of living that most of us accept as normal. That's Cassie."

Rebecca was right. I see it now. I used to grow so impatient with Cassie's quirks but now I can at last accept the fact that she wasn't responsible.

I've always tried to do what was best for her. She was such an enchanting child. Big opal-blue eyes, abundant red-gold hair, small-boned, plump little body. She was a born mimic. Even then she mimicked me. But if she saw that it disturbed me, she always stopped and looked upset, and if ever I scolded her, even lightly, she broke into tears. On tour she would often make fun of our elders, which shocked me, because I was so serious, so deathly afraid of antagonizing adults.

I had much better results disciplining her than Mama did. Mama coddled her too much. Everyone spoiled her because she was such a darling funny little girl.

Later, when we were adults, Rebecca said, "I can't understand it. Cassie adores you. But she's never herself around you."

"What do you mean?" I asked.

"She's *uncomfortable* with you, Vanessa. She's tense. As if she's terrified of your disapproval."

"That's perfectly natural, I should think. The younger one always looks up to the older. Especially because Mama always consulted me." Still, I remember her saying, "Why don't you ask me sometimes what *I* want? Everybody tells me what to do. Nobody asks what *I* want to do."

But we meant it all for her best. Mama didn't want to upset her. She felt that Cassie was delicate.

I tried to help Mama bring up Cassie. You have to understand, Dr. Cooke, we weren't two little girls living in a house with Mama and a papa, going to the same school year after year, having the same friends, putting down roots. Such children can be spoiled and bratty and their parents, neighbors and teachers can be tolerant and forgiving, thinking they'll grow out of it.

It was different for us. We were children with children's needs, but we were living in a transient world made up almost entirely of adults. And the grown-up faces changed from season to season. New people, new towns, new situations. Nothing was stable or permanent. Except Mama.

I already knew that on today's behavior depended tomorrow's bread. If we were brats, the company manager would get rid of us. I was serious beyond my years. Disciplined out of necessity and fear.

It was my responsibility to look after my little sister. Cassie's instinct for rebellion was uniquely hers, inherited, I believe, from our father. None of it came from me, I was always older and more serious than my chronological age suggested.

I was her model. Even after we grew up, she measured perfection for herself by my standards.

Whatever was mine, from a new dress to a new role was, in her mind, always superior to what she had.

At the same time she was always so eager to do something for me. To show her affection by some gesture. But then she'd announce glumly, "Anything I would do for Vanessa wouldn't turn out right. She does everything better anyway."

When we toured as children, Mama, Cassie and I shared a room.

Later, when we lived in Manhattan apartments or Beverly Hills houses, we all had separate bedrooms. Mother always occupied the master bedroom, dressing room and bath. Sister and I both had big rooms, with spacious closets and private baths. Each day, the maid tidied. But after Cassie got dressed, her place looked like a rag bag. Dresses scattered on the chairs and carpet. Cassie never settled on the first dress she tried on. Drawers open, hats, bags, scarves, shoes littered everywhere.

It was the same when we were little. What set us apart from other children were our white, long ribbed stockings. Each year Mama bought two pair and every night before bed she washed out the stockings worn that day. But they weren't always dry by morning and we girls had to wear day-old stockings. It was very important to keep them as clean as possible, but Cassie's were stained after five minutes' wear. Mostly at the knees. She seemed to stumble over every rock in the road or stone in the grass. Her knees were always scabbed, and she pulled at the scabs, never letting them heal completely. It drove me wild. When I'd see her rubbing her left knee, or applying that horse liniment they used for sprains and aches at the circus, I'd tell her, "If you'd look where you were going you wouldn't take such falls. Your head is in the clouds."

But no matter how much Mama or I pleaded with her, or reprimanded her, Cassie never changed.

Mama would say with a resigned sigh, "Cassandra needs five people to take care of her."

When we were in our teens and twenties, she was remarkably healthy and bursting with vitality. I suppose now you'd call her behavior hyperactive. She could work all day at the studio or, if she was in a play, all evening, and then go out for dinner and dancing with one of her beaux until dawn without showing the slightest fatigue. She was marvelously thin in those days. And hysterically funny. But it wasn't the kind of humor you can put into words. You had to see her. She'd be looking at you so angelically and suddenly she'd stick out her tongue. She still sometimes sticks out her tongue at me. But she was very amiable and good-natured. Unless we forgot to have chocolates in the house. She was crazy about chocolate, and she always had to have some after dinner. She'd sit there like a child, licking the melted chocolate from her fingers. If the box were empty and we forgot to replace it—I never touch sweets—she would have a temper tantrum.

"You never think of me," she'd scream. "I don't count for anything in this house. You're the big shot here, Vanessa, only you."

In our family we never complained of sickness. We weren't Christian Scientists but we did have a positive attitude toward health. If we were ill, good manners kept us from complaining. Whenever I felt unwell—there was a period when I suffered from cluster headaches—I overcame the weakness before it could cripple me.

We were too aware of each other's feelings to spread anxiety. We did what had to be done without fuss. Pains, aches, fever— we hid our misery from the director, terrified that he might replace us.

Work was our salvation.

Hard work and self-control saved me from untold psychosomatic ills, I'm quite sure.

But not Cassie.

She was the vision of perfect health. Yet I think the seeds of her illness were planted early. She was a colicky baby. Mama was up nights with her, walking the floor. In her teens she developed the nervous indigestion that has plagued her ever since.

The small things one remembers . . .

"Flossie, I'm so cold!" When she was on tour or on Broadway, Flossie accompanied her. "Feel my hands, Flossie. They're *ice!*"

And Flossie, massaging her hands, would soothe her. "It's your circulation, Miss Cassie."

"There's ice inside of me, my veins are filled with ice."

"Maybe you should see the doctor, Miss Cassie."

"Don't tell Vanessa. I don't want to worry my sister."

"I won't tell, Miss Cassie. *If* you go to the doctor . . ."

"I promise."

But she never did, not in those years of her growing fame, not until these last ten years when her doctor was always on call, always trying to soothe her. And then the Valium syndrome began. . . .

Whatever was bothering Cassandra and led to her present illness, it developed slowly, in such subtle ways that it took us a long time to become aware of it. I've said she was accident-prone.

I blamed that condition on her impulsive haste. She was *always* in a hurry, even when going nowhere. Until the past few years she was always so active she couldn't sit still. During the filming of *Jesus Christ—Son and Savior*, she persuaded one of the extras to let her ride his horse. She'd never ridden before but it was a dare from her girl friend Rosalind Terhune, who also played a small part in the film. Cassie mounted, picked up the reins and the animal took off. He ran wild, and the extras were too paralyzed to catch him.

Cassie held on, screaming. I could not tell whether from joy or fright. I called out for somebody to stop her. It was a low-hanging branch that finally did. She fell, the horse ran off and Mr. Fodor carried her into his office. She had a mild concussion. When she came to, she said, "I'm glad it didn't happen to my sister. She might have been killed."

I happen to be an excellent horsewoman, which she seemed to have forgotten. Nothing so foolish as that accident could have happened to me.

The filming of *Jesus Christ—Son and Savior* was a difficult time for me since I was playing two roles, Mary, Mother of God, *and* Mary Magdalene. I felt these weeks should be a time of contemplation for me, a withdrawal from the world. I read the Bible, especially the New Testament. I thought of the Virgin Mary, and I tried not to think too much of Mary Magdalene. Cassie was blossoming, full of high spirits, clowning all over the place with her friend Rosalind. Both girls had small parts in the film but were expected on the set at all times, and I must say they were both a source of some aggravation to Mr. Fodor. Rosalind's energy was as boundless as Cassie's. They loved to dance and the character of the partners didn't matter as long as the young men were skillful dancers. Richie (Richard Doyle) didn't approve. He didn't dance, his strict Irish Catholic mother allowed no frivolities in her sons' lives. Cassied loved him, but she also loved her good times.

Mama and I tried to harness her exuberance, but with little effect. She just didn't show much sense, but everyone loved her.

No wonder she was always Mama's pet, her favorite daughter.

The basics of loving always eluded her. When Flossie first came to her, Cassandra was living in her own apartment, two rooms in a residential hotel that she used just as a place to hang her hat. Naturally, Flossie took over. She knew how to cook for Cassie, including the chocolate nut brownies and fudge Cassie always had to have. She gave Cassie the devotion she might give a beloved child.

Cassie has always lived her own style. She kept ridiculous hours. She ate when it pleased her, slept little or much, depending on her whims, turned down roles that were later given to Constance Talmadge and Dorothy Gish.

She had numerous friends and many suitors, and they rang her at all hours and she didn't mind, although it must have interfered with her rest. She was generous with money and it seldom mattered who asked for help. She gave.

Before crowds began to disturb her, we traveled a great deal on the luxury ships that crossed the Atlantic. She loved the ocean and she always made the trip lively and eventful.

Our friend Rebecca says that my presence at a party does nothing for it. But once Cassie appears on the scene, it becomes as exciting as a circus parade.

For some reason I can't explain, while her nature was warm and sympathetic, she lacked the capacity to look after others. Except for animals. She was obsessed with our little dogs, she couldn't bear to see an animal in pain. When her little apricot poodle developed kidney trouble the world stopped for Cassie. She seemed paralyzed. As always in an emergency, she sent a frantic call to Flossie.

In our family, Cassie worried and I spent endless hours soothing away her fears.

"Cassie, why don't you have a drink?" Rebecca often suggested. "It would help you relax."

Alcohol is anathema to her. I suspect it stems from the memory of our father's weakness.

She has always been compulsive about her weight, too. The lovely curves of her body disgusted her. She wanted to look like a boy. It's true that when she was younger, we used to tease her about her tendency toward plumpness. But we never thought she'd become so compulsive about dieting.

She lost weight. She gained weight. She lost it again. Her seamstress was forever taking her clothes in or letting them out.

Actors who appeared with Cassie suggested her nervous eating was worse whenever she prepared for a new play. She would fret over the script, unsure of her judgment. Apprehensive. Once she signed the contract, her anxiety seemed to obliterate all sensible thinking. Can I play the part? Will I be good? Will the critics pan me? What will Mama and Vanessa think?

"Cassie, don't be so fearful. Remember all your successes," we reminded her. But it did no good. Her body exhausted, her mind racing like a caged creature, she would simply collapse.

No appetite.

"Just one bite, Miss Cassie." Flossie would coax her. "One little bite."

"I can't, Flossie. It gets stuck."

In retrospect, I believe the movies were easier for her than the theater. The pressures of making a film made no demands on her. She never showed the slightest interest in any area but her own role. Movies were a lark. Like Rosalind Terhune, Constance Talmadge, Bessie Love, Dorothy Gish, Clara Bow, she was adored, pampered and idolized. I realize now that for her, the movies were ideal. That is, the silents. She listened to the director, followed his orders and that was it. She sailed through each film on her natural gifts, charm and Mr. Fodor's training. Few directors demanded more of her than she could give.

I've always regretted the fact that she never lived up to her potential as a great comedienne.

To take the initiative, to experiment, to try new forms were beyond her capacity.

In the '30s when we both returned to the theater, Cassie was confronted by a new set of conditions. She respected the theater and wanted very much to be accepted by its people. Movie critics scarcely touched her either by flattery or carping. But to face a sophisticated Broadway audience seemed to set off fresh anxieties. On the stage, she was a star and a victim.

I shudder at the memory of Cassie showing up the first day of rehearsal. Her hands trembled as she held the script, her eyes were unfocused, her throat parched. She went through a series of successful performances in hit plays with outer gaiety, and inner anguish. The ills of Job seemed to afflict her. Medicine for gall bladder, for ulcers, for constant stomach pains, nerves so tight she could scarcely control herself. But on stage she was superb, gay, charming, fun to watch, to listen to. She made the audience have fun all the while she was suffering.

Until just before World War II when she played on Broadway with a man she greatly respected and perhaps was learning to love.

Luther was a beautiful man who'd posed in his youth for Rodin's "The Kiss." He was a brilliant actor who deserved stardom. But in his case a success was usually followed by a failure. A "yo-yo syndrome," one critic called it. "As though he can't accept his own worth and seeks failure."

Oddly enough, now that I think on it, it was a trait he shared with Mr. Fodor. "Guilt after success," Rebecca Kahn says, "the need to expiate for success undeserved, a self-punishing prophecy." Strange that Sister and I should both find men of this caliber attractive.

When I heard about the basic reason for his failures I debated whether to inform Cassie. She was obviously happier than I had seen her since Richie's death. The play was successful. It was about a couple based on Pierre and Marie Curie who'd discovered radium, and the warmth of their love and respect for each other. It made for good solid theater. Cassie and Luther were ecstatically happy.

Dr. Cooke, in the theater there are no secrets. Players are one big gossiping family. The first mention of Cassie's and Luther's affair was in that awful Walter Winchell's column, with Winchell sounding so pious and hypocritical. "Flash. The star of *Pierre and Marie* has been on the wagon for nine months. The famous younger Oxford sister who plays opposite him is the reason. He's no longer one of the regulars who dry out periodically at Stamford Hall ..."

Cassie didn't read Winchell, but her friends did.

"Did you know about his weakness?" I asked her.

"Not in the beginning."

"You aren't thinking of marrying him?"

I could imagine nothing more catastrophic for our Cassie, who hated liquor, than to be involved with an alcoholic.

She didn't answer and I wondered if she'd made a commitment to him. He came to dinner several times and he was courteous and charming, with a sense of humility that enchanted

Mother. He spoke of future plans for himself and Cassie, mentioning Alfred Lunt and Lynn Fontanne. A partnership would insure Cassandra's future in the theater, he said. Audiences loved great acting teams.

"Do you think he can stay sober?" Mama worried, remembering no doubt how often Father swore off drink only to lapse back into hopeless alcoholism again.

Both of us were disturbed, wondering what measures to take. The play continued to standees, the press was generous with photographs and articles and interviews about this new acting couple. I rejoiced for Cassie. I prayed that Luther would not crack under his success.

One afternoon, he took us to lunch at the Tavern on the Green. It was a charming occasion, and afterward we all decided to walk through the park to Fifth Avenue.

Mother and Sister walked ahead, Luther and I behind them.

"I'm so sorry we've not had the opportunity to know you as Cassandra does," I said. He had always been somewhat distant with me, but more receptive to Mama because he could sustain his charm with her without being afraid she might see through the surface to the weakness beneath. But my vision was distressingly clear. I wanted him to be perfect, to be worthy of Cassie's love and devotion. He was not.

"You will, I hope." His voice was resonant. "Cassie is just beginning to come into her own," he said. "Cassie's future is limitless. Not only the modern comedy, but the old Restoration comedies would be great for her. She has the beauty, wit and the subtle touch of the great comediennes."

"Oh, I'm so happy to hear that!" To express my gratitude, I linked my arm through his. "You know, Luther, since you are now so close, almost family, whether you marry or not, I want to tell you I am glad you are older than Cassie. She needs a very strong man. Some might even say a father figure, or whatever it's called."

"Now, Vanessa—"

"I'm not talking Freudian gibberish." I held back, so Cassie and Mama wouldn't overhear. "I must confess something only Mama, Cassie and I are aware of. Cassie adored our father. So did I. He was an extraordinary man, literate, charming, Black Irish, I think, in temperament. He loved us but not enough to overcome his alcoholism. He had a very low frustration tolerance and never realized his potential, and when he was upset he turned to the bottle."

Then I told him a frightening incident in our lives that I hoped would make a strong impression on him.

I told him of the time Cassie and I went to visit our father, when we were already with Mr. Fodor and he was in California, deciding on a location for his new film venture. Cassie, Mama and I had a lovely vacation together until it was interrupted by a letter from Mama's sister, our Aunt Annie.

She had a letter from a friend of father's. He was sick. He wanted desperately to see us.

"What do you think, Mama?" It was during our nightly family talk and we were sitting in the kitchen, in robes and nighties, sipping hot Ovaltine.

Mother shrugged.

"If Father needs us . . ."

"You must decide for yourself." She spoke softly without inflection, as she always did when I asked her what I should do and she answered that I must make my own decisions.

"I must go." I tried to sound resigned, as though it were a duty I couldn't shirk. But the excitement I felt was difficult to contain. My longing to see Father would come to pass: "Did Aunt Annie give his address?"

"Yes." She held the letter out. "A state hospital."

Someone said that doing your duty is a spiritual reward that brings joy to the soul. I felt so good. It is hard to explain, but I was aware of a deep spiritual feeling, the kind that the nuns must experience when they go on retreat.

"If you go, Cassie should go with you." Mama was surprisingly firm about it. When we told Cassie she burst into tears of joy. She couldn't wait, she wanted to go immediately to Father. I reminded her that she must be kind to him, not aloof and angry as she often had been. Mama saw us off on the train.

We got off the coach at midnight at this dark, deserted hamlet. The station was shut. There was nobody around but a couple of Negroes. You can imagine how terrified we were. I was fifteen, Cassie was fourteen, and for all of our experience touring with

Mama, we were uneasy about this adventure. I don't know what we had expected—surely a lighted station, some houses, a nearby hotel or boarding house. But this was all darkness and it reminded me of one of Mr. Fodor's films, where two girls are trapped in a haunted house with a rapist.

Cassie clung to me. She was shaking and about to cry. I gritted my teeth. Pulling Cassie along with me, I marched to the station and knocked on the door. Somewhere a dog howled. I pounded again. "Open up," I shouted.

One of the dark figures ambled over to us. "Ain't nobody there, ma'am. Station master locks up at ten."

"Where is the town? Which way?" I made my voice sound low and stern with authority.

"Right around the corner, ma'am. Jest a block. I c'n show you."

He motioned to the other fellow who came over. I said, "We are here to visit our father, who is sick."

"Where is he stayin', ma'am?"

"With the sheriff. Will you show us the way?"

"Some of the way, ma'am." His voice thickened. I hoped he was sufficiently scared not to get any wrong ideas. They offered to take our bags; Cassie clung to hers but I said to her in an undertone, "Let them carry it."

We followed them along a wide dirt road. I knew what Cassie was thinking. We had both seen Mr. Griffith's *The Birth of a Nation* and remembered Mae Marsh preferring a shocking death to rape by a Negro. The sheer horror of that scene filled our nightmares for weeks afterward. Now I could see that Cassie felt we were facing a similar situation in real life.

Each step was endless. Cassie clung to me as we half-walked, half-stumbled in the dark. No moon showed us the way, nor were there any lights. Oh God, I prayed, keep us safe! There was a cut in the road, and to our eyes, accustomed now to the dark, a few houses appeared, dark blocks without lights except for a faint pinpoint here and there. They looked like row houses, all linked together, and finally there was a light on a sign on a two-story house that said "HOTEL." I called out to the Negroes, "I think we'll stop here for the night. It's too late to visit our father." They set the suitcases on the steps. In the dim light I could see they were quite young, their caps pulled down over their faces.

I opened my purse to tip them, and one said, "No, ma'am, much obliged anyway. Ma'am . . . ?"

"Yes?"

"Jes' don't tell the sheriff nuthin' . . . I mean . . ."

"I understand. I thank you very much."

I behaved like a lady and they responded to it. When the owner of the hotel finally opened the door and showed us to a room, we felt safe at last. Cassie burst into tears. Of relief, I suppose.

"Vanessa, you're so brave. I'd be so scared without you. Don't ever leave me behind . . ."

I held and hugged and kissed her, I understood how much she needed reassurance. Then we ate our sandwiches, which Mama had made for us. They were a day old but they tasted good. Finally, just before she fell asleep, Cassie asked me, "Vanessa, what did you mean, saying Father was staying at the sheriff's? Is he in jail?"

"No silly I just said that to scare those boys . . . in case they had any ideas."

I held her in my arms all night, she was shaking so.

It was worse the next day. We hired a horse and buggy and driver to take us to the place, which was five miles outside the dreary little town. This was mining country, very depressing. But I resolved to be strong for both of us, and I maintained my strength. As we approached the institution, we saw a building of yellow brick with turrets and long, narrow windows. Barred windows. Cassie was clutching me again. We reached the entrance where the road cut into the dingy parched grass and weeds. We stepped out of the buggy. I had already made arrangements with the man to wait for us, and he took out a feedbag for his horse and prepared to lounge in the grass. I rang the bell.

"We've come to see Mr. Oxford. Mr. Patric Oxford," I told the man in a kind of uniform who opened the door for us.

He looked at us up and down. I assumed my best ladylike air. "This way," he said gruffly.

It was the smell that most affected me at first, not only a hospital smell but a mixture that told of something worse than ordinary sickness. Later I learned that it was from the medication they gave the patients every night to keep them sedated.

There was a bare desk in the office, and behind it sat a heavy-set older man who looked like he'd been in the sun too long. His skin was mottled, and the fat melted into his heavy jaw, forming double chins. He was chewing a stale cigar. He summoned a nurse to take us to see Father. We passed some sights I will never forget. One man was standing upright, his arms outspread, his muscles rigid, as though he were made of plaster.

"What's wrong with him?" I asked the nurse in a whisper.

"He thinks he's a tree," she said. "Try not to mind what you see."

I tried not to, mostly for Cassie's sake. But she saw everything. The half-naked girl crumpled in the corner, her mouth drooling, mumbling to herself. Two stringy-haired women clawing at each other until a man in a white jacket separated them, and then one threw herself on the floor, wailing like a baby, pounding her head against the wall. The long, dank ward of men lying on messy beds, men who looked like corpses. The smell of urine. And Cassie growing white.

Then we saw Father.

Was this our father? He lay in bed, curled up, knees to chest, scrawny fingers clawing the coverlet, the way Cassie used to hold tight to her security blanket when she was a little girl. What had happened to his beautiful face? He was all gray, his eyes sunken. He wasn't even aware of us.

"Wake up. You've got company. Look who's here."

The nurse got no response. I approached the bed. Cassie backed away...the smell...we waited. He was shut away in his private world. Finally the nurse said, "He doesn't remember." She sounded genuinely sorry.

The man in the office asked if we had any luck. I shook my head.

He said something about dementia praecox.

We left. Outside, Cassie vomited.

He was a catatonic schizophrenic. I learned that later. And it wasn't merely the alcohol—he had, what did they call it, a wet brain, or something.

I told Luther only about the alcohol.

"Now you understand why the sight of a drink sends poor Cassie into hysterics," I said.

The play about the Curies celebrated a year's run, and we were celebrating with a party backstage. Luther got drunk. The next few days he played his part in an alcoholic fog. Cassie was so in love with him that his weakness, rather than disgusting her, became a challenge. She felt it her duty to help him regain his sobriety. As he began having trouble remembering his lines, Cassie learned his as well as her own and managed to prompt him and save his reputation.

But not for long. Attendance fell off. His understudy was obliged to pinch-hit more and more often. Cassie developed an ulcer. Luther finally dried out, and then broke with her.

"I can't make it even with you," he said. "I'm finished, Cassie. I don't want to end up like Vanessa said your father did." He spent the rest of his life in England. The last we heard he was traveling in the provinces with some third-rate company, and he finally collapsed with malnutrition and degeneration of the liver. Cassie never spoke of him again. Looking back, I realize her feelings were already going flat. She once told me that she hated me because I had told him about our father, that I had terrified him so much that he left her and then drank even more heavily to forget his fears. Perhaps . . . but even so, I am convinced she was better off for getting rid of him. He would have destroyed her. Don't you agree?"

She started having new trouble when she played in *The Drudge of Oliver Street*, a charming Cinderella role with all the warmth and insight Sir James Barrie gave his women. She couldn't speak her lines, although she knew them well. Mama and I held countless conferences. We didn't know what to do. I don't, I'm afraid, believe very much in psychiatrists—you know my feeling about Freud, which I made clear to you before—but if it would help Cassie, I was willing for her to have analysis. She refused. Friends are better than psychiatrists, she said. They listen and they love.

As a last resort I suggested we do a play together. My presence, I hoped, would restore her to her old state, which was always a little off-center but reasonably stable, I felt. We decided on a new play by an English dramatist who had taken the friendship of Virginia Woolf and V. Sackville-West and had created, with delicate, sensitive insights, the love story of two brilliant women.

Cassie was given her choice of roles, which had been customary in the past when we had appeared together. She chose Virginia Woolf.

We began rehearsals with high hopes. There had been *The Well of Loneliness*, and *The Children's Hour* by Lillian Hellman, but nothing comparable to this drama, which was a probing into the lives of women long before the beginning of the feminist movement.

Cassie hated the play. "I can't do it."

"Yes, you can!" said Valentine, the young director.

"I don't *understand* them." Cassie seemed frightened. Valentine said privately to me that Cassie closed her mind to the fact that women could love women as well as men. It was a psychological situation that he understood, being homosexual, and that made him a good director for this play.

"Yes, you can, Cassie." We tried to convince her together. "You'll be *great*."

We were to open in Cleveland. Cassie was in a state. No sleep, no food, memory uncertain. She was a wraith. It was a nightmare for the cast.

And for me, too, I confess.

When Cassie suffered, I suffered. Aware of her helplessness, wanting to protect her, to give her strength, I summoned Mama to the opening. Together we would hopefully find a means to help her. Well . . . if rehearsals were awful, the opening was a disaster. I don't know how we lived through it. Cassie couldn't remember a line. I fed her cues and, whenever possible, her lines. As did everyone who had a scene with her. When the curtain was finally rung down we were all drained and defeated.

I felt the audience should have their money refunded.

"Don't say that in front of Cassie," Mama cautioned me.

"Perhaps it would wake her up to what she's doing to us all," I said. But of course I did keep quiet. Valentine spoke his appreciation of my tact and support of Cassie.

As the tour continued, Cassie eventually proved excellent in the role. Perhaps her fragile and depressed emotional state evoked the skill to portray Virginia Woolf's rare sensitivity and her self-destruction. Cassie always received the greatest number of curtain calls. Deservedly, of course.

She was still tense and sick before each performance. She ate little. Even the homemade chocolate and fudge she loved now made her squeamish. Friends who had played with her at other times now told me this pattern wasn't new. I hadn't performed with Cassie since our last film for Mr. Fodor so I had no idea of how she felt.

I knew I must never play with her again, otherwise, as you can understand, I would become identified with her. And I could not *afford* failure, either monetary or critical. *Our* future depended on my success.

I hesitate to write this and yet feel that I owe it to you since you, Dr. Cooke, will be restoring her to health.

Rebecca once said, "Vanessa, I hate to say this, but you are Cassie's ulcer." The words stung. Coming from anyone else, I would consider them cruel. But Rebecca didn't mean to be unkind. She is just so honestly concerned, especially where Cassie and I are concerned. She *means* well.... Now I wonder if others have also misinterpreted my feelings for my sister. I've wanted only to help her, but somehow there were always barriers between us that as sisters we found impossible to surmount. We love each other. We are proud of each other's achievements. Often Cassie has shown a talent far beyond my expectations, when she has been nearly as good as I.

During one of our endless conversations about my sister, Rebecca once said, "I have never seen such a love-hate relationship!" But I cannot believe Cassie hates me. She admires me. She wants to emulate me. My opinion means so much to her. She is always fretting whether I will like what she is doing. And why not? After all, when I praise or criticize her, it's always been for her good. She knows that, deep down.... Is anger the other side of love? Men who have professed to love me have later turned on me in absolutely murderous fury. I can withstand their hatred. But not Cassie's. What she, Mama and I went through together was enough to weld us for eternity. No man has ever meant as much to me as Mama and Sister.... Indeed, I might have married Piers van Cleave, who produced my finest film, if he had not been so jealous of my devotion to them.

But Cassie's sick now, and I am in despair. Could I have helped her more? Was it wrong to insist that she remain in the theater?

But she's never had any other interests. We were both actresses from childhood on.

Dr. Cooke, I have been searching in the corners of my mind, wondering if I have overlooked something she tried to tell me, something that I was blind to.

From the time I was a small child I was alert to opportunities not only for myself but for my little sister.

You see I learned early that *acceptance* means security. That was most important for a youngster who'd seen her mother and sister actually hungry.

Our prospects for food and shelter improved after I went to work for Joshua Fodor. It became necessary then to work for a new set of values, to be so good that I would become an indispensable member of Mr. Fodor's company. I concentrated on what he wanted. I worked hard for our future. I had to do things that I could not talk about, even to you. But whatever I was obliged to do, I did for Cassie and Mama.

Cassie was interested only in herself, except where Mama was concerned. After Mama's coronary, we both protected and cared for her. Rebecca said that Cassie made a cult of Mama's heart condition. Perhaps I did, too. Men who loved me couldn't understand the depth of our feeling toward each other. They resented my devotion to my family. This has always baffled me. It seems immature and selfish, for certainly a true love shouldn't need to demand complete and exclusive attention from the loved one. No one could ever accuse Mama of interfering in our lives. She was there when we needed her, but she was unobtrusive and she never tried to influence us.

Our devotion to her was not a demand on her part. Don't forget she was both father and mother to us, and she managed with tact and gentleness to put us on our own early in our lives. Nevertheless, memories of childhood insecurity continue to haunt Cassie. Away from Mama, at first we were too small, scared girls, weak and defenseless. We were pygmies in a world of giants, and no matter how kind the giants were, we remained at their mercy. We molded our personalities to their whims. We stayed quiet, meek, unobtrusive. I grew a shell to protect myself. To survive. Poor Cassie was not able to.

I thought back to our childhood those nights recently while

I sat by her bedside. Sometimes when she cried out in her sleep, her sobs were heartbreaking. I held her, wanting to protect her. And always in those moments a picture drifted into my mind.... Two small girls, shivering in a drafty dressing room in some bleak midwestern town hall, waiting for Mama to come and fetch us, knowing that before long she would lead us home.

I pray, Dr. Cooke, that you can save my sister.

The only other man who might have is long since dead. His name was Richie Doyle. He could not control his sexual impulses and was unfaithful to her. I think that's why he killed himself. Even now I wish I had been able to warn her about what kind of person he was, but of course I did not know anything about it ... until it was too late for me to do anything about it....

Vanessa looked over the long letter, decided it was fair, honest and compassionate, and sent it off to Dr. Cooke with a prayer that it would do some good. And with the feeling that she had done her best. As always.

THE PRESENT: SUE AND VANESSA, AND WHAT TO DO WHEN THE STARLIGHT DIMS ON A CAREER AND A LOVE AFFAIR

THE STREETS were car deep in fog and rain. Vanessa and Rebecca stepped out of Dann's car and scurried under the awning to the snug security of Vanessa's apartment and a tea tray fragrant with clove-studded lemon, cinnamon toast and Fortnum and Mason's special blend of tea leaves.

Vanessa leaned back in the bergère, overcome with fatigue. She

did not mention her exhaustion to Rebecca, who was apt to remind her tartly that neither of them was sixteen and fatigue was
inevitable—especially after the emotionally draining experience
of visiting Cassie at Sunset Hill. But Vanessa never shirked her
obligation to Cassie and she wasn't about to start now. The tea
would restore her. Images of her visit to Cassie ran through her
mind.

*Cassie was supposed to be less agitated. But when she spoke
she twisted her hands so her fingers seemed to claw the air, tension
was like an electric charge around her.*

"Get me out of here," she screamed. "I want to go home."

*She squeezed the poodle so, he yelped in pain. She smothered
her face in him.* "Get me out of here—"

*She's receiving therapy. She was so hyped up that she moved
compulsively from her bed to a chair and back again.*

*Dr. Cooke asked when this "episode" began. At the time of
the retrospective? Was there anything about the retrospective to
disturb her?"*

She said she couldn't imagine, which might have been mis-
construed as a lie by those who didn't know her, but it was no
lie. What if she saw only what it suited her to see. This was how
she survived. Would it have been better if she were more like
Cassie? On the thin edge of insanity?

If only she could inoculate Cassie with her own strength!

Meanwhile she was at a professional dead end. Mrs. Kramer had
received no offers for her services. Interest generated by the Fodor
retrospective seemed to have tapered off. She pondered how to
rekindle it.

It was Cassie, ironically, who received an offer to play in a
comedy aboupt a madcap heiress who refused to allow age to
intimidate her. It offered some penetrating wit on the problems
of outliving one's friends and lovers. Of course Cassie couldn't
accept the role, being full of tranquilizers at Sunset Hill. So
Vanessa graciously offered to pinch hit for her, as she had before
whenever Cassie was indisposed (some of her greatest successes,
including *Camille*, came about in this fashion).

"They've sent the script to Katharine Hepburn," Mrs. Kramer
reported back to Vanessa. "Their feeling was that you were too
... too spiritual for the part."

Vanessa now pondered, as she sipped her tea, whether Mrs. Kramer was the right agent for her. Perhaps she'd begun to take Vanessa for granted. At the same time Vanessa contemplated hiring a publicity man. Never before had this been necessary, but life had changed. You couldn't count on people remembering you unless you made news. It was all too degrading, but Vanessa knew the time of refinement was past. She would speak to Sue's friend ... Charlie ... about doing some publicity. Of course the *important* thing, she told herself, was to keep Joshua Fodor's image and his memory alive. And the best way to do that was for Vanessa Oxford to get back into the limelight herself....

Inaction made Vanessa restless. She always had to be doing something, except, of course, for her periods of contemplation. To wake up to a blank calendar made her itchy.

Besides, Sue was nearly finished with the filing, collating and arranging of the material of Vanessa's productive film and stage years. Sue planned to take a brief vacation in Williamstown with her father and then return in the autumn to the Film Wing as a full-time assistant to Mrs. Elsberg. The Film Wing was pleased with the results of her work on Fodor and the Oxford sisters. Her next project would be to compile oral histories of the careers of famous film directors. Mr. Friedlander planned to expand the book department and was counting on Sue to take charge of that too. And Sue was delighted, grateful for the challenge. Mrs. Elsberg was a joy to work with.

Vanessa made it clear that she was unhappy to see Sue leave. She had even made a tentative offer to take Sue on as her secretary, a suggestion Sue delicately refused. She'd learned a great deal about the Vanessa Oxford mystique, much of it good, much of it rather shocking.... Not that she thought any the less of the elderly actress, but she did want to get away, away from the intensity of the Oxford ménage, out into some fresh small-town air with fewer dark notes playing in the wings.

Meanwhile Vanessa hadn't forgotten her plan to meet with Charlie to pick his brains about publicity, which she never called publicity. She referred to it as "information awareness." It sounded less crass that way.

"Charles, this is vital for me—how do we keep the Fodor image alive in the public's mind?"

Charles was a dinner guest and Vanessa had asked Sue to stay on too. They were seated in the dining room of Vanessa's apartment. Flossie was serving poached salmon with a green sauce and fresh peas with mint and a choice white wine.

Vanessa was at the head of the table, cool in exquisite white lace and muslin cut in Empire style that came from one of her trunks stored in Dann's basement. Beside her, Sue in a denim skirt and white T-shirt felt like a peasant. Charlie had added a denim jacket to his jeans, as well as a knotted silk scarf, as a concession to his hostess. Sue was grateful that he seemed to be enjoying his visit.

"There are any number of angles," Charlie said as he put down his wine glass and concentrated on Vanessa, who rewarded him with her total attention. He took a small notebook out of his breast pocket. "We're lucky. The timing is great. Interest in old films is building. When did you make your first film for Fodor?"

Vanessa was visibly distressed. "Must we mention dates?"

"I read somewhere that old movies are now being used in remedial reading classes," Sue said, seeing Charlie was off on the wrong foot. "The students read the simple subtitles and then discuss the film.

Charlie's reaction to Sue was pure gratitude. It fed his ego to be the center of attention of two women, even if one was old enough to be his grandmother.

"I know," he said. "We've been sending the schools some classics along with shorts on music and sports. It might be a good idea to arrange for Miss Vanessa's appearance at some of these classes.

"The School of Arts at NYU is awarding scholarships to students who want to major in cinema studies," Sue contributed.

"Now there's an idea!" Vanessa warmed to it. "Suppose I offer a scholarship in the name of Joshua Fodor. Could that be arranged, Charles?"

"I've never known a school to turn down money. I'll sound out the head of the film department. By the way, are any of your films still shown in Europe?"

"Oh, yes! Particularly *The Passions of a Portuguese Nun*. It's a great favorite in Berlin. And the Russians are always screening *Jesus Christ—Son and Savior,* it's developed into an underground favorite. Of course, in recent years, it's been screened all over Europe. I know *Variety* didn't believe me but I'm convinced that in time *Jesus Christ* will surpass the receipts of *The Birth of a Nation.*"

Sue was curious. "Who gets the revenue from it?"

Vanessa shrugged, as though puzzled, and didn't reply.

"Pity Fodor didn't live to enjoy the proceeds and the belated recognition," Charlie said.

"Isn't it! That's why I want so much for him to receive the recognition he deserves."

"I'll do my best to help you," Charlie added. "I'm taking off for London and I'll see what can be done there."

Sue was startled, then suddenly felt depressed, and was surprised that she did.... Charlie was, after all, always on the move, shuttling from New York to Beverly Hills to London. Why should she feel this sudden emptiness, this sense of loss? She hadn't been seeing much of him since she'd gotten involved with Dann. Charlie was merely a friend. Or was she afraid to admit that he was something more than a friend ...?

Charlie explained that he would be in London on business for his boss, and then go on to Italy, hopefully to make arrangements for a film of his own. "Sue, you remember the galleys on the book about the young woman who can't find out who's the father of her child—and ends up not giving a damn?"

Vanessa was startled, a blush of color staining her cheeks. "Oh, my," she murmured, sounding genuinely shocked.

And at that moment Sue found herself thinking—a child ... I wonder, did Vanessa ever have a child by Fodor?

"I'm going to Italy soon myself," Vanessa said. "I always spend two months of the year in northern Italy." Vanessa went to her desk and wrote on a sheet of Tiffany notepaper. "Here's my address. I'll be staying with Dr. Harold Kellogg. Perhaps we could arrange to meet in Rome."

"Good. One thing more, Miss Oxford. Could you tell me something about why Fodor never recovered his reputation after the failure of *Jesus Christ—Son and Savior?* What was responsible?"

Tears filled Vanessa's eyes. "The world moved on, but he did not. I've always felt his final choices were so dreadful, it was as though he willed himself to fail."

"She may have loved Fodor," Charlie said, "but there's a savage note in her voice when she mentions his flops. They seem to give her some kind of satisfaction."

"That's because he jilted her for a much younger girl," Sue explained, repeating what Rebecca had told her. "Not that Vanessa was old, in her early twenties, I think. But the girl who replaced her was fourteen."

They'd left Vanessa's apartment and were walking west toward Fifth Avenue. It was a clear night with a pale distant scrattering of stars, not yet dimmed by the city lights.

Still under Vanessa's influence, Charlie shook his head in reluctant admiration. "They don't hardly make them like that any more. I bet she's never had a feeling she could call her own, that wasn't in some kind of script."

"It's not all Fodor. Rebecca says she'd written the script for her future before she'd ever met him. You know, in a way, once you get to know her she's sort of transparent even though she does everything by indirection. One day she asked me what books I kept on my night table. I knew there was a reason for it. She never asks a useless question. So I reeled off some names I figured were suitable . . . the Oxford Book of Verse, War and Peace, things I thought would impress her. A couple of days later she was on a radio show and she mentioned the books she dipped into before falling asleep. They were the same ones I'd told her about. She's like a sponge."

"With no humor."

"None that I can see. . . . Cassie's the witty one. She'll come out with things like, 'Men are the greatest playthings after you've outgrown teddy bears.' She also can be cruel, I'm told. Rebecca said she once told Vanessa that the play Arsenic and Old Lace was written about her. I guess humor doesn't much go with Vanessa's kind of success. Cassie is very lovable, while Vanessa— well, I still admire her, I think she's really extraordinary. But I don't think I could feel close to her—ever."

Charlie's thoughts were still on his promises to Vanessa. "I think one of my pals is promoting a photographic display of the most beautiful women of the last fifty years. A showing at Saks or Bonwits for the benefit of the American Cancer Society. I'll call him and make sure our shy retiring Vanessa is included."

Sue was grateful. "She'd like that."

He pressed her arm. "You understand I'm doing it for you."

"I understand, and I thank you."

"You know, I kind of wish you were coming with me."

Sue's smile was uncertain ... reflecting how she felt. Each time they'd met since her affair with Dann began she'd been aware of this conflict—pleasure at having put Charlie in his place, and an undiminished yearning for him. Tonight, her gratitude for his kindness to Vanessa had compounded the feeling. He was smiling at her, warmly, showing the Charlie behind the slickster P.R. facade. She felt tender toward him. She held his hand and, without speaking, they went to her room. He took off his jacket, turned on the radio to an all-night FM station and walked around looking over her books and magazines and the new lithographs her father had sent her from Mexico.

"Tell me about your film," she said.

He fixed himself a scotch on the rocks, and went into detail about financing and releasing a film and the problems in signing up a cast. As he warmed to his project, she became aware of his judgment and integrity, qualities he often disguised, as though ashamed of them. He was delighted with her interest and gave no indication of wanting to leave, and in her heart Sue admitted she didn't want him to go. They were comfortable together, the way they'd been in their evenings at NYU ... easy, relaxed, in harmony. She knew he would stay the night. And the promise of that along with the tenderness she felt elated and unnerved her. . . .

"I could very easily make a habit of this," he said, holding her close. Their lovemaking had been leisurely and lovely, and when he'd fallen asleep with his arm around her she'd tried not to move, afraid to disturb him. When she heard his voice now and opened her eyes, it was light, with a morning sun that even the city pollution couldn't ruin. They kissed tenderly. He got out of bed.

"The next voice you hear..." and from the small refrigerator behind the teak screen he was bringing her a glass of chilled orange juice, which she accepted, offering him a sip and drinking the rest. "You're a good man, Charlie Bryson."

He sat down on the bed and scooped her up in his arms. The daybed was narrow but wide enough for their pleasure. Her dark hair was tousled and the remnants of eye makeup gave her a faintly bawdy air. They were still euphoric. It was for each of them, she felt, something unexpectedly lovely. "Oh, God, Charlie," she said, "I feel so wonderful."

"Well," he said, "I guess I improve with use."

Whereupon she gave him a good lovebite on the neck, and held him hard and tight against her, not wanting to give up the moment.

She hated to see him leave. When she was alone in her room she lay quietly on the narrow bed, eyes closed, savoring.

And then... *What in the world is wrong with me? Sure, I'm angry with Dann, but is this my way of showing I don't care what he does? Because that's not true, I do care, dammit, Dann. Charlie? What kind of a girl am I, anyway?*

Dann was sex. She recalled the afternoons when she'd sneaked off to meet him for a "matinee." The depth of passion he aroused in her often shocked her. She didn't want to think of him now, after being with Charlie, the rough sunbleached mane of hair, the outdoor skin, the stubborn jaw and the body like some beautiful machine designed to bring her to unbelievable heights. She couldn't stop herself from wanting him.

But she didn't like herself for this infatuation for Dann—a sort of physical tyranny, it couldn't lead anywhere. On a permanent basis she had an instinctive feeling it would end badly. By its very intensity it was an affair of diminishing returns. He would soon be bored. The girl who married Dann, she reflected, had better keep her bags packed.

One night recently when they were resting on the bed in Dann's place, drinking champagne, she had the uneasy conviction that the affair had already reached its plateau. He suggested tentatively that sometime it might be amusing to have a threesome. She quickly refused. No kinky sex for her. Later, she thought about his suggestion, wondering whether his enthusiasm was flagging. Was there another girl?

Dann's devotion to Vanessa didn't help much either. Well, after a fashion it did. Because the clandestine air about their moments together stimulated them sexually. Several times recently he'd had to break dates with her because Vanessa's need for an escort had priority.

The last time she'd seen him he'd come by her place at two in the morning. It was difficult for him to get past the doorman, who rang Sue from the foyer, obviously disapproving. And Dann was obviously hung over and grumpy.

She wasn't very cordial. Not that it mattered.

He was impotent with her for the first time, and said angrily, "If you lived with me, this wouldn't happen, damn it."

His manner irritated Sue. His manhood seemed more at issue than her feelings. She contrasted it with Charlie's wry reaction their first time. . . .

"And what would you do with me when Vanessa came to see you? Hide me in the closet?"

He was furious with her, so furious that he got up, dressed and strode out, slamming the door after him. That wasn't his Indian genes, she thought. It was just his bruised male ego.

He was still exciting to her, though, but now she had Charlie to think about. Sweet, loving Charlie. Not a sex machine in bed, and not movie-star handsome like Dann. But a very human man who was capable of tenderness as well as passion. She needed both when she made love, or to be in love. *Maybe*, she thought, *she needed Charlie. Maybe it was as simple as that.*

THE PRESENT: VANESSA UP CLOSE

THIS WAS a red-letter day.

Dr. Preston Cooke rang me up with good news. That is, cautiously optimistic news. Cassie was making progress, he said. If it continued she could come home the next weekend.

This wonderful news—(dear God, how I had prayed for it)—presented a few problems:

1) I could not postpone my trip much longer. I had to be off soon for Italy.

2) In that case, what would happen to Cassie on her release? Who would look after her?

Flossie had gone home to South Carolina to be with her ninety-year-old mother who had terminal cancer and needed constant nursing.

Rebecca? Cassie certainly would be welcomed in her country house, and I suppose I could arrange for her to have a nurse companion. But suppose Cassie went into another tailspin? She might be dangerous to herself and others when she was agitated. I couldn't impose on Rebecca, who was trying to work on her autobiography between bouts of crippling arthritis.

Could Sue stay with her? I'm truly fond of Sue; she's a lovely girl, well bred, tactful, dependable. Still, if in a wildly garrulous moment Cassie felt the need to talk, there was much Sue shouldn't know. *An agitated Cassie was not to be trusted.*

Oh dear, what should I do?

My obligations in Italy were waiting for me. It was important for me to take care of them. Dear Harold Kellogg could do so much and no more. . . .

Dann and Sue were driving out to Sunset Hill with me. Sue

remembered to stop at the optometrist to pick up a new pair of bifocals for Cassie, who was forever misplacing her glasses and was nearly blind without them.

I didn't suppose Dr. Preston Cooke would consider keeping her as... not a patient, but a *guest* until my return home in September. It could be September, right after Labor Day, as always. But circumstances might have changed. From what Harold said the last time we talked by trans-Atlantic phone, I might come home earlier—or much later.

I had to close my eyes and concentrate.

What would be best for Cassandra?

Vanessa and Sue were in the front seat of Dann's new Mercedes, and there was ample room for all three, fashionably thin as they were. Dann in beat-up recycled jeans and a T-shirt, Vanessa in handwoven cotton, a gift from a Pakistani admirer, its loose, easy lines protecting her against the morning's heat. Sue in frayed denim shorts and a striped red-and-white French sailor's jersey, a scarf protecting her hair, welcomed the brilliant sun and the wind. As they sped onto the Merritt Parkway, Sue pretended interest in the rich green strip fronting the road with its laurel, evergreens and dogwood. But she was aware of Dann, his strong, tanned hands holding the wheel without strain, the rough blond hairs on his arms. The attraction was still too strong. Whenever she was working at Vanessa's she was inclined to think about him much more than she did in her own room. Each time the telephone rang she tensed up, wondering if it were he, and whether his calling Vanessa was perhaps an excuse to speak to her....

What a pity there wasn't some pill you could take to treat a sexual attraction, the way aspirin banished a headache. Sue knew it was an unhealthy fascination, that the aftermath could cause her great pain. She wondered, too, whether her night with Charlie was mostly a subconscious reflection of her too intense involvement with Dann? She hoped not.

Cassie was sitting on a Boston rocker on the front porch of her cottage, the apricot poodle on her lap, Dr. Cooke standing nearby talking to her. They were diverted by the sound of the Mercedes and, although Cassie remained seated, her face did reflect a kind of welcome. As they came up the steps Dr. Cooke greeted them more warmly than usual; evidently he was pleased with Cassie's progress.

"Have a nice day," he said, waving and walking off.

Sue immediately gave Cassie her new glasses.

"Thank you, thank you." Cassie nodded her head. She was nicely dressed in a lemon linen shift, banded in green and white. Her hair was combed off her face and tied at the nape of her neck with a bright silk scarf.

Vanessa leaned down and kissed her on the forehead. Cassie tensed. Sue noticed and thought, astonished, she didn't like her sister to touch her. But when Dann took her by the hand and led her to the car, she walked with him like a well-behaved child.

"Sister, we are going to take you for a little drive and we'll stop for ice cream. Would you like that?"

Cassie nodded but said nothing. She got into the rear seat with Sue, and they sat close together. Vanessa joined Dann in the front, but she was partially turned so she could talk to Cassie.

"Now, Sister, you'll be good, won't you? You won't try to open the door and run away, will you? Dann is driving fast, fifty miles an hour, and you could be hurt..."

Again Cassie nodded. She seemed to be calm, not tense or rigid, and Sue had the feeling that she would do whatever was expected of her, that it was a strategy for...what?

They drove through New Canaan, past great houses set back from lawns and foliage reminiscent of England, and it was quiet in the car except for the music coming from a tape. It was Strauss' "Graduation Ball," which was one of Cassie's favorites, as Dann knew. The air conditioning in the car couldn't compete with Vanessa's expensive perfume. Cassie sneezed, and Vanessa handed her a tissue. "Wipe your eyes, Cassie. Are you crying?"

Cassie shook her head and hugged the poodle in her arms.

"Dear, why don't you let him sit between you and Sue? He's wrinkling your dress."

Cassie managed a smile, an expression that lifted her lips and left the upper part of her face blank. She raised the poodle to her cheek, and he responded with tiny affectionate licks.

Vanessa shrugged, then asked, "How long did it take you to dress this morning, Sister?"

Her question seemed to have caught Cassie unaware. She frowned, as though trying to remember.

"I hope you're over that awful habit of trying to decide what to wear when you get up."

Sue tried to soften the building tension. "I have the same problem. I wake up and think, decisions, decisions! When to get up, what to wear, what to have for breakfast..."

This time Cassie's smile was warm. Her right hand left the poodle's back and reached for Sue's. Dann was quiet, and Vanessa was now silent too as they traveled through the residential section of New Canaan and swung across winding old roads toward Stamford. They cut across the highway to a shopping center, blazing hot in the midday sun.

"There's a shop that sells homemade ice cream," Vanessa said. "You sit in the car, Cassie, dear, and Dann and I will get you some."

Now that they were alone in the car, Cassie turned toward Sue and smiled.

Sue said, and meant it, "It's *good* to see you, Cassie!"

"I like you." Cassandra said it with the direct simplicity of a child.

"Thank you. I like you too." They held hands and Cassie squeezed her palm. *She is better*, Sue thought. *She must be nearly well, otherwise Dr. Cooke wouldn't allow this outing—*

"I want to go home," Cassie said abruptly.

"To Sunset Hill?"

"To my hotel. To New York. Guy doesn't like the country. It's dark and he's afraid of the dark."

"I'm sure you can come home very soon"—Sue felt apprehensive—"the doctor seems very pleased with your progress."

"I want to go home *now*."

Fortunately Dann and Vanessa were cutting across the parking lot, Dann carrying the lower part of a cardboard box with four tall plastic containers of ice cream topped with twirls of whipped cream, a maraschino cherry in each center. Vanessa was carrying a larger package wrapped in tissue paper, holding it as one might hold a child.

Cassie looked pleased at the prospect of a treat. Sweets weren't part of her diet at Sunset Hill.

"A chocolate fudge sundae, Cassie," Vanessa said, opening the car door. "Doesn't it look yummy? You've been so good. The doctor is pleased with you. You've earned a treat."

Dann handed the ice cream to Cassie while Sue spread a napkin on her lap, gently nudging away the poodle who was begging for a taste.

Cassie accepted her reward and began to lick the plastic spoon, small sounds of pleasure coming from her lips. Dann and Vanessa were standing beside the car's open door, enjoying their ice cream. A strange pair—Dann, cowboy-lean in his denims; Vanessa, the Victorian lady in her loose cotton.

Vanessa shifted the bundle from under her arm onto Sue's lap. "Cassie, look, we've brought you a present."

She looked to Sue to open it. Cassie was watching too, spoon poised midair while Sue unwrapped the tissue paper.

It was a doll. A beautiful doll with yellow curls, a porcelain face with enormous blue eyes that opened and shut and a tiny flower of a mouth. Vanessa took it from Sue and placed it on Cassie's lap. The poodle growled.

Cassie's reaction was worse than a growl. The wildness that had seemed subdued flared up, a maniac gleam was in her eyes, her mouth became loose, distorted. The changeover gave Sue the shudders. Is this what the doctor meant when he'd told Vanessa (who'd told Sue) that poor Cassie was an ambulatory paranoid schizophrenic.

Using the doll as a weapon, Cassie lashed out at Vanessa, who jumped back as the doll's porcelain head was smashed to fragments. The half-eaten sundae dropped to the floor of the car, staining Cassie's dress. She opened the left door and, clutching the poodle, slid out before Sue could stop her. Dann ran across the lot and finally caught up with her. Whatever he said seemed to calm her, and she allowed him to lead her back, his arm protecting and guiding her. People were watching curiously. The parking lot attendant stared, wondering, no doubt, if he should alert the police.

"Oh, my God! My God!" Vanessa was saying. "I should have known."

Dann tried to help Cassie into the car, settling her in the front seat.

"I know what you're trying to do," Cassie was screaming at Vanessa, her fingers outstretched like claws, seeking Vanessa's face. "You're trying to drive me crazy . . . well, *I'm* sane. If anybody is nuts, it's you, dear Sister—"

"Cassie, *please!* I didn't mean anything by it. I swear to you I just saw this pretty doll and it made me think of all the years you wanted a doll and Mama couldn't afford it—"

"Bullshit! I know you and your tricks, Sister. Always calling me your dear fat little sister, always making fun of me, always belittling me to *him*. Well, I screwed you up but good, didn't I? After he made love to me, he never touched you again, did he? *Did* he?"

Somehow they got Cassie back to Sunset Hill Inn, but she was so agitated that it took two nurses to carry her back to the cottage. Dr. Cooke was angry. He said this setback might result in a longer stay at the sanitarium.

"Of course, whatever you say, doctor"—Vanessa was choked—"and for as long as you think she will need your help. I'll be away, but my friends here, Dann and Sue, will be available in any emergency . . ."

Dann and Sue walked back to the car, miserable, while Vanessa remained a short while to continue her consultation with the doctor. Standing at the hood, waiting, Dann turned to Sue.

"Still mad at me?"

"Not really."

"You didn't show much interest today—"

"Under the circumstances—" she began, still too shaken to fence with him.

"Tonight?"

She shrugged. Vanessa approached and suggested they all sit together in front. They drove off, the car quiet and powerful as it glided through the traffic.

Vanessa was crying quietly. Sue put her arm around her shoulder.

"I meant only good for her. Why did it turn out so badly? Why does it *always* turn out so badly?"

It was the first time Sue had seen Vanessa weep. Tears ran down her pale cheeks, her shoulders heaved. Dann took his eyes from the road and put his hand over hers.

"Take it easy, Vanessa, it'll be all right. Remember, that's what you always say."

And after a while Vanessa's tears stopped and they reached the city's outskirts in a kind of numb silence.

At her door Vanessa thanked Dann, her eyes shimmering, and asked Sue to escort her to the apartment. Dann tried to signal Sue but stopped abruptly as Vanessa intercepted his glance.

Once in the apartment Vanessa said calmly, without missing a beat, "Perhaps we can work on that article for *Guideposts*, Sue, unless you have an appointment?"

Sue was startled. "What? ... Oh, sure, I'm free." She picked up a pencil and dictation pad and followed her into the bedroom, where Vanessa stretched out on the chaise, looking spent but very much in control. *My God*, Sue thought, *what extraordinary recuperative powers, what an exercise in will over body and circumstances* ... well, nothing to do except try to keep up.

Vanessa wanted to sumbit an article to Dr. Norman Vincent Peale's inspirational magazine, *Guideposts*, being a strong admirer of Dr. Peale's philosophy and believing that his magazine was the perfect forum for her own observations and purposes. She wanted to justify Joshua Fodor's fall and she realized that to do so she must mention the change in life styles from his beginnings fifty years ago to the present. "After World War One, Mr. Fodor's concepts no longer were in harmony with the complex social systems in the world," she lectured Sue. "Old morality was put on the shelf. New morality was welcomed. And Mr. Fodor was a 19th-century romantic, out of his time now. His films continued to dramatize the old codes that his immigrant parents had sought out as guidelines in a strange new world. He couldn't and wouldn't disappoint his first loyal audiences."

"But it is necessary to explain him, to make excuses for him?" Sue asked. "Mr. Fodor is now accepted for what he was—"

"Well, I thought it would be a good way to express my own feelings about today's morality as well," Vanessa said. "Dann took me down to the East Village the other night, there was a rock group he wanted to hear. I hadn't been in that part of the city for"—she shrugged—"more years than I can recall." It was an unforgettable experience, she said. The girls all looked alike. The fashions in eye makeup were grotesque, with eyebrows blotted out, sockets and lids darkened, making them look like baby raccoons. Jeans or tight pants sitting on meager little hip bones; revealing T-shirts; hair parted in the middle, long and free flowing; girls on pills and drugs, street waifs prowling the streets, yet oddly innocent.

"They are the stuff of nightmares," she said softly.

"Many of them will grow up and change." Sue wanted to comfort her, sensing a pain that Vanessa was trying both to hide and to reveal.

"The new morality offends me because it is destroying our womanliness." She was looking at Sue. "Don't you agree, dear?"

"I'm not sure—"

"This unisex business, for example . . . I think girls are foolish to have anything to do with it. Just as they're foolish to get involved with . . . bisexual men."

"But aren't bisexual men supposed to be fantastic lovers?" Sue was simply trying to make talk, but the conversation was actually making her uncomfortable.

"Whoever told you that?"

"This girl, 'Liv,' who lives on my floor. She's a one-woman walking encyclopedia of sex sex sex."

"Oh. Well, I'm glad it wasn't Dann who talked to you."

Sue could not hide her surprise. "Dann?"

"Jeff . . . and Dann . . ." said Vanessa and that was all she said as they got back to work.

By dinner time the correspondence was brought up to date and Sue had typed the notes for Vanessa's article. "Will you have dinner with me?" Vanessa asked.

"I think not, but thanks all the same. I'm a bit tired—"

"I know . . . D'you think I should call Dr. Cooke?"

Sue shrugged. A faint frown marred Vanessa's serene brow. "Perhaps I should have Dann telephone. Doctors always take a man more seriously."

She walked Sue to the door. "Thank you for everything, dear. You've been so kind."

Sue smiled weakly. When she pushed the elevator button, she realized that Vanessa had kissed her goodbye on the mouth. Not one of those meaningless kiss-kiss gestures that most women offer to each other, and which usually land in the air. She'd never thought of it before, but now she remembered that Vanessa had always kissed her on the mouth.

Letting herself into her room, Sue tossed her bag on a chair, kicked off her slippers, stripped and ran a bath. She felt the tension in her muscles, the ache in her temples that were the beginning of a bad headache. She was tired and depressed and she knew with perfect clarity that the time had come to make a break. A clean break. Her Aunt Harriet was right. Vanessa was kind and gentle and sweet and she had a spine of steel and was voracious in her need for people. Sue shivered. The warm bath was doing her no good.

She wished Carlie were there. She needed to talk and there was no one else, not even Aunt Harriet, who was away for the weekend. And Dann was certainly the last man she could discuss her feelings with.

She got out of the tub, padded into the bed-living room and slowly dried herself. She'd lost her sense of herself, what she believed in . . . something was going terribly wrong with her life. She decided to take off for her vacation immediately, for the clean, sweet country of Williamstown and her father's sensible, understanding companionship.

The telephone rang. Once, twice, a half-dozen times. She made no effort to answer it. The shrill sound stopped. And started again.

She was being a coward. She didn't want to face him. She was afraid of explanations. But his hold on her was still strong. By the time she picked up the telephone, the ringing had stopped.

She stood there holding the buzzing phone, thinking about what Vanessa had implied about Dann and Jeff.

Was it possible?

Or was it a fabrication of Vanessa's to keep Sue away from Dann, or to end what she suspected had been going on?

Or was it her way of warning Sue away from a relationship that one day could only hurt her?

It was a mystery. Like Vanessa herself.

THE PRESENT: SUE—AND WHY SHE CAN'T, AS THEY SAY, SPLIT

ARRIVING AT Vanessa's apartment the following morning, Sue found the Vuitton bags open on the luggage racks in Vanessa's bedroom and the bed strewn with dresses, suits, lingerie.

"I had a disturbing call from Italy," Vanessa said, plainly upset but continuing to fold garments and put them in the bags. "I must leave immediately. I've booked the evening flight to Milan."

Sue was startled. Vanessa made no explanations. But perhaps it was fortuitous. With Vanessa gone and the work completed, there was no reason for her to remain. She could take off for Williamstown next weekend.

"I called Dr. Cooke and apprised him of this emergency. He is arranging for Cassie to remain at Sunset Hill until my return. Sue, I took the liberty of assuring him that you and Dann will visit her every few days. He believes this will be good for her." Seeing Sue's hesitation, she added, "I hope it doesn't interfere with your plans."

"Well, actually, it does. I meant to go home."

"Could you wait for just a few weeks? At least until Flossie gets back? I'll call Rebecca and she can spell you."

As simply as that, Vanessa had arranged it all for her convenience. Cassie would be looked after. Dann and Sue and Rebecca would guard her.

What was her business in Italy? Sue wondered. What was this big emergency?

Vanessa was gone now, and Sue was grateful to have time for herself. She went through Vanessa's files, making certain everything was in place so that whoever worked on them later would have no problem. She had already checked in at the Film Wing, going over the fall schedules with Mrs. Elsberg. Working with Vanessa Oxford had been an experience, and she wouldn't have missed it but she was relieved it was coming to an end.

The only unfinished business was Cassie.

Strange, when she had first met the sisters she had idolized Vanessa. She'd admired Vanessa's strength, her courage, her uncanny talent for arranging situations to her advantage. But the longer she knew Cassie, even after her breakdown, the more her loyalty and affection turned toward the younger sister.

When Vanessa had been busy with personal matters, Sue had spent considerable time with Cassie, and on several occasions they'd attended screenings of Cassie's European films at the Film Wing, and Sue had been astonished and impressed by the range of Cassie's talents. But she'd also discovered that Cassie couldn't accept a compliment without putting herself down immediately afterward. Once when, at Vanessa's suggestion, she'd taken Cassie to see the ballet *Copelia*, Cassie had shown great sympathy for Copelia, and when the lovely doll ran down and collapsed, Cassie had said softly, "That's how I feel . . ."

But she also was aware that she needed some help, even if on her terms only. She remembered the time she'd gone along with her to her Park Avenue internist, and Cassie had literally begged for some kind of psychic energizers.

"Cassandra, you've had everything from Elavil to Tofranil and none has done you any good." The doctor, seated behind his desk with her thick file before him, kept his voice moderate and patient, but his eyes regarded her with the sharpness of an X-ray, searching through the surface to the anguish beneath her bright impudent manner. "You haven't given any of them enough time to work. Cassandra, sometimes I wonder if you want them to work."

"Now, Dr. Levine—"

"Cassandra, what are you running away from?"

"Madness." Said simply, and therefore shockingly.

Sue, sitting there in the doctor's office at Cassie's request, shuddered.

"Self-induced?" the doctor suggested.

"My father died in a madhouse."

"And mine was a Bowery bum. Look, Cassandra, I'm no psychiatrist, but I am your doctor and friend . . . and it's my humble unprofessional friendly opinion that part of the problem is you and your sister. You've always been under her thumb, and it just might be that you'd do anything to get out from under—including getting sick. Anyway, why don't you at least try to face your problem head-on instead of hurting yourself? Go get some competent advice from a psychiatrist . . . I'll be glad to recommend—"

She avoided his challenge, as she always had, by changing the subject. "Doctor, do I need hormone shots? Why don't you give me hormone shots like Dr. Wilson gives his patients?"

"Because you don't *need* them. For a woman beyond menopause your estrogen count is unusually high—"

"So you won't help me, doctor, after all these years, you're turning your back on me?"

"I'd never turn my back on you and you know it. But you need help in an area where I'm just not knowledgeable enough. Cassandra, again, I wish you'd see a psychiatrist."

"Whatever for? I know my problem, you know my problem . . . it's Vanessa." Abruptly she got up and leaned over his desk, her expression suddenly pleading. "But at least it's a problem of love. Well, isn't it?"

"Is it, Cassie?" . . .

From that day on Sue had found herself equipped with antennae that gave her fresh insights into the relationship of the legendary sisters.

She could see the difference between Cassie with her friends and with Vanessa. With her cronies, Cassie had still been relaxed and witty. With Vanessa, she'd displayed what seemed an hysterical need to please.

It was a unique hypocrisy . . . if it could even properly be called that. Cassie was honest, almost painfully so in her dealings with the world, and as a result she was often humiliated, misunderstood and exploited. While Vanessa, Sue realized, had a pragmatic moral double standard. "If it doesn't touch her," Cassie had once said in a revealing moment, "Sister can be a monument of virtue and righteousness. Otherwise she judges morality by her own needs. If it helps her, it's morally right." . . .

Sue wondered if Cassie would ever recover, and despite her need to get away from the Oxford sisters, she wavered in her decision to leave immediately.

Meanwhile, she heard from Charlie, who was briefly stationed in London and had heard from a friend in Los Angeles.

"There's a good chance that the American Film Institute will honor Joshua Fodor with a posthumous Life Achievement Award," he wrote. *"If that should fall through, he's likely to be given a special award in recognition of his achievements. Some previous personalities singled out were John Ford, James Cagney, Orson Welles and William Wyler—he'll be in good company. Miss Oxford should be pleased."*

Sue was certain of that.

It was Saturday morning, and Sue was cleaning her room, which gave her a good feeling. She sorted out garments for the cleaners and others for the Thrift Shop, and was filling up a Bloomingdale's shopping bag when Liv walked in.

Liv was her usual irrepressible self, flowing, long blonde hair, blue eyes heavily made up, denims fashionably frayed and faded, and barefoot. She was holding a glass half-filled with a bloody Mary.

"Hi, what's all this?" She nodded toward the shopping bags.

"Extra baggage."

"Anything unusual in it?" Liv set down the glass on a side table and started pawing through the bag. "I'm scrounging for a charity auction for unemployed young actors. It's going to be at Lincoln Center and I've already collected good loot."

"Nothing here's worth putting on the auction block," Sue said.

"What agout those lithographs on the wall?"

"No, my father brought them from Mexico for me."

"Oh, come on, honey. What's a gift if it isn't a sacrifice? I, *par example*, am giving up my mother's collection of Battersea boxes."

Liv was a girl who always said "yes" and never accepted "no." As a reward for Sue's contribution of one of her lithographs, she took Sue off to the Saturday auction where, at one of the tables set up for guests, all of whom looked frighteningly affluent, Liv introduced her to an elderly woman with a gray wig, a face heavily wrinkled and a designer dress weighted down at the neckline with authentic jewels. Liv then took off with her friends, having deposited Sue at a choice table. The elderly woman seemed lonely and ill at ease among the couples, and Sue promptly shared her interest in the auction with the woman, who introduced herself as Mrs. Matthews.

"You know, I've enjoyed everything connected with the theater," Mrs. Matthews confided between bites of cold fried chicken. "You see my husband was a doctor to many of the stage luminaries for over fifty years—"

"What interesting stories he must have," Sue said.

"*Had*," Mrs. Matthews corrected her, tears filling her eyes. "He passed away last year."

"Oh, I'm sorry. It must be difficult for you."

"Awful. I lived my life vicariously. He had so many friends on Broadway and they were always so nice to us when he was alive. . . ."

"What lovely memories you must have."

"Yes, I do. He used to tell me about his patients. You'd never realize they were human, like all of us."

Champagne accompanied the box lunches and two hundred well-fed guests were now primed for the auction. The auctioneer was a professional who could easily have passed for an actor, handsome, mod but not extreme, with a voice to inspire a sense of competition in the audience. Liv's Battersea boxes brought a hundred dollars each, Sue's Mexican lithograph brought two hundred.

"I contributed a beautiful teakwood box that Katharine Cornell gave the doctor," Mrs. Matthews confided as the auction continued.

"I wish Miss Oxford had been here," Sue said. "I'm sure she'd have found something choice to give."

"Miss Oxford? You know her?"

"Why, yes, I've been working for her."

"Now, isn't that interesting! She was one of my husband's patients." She leaned closer to Sue. "As a matter of fact, and I shouldn't be telling you this, but . . . well, he took care of her years ago when she was pregnant."

Sue's heart jolted.

"When was that?" she asked casually.

Mrs. Matthews plunged on, professional discretion to the winds. Besides, talking about her husband's famous patients was always good for inciting curiosity in people who might otherwise ignore her. "Let me see ... it must have been around 1920 ... maybe 1921."

"Was he her obstetrician?"

"No, no! She went to Italy, or was it Switzerland, to have the baby."

"Isn't that odd, I know Miss Vanessa very well—"

"Not Miss Vanessa, the other one. What's her name?"

"You mean Cassandra? *Cassie?*"

"That's right! Cassandra Oxford. She was a lovely girl. But I never heard any mention of her child." She rubbed her forehead. "It ... it would be middle-aged now, I suppose. I still think of the Oxford girls as young, you know, the way they were in the Fodor films. Somehow it doesn't seem all that long ago."

Sue made an excuse that she had forgotten an appointment and quickly left the old woman. She went straight home to think about what she had just discovered.

Sue's thoughts on Cassie:

1) Poor, poor Cassie
2) How did it happen?
3) Who was the man? She had never married. So the child was illegitimate.
4) Why didn't she have an abortion?

It wasn't against their religion, but it may have been against their moral principles. Cassie was so tender with animals, so compassionate with people that it was difficult to think of her destroying life. ... Then too, Cassie was young, people looked differently on abortion. A half-century ago women performed abortions on themselves or went to quacks and died of awful things like septicemia. Sue badly wanted to talk to her Aunt Harriet or Rebecca about Mrs. Matthews' astonishing revelation. No doubt, Rebecca must know about it, being so close to both sisters. ...

"Cassie has always felt unloved," Rebecca had once told her.

"Like a non-person. She's been hurt in love, but she'll hold onto the memory of a love affair and suffer. She's always chosen men who wound her, men who give her passion but never a commitment. I wonder if anything can make up for the emotional deficit in Cassie's childhood...."

Cassie never showed herself any mercy, Sue realized, and Vanessa apparently never allowed Cassie to accept her limitations, or her failures.

How much of her retreat from reality, Sue wondered, was indeed a need to separate herself from Vanessa, as Dr. Levine had suggested. And at the same time to punish Big Sister? ...

Was it true that the answer for her was in the dark, lonely realm of the split personality?

Sue couldn't fall asleep for brooding about Cassandra. *Perhaps while Vanessa is abroad I should spend more time with Cassie. If she's allowed a weekend pass, perhaps I could bring her to New York, and we could share two days. It might do her good....*

In any case she put out of mind any thought of her vacation. It would have to wait. Meanwhile, she'd call Dann and ask him to drive her out to Sunset Hill Inn. She hadn't seen Dann since the afternoon Vanessa left for Italy, although he'd telephoned her several times, and on each occasion she'd had a legitimate excuse for not seeing him. She was still divided in her feelings. She didn't think she should see him but she did want to, dammit!

Oh, if only Charlie were here....

Before she could telephone Dann about Cassie, he called her.

"Look, we've got a problem." His voice was tense and anxious. "Cassie has disappeared!"

"*What?* You're kidding—"

"I wish I were. Dr. Cooke just called, they're looking through the woods, she may have gone for a walk and got lost..."

Sue was aware of a sinking feeling. She didn't believe Cassie was lost. A chill took hold of her... had Cassie finally come to terms with her dark obsession...?

"What do you think we should do?" she asked him.

"Wire Vanessa. As much as I hate to. But she should hear it from us before it comes out in the papers."

"Should we call her?"

"Better to wire first, then call when we have a little information. We've got to get out to Sunset Hill. Can you be ready in fifteen minutes?"

"Yes."

"Okay, meet me downstairs, outside your place."

There was little talk between them as he swung the Mercedes toward the East River Drive, but for once their silence was companionable, tempered by their concern over Cassandra.

"I feel responsible. Vanessa left her in my care—"

"*Our* care."

"Mostly mine, though. After all, you haven't known Cass long and it isn't fair to burden you—"

"All I hope is that nothing serious has happened."

"It would break Vanessa. In a special way, her life revolves around Cassie—"

Try to put yourself in Cassie's place, Sue told herself, not really hearing him. *Where would you go? What would you do?* Cassie didn't want to stay at Sunset Hill. She'd said she wanted to go home.... "Dann, did Dr. Cooke say anything about her poodle?"

"No. And I didn't think to ask."

"If she left of her own accord, she took the poodle with her—"

"You're right! We'll stop at the next service station and I'll put in a call."

While the car was being filled up, Dann went to the telephone booth. He returned shortly, dejected.

"The pup is missing, too." He paused by the door of the car and lit a cigarette. "What d'you think we should do?"

"We may as well go on, we're already near New Canaan ... It's better to be there and find out what we can than to brood at home."

But after several frustrating hours with Dr. Cooke, they grew restless. The police had been alerted and were checking on the possibility of a hitchhiker on the Merritt Parkway. Meanwhile they were still combing the woods and now were dragging the pond beyond the sanitarium.

"Let's go back," Dann said. "We'll call Vanessa from my place. My God, what do we tell her?" ...

Before Dann could insert the key in his lock, Jeff had opened the door of the townhouse.

"There's a lady here to see you," he said.

Cassandra. Sitting in an easy chair, the poodle on her lap, no sign of nervousness or agitation about her.

She was there on a mission . . . "It's down in the basement," she said tersely. "I'll know it when I see it."

She reluctantly answered their questions. How did she get there? Took a cab. From New Canaan? From New Canaan. Where did you get the money? Do you think I would let them take away my money? I always have some mad money stashed away.

"I'm delighted you did, but why did you come here?" Dann asked.

"Because you have something I want."

Dann looked baffled. Cassie turned toward the staircase. She knew the house well, since some of her belongings, along with Vanessa's, were stored there. Dann motioned Jeff to go along with them as they descended the stairs to the basement, single file. Cassie, holding the poodle, wrinkled her nose at the smell of film developer. It was her first show of any feeling.

She didn't pause nor did her gaze wander. She knew what she had come for. It was standing on Vanessa's theatrical trunks, large and oblong, wrapped in heavy brown paper. She pointed to it.

"Take it down," she said, and Dann and Jeff did as she asked.

"Take off the wrapping," she ordered.

Sue watched her, puzzled. There was nothing at all sick or agitated about her; she seemed remarkably in control. She watched as the men cut the cord and tore at the heavy paper until it came apart.

It was a painting. "Piers van Cleave commissioned it when she finished *The Passions,*" Cassie said clearly, as though delivering an art lecture. "It was originally done by a great French painter, but when she walked out on him Piers had some changes made. Look closely, my friends, so you may see the authentic Vanessa Oxford."

The painting of Vanessa was a three-quarter pose. She was wearing the headdress of a nun. Her body was nude. Instead of breasts, there were two small, open cashboxes, with green currency and stock certificates drifting down the front of her. Just below her hands, palms clasped together in the Near Eastern greeting she so often used, there emerged from the nest of blonde pubic hair an erect penis.

As she looked at their shocked faces, Cassie laughed hysterically, then stopped, suddenly and completely. She spoke in a clear, determined voice.

"I've always wanted this portrait of Sister. I shall take it back to Sunset Hill with me, and I shall bring it to my sessions with my therapist. Maybe then he'll understand."

She got up and set the poodle on the floor, clutching his leash. "I'm ready to go back now."

Sue took her into the guest bedroom and suggested she rest and Cassie agreed, admitting she was a bit tired...but happy.

Vanessa's reaction to the news of Cassandra's disappearance and discovery was swift and certain.

"Sue, I want you to bring Cassie here."

"To Italy?"

"She isn't safe at Sunset Hill. God knows where she'll go next. I'll book a flight for you. Come as soon as possible."

THE PAST: CASSANDRA REMEMBERS THE NIGHT OF HER LIFE

CASSIE'S MIND wandered back over the years as she dozed in Dann's townhouse....

How could you love and hate at the same time? Her feelings always got mixed up. The first time Vanessa brought her on the set, she couldn't stand Mr. Fodor. Something about him gave her the creeps! But after he offered her a steady job and more money than he was paying Vanessa, she kind of liked him. *He's on my side,* she thought. *He likes me better than Vanessa. That's a new one, for sure!*

When he was rehearsing her, though, she couldn't stand him. He drove her crazy, making her do the scene over and over again. Then other times, mostly on location, he was really fun. He teased the girls in the company and clowned around with them and when they were all laughing, he'd put his arm around Peg or her and she didn't mind at all. She knew he was kind to everybody working for him. But if there was so much goodness in Mr. Fodor, why did she hold back, why was she so uncomfortable when she was alone with him? Was it because of Vanessa? Cassie knew Vanessa had priority, she and Mr. Fodor were inseparable and Vanessa got most of the choice parts in the new films.

But Mr. Fodor had plans for her too. Sometimes, late in the afternoon when the others had gone off and Vanessa was nowhere around, he'd tell her about them. She felt kind of guilty about it, as though she were betraying Vanessa. At the same time, though, she felt good. Here was Mr. Fodor, who could have any girl in the whole world, telling her she was beautiful, she had a soul, and a brilliant future as a comedienne.

He was disturbed about the plans she and Richie had to get married. Not that he had anything against Richie. But he said Richie was too inward, too moody, even though it was his superstitious neurotic mother's fault. He was afraid that marriage with Richie would ruin her future.

And after Richie died and darkness closed in on her, it was Mr. Fodor who comforted her. Vanessa was no help to her. Mama couldn't understand why she'd turned so against Vanessa. But she knew Big Sister. Something must've happened when Vanessa and Richie were out of town together. Oh, she *knew.* She didn't need the priest saying that it was just a tragic accident.

Mr. Fodor was always there. When she'd wake up from her sedated sleep he was in the living room, sitting with Mama. He came in the morning before going to the studio; he stopped by in the late afternoon. He was comforting. She couldn't explain it, but she knew that he cared how she felt, that he wanted her to get well quickly and it wasn't selfish, it had nothing to do with his plans for her. And after a while, when the awful pain eased a little and she no longer went to sleep thinking, *God take me,* and woke up in despair because God hadn't, he was always there with her, and she began to look forward to his company.

It happened during that bad time when *Jesus Christ* was causing him so much heartache and Vanessa was on the road, seeing distributors or making personal appearances.

Mr. Fodor often took Mama and her out to dinner. Sometimes when Mama was tired, he took her out alone and she enjoyed herself as much as she could those days. Richie's mother had come to see her and the meeting had upset her for days. "You ruined my son!" the woman screamed. "If it weren't for you and your sister and that man—that Fodor—my son would be alive today!"

She told Mr. Fodor about it and he told her she had to forget her, that the woman was mad and that if anyone had ruined Richie, it was she.

The following day he took her for a drive, and then they left the car and chauffeur in Greenwich and they walked until she felt exhausted. She remembered the day was clear and cool, with the trees suggesting autumn in their coloring and the chrysanthemums in stately gardens in rich full bloom. She never knew how they got to the shore, but it was an isolated stretch of beach, fronting the big Victorian houses already shuttered for the winter. Mr. Fodor saw her fatigue, and he stretched out his suit jacket and she lay down in the shade of some Australian pines, and all she could think of was Richie, and the tears began to flow.

"Don't cry, little one." He took her in his arms, cradling her, his embrace protective, as though she were a small child who needed his love. "Don't be afraid, Cassie. I'll take care of you. I've wanted to since the first time I saw you. Remember when you came into the studio and weren't sure you wanted to be in 'flickers' because you felt yourself a legitimate actress?"

In the midst of tears, she smiled. "Wasn't I the little prig! 'I belong to the theater,' I said. Why didn't you send me packing?"

"Because I sensed your talent, Cassie. I knew you had the makings of a fine actress."

She hesitated. "Like Vanessa?"

"Superior to Vanessa. Vanessa's acting comes from her mind. Yours, I knew, would come from the heart."

"But Vanessa has done so much more than I—"

"Vanessa is ambitious, Cassie. You're not. Vanessa *makes* things happen. You're content to drift along—"

"Is that the reason you've always kept after me and nagged?"

"Not *nagged*, Cassie—inspired. You've no idea what you can do. I do. I have plans for you—"

"But what about Sister?"

"It will be our secret, Cassie. Until the day she sees you in a film. And then she will know. . . . Would you like that?"

Her reply was impulsive. "I'd love it, but I can't believe it will really happen—"

"It will, I promise you. Have faith in me, Cassie. Will you do that?"

"Yes, sir."

He laughed. "Can't you say Joshua?"

She was startled. Of course she couldn't use his given name. "Will you try, Cassie? Say it."

She hesitated.

"Say it. 'Joshua.' "

"I couldn't. Suppose someone at the studio heard me?"

"Say it when we are alone. The way we are now. Do you realize that this is the first time we've ever been together without anyone around. Do you, Cassie?"

"Yes, yes, I do."

"Cassie, tell me, dear one, was there ever anything . . . intimate . . . between yourself and Richie?"

"Oh, no, *never*."

"He had great respect for you? He loved you and respected you?"

"Yes . . ."

"Cassie, was it because you are a virgin?"

She was crying again, her eyes closed, feeling the warmth of Mr. Fodor and wanting to be closer to him . . . to pretend it was Richie . . .

"You're a virgin, Cassie, but I'm afraid Richie wasn't, there was—"

"Please, don't," and she had her hands over her ears to shut out the possibility of hearing what she already knew . . . Sister and Richie . . . and now the tears were a torrent, and his arms held her to comfort her, but after a while there was a change in the way he was holding her, and he was opening her shirtwaist and his mouth was exploring her, touching her nipples, and something strange was happening to them, they grew thick and erect, the way they did when Richie had kissed her, and then his hand was underneath her skirt and his mouth was everywhere, on her flat little belly, and down below. "Don't be afraid, dear one." His voice was soft, crooning, as he settled himself at her side. "I'll help you forget all the hurt and sorrow, you are very precious to me, Cassie..." And he was doing things to her, she felt an intrusion that tore at her, and he pulled back and entered very, very gently....Yes, he was very gentle, even though it burned and tore, and all she could think of was Richie...and that was how it happened—the first and only time—and in her confused mind he and Richie were melded together.

In the morning, she hated him.

And Vanessa.

She wanted to kill them, but instead she began slowly to kill herself, in a hundred different ways, over the long years of her life.

THE PRESENT: SUE— STRANGE INTERLUDE

She was in shock. Cassie's disappearance, Cassie's return and that monstrous portrait had been too much for her.

Now she really wanted to get away from the Oxford sisters, and Vanessa was insisting she bring Cassie to Italy.

Why? To keep Cassie from telephoning the press, to keep her under guard in a place where she couldn't make trouble for her sister?

Why Italy? What was this place Vanessa visited? And who had called her in Italy and reported an emergency?

Sue's first impulse was to contact Rebecca and ask her advice. Rebecca would know what was best for Cassie.

But Rebecca wasn't home. Her housekeeper told Sue that she had gone to Bridgeport Hospital for physical therapy, her sciatic nerve was giving her trouble again, she wasn't expected home until the following day.

Sue decided to talk to her Aunt Harriet even though Harriet wasn't likely to be too sympathetic, disapproving as she did of Sue's association with Vanessa. Still, Sue did trust her judgment.

And on top of the crisis with Cassie, there was the matter of the photographs that she and Charlie had unearthed in the Fodor packing cases. At Charlie's suggestion she'd kept them in her room, but their presence made her feel like a fence for stolen goods. She'd thought of turning them over to Rebecca, then decided against it. Rebecca and Vanessa had no secrets from each other, which meant that Rebecca would return them to Vanessa and cause Sue embarrassment.

When she telephoned upstairs, Aunt Harriet invited her for dinner.

The meal went well, bringing out warmth in Harriet she seldom displayed, and it was the first time Sue was completely at ease with her aunt. She decided to risk her indulgence.

"I want to show you some pictures." She took out the prints from the manila envelope, explaining how she happened to discover them.

Aunt Harriet stared at the photographs. "A child prostitute of the Victorian era?"

"Vanessa Oxford, as taken by Joshua Fodor."

"My God, shades of Lewis Carroll! So Fodor was one too."

"Another proper Victorian," Sue said ironically, pleased that Harriet's reaction coincided with hers. "I understand Fodor loved all his little girl actresses, and they adored him."

"Naturally . . . the father image . . . was there a scandal?"

"No. Apparently he was so good to all of them, so very thoughtful and generous, that they united, the company and the girls, to keep his secret from the world. But wouldn't you think it was an awful experience for a very young girl?"

"I'm not so sure," Harriet said. "Some girls, even in prepuberty, are instinctive little witches. They enjoy leading a man on. To them it's nothing more than a game to be enjoyed for its power over a man, seeing him so excited and out of control."

"I should think it could make some girls frigid for life."

"Not Vanessa Oxford, not from what you've told me about her. If anyone suffered, I suspect it was Fodor. Can you imagine how his famous Victorian sense of morality conflicted with his perverse desires? . . . Was he married?"

"Yes, but I understand he didn't live with his wife."

"I'm not surprised," Harriet said. "I suspect normal adult women disgusted him. He was probably terrified of sex with a mature woman, probably felt inadequate with her."

"Rebecca Kahn said that after he finished the Christ film, he lost interest in Vanessa."

"How old was she then?"

"I guess about twenty-one."

"That's your answer . . . too old. For Fodor, Vanessa was a sexual has-been at twenty-one."

"What d'you suggest I do with these pictures?"

"Get rid of them! Burn them or tear them in little pieces and flush them down the john."

Harriet gathered her papers and shoved them into a leather folder. "I really do think it's time for you to leave Vanessa. She cannibalizes people." It was a strong way of saying what Sue already had decided, but she couldn't just desert Vanessa, not now. . . . She didn't bother to ask her aunt's opinion on taking Cassie to Italy. She already knew what she'd say—no.

To add to Sue's dilemma, even Rebecca was against the trip with Cassie to Italy. She was uncharacteristically emotional about it.

"I can look after Cassie," Sue said. "She's very gentle—and I think she likes me."

"She's also not responsible for her behavior."

"I can't let her down."

"Sue, you're so deeply involved with the Oxford sisters that it's time you knew the truth about them." And she promptly came into the city, fortified against pain by aspirin and Indocin, met Sue at Vanessa's apartment, and proceeded to tell her the true story of the Oxford sisters—a story she would never tell the world.

THE PRESENT: REBECCA—THE REPOSITORY OF THE TRUTH

Sue, as you've gathered, I'm very much against your taking Cassie to Italy. It won't benefit Cassie and it may be a hazard to you. Escorting her on an overseas flight, without sedation, without the presence of a psychiatric nurse isn't going to sit well with the airlines, either. I suspect Vanessa hasn't given her plan her careful objective thought. She's running scared, so she says *do it* and expects miracles.

I assure you my objections are based on facts that I never expected to share with you or anyone else. You once asked why I didn't write Vanessa's story and I laughed it off, saying, "Who would believe it?" I meant it: who *would* believe it?

There were many fortuitous moments in Vanessa's and Cassie's lives—high among them the increasing involvement of star-maker Joshua Fodor in their careers... You once asked me if Vanessa had a child by Fodor. You said there was gossip at the Film Wing.

Well, Vanessa did not have a child by Fodor. Or by anyone else. Vanessa could not have children. A gynecologist in Switzerland told her there was no physical reason for it, but that there's much we don't know about the *mind's* influence on our hormones.

As you know, though—Sue had told her about the chance exchange with the doctor's gossipy widow—there was a child. Cassie's child.

What you don't know, what I avoided telling you, was that the father was Joshua Fodor.

I see you're shaken. Well, it shook me when I first heard she was pregnant. She asked me to meet her at the Plaza for tea and when she came into the Palm Court, I saw that tea was not what she needed. This was after Richie Doyle's suicide, which had thrown her into a tailspin. We were all frantically concerned for her, but somehow she pulled herself out of the depression and went back to work. She was committed to a series of comedies with a company that was an offshoot of Fodor's, a company that had already made a great deal of money for him (but not enough to bail him out after the failure of *Jesus Christ—Son and Savior*).

After her return to the studio, Fodor was very kind to her. Whether he felt indirectly responsible for Richie's death, we'll never know. What we do know is that he himself directed her first vehicle for the new company. This in itself was unusual, since comedy was hardly his forte. I don't know how Vanessa felt about it; outwardly she seemed grateful that Cassie was willing to start working again.

On film, Cassie retained her quicksilver zany charm. Off-screen, she alternated between elation and depression, serenity and agitation. She still couldn't get up in the morning or decide what to eat or how to get to the studio. "Decisions, decisions," she'd fret. "Mama, what shall I do?"

Fodor took care of her. I was out on the coast at the time, and lived with them and I'd never seen him so gentle and paternal with anyone. Certainly not with Vanessa, who had in her oblique, subtle way learned how to manage him. Vanessa was never confused by options. She had only one goal: to succeed. She willingly paid the high cost of being a star. Cassie, though, was a leaf in the wind. Cassie needed a strong paternal hand to guide her.

One day, when Mr. Fodor drove her home, she stood with him at the car, smiling up at him. I saw them from the door and I thought, surprised, *She's flirting with him!*

Vanessa still was important, she was his strength. But there were younger girls underfoot, a new flock of nymphets. Cass was only a year younger than Vanessa, but she was always younger than her age, always vulnerable and young. It was the quality Fodor needed, that he couldn't live without. He was a true artist, no question, but terribly flawed as a man.

I suspect Cass led him on. What drove her to it, I can only guess at. Maybe it was Vanessa. The love-hate between the sisters was unbelievable, although on the surface love was all predominant.

Until Cass came to me that day in the Palm Court with her awful secret.

She tried to carry it off lightly. "I suppose every great man is entitled to sire a few bastards," she said, but then the tears poured and she whispered, "Oh, Rebecca, whatever shall I *do?*"

I asked if he knew a good abortionist. Every studio had the address of a cooperative gynecologist who'd relieve their little stars of unwanted burdens.

Not Fodor. *He* was too much a gentleman to know of such things. Cassie told me that he'd never had this problem before . . . she'd discovered this by some judicious questioning of his secretary, Thelma. I didn't quite believe it. He was often secretive to the point of paranoia. Since I knew of no other sources, there was only one other person Cassie could turn to.

To Vanessa.

Cassie begged me to come with her to see Vanessa. . . . "I can't face her alone. She'll hate me, she'll kill me."

There was no expression on Vanessa's face, just cool, quiet poise.

"Are you *sure*, Sister?"

"Quite sure."

"How long?"

"I don't know, I don't know!"

Cassie was like a child suddenly exposed to some horror beyond her comprehension.

Big Sister took care of everything. The trip to the German spa ostensibly for therapy for her injured right hand. The newspapers ran the item. Everybody said, Wasn't it wonderful of Cassie to take all that time off to attend her sister. . . .

They were gone a year. I understand Vanessa's dear friend Dr. Harold Kellogg took care of everything, including Cassie's post-partum psychosis. When she was reasonably well again, she stayed abroad to do a series of films and Vanessa returned home. . . .

So many unanswered questions:

What happened to the child?

Even before the infant's birth, what went on between Vanessa and Cassie while Cassie was waiting out her pregnancy?

How did Vanessa feel, watching her little sister's body swell with Joshua Fodor's child?

Even if she didn't blame Cassie—being aware of Fodor's special weakness, did she feel anger, perhaps even hatred?

Vanessa, who could bear no children, had to live with the knowledge that the most important man in her life was bound to her little sister. Did she fear what Fodor's reactions would be if he knew the truth? Might he feel elemental male pride at the thought of being a father? After all these years of being a father figure to his company, he might rejoice at becoming an actual flesh-and-blood father. A king. And Cassie would be the queen . . . ?

Knowing Vanessa, I suspected she spirited Cassie out of the country for a double reason:

To avoid any danger of scandal. No matter where Cassie had the child in the States, somebody was bound to recognize her.

To keep Joshua Fodor in the dark.

I've often wondered if she stayed with Cassie until the child was born. I don't know what its sex was. I don't know what happened to it. (Would Dr. Harold Kellogg know?) What did she tell Cassie? How did she persuade Cassie to give up the child. Or wasn't persuasion necessary, considering Cassie's later revulsion against Fodor.

Knowing Vanessa so well, I have a suspicion that she is aware of its whereabouts. Vanessa never lets go of anyone who is important to her.

What a traumatic experience for Cassie! I keep thinking of what she has lost—the joy of rearing her child. She would, I'm convinced, have been a good mother. Perhaps not in the conventional sense, but with her generous outlook she would have given so much to a child. Has the child grown up in the household of some Italian farmer—or perhaps in the theater, or even in a religious sect?

What more terrible punishment could Vanessa have inflicted on Cassie?

You bore the child, Little Sister. But I arranged its life.

Unless, of course, the child died.

So now, Sue, you understand why I was frantic when you told me about Vanessa's decision to have you take Cassie to Dr. Kellogg's villa.

Is she determined to lead Cassie to the brink? All poor Cassie needs now is to come face to face with Joshua Fodor—

No, dear, I'm *not* off my rocker. It's true. If she goes there, she will meet Joshua Fodor.

He is not dead.

Joshua Fodor is alive, although not exactly well, in the Kellogg villa in Italy.

Now, having told you this much, I may as well bring something else out in the open. Vanessa and Cassie are my friends, and, I suspect, my obsession. Strangers seeing us together, even at our advanced years, have often hinted at a lesbian relationship. Not true. Ours is an extension of those early adolescent years when we literally swore eternal friendship, when we gave each other courage and support because we were the outsiders in a small, rigid, conformist community. And we kept loyally in touch all of our mature years, which in itself is rare for a friendship based on loneliness, rejection and need. I was lonely, really an outcast, and took my refuge in the make-believe of literary fantasies. Vanessa was lonely and found the answer in Joshua Fodor and her films. Cassandra was lonely and looked for relief among her many and varied friends, but never found it.

Somehow, though, we sustained each other.

Cassie has loved me without question or reservation.

Vanessa insists that she has learned much from me.

I know how much I owe Vanessa. Not only for her generous help in my career, not only for the financial help she gave me during the Depression when she herself was hard put. But also for the dreams she ignited in me by her very presence, by her girlish ambition to become a great actress. Before meeting her, living in the isolation of that tiny Jewish community, I never would dare to imagine a world beyond that little midwestern ghetto. She made so much possible for me.

I want the very best for her and Cassie, and sometimes when I see her behaving foolishly and closing her ears to advice and common sense, I suffer.

She certainly behaved foolishly, even irrationally, in the final affair with Joshua Fodor. Again, she wouldn't pay attention to my advice. She was determined to save him. No matter how she tried to convince herself she was finished with Fodor, the umbilical cord severed, her deep feelings rose to the surface whenever he was in trouble. Vanessa was there when he needed her. Even if he didn't want her.

Cassie, in her anger, her madness, managed to telephone the newspapers the other day and tell them: "You want the truth about Joshua Fodor's accident? Ask Vanessa Oxford." It was an anonymous tip. I don't believe they followed it up. Perhaps the interest in his disappearance is dead. To most people today he's as dated as Judge Crater, who also, as you'll recall, disappeared long ago and was never found.

The headline from the *New York Times* a half-century ago read: NOTED DIRECTOR MISSING AT SEA. JOSHUA FODOR AND COMPANY FEARED LOST IN STORM OFF FLORIDA KEYS.

Joshua Fodor didn't need a guardian angel as long as he had Vanessa.

Even after his callous rejection of her for a very young girl, even after she'd made her great film, *The Passions of a Portuguese Nun*, which proved she didn't need him professionally, she was always waiting in the background when he was in trouble. To gloat? No, to help. And to prove to him that *he* couldn't function without *her*.

The obsession increased with time. As she grew older, she allowed herself to remember the good in their relationship. Perhaps, to herself, she acknowledged the truth: that only Joshua Fodor could have packaged her sparse and particular talents. She was in a position to help him. And to hurt him, if he didn't go along with her wishes.

Fodor brought a company of fifteen to Palm Beach for scenes of his new film, *The Confessions of a Woman of Pleasure*. Even after the failure of his *Marie Antoinette*, he found a rich investor to underwrite his new venture. The film combined his Victorian rectitude with his lascivious needs. His new nymphet, Doreen Douglas, was to have the lead in this presentation of *la belle époque* in Paris, that period of elegance, extravagance, frivolity and wit when the famous courtesans—the Grand Horizontals, as they were known—ruled male society. Borrowing from *La Dame aux Camélias*, he created his own vision of the delicate courtesan Marguerite. It was an appallingly unsuitable part for Doreen

Douglas. But Fodor was still unshaken in his belief that he could create artists out of ordinary clay.

While he was filming in Florida, Vanessa happened to be visiting friends in Palm Beach. It may have been a coincidence but, as I recall, Vanessa was often in the vicinity when he was filming or working on a business deal. She'd put aside whatever pride she had. We didn't discuss him in those days. She seemed in many ways more secretive than ever, a trait she'd probably borrowed from him.

This was shortly after her mother had died of a massive coronary. Vanessa's friends, the very rich Weymouths of Philadelphia, insisted on bringing her to their Palm Beach villa for a mourning period, and while there she sent a note to Fodor, who was staying at a West Palm Beach guest house. He telephoned. She greeted him warmly and invited him, on her hosts' behalf, for dinner.

He charmed the Weymouths and their guests. Soon after, Mr. Weymouth, a reserved man not much given to grand gestures, generously offered Fodor the use of his yacht. When Fodor took his company down to the Keys for water scenes, Vanessa went along. I can't imagine how they would have behaved to each other during that trip, but I could imagine Vanessa, in a wide-brimmed straw hat, swathed in veils and in a long dress against the sun, sitting inside while Fodor rehearsed his people on deck.

Vanessa told me later that she was already concerned about him. There was something lacking in the film, even though the basic story was sound. He'd lost his touch. He was plagiarizing himself. And he was drinking, which shocked her.

They left Palm Beach at midday, heading toward the Keys. The Weymouth yacht, *The Seagull*, a 70-foot craft equipped with a 200-horsepower engine, had had engine trouble before leaving port. An Atlantic storm was threatening. A Coast Guard cutter and airplanes were alerted to warn *The Seagull* of trouble.

The Seagull was caught in the heart of the storm. Its motor conked out. Helpless against gigantic waves, it foundered. Most of the cast was lost, although the Coast Guard did rescue a few in the rough waters. The survivors' report was that the last they saw, Joshua Fodor and Vanessa were clinging to a plank, both wearing lifejackets, and holding on to each other.

The storm that swept in from the Atlantic built to near-hurricane strength, and in its wake hundreds were lost and towns were wrecked. It was believed that Joshua Fodor and Vanessa had drowned.

I was heartsick. It was dramatically right, I knew, that Fodor and Vanessa should have perished together, like lovers in one of his better films. But it was also as though a part of me had been lost, never to be replaced.

Five days later, newspapers carried miraculous news: Vanessa Oxford had been found. She was in a very weak condition, but not seriously hurt and was recovering with friends in Nassau. How she got there was never explained.

Joshua Fodor was presumed lost in the storm.

There was a memorial service in New York for him, Hans Rolfsma came with various others of his company. Doreen Douglas was among those rescued by the Coast Guard and of course she attended the service. Vanessa was the chief speaker (and the chief mourner) and she ended her eulogy with a glowing tribute.

"He was everything to us. Father, teacher, friend..."

Lover? She didn't mention that. It was the beginning of her idealization of him to herself and to the world.

Afterward, in her apartment, she seemed another person, revealing a strength that she usually hid behind her little-girl mannerisms.

"Rebecca, I must go to Mexico," she said. "I would be grateful if you'd come with me."

I said I would.

"There is so much to do." She ran through a long list. She was resolute. Practical. Then she added, almost as an afterthought, she was so casual, "Rebecca, my first obligation is to get Mr. Fodor out of the country—"

Vanessa never ceased to astonish me. But her casual statement that morning was beyond my comprehension. Fodor was alive! When they were washed ashore, battered, exhausted, he'd had a heart attack. But he was still breathing, and, out of instinct, Vanessa had poured her breath into his mouth, trying to breathe for him. They were rescued by fishermen and brought to a small village that had a primitive hospital. They had no identification and by some instinct of self-preservation, Vanessa didn't give Fodor's real name. Nor her own. When the storm subsided she left Fodor in the villagers' care and returned to Nassau, where she was treated like a miracle saved from the sea. The Weymouths quickly arranged for her to cash a sizable check, although they didn't know why she needed it, and being as polite as they were rich, didn't ask.

By the time she reclaimed Fodor she realized her initial fears were accurate. Fodor was restored to life but the few minutes his heart had stopped had created irreversible brain damage.

"He's a vegetable." There was such anguish in her voice. "His memory is gone. He's just a shell of the man he was." Her hands were clenched, the scarred one appropriately close to her breast. "*Nobody* must ever know what has happened to him."

Vanessa, pragmatic Vanessa, had it all planned out.

Somehow Joshua Fodor had to be gotten out of the country and brought to Italy, there to be put under the care of Dr. Harold Kellogg. If anyone could restore Joshua to normalcy, it would be her dear friend and doctor.

She had arranged it beautifully. Joshua would be taken to Mexico on a small fishing boat. There would be a new passport for him (it always surprised me how resourceful, even illicit, Vanessa could be if circumstances demanded it). We would then arrange for Joshua to be sent by a Colombian freighter to Italy.

"It won't be safe for me to go, I'd surely be recognized," she said. "Rebecca, you are the only one I can trust. Harold will look after him"—her voice broke—"oh, that brilliant inventive mind . . ."

It never occurred to me to refuse.

"What will happen to his film?" I asked.

She shrugged. "First things first, dear Rebecca."

During the fortnight that I shared with Fodor on the freighter, I saw no sign of the man I'd known. He had totally lost his memory. He was a gentle, quiet, undemanding giant. Most of the time he sat in a deckchair or remained in his cabin. The male nurse who'd accompanied us dressed him, fed him and read to him (although we weren't sure how much he understood). He made no trouble. Every moment I spent with him, I shared Vanessa's anguish. And also her determination to keep his pitiful condition from the world. How his enemies would gloat if they knew what had happened to him! In Hollywood, nothing was sacred and only the knife in the back was respected as the sensible way to treat foe *and* friend.

I left Fodor in the capable, compassionate care of Harold Kellogg.

On my return to New York, I found that Vanessa had taken over the production of *The Confessions of a Woman of Pleasure.* I don't know how she managed it—except she does have many friends and admirers in the legal profession—but she got herself appointed the conservator of his estate, too. Then she went to work on the film. She fired Doreen Douglas, who had no desire to continue in films now that her sponsor was gone. She revamped the cast, and she directed the film as well as acted in it. It was, as you know, enormously successful, and critics said that it was as though all she'd learned from the Master—his best, his most productive—shone with radiance in this work. . . .

So all these years Joshua Fodor has been living in comfortable retreat, protected, coddled, under Dr. Kellogg's care. Vanessa visits him each summer; she spends July and August with him. She insists that he recognizes her, that he's more gentle, more affable and less remote when she is with him.

Who knows? We see what we want to see.

That's it, Sue. The true story.

Do you see now why Cassie must not go to Dr. Kellogg's? I don't know whether Fodor would recognize her, he's so old and frail now. But we mustn't take the chance. And what would happen to her fragile hold on sanity if she saw the father of her child again after all these years, reduced to a mindless ancient wreck of a man?

Vanessa's reaction to her best friend's logical pleas?

Rebecca, don't interfere.

Sue, get Cassie on a plane. If you can't manage alone, Dann will come with you. Dann will do anything to help me.

So they all did as Vanessa demanded.

Sue simply could not refuse.

In spite of Rebecca's and Aunt Harriet's opposition.

It never occurred to Dann to refuse. He'd do anything for Vanessa. Besides, he thought, being together with Sue again might revive their affair.

THE PAST: DEEP, DARK, DANGEROUS

Hidden in a secret compartment of Vanessa's desk, where no one will find it except perhaps after her death, is a clipping, yellow with age, from a privately printed Hollywood magazine, editor and publisher unknown.

Joshua Fodor? He didn't like any girl child who was more than ten years old.

Well, let's stretch it a little. The typical Fodor actress was thirteen years old and would never age, if she wanted to stay in his company.

She responded to him because she knew her power over him.

Several international film luminaries can trace the origin of their fame to the great director's pedophile inclinations.

One of them is revered as a model of purity and a paragon of womanliness.

To turn an old phrase into a new truism of our modern amoral age: She got that reputation by putting her mouth where the money was.

Need we draw any pictures to make it any clearer? Hmm???

THE PRESENT: CASSIE, SUE AND DANN

ALITALIA NIGHTFLIGHT, a Boeing 747, leaves Kennedy at 7:30
P.M. Wednesday evening and arrives at Milan's Malpensa Airport
at 9 A.M. Thursday morning. Among the passengers:

Cassandra:

"I am a vagina." What a theme song for one of those fancy
bordellos Vanessa and Piers van Cleave were always frequenting
because Vanessa maintained an actress should understand every
aspect of life. Dear Sister, always a logical excuse for all of her
behavior... the Thorazine is working... I am so calm, no shakes,
no agitations, no flutters in the chest... fans were always sending
us gifts, homemade fudge because they read that I love chocolates... letters... poems... who sent me the poem... Christina
Rossetti's... *"For there is no friend like a sister... in calm or
stormy weather... to cheer one on the tedious way... to fetch
one if one goes astray..."* ... Vanessa on Ed Murrow's program,
Person to Person, The Fabulous Oxford Girls—"The human emotions behind the saints fascinate me... I would love to interpret
the role of Mother Cabrini..." ... "And you, Miss Cassandra,
what do you think of your sister?" "Vanessa is my best friend...
she is always rescuing me from disaster..." But of course that
dear, gentle sister of mine often rewrote our history to satisfy her
needs... "I am so serious" ... "My sister is the bright, witty
one..." The reason for the laughter... when you made people
laugh they were kinder to you... so you were funny and people
said: *Darling, darling Cassie* ... and it helped... it still helps when
you live in everlasting fear... fear of strangers, fear of strange
places... with only Mama to keep you safe... Mama... such a
life... so undemanding... closing her eyes to Vanessa's shocking

behavior, wanting to believe when Sister said, "Don't worry... everything will be all right..."

I was too old for Joshua Fodor, known affectionately as The Master...a new generation of little girls was making film history under his guidance...but he'd been after me since I was their age...and I'd put him in his place...not so with Sister...he whistled and she was there...she didn't fool me any, parading around in front of the other girls, flaunting her influence on him ...Mr. Fodor and Miss Vanessa...

Even after I skipped having the curse a couple of months, the truth was beyond me...I couldn't believe that what had happened between us would result in that...I knew from the other girls what he liked to do...but he didn't try any funny business with me...I was a virgin, which he found *very* exciting.

A virgin...I'd held out...Fear? Maybe? But mostly because of him...Richie...I wanted my darling to be the first...except my darling sister got to him first...

Richie dead? It can't be, but it is. Vanessa was the one to break the news to me...Vanessa and Mr. Fodor...Richie had blown his head apart but he looked beautiful in death because the undertaker was such an artist...Richie was dead but there was still a bit of life in me...

Mr. Fodor was the first tenant of my vagina. His lease was brief. A few seconds of tension, an explosion, his strange laugh as he peaked...

My equipment was no different that Vanessa's, but she used hers more *sensibly.*

No babies for Sister...no contraceptives...no abortions... she was a receptacle trained to give a spasm of relief to an adoring male who'd pay dearly for his moment...

Something tiny in the womb that persisted in growing, nothing to do with me, I had this terrible need to expel it, to make my body clean and inhospitable again...but it was late, too late... the little living thing clung there, unwilling to leave its warm nest...

Sister said she would take care of everything. Trust me, she said. I did.

The lithium is horrible...it makes me upchuck...the Thorazine helps me without hurting...I am prepared for whatever comes...He's at the Kellogg villa...I know it...she's never fooled me...I have read her mail...I have questioned Rebecca in such a way that she didn't have to answer outright, but she doesn't know I know. None of them do....So we will meet again.

I am calm. There is a caul around my body, like the afterbirth that wouldn't come out when it was born....Does he know there was a child?...Once I asked Rebecca if he ever knew and she said no, Vanessa had never said a word to him...of course, if it wasn't *her* child, she'd keep it silent as the grave....If I see him, I don't think it will mean anything to me...except for a year out of my life...a missing year...how could it...?

Did it matter that much? What is a year? What is a day?... Richie loved me and I was so very young...I believed in dreams, and a world of good without evil. Ha. Double ha.

The nice doctor at Sunset Hill has asked me about my cuts, my bruises, my spills, the operations that he says were unnecessary. All he will say is that my self-destructive impulses are an act of aggression against Vanessa.

I'd rather believe Rebecca. Rebecca says that every personal crisis...if handled properly...can become the seed for growth...
Ha.

Growth. Who wants growth?...I want a nice quiet place, dark as the womb, where I can curl up and sleep...

Like this man-made nest roaring through the black sky....

Sue:

In the dim light, a stewardess walked softly up the aisle, carrying a blanket for the old lady who was lying with her head back against a pillow. Sue, seated beside the woman, took the blanket with a grateful smile. She covered the sleeper gently, over the shoulders and around the chest and tucked it behind her back so it was almost like a swaddling cloth.

Charlie once said he'd like to take me to Italy, and I just laughed it off, Sue thought, and now I'm on a flight with Dann and there is no thought in my mind, no feeling in my body except the urgency to get Cassie safely to Vanessa.

She glanced toward Dann slouched in the seat across the aisle.

He seemed absorbed in his thoughts, the photography magazine unopened on his lap.

"She's sleeping," Sue said, thinking perhaps she and Dann might have a little while together.

"I want to thank you for coming with me," Dann said, leaning toward her. "It was very good of you."

She was aware of something in his voice that told her he was part of the Oxford family, that the sisters were his primary concern. Not her. It was a strange relationship but it proved the power of Vanessa's hold on her admirers. "I owe her so much," Dann had said to Sue in a moment of confidence. "I can't ever repay her." ... *I let myself get too dependent on him. He used me. I used him. But there never really was love. He's in love, if at all, with Vanessa's image.*

"I'm going to try to get some sleep," she said, and curled up in her chair. They were thirty thousand feet in the air, streaking through space, and the awareness of their isolation struck a note of loneliness in her. She wished Dann would come over and put his hand over hers. Oh, for a warm body to banish this loneliness ... *I don't want to end up like Cassie or Vanessa ... I want to be with a man I can love, I want to share ... I want to see Charlie again....* She was unaware of the tears spilling over. When she fell asleep, they were still damp on her cheeks, and she began to dream about Charlie....

It was a place of sunlight and shadow, of antiquity and modernity. It sat not far from some Roman ruins and a spa known for its radiated mud baths to which the French and German upper classes came annually for the cure.

Dr. Harold Kellogg's retreat was a Mediterranean villa surrounded by magnificent terraced gardens, all lovingly restored by the profits from Dr. Kellogg's line of vitamin supplements and his books on health, beauty and perpetual youth. Dr. Kellogg was a "naturopath" whose title had come years before from a diploma mill, but he was prescribing megavitamins long before Dr. Linus Pauling became their champion. And his diets, which stressed the well-balanced meals suggested by the New York Health Department obesity clinic, had given him a loyal following among people who made the news.

Dr. Kellogg himself was the finest exemplar of his own health theories, looking like a man not yet fifty though he actually had passed his seventieth birthday. Food, exercise, the fabulous radiated mud baths, a little tuck here and there on his chin and around his eyes, and he was still handsome, energetic and equally devoted to his male and female acolytes. His villa, once the summer home of Italian royalty, was spacious enough to accommodate a few carefully chosen guests (who paid astronomical fees for a fortnight of diet, massage, mud baths, and his mini-sermons on respect for the body, which he believed was in God's image).

No more than five guests were accommodated at one time, and none of them had ever been aware that the suite of rooms at one end of the rear wing was occupied by a very elderly, senile gentleman. A certain section of the grounds was off limits to guests, who showed little curiosity about anyone except themselves. Dr. Kellogg's staff was schooled to give its guests the most loving care— "it must resemble a regression to infancy," Dr. Kellogg instructed his people. "During their stay here, they have no need to think for themselves."

It was noon and the gardens were brilliant under the warm sunlight and the blue cloudless sky. The guests were resting until lunch, somnolent from their massages and exercises and ready for the delicious foods.

Vanessa was too keyed up to rest. Dressed in a peach linen sheath, a big woven straw hat covering her hair and face, she strolled in the garden, waiting impatiently for the car to arrive.

She did not question her decision to send for Cassie. Although she hadn't consulted Dr. Kellogg until later, he did agree with her. He'd had some reasonably good results with megavitamins for schizophrenic patients, and she was counting on his skill to restore Cassie. It had done something for Joshua. Not as much as they'd hoped originally, but Dr. Kellogg's supervision had kept Joshua alive and reasonably well.

She walked along the gravel paths in the garden banded with flowers—the hillside on which it rested was a part of the villa. There were Roman tiles on the roof and the stucco walls were pink with a touch of ocher. White rattan chairs and lounges surrounded the glittering sapphire pool and the nearby pavilion was shaded by full, striped red-and-gold curtains against the midday heat. Olive trees grew on the lower level and the terraces spilled over with tulips and irises, bordered in lavender blossoms. On the lower terraces the vegetables were rich, colorful and abundant. On low tables were vivid still-life baskets spilling over with fresh produce and cut flowers.

It was a place of serenity, and the sense of peace she received here for two months each year enabled Vanessa to return to civilization and cope for the rest of the year.

Now her mind was busy with plans for the future. She would send Sue back after the weekend, perhaps treat her to a week in Paris. But Dann must remain here. She would need him while she coped with Cassie and until she made sure Cassie was installed in the one place where she, too, would find peace. . . .

"Dann!" Vanessa kissed him on the mouth and embraced him. "It's so *good* to see you." Still holding his hand, she turned to Sue and embraced her warmly. The chauffeur had stepped out of the red Fiat and was waiting for Cassie to move. But she remained seated, immobile, watching the enthusiastic reception given her two companions. The poodle was out of his crate and was on her lap, still shaking with fright two hours after their landing in Milan. Sue thought suddenly, it's Sunset Hill all over again, there will be a scene . . .

But Cassie had evidently reconsidered it. She handed Guy over to Sue, accepted the chauffeur's hand and walked toward the group. "Sister." Her voice was cool, her manner aloof as she acknowledged Vanessa.

Vanessa made an attempt to embrace her but Cassie remained rigid. Housemen carried the luggage into the villa. Now a tall, erect man with a handsome sunburn and a crest of white hair walked briskly across the lawn. He was wearing cotton slacks and a blue sports shirt, and he gave the impression of tremendous vitality.

"Cassandra, my dear." He kissed her hand. She looked carefully at him.

"Sister, you remember Dr. Kellogg," Vanessa prodded.

"Of course. He's been taking care of Joshua all these years, hasn't he?"

They were all startled by the clarity of her voice. Such poise and assurance, Sue thought. It must have taken a tremendous amount of will, and if she could somehow manage this, wasn't there hope for her, after all?

Dr. Kellogg guided Cassie, holding his palm to her elbow, and pretended not to have heard her. So did Vanessa.

"Come, my dear. You've not seen my house yet."

Following along was Dann, walking between Vanessa and Sue, loaded down with his camera and equipment.

"There's so much to photograph here," Vanessa chattered. "Marvelous old ruins ... we can go off on picnics ..."

The reception rooms on the first floor had marble floors. The ceilings were painted cerulean blue with a suggestion of clouds. Dr. Kellogg was showing the rooms to Cassie, concentrating on her to the exclusion of the others.

"I've used the colors of the sun," he said. "Yellows and oranges, mostly, and soft celadon greens." He had retained some of the grandeur that came with the villa, such as the heavy carved furniture, but he had lightened it with white cotton draperies and slipcovers, plants and blooming flowers. The windows were shaded with growing vines to protect the house during the hot months.

"It's a dream house," Sue exclaimed and thought how marvelous it would be to live here with a man you loved. Dann was silent, except for a comment that every corner of every room was an exciting prospect for his camera.

Sue and Cassie were to share the bedroom next to Vanessa's for the next few days. The chambers were shadowy, fragrant with the lavender of fresh sheets and the perfume of flowers in antique vases.

"There's a connecting door to my room, Cassie," Vanessa said. "So you won't be afraid."

The jet lag had caught up with Sue. "If you don't mind, I'll skip lunch. I'm more sleepy than hungry."

"I'll stay with Sue," Cassie said. "I'm sure you and Dann have much to catch up on."

She's normal, Sue thought. She's as normal as Vanessa. What has brought her back to reality?

THE PRESENT: WHAT SUE WANTED
TO KNOW BUT WAS TOO POLITE TO
ASK

Sue was resting in the handsome bedroom she was to share with Cassie until Cassie's future was decided upon. Cassie was downstairs in the doctor's examining office submitting to tests. Tomorrow she would have the six-hour glucose tolerance test on which Dr. Kellogg based his treatment.

To Sue, Cassie's attitude since they'd left Kennedy was hopeful. She was rational, pliable, alert. For whatever reason, the important fact was that she had improved. Whether it was only temporary ... well, it was too soon to tell. If only the sisters could avoid a major confrontation!

I can't leave, Sue thought, *until I see how Cassie makes out. It will be all right: Vanessa's favorite Valium. I only hope it works this time.*

Sue admired Vanessa's calm determination. She had that rare and sometimes dangerous gift, the ability to arrange people's lives to serve her purpose ... how easily, for example, she'd arranged to have Sue bring Cassie to her. That Joshua Fodor and Cassie were in the same house didn't seem to disturb her at all. Her sense of what's right might be distorted but she certainly worked it to her advantage!

Vanessa stopped in the doorway and invited Sue into her room. There were fresh flowers everywhere. She recalled Rebecca once saying that gifts of flowers meant much to Vanessa, signifying that she was still loved and remembered. At home she cared for them as though they were her children. Each night they were brought into her bedroom, which she kept very cold, and then in the morning were returned to other places in the apartment.

A large framed photograph of the Oxford sisters stood on the marble bureau top, taken when they were young Fodor players. They were close together, cheek to cheek, like Siamese twins, but if you looked closely you saw that it was Vanessa who was curved toward Cassie and that it was Cassie who was looking away.

Vanessa motioned Sue to a comfortable easy chair. The room was quiet, the wooden shutters drawn against the sun. In her simple linen shift, Vanessa looked almost girlish. But the shadows under the eyes and the lines around the small, prim mouth betrayed her years.

"You know the truth now," she said. "I've heard from Rebecca."

"Yes, I think she had some qualms talking to me, but under the circumstances—"

"Sue, I trust you." Vanessa's luminous eyes were moist with a suggestion of tears. She appeared to be truly suffering.

"How is Mr. Fodor feeling now?"

"Somewhat better, but it's touch and go. He had a setback, that was the reason Dr. Kellogg called me. Today was a good day, but he is so old and so frail."

"Did his memory ever return?"

Vanessa shook her head. This was no time for shame or reticence or masquerade. She could trust Sue, she felt, like Rebecca. Or Dann.

"His condition is quite different from Cassie's. Her mind has censored all memories she needs to wipe out. Most of his brain cells are dead. We don't know how much he understands, if at all. Dr. Kellogg has had consultations with specialists. One man has had extraordinary success with his spastic patients, he starts them off in the beginning by crawling on all fours.... We tried it with Joshua. It must have been a strange sight—I got down on my hands and knees and crawled and he watched me, totally indifferent. It nearly destroyed me."

She walked over to the window and opened the wooden shutters. Below her, gardeners were caring for the flower beds, and she said, mostly to herself, "Simple people ... simple needs ... simple satisfactions ..." Then, turning to Sue, "There's been some work in pacemakers for the brain, but Dr. Kellogg says it is too late. Joshua has had several small strokes. He's done well under the care of the staff. Dr. Kellogg did warn me, years ago, that we had a dangerous choice.... Perhaps he's better off as he is."

It was characteristic of Vanessa to absorb the inevitable into her own philosophy, Sue thought.

"When we were washed up on that beach in the storm—I tried to revive him by artificial respiration. I literally breathed my life into him. He was rational for a moment. He was trying to speak and when I bent down he whispered, 'I never thought it would end like this.'... *Oh, dear God...*"

Vanessa, who had boasted she never wept, began sobbing now, and Sue cradled her thin, fragile body in her arms, grateful that finally she'd allowed her grief to pour out. "He had no malice, not ever. He couldn't fight those Hollywood sharks. He was always a generous, courteous man of great talent, with one terrible weakness that destroyed him."

Sue led her to a chair and persuaded her to sit.

"He burned himself out. Rebecca always said that the sum of the incidents in his films was greater than the whole. That's been true of his life. And now it's too late... *too late...*"

The mascara stung her long, still-thick lashes, and Sue tenderly wiped her eyes with a tissue.

"I spend every afternoon with him, when he wakes up from his nap. I show him old pictures and read to him from his old scripts and ramble on, trying to recall what will please him.... I even tell him how after we parted I always conjured up an image of him in my mind. I mean, when another director, at Metro or Fox, was supposed to be guiding me... Oh, Sue, it's such a tragedy! How they would gloat in Hollywood if they knew what has happened to him, his helplessness."

"Most of his contemporaries are dead," Sue said, hoping to comfort her.

"Yes, I know. Perhaps it's best if he just drifts off quietly. I've tried to do my best for him, I have . . . but it's not been enough. . . . If only he at least could have understood when I told him about the retrospective and the movie house named for him, and the great financial and artistic success now of *Jesus Christ—Son and Savior.* Oh, Sue, I feel that somehow I've failed him—"

"I think you've done beautifully . . . And don't forget, without you, he might have died in that storm—"

"Perhaps it would have been better." She was rubbing the scar on her injured hand. "I owe him so much. Without him, there'd have been no Vanessa Oxford. No Cassandra Oxford, either."

"Vanessa, it isn't like you to reproach yourself." Sue was embarrassed for her, and at the same time deeply touched.

"My best hasn't been good enough. Oh, Sue, what can I do?"

Let Cassie go, that's the best you can do, Sue thought, but of course she said nothing. How could she? . . .

Vanessa's eyes were closed now. She was very still.

"When I was young," she whispered, "you had to be Little Orphan Annie. With a Daddy Warbucks to look after you." . . . Young, but *never* a child, a very determined young person who knew what she meant to be, who seemed the ethereal image of every man's dream of the perfect woman . . . "Rebecca used to say, 'Vanessa is like the lions guarding the entrance of the Public Library. But Cassie, Cassie is a Calder mobile, stirring in the wind.' Of course Rebecca has a way with words, she does sometimes get carried away— Oh, Sue, have I ruined her life?"

A war-torn landscape, one she was painfully familiar with, rough stones, dark treacherous alleys leading to a dead end.

And suddenly out of nowhere a big, faceless woman . . . as terrifying as death, and she is saying "Come, I'll take you to your mother's house." But death wanders away, and she finds a young couple quarreling bitterly. She doesn't feel welcome . . . there are spoiled fruits and grapes picked over and everything she sees is decayed, dead . . . The one to blame—the culprit—she must destroy the culprit . . . in order to save herself—

"Vanessa! *Vanessa!*"

Who is screaming? Why am I in the big room Sue and Cassie are sharing for the night? Why am I on Cassie's bed, my hand seems to be reaching for her throat and Sue is pulling me away . . . ? Oh my God, *no.* The night terrors still haunt me. Only now they make me *do* things—terrible things I can't live with. . . .

"It was a nightmare," Vanessa said after Sue had bathed her

face, given her a drink of water and guided her back to her bed. "Is . . . is Cassie all right?" She couldn't look at Sue as she asked it.

"Cassie is fine, dear . . ." Nor could Sue look at her as she fought to keep herself under control.

My God, Vanessa thought, *I must get her out of here. She isn't safe here. We cannot live together anymore. There's no more pretending. I'm too tired to pretend and it is too dangerous for Cassie . . . and for me. I too will go mad."*

"Come, Sister," said Vanessa.

"Where are we going?" Cassie asked.

"We've found a home for you, dear. Where you will be happy."

"Why can't I stay here? I like Harold."

"Harold will be treating you, dear. But there's no room—"

"The villa once held Italian royalty and their staff. Surely there is one small room for me."

To Sue, who was present, Cassie sounded sensible and rational. It was Vanessa who was growing tense, almost hysterical.

"You will go, Sister. I know what's best for you."

The cloud momentarily lifted. "Vanessa," she said, "it's so late . . . so terribly late. What happened to the child?"

Perspiration glistened on Vanessa's milk-white skin and pain flooded her eyes.

"Come, Sister," she repeated. "Let's go, quietly now. We don't need Harold's nurses . . ."

Dann was off on a walking tour for the day with his camera. The Italians fascinated him. One of the gardeners was driving the station wagon, with Vanessa in front and Cassie and Sue in the rear seats, the poodle wedged between them. Sue was tense about Cassie, but Cassie seemed remote, withdrawn again. The question she'd addressed so poignantly to Vanessa no longer seemed to trouble her. She had closed her mind to it, as she had to many other problems. They drove along the dusty road, close to the vineyards and the upper levels of vegetable gardens. The country, although parched, had a certain medieval richness. Sue's glance returned to the front seat. She realized how strong Vanessa had been . . . how well she'd managed to avoid any scandal . . . *Don't worry. I'll take care of everything* . . . No wonder it had finally taken its toll. . . .

They drove past the ancient church. A priest was coming down the walk. He was middle-aged and very thin, his dark cassock falling in heavy folds around him. His features were delicate for a man and the advancing years had not roughened them. His hair was fair, his opalescent blue eyes well spaced, his nose blunt, like a boxer's. His mouth was small and sensitive. He had the noble Oxford brow. Sue saw the family resemblance immediately and wondered if Cassie noticed it. But Cassie said nothing and seemed to see nothing. She was a solitary voyager in her own world.

He nodded, evidently recognizing Vanessa. She returned his greeting as the car turned into the driveway leading to the convent.

Vanessa looked over her shoulder at Cassie.

"The Order is old and beautiful," she said. "And the Sisters are very nice, they will look after you well, Cassie. This will be your home and you will be happy here." And there even is, she thought, one priest who will look after you with most special care. . . .

Suddenly Sue remembered the day she'd been filing a copy of Vanessa's will, and Vanessa had said, "When my time comes, I am bequeathing all of what I have to an Order in Italy. The Order has done much for me. And for Sister. I hope she'll never know how much."

Lunch in the pavilion:

Lunch on the pavilion:
Present: Vanessa, Dann and Sue. There were two empty chairs. Dr. Kellogg was missing because he'd been working in the laboratory and recently had begun to use his lunch hour for meditation. As they waited patiently in the shaded pavilion, an orderly in white was pushing a wheelchair across the lawn toward them.

For the first time since her arrival three days ago Sue met the famous invalid. So this was the great Joshua Fodor! He was shrunken, incredibly aged, but his cream-colored summer trousers, yellow linen shirt and blue alpaca sweater fitted him faultlessly.

His sparse gray hair was clipped neatly and his long clean-shaven face was remarkably placid, the face of one who had escaped the tensions and pressures of life. There was a lack of guile in his features, the deep-set eyes now washed out with age, the remodeled nose, the strong, obstinate chin.

The butler fetched the tray and served them. Vanessa cut up the breast of chicken, tucked the napkin into Joshua's shirt to protect him, and without embarrassment fed him. Whenever the food dribbled, she wiped his lips. Gently. Patiently. Lovingly.

Watching them, Sue could only think of what Vanessa had told her his last words had been on that beach in the Florida keys . . . "I never thought it would end like this." . . .

"Sue, Sister Carmelita will drive Cassie over after lunch," Vanessa was saying. "She wants to say goodbye to you."

"I'll be leaving at one-thirty," Sue said.

"I wish you'd let me drive you to the airport," Dann said. He looked upset but his discomfort made no impression on Sue.

"I believe Vanessa has plans for you this afternoon."

"I thought we'd go down to the ruins," Vanessa said, "and take some photographs. Perhaps Vogue will be interested."

"Can't it wait?" Dann asked, sounding annoyed.

"Of course. Another day."

Salad and sweetish goat's cheese and fresh strawberries were served. Sue could wait no longer. She blotted her lips, put down her napkin and prepared to return to the villa for her bags.

She shook hands with Mr. Fodor. His skin was dry and wrinkled, his expression pleasant but empty. She turned to Vanessa, who embraced her.

"Sue, there's one little matter I forgot to take care of. You remember at the retrospective . . . there was one of Mr. Fodor's first leading ladies . . . Lorraine North? She's having problems and I've been sending her a monthly check. Call the bank and arrange to have it continued while I'm away."

Oh, Vanessa, kind and selfish, thoughtful and self-centered.

Dann walked her to the waiting car. The chauffeur had taken care of her bags.

"I'll see you when I get back," Dann said, but he said it as a question.

He's such a beautiful man, Sue thought, and I've learned

something from him I'll not forget. . . . But he *is* a part of the Oxford family, and I am about *not* to be. . . . She still had regrets about her decision, but she knew it was the right one.

He leaned down, put his arms around her and kissed her hand, reminding her of earlier times, and pleasures.

"Perhaps I can fly over to Paris to meet you."

"I'm going to London."

"To meet someone?" He knew the answer before she could reply.

Charlie Bryson was expecting her.

The chauffeur started the motor, the car began to move.

Across the lawn, Vanessa was pushing Joshua Fodor in his wheelchair. The sun was shining on her. She was the picture of serenity and fulfillment.